NICOLAI'S DAUGHTERS

NICOLAI'S DAUGHTERS

Stella Leventoyannis Harvey

Author's Note
This is a work of fiction. I have used historical information, but have changed certain details to fit my storyline. I take full responsibility for any errors or inconsistencies I have made in the historical aspects of the novel.

Cover design by Doowah Design.
Photo of Stella Leventoyannis Harvey by Joern Rohde.

This book was printed on Ancient Forest Friendly paper.
Printed and bound in Canada by Hignell Book Printing Inc.

We acknowledge the support of the Canada Council for the Arts and the Manitoba Arts Council for our publishing program.

Library and Archives Canada Cataloguing in Publication

Leventoyannis Harvey, Stella, 1956–
Nicolai's daughters / Stella Leventoyannis Harvey.

ISBN 978-1-897109-97-7

I. Title.

PS8623.E944N52 2012 C813'.6 C2012-905576-X

Signature Editions
P.O. Box 206, RPO Corydon, Winnipeg, Manitoba, R3M 3S7
www.signature-editions.com

To Mom and Dad
with much gratitude and love

All the generations of mortal man add up to nothing. Show me the man whose happiness was anything more than illusion, followed by disillusion.

— Sophocles, *The Theban Plays*

1

1986

Each day was the same as the one before. He'd wake up and stretch out his arm to pull Sara close, snuggle into her. His hand would feel the empty place beside him. Then he'd remember that she was gone and the ache would begin again, starting at his temples, stabbing him in the eyes, wrapping itself around his jaw. Every muscle hurt. His strength had been sucked away. Each breath made the room spin, his stomach twist. How could he still be breathing? It wasn't right.

When he could manage to get himself out of bed, he couldn't be bothered to get dressed. He stayed in his underwear all day, walking back and forth from the kitchen to the living room to the dining room, unsure what he was supposed to do with himself.

Most days, he flopped onto the recliner and stared at the pictures Sara had hung on the wall above the couch, as if they could somehow show him how to move forward without her. Even with his eyes closed, he could see the framed pictures—their wedding day, their camping trips, the baby pictures. He'd never asked for this house, this kind of life. He'd always known that good things couldn't last for people like him. How could he have thought that God would allow him this bit of happiness?

When he'd first arrived in Canada — far from Greece, far from his father — he'd taken language lessons, and then enrolled in university. He washed dishes to support himself and lived in a room the size of a closet. After university he'd talked his way into a great job at one of the city's top publicity firms, then left it to strike out on his own. The first few years were lean, but business gradually picked up. His clients were loyal, and became almost like family; they knew there wasn't anything he wouldn't do for them. And things just got better after he met Sara. When he lost the occasional contract, he'd be sure it was the beginning of the end, but she'd say, "More work will come. Wait and see." She never once stopped believing in him. He even began to believe he was the man he saw reflected in her eyes.

It had been Sara's idea to buy this old house in the suburbs. "Who wants to live in a condominium?" she asked when they finally had enough money for a down payment. "We'll fix it up. It'll be great. Wait and see."

"In a condo, someone else takes care of everything," he'd said. "We wouldn't worry about a thing."

"You appreciate it more if you do it yourself." She kissed him. "And besides, I want a yard where our child can play, where our dog can run around, a garden I can grow things in."

"And a white picket fence?" He shook his head dubiously. "We don't even have a child."

But then they did have the child, and the yard, and the garden, although Nicolai drew the line at a dog. It was a charmed life.

He remembered the day they moved into the house. Their furniture hadn't arrived yet, and they slept on the floor that first night under their light jackets. They lay in each other's arms and talked about how the old chair would go in their bedroom and be ready when the baby came. He couldn't imagine being happier. And then Alexia was born and his chest ached with a joy he didn't think was possible. Did he deserve this happiness? It had scared him to think about the answer to this question, but he didn't talk to Sara about it. He went to work, ignored his worries and prayed every morning for God to watch over them. At night, after Sara fell asleep, he whispered his thanks.

None of it had meant a thing. Even God had abandoned him. How could he believe in a God that would do that? Maybe He knew what Nicolai had always known: he never deserved any of this. Wasn't that what his father always told him?

And now he needed to start over again. He'd done it before, he told himself. He could do it again. But not just yet. He wasn't ready to think about all this. Sara had been gone only a few weeks. Or was it just a few days? He needed more time.

"We'll get another opinion," Sara had said in the doctor's office. Later, lying in bed, his head on her chest, she gently tugged his hair through her fingers as if braiding a doll's curls. "The chemo will help. You'll see."

He listened to her heart beating, breathed in the scent of her just-out-of-the-shower skin. How could he manage without this? Everything he'd accomplished was better because of her. All he had to do was make her happy, protect her.

He couldn't even do that.

The chemo didn't help and Sara insisted on getting her affairs in order. Nicolai was reluctant, but when she forced the issue, he went with her to Stuart's office. She wanted the details—a trust fund for Alexia, a plan for the house, donations of her eyes, heart, lungs—all of it written down. She gave herself away to strangers. What would be left for him?

When the envelope from the law firm arrived, he hid it in the cupboard above the fridge. She asked him if it had come. He shrugged, said he hadn't seen anything.

"I'll call Stuart tomorrow," she said. "I have to get this done." She leaned against the counter, put her head down. He rubbed her back. Her T-shirt bunched. She sighed. "There's so much to do."

"I have it."

She turned and met his gaze; her face was so small and pale. Why had he put her through this charade? He was scared. He couldn't help it.

He pulled the will from its hiding spot.

"I'm handling it," he said. "You just get better."

"This is important to me."

"No. Getting better is more."

She shook her head. Hugging the envelope to her chest, she'd reached for him.

Nicolai woke to the sound of knocking on the bedroom door. His mouth felt like he'd chewed sawdust. He wrung out a ball of spit and swallowed, ran his heavy tongue over his lips, gnawed at a piece of dry skin with his teeth and peeled it back until he tasted blood.

Alexia knocked at his bedroom door. "Are you okay, Daddy?" Alexia called.

"Why aren't you at school, Alexia?" he yelled through the door, his fists balled on his lap. He heard her footsteps moving away down the hallway and immediately regretted yelling at her. It wasn't her fault. Why was he such a shit? He was becoming more like his father every day. Sara wouldn't have allowed him to talk to Alexia that way. But Sara wasn't here, was she? She'd left him to deal with life without her. He punched the mattress.

The door opened and the light in the room flicked on, bit at his eyes.

"I made you breakfast, Daddy." Alexia was silhouetted in the doorway, holding her mother's breakfast tray, her arms straining with the weight. He tightened his fists, released his fingers slowly and concentrated on the comforting ache. He sat up, and was overcome by a wave of nausea. He fell back against the headboard until the nausea passed.

She advanced gingerly with the tray, as if afraid the floor might collapse underneath her. Her smile stayed fixed. She set the tray down beside him and nodded for him to move over.

Her long, ash-coloured hair dripped water onto her nightie, onto the sheets. "I had a shower all by myself," she said.

"Good for you," he said.

Her hair glistened with leftover shampoo and her nightie was soiled with peanut butter, smears of jam and splatters of yellowed milk. "I can take care of us, Daddy." Her hazel eyes burrowed into him.

He looked away. "Daddy doesn't deserve you."

She poured milk into a cup for him, spilling some drops. "Damn," she said, just like her mother used to whenever she stubbed her toe, accidentally dropped a plate or burned the bread she'd forgotten in the oven.

Alexia held up one piece of the toasted peanut butter and jam sandwich she'd hacked into awkward triangles. Strawberry jam oozed onto the white antique plate, Sara's favourite, the one she brought out at Christmas, Easter or Thanksgiving. Alexia put the first bit of sandwich up to his mouth as if feeding one of her dolls. "Okay?" She opened her mouth to show him how it should be done.

He took the piece from her and wondered how she'd become such a serious little girl. He bit down and acid welled in his stomach, scaled up his throat. He gulped hard to keep himself from throwing up. When he finally spoke, he said, "You're strong like your mother, *paidi mou.*"

Alexia shrugged, kept her eyes on the tray. She moved the creamer, the sugar bowl and the plate from one side of the tray to the other, wiped the spilled milk and moved them back. She did this once, then a second time and a third, as if unaware of what she was doing.

When she was done, she looked around his room. Sara's chair, a beat-up leather discard she'd rescued from the flea market dumpster, was buried under a heap of dirty clothes. In that chair, Sara had breastfed Alexia and rocked her to sleep, read to her, the two of them snuggled under the plaid throw she'd bought when she got pregnant. The throw lay twisted on the floor along with Nicolai's old work shirt, a dress shirt, khakis and his funeral suit.

Alexia walked over to the piles of clothes and picked up everything, including his suit, and dumped it all into the hamper. Bending into the hamper and shoving all her weight on top, she squished the pile down. He should have said something about things needing to go to the cleaner, but just then she picked up the throw in front of her mother's chair, sniffed it, rubbed it against her cheek and hugged it into her chest. He held his breath.

She turned, caught his eye and began to fold the throw. "It's pretty old. I guess we should get rid of it. Okay, Daddy?" She dropped it on the chair and came back to sit beside him, stroked his hand, and then picked up another piece of the sandwich, ready to pass it to him.

He was trying, but he could barely take care of himself, let alone an eight-year-old. If he managed to cook something for them, he didn't have the energy to eat. He'd make macaroni and cheese or a tuna casserole and leave it on the counter with a note: "Daddy's not feeling well. Warm this up in the microwave. Make sure to do your homework." Then he'd fall into bed, exhausted, away from the constant worry in his daughter's eyes. He knew they couldn't go on like this.

He had to get away, even if it was just for a little while. As soon as the thought occurred to him, he knew in his bones it was true. He felt his shoulders relax and the throbbing behind his eyes ease. He needed to put his life back together before he could take care of someone else. But where? The question rolled around in his head.

A week later it came to him.

He called a company to clean the house. Four Merry Maids with buckets full of cleaning supplies swept, emptied, sprayed, vacuumed and washed every surface. As he drifted around the house, he found Alexia talking to the women, asking questions about the supplies they brought, what cleaning products they used on the counters and the floors, how often the fridge needed to be cleaned, how to use the washer and dryer. She scribbled notes or asked them to write things down for her.

He heard one of the Merry Maids say to her, "Sweetie, you're not big enough to do all these things by yourself."

"I am so big enough," Alexia said. "I have to take care of my daddy." She continued to write the names of the products they spelled out for her. They stroked her hair and shook their heads.

"Stay out of their way and let them do their work, Alexia." Everything was backwards. He was supposed to take care of her. Why couldn't he? He gripped the coffee cup in his hand and brought it to his mouth, swallowed too quickly and burned his tongue. He just couldn't.

Later Nicolai brought home a box of *bougatsa* and *baklava* and put it down on the kitchen table. "Let's have something sweet."

"Okay Daddy, now that the cleaning ladies showed me how, I'll be able to do it after school," she said.

"Daddy's going to sell the house."

She was reaching for a slice of *bougatsa*. She pulled back her hand, stuck it behind her back. Her bright hazel eyes were questioning. Her T-shirt sat askew over one shoulder as if too big for her. She fixed a smile in place and yanked at her shirt. "Something new would be good."

"Go on, have a piece of *bougatsa, paidi mou*. It's your favourite."

"Will I go to the same school?"

"You could go anywhere."

"I can do it, Daddy." She put her hand over his.

She was such a good little girl. Maybe there was another way. He should try for her, for Sara. He shouldn't put Alexia through this. He knew that Sara wouldn't want him to give up. But he wasn't giving up. He was trying to do his best. He couldn't take care of anything. That was bloody obvious. Maybe he could try. Life might get better. But if he got away even for a little while, maybe he'd come back a better person, more ready to be what she needed, less angry. He'd already made up his mind.

He moved his hand away, picked up the box, passed Alexia a slice of *bougatsa* and took one for himself. They sat across from each other. She talked about the new house they'd buy, the bigger yard they might get, where she'd go to school, and how it was time they got a dog. Warm custard dripped onto their chins, through their fingers and onto the table. She giggled.

He couldn't remember the last time he'd heard her laugh. "Talking with your mouth full," he said. "You're Greek."

She nodded, swiping one dollop of custard after the other from the table.

He had practised what he would say, but now as she sat in front of him licking custard from her fingers, he couldn't find the words. He bit at his lip. He wasn't sure when he'd tell her, but he had a ticket for a flight leaving Vancouver for Toronto and then on to Athens a week Thursday. Why Greece? He wasn't sure. He'd left it before to start something new, but nothing had worked out as planned. It was the only place he could think of. And besides, he'd be with his mother and sisters. If nothing else, they'd take care of him. He could use that. And if his father hadn't changed, they'd buffer him from the old man. There was lots of time to tell Alexia.

"What kind of house do you think we should get, Daddy?"

She did deserve better than him. He shrugged. "Let's see what happens."

He told his clients he was taking a break, reassigned his files, took Alexia to school each morning, put the house up for sale, got rid of what he could and called the Salvation Army to pick up the rest. He told Alexia she could keep anything she wanted.

"I don't need a lot of stuff," she said, then picked her mother's antique serving plate, a framed picture of Sara and some books—*Moby Dick, Hansel and Gretel* and the entire Dr. Seuss series—her mother had bought her. She pasted a picture of the whole family, all three of them, taken when she was four, into her notebook. She told him she liked this picture best of all because they were together for a weekend away so he wasn't worried about work and could spend all his time with them, like a family.

Her mother's special reading throw went to the Salvation Army. She put it into the garbage bag herself, turned and looked around. She quickly grabbed some towels beside her and covered the throw. Later she piled a few tea towels and a set of sheets on top. "I'm not little anymore," she said.

Throughout the week, she was helpful and chatty. "I don't think we need this in our new house, Daddy. What do you think?"

"I'm trying not to."

"Can I help pick the new house?"

"We're not going to look for a house right away," he said. "We're going to stay with Uncle Stuart and Auntie Mavis for a while."

"Oh, good. Then we can take our time, right, Daddy? I know we'll find just the most perfect house." She patted his hand.

He couldn't meet her eye. "Why don't you go finish up with those toys?" he said, letting go of her hand. He walked over to the window. She went to her toy box, fishing for pieces of her Lego set, the one she planned to give away.

He leaned against the windowsill, heard a lone bird screech outside, but couldn't find where it was perched.

His flight was at three o'clock. That would give him just enough time to pack the rest of the boxes, close up the house, take the keys to the real estate office and have a quick lunch with Alexia before dropping her off at Stuart and Mavis's. He still hadn't told her that he was going away, hadn't been able to find the right time to do it. He hoped she'd understand. If he kept moving, focused on the list of things he had to do, he'd get through it. For now, all she needed to know was that she wasn't going to school today.

"You won't need a lunch today," he said.

"How come?" She was standing at the kitchen counter dressed as usual in her school uniform, the navy-blue skirt and the regulation white blouse making her look more grown-up than she was. She pushed the jar of peanut butter away and put the knife down, left her sandwich only partially spread.

"I called the school and told them we're spending the day together. We have to say good-bye to the old house and move to Uncle Stuart's place and..."

Her head was cocked, her forehead furrowed. He was sure she'd caught the hesitation in his voice. He couldn't meet her questioning eyes. He put the peanut butter into one of the boxes, rinsed off her plate and knife, added them to the box.

"Well, looks like this is the last of it. We'd better get going." he said.

She followed him out to the car.

After he dropped the keys at the real estate office he took Alexia to a nearby Greek diner, where they split an order of calamari and a Greek salad.

He couldn't delay it any longer. "Daddy has to go away on a business trip." He turned his chair towards her and moved hers so that his legs hugged her chair and she faced him. She sat like a caged bird, picking at her thumbnail. He put his hand over hers.

"When?"

She stared at him with those eyes that made him feel worthless. He reached over to wipe off a drop of olive oil on her chin with his napkin. Alexia took it from him and wiped her mouth, then sat on her hands.

"When, Daddy?"

He bit at the inside of his mouth, stared at the closed door just beyond where she sat. His voice cracked, he cleared his throat, then ploughed forward. "This afternoon," he said and cleared his throat again.

"Where are you going, Daddy?"

"Greece. I have to go do some work there, so you're going to stay with Stuart and Mavis for a little while. They're your godparents. So they're just like your real parents except they'll probably let you get away with more stuff."

"When are you coming back?"

"I don't know yet," he said. "I have to go find out how hard it's going to be."

"I could go with you, Daddy. I could ask for homework and do my school work while we're away. Honest. We could call my teacher now. I know she'd let me do it." She jumped off her chair, pushed it back out of his reach, wiped her mouth with the napkin again and threw it on the table.

"*Paidi mou,* I'll be busy working. And besides, you like school, your friends. I promise you, next time we'll go together and then you can meet all your aunts. They're crazy but really, really nice. You remember when Aunt Christina was here?"

Alexia nodded. She opened her mouth to say something, choked and coughed. He stroked her back. A single tear ran down her cheek. He wiped it away with his napkin.

"You shouldn't talk and eat at the same time," he said. "You're just like them."

"Why don't we go this summer then?" she said. "School will be out in a month. We could go together then."

"I have to go now, Alexia. I'm sorry."

"Mommy would want us to stick together," she said, her voice breaking. She grabbed her glass and gulped water just like Sara used to whenever she was about to cry and wanted to control the impulse.

He reached for her. If he could explain that he was having a bad time without Sara, that he felt angry and helpless all the time, that this would be better for both of them at least for a little while, he was sure she'd understand. But then she might think it was her fault and he didn't want that either. He'd said what he had to say. There was nothing else.

She put the glass down, excused herself to go to the bathroom. Nicolai held on to the back of her empty chair.

When she returned, she had somehow managed to find her serious little girl composure. She asked him about the work he was going to do and he made up a client. A large shipping company needed a new marketing campaign. She listened, asked questions, nodded and asked more questions. He surprised himself with the answers he so quickly came up with. He smiled, made jokes about the challenges of working with Greeks who showed up late for meetings, tapping her shoulder now and again as if she were a client he had to charm. It was a lie. They both knew it.

After lunch, he dropped her off at Stuart's. He left his car there and called a cab.

"Everything's going to be fine," Stuart said. He tried to put his arm around Nicolai's shoulder. Nicolai bent down to hug Alexia.

"Don't worry about a thing," Mavis said. "You know we'll take good care of her."

Stuart had been his best man. When Sara was alive, Stuart and Mavis were over at the house every Sunday for dinner. They'd dropped off food for him and Alexia after Sara died. He'd called them a week ago to ask them to take care of Alexia. Stuart had wanted to talk. Then Mavis phoned for one of her friendly chats. He couldn't. Not then. Not now. All he could think about was getting away from their concerned nods, from Mavis's warm hand on his back. He didn't need her sympathy.

"Take as long as you need," Stuart said. Mavis crouched down and put her arm around Alexia's shoulders.

Nicolai knew Sara wouldn't understand. She loved her friends, but they weren't Alexia's parents. "She needs you," Sara would say to him whenever he was late for supper or worked weekends. No, he said to her now, Alexia needs better than me. He looked up at the waiting cab.

"You'd better go, Daddy. He's waiting," Alexia said. "Don't worry. I'll be good." She held his hand as if he needed the support.

He had to do this for both of them. "See you soon, *paidi mou*."

She nodded. He hugged her. Her arms wilted by her sides. He turned and got into the cab and waved at her over his shoulder as it pulled away. Long after he'd gotten to the airport, checked in and got on the plane, he could still see her brave little face.

2010

Alexia lay fully clothed under the bedspread, her linen pants and silk blouse hopelessly wrinkled. I can take them to the drycleaners later, she thought. When he gets better.

She hadn't slept in this room for ages. Ten years. Maybe more. An adult, and somehow still the same little girl who had once taken care of him. On the dresser, the brush and mirror set Nicolai gave her the year she turned thirteen. She hadn't taken it with her when she left for university or when she moved into her own condo after law school. The pink mother-of-pearl was meant for a little girl. Someone else, she thought. Not me. She'd left behind most of the things he'd given her over the years: the Canadian dollar bill he said was the first he'd made in this country, the glass eyeball he brought back from Greece to ward off the evil eye, the marble worry beads too big and clumsy for her hands. Not enough room in the dorm, she'd said. He tapped his fingers against his leg and gnawed at the inside of his mouth like he did when he was disappointed or nervous.

And now here she was, back looking after him because he was too sick to take care of himself. It was just like him not to tell her about the cancer. "If it was too hard for you to tell me in person, you could have told me on the phone or sent me a note."

"I didn't want to worry you," he said, shaking his head.

"Dad, we can find a solution to this."

He smiled and held her hand. "You always take care of things."

"So let me help."

That boyish grin was not an answer. I bet he told his mantra-chanting girlfriend, she thought. As if that airhead could do anything to help him. She'd show him this could be fixed.

She'd called his doctor, insisted on another treatment plan. She printed some articles she found on the Internet about new procedures in Mexico and India. There was always something that could be done. Problems didn't exist that effort couldn't solve. That's how she lived. And it worked. She was the youngest partner in her firm. She'd wanted it and she'd gotten it when she was only twenty-nine. She'd get his health back, too, by herself if she had to.

"Some things we have to accept," Nicolai said and stroked her face.

He was such a fatalist. But, she wasn't ready to give up.

She kicked off the covers, went to the dresser and fingered the mirror. When he gets better, I'll take this back to my place, put it on my dresser. He'll like that.

She heard his voice coming faintly from the room down the hall.

"Dad?"

No answer.

She opened his bedroom door. Stagnant, humid air. The thermostat turned up because he complained of being cold. She listened. His snore was steady.

She opened the blinds and realized she shouldn't have bothered. The sky was overcast. Threatening. He needed sunshine. A clear sky full of promise. It wasn't too late.

She'd made him a Greek salad, roasted a leg of lamb and squeezed three extra lemons on his fried potatoes. He loved them that way. He hadn't touched any of it. At least he'd managed a cup of clear broth once and sometimes twice a day in the time she'd been here, protecting him from his bad dreams, his regrets, this stupid disease.

As she sat down on the chair beside the bed, he jerked awake.

"I woke you up again, didn't I?" he said. The covers moved as he yawned.

"I was just getting up anyway." She cupped her hand over his forehead. "Do you want some water?"

He patted her leg. "You've done too much. What about your work? You should get back to it."

"I think we should see another doctor."

"We need to talk." He tried to hoist himself up in the bed.

"Where are you going?"

He lay still.

"I have a list of doctors I found through the College of Physicians. I've made an appointment to see one of them the day after tomorrow; your medical files have already been transferred. We're going together."

He closed his eyes as if her voice caused him pain. "I made a mistake years ago."

That again. How many times did he have to apologize for leaving her after her mother died? She'd heard it all before. She'd tell him the same thing she always did when he got down on himself. "No harm done." Please. Let's not dredge up this old story.

"When I left you ..."

"Dad, the past is the past. Forget it. Let's just focus on how we're going to fix this problem we have now. That's all we should be worrying about."

She stood. "I'll get you some water."

He shook his head, tried to lift himself up again and coughed. He sank back against his pillow and hacked. "You have a sister."

She put her hand on his shoulder. Why did he keep doing this? "You don't know what you're saying." He was delirious again. The morphine. It could do that. She touched the jaundiced skin of his cheek. The white stubble pricked. She pulled away. "You're stuck with me, Dad. There's no one else." A laugh caught in her throat.

He grabbed her hand, pulled her close. His breath was sour. Perspiration beaded his upper lip.

"No one knows," he said finally. "Too many secrets. I'm sorry. So many things."

"Dad, you've just been dreaming. It's okay. When you're better, you'll see." She patted his hand. She caught a whiff of her blouse. She needed a shower, but how could she leave him like this? The morphine wasn't keeping up with his pain. She'd call the doctor in an hour; see if they could get in today.

"*Paidi mou,* I'm telling you."

"It's just a bad dream. Lay back now. Rest and get better."

"It's true, Alexia." He stared at her, his eyes ablaze for the first time in weeks.

She stood and pulled her sweater tight around her.

"What do you want from me?" she said, regretting the words as soon as they were out. Patience. She had to be patient with him. He needed understanding now. It doesn't matter what he says, she told herself. He'll forget about it later. It's meaningless. Stop reacting.

He shook his head like a disappointed little boy. "I'm sorry. Can't explain." He closed his eyes. "Don't live like me."

He drifted into sleep again. It had to be the morphine. In the two weeks she'd been here, he'd called out to her almost every night, and each time she'd gone to him, he talked gibberish. In the morning, he didn't remember a thing. He shivered in his sleep as though freezing hands had been laid on his warm chest. She leaned over him and tucked the comforter around him. His chin was ice cold.

A sister? What next?

"Haven't I been enough family for you?" she whispered. "Haven't I taken care of you?"

Flipping and rubbing worry beads was how her father sorted out his problems. They were in the pocket of his pants now. He was enmeshed in silk, like the sheets he brought out when he had a friend over to the condominium. He hated silk sheets. He'd told her: silk for friends, flannel for him. But Erica, his last in a chain of thirty-year-old girlfriends, had insisted on the silk lining.

"You think you know my dad better than I do?" Alexia had shot at Erica in the funeral home. Ross, the ruddy-faced, broad-chested funeral home director sat at one end of the boardroom table like a tired referee. He seemed stuffed into his clothes, his neck scored by his tight collar, his suit creased around his arms. Erica sat on Ross's left, a thin stick. Her father had liked his women androgynous.

"We were soul mates." Erica dabbed at her eyes. A fluff of Kleenex stuck to one edge of her nose.

"After six months?"

"Almost seven." She sniffled.

Ross rubbed at his nose. Erica followed his lead. The shred of Kleenex floated to the table. Alexia glanced away just as Erica caught her eye. Ross's face turned a darker shade of red. When he spoke, his tone was conciliatory and his smile as cold as the marble headstones he'd shown them. "Let's compromise, shall we? Nicolai would have wanted it that way."

Alexia doubted Ross knew what her father wanted. She didn't, and she had known him all her life. Still, she argued about the casket, the fabric that lined it, the time of the service and the words to be written on the headstone. Erica paced.

Finally they agreed: Alexia would pick the headstone and casket; Erica would choose the casket lining.

"It's the most important part," Erica said. "It's what's closest to him."

Alexia thought about changing her mind, putting Erica in her place. I don't have to let you be a part of any of this, she thought. You're just another one of his bimbos.

Ross bowed his head and gripped the sides of the table as if expecting an explosion. He wasn't the only one in the room who was tired.

At the funeral, people Alexia didn't even know touched her arm and hugged her. Others nodded in her direction. They sat against one another, filling the long pews of the Greek Orthodox Church. Alexia saw the priest's lips move, didn't register a word. She scanned the high ceilings, the replica gothic arches, the walls that seemed to glow against the cherry-coloured beams. A strip of wooden relief carvings lined one wall. Christ's journey to the cross. Another step. Another fall. The third carving dangled slightly lower than the rest. Hadn't anyone bothered to measure before hanging them?

Erica sat in the pew on the opposite side. She wore sandals, a black skirt, and a see-through peasant shirt that enhanced her alabaster skin and flat chest. Alexia's heels pinched her feet and her suit felt stiff. She poked at her French braid. She had wound it up too tightly this morning and now it made her scalp itch.

She sat between Stuart and Mavis. Stuart patted Alexia's hand. Stuart had been her father's friend since he immigrated to Canada. He became his first and only legal advisor after Nicolai opened his public relations firm. He was more than Nicolai's lawyer; he and

Mavis were Nicolai's best friends and her godparents. It was Stuart who got Alexia interested in law. He often took her to his office and just let her hang out, among the paper and books.

She felt Mavis's arm around her shoulders like a warm shawl.

She shifted in her seat, saw her boss, Dan, a few rows away, wondered what he was doing there. She supposed he had come to represent their firm. Still, it was nice he took the time.

She slipped off her shoes, twisted the handkerchief that had been her father's, the one her mother had given him. It had yellowed over the years. She'd kept it under her pillow after he died, rubbed her cheek and sniffed it when she thought of him. She couldn't bring herself to wash it.

She tried to remember one of her father's corny Greek expressions, one that actually made her laugh.

"If you don't learn how to relax, *paidi mou*," he'd said one day, "you'll get old." He was in bed with the flu. She cleared the half-empty glasses of water on his nightstand.

"Look who's calling the kettle black."

"Greeks have a similar expression. *Epe a gaitharos ton petino kefala.*"

"Huh?"

"The donkey called the rooster a big-head."

"I guess that's similar."

He'd laughed. She kissed his flushed cheek and handed him the soup she'd picked up at the market.

It didn't rain or even spit on the day of his burial. And it wasn't a Tuesday. She made sure of that. He hated doing anything important—going to the bank, paying bills, signing any major deals—on that day. "It's bad luck," he'd say. "We Greeks lost Istanbul on a Tuesday." Whenever she'd tease him about his superstitions, he always had the same comeback as if it explained everything. "This is who we are."

Her father would rest for eternity in Vancouver's damp ground in a casket beside the one that held her mother. He always told her he wanted to be buried beside Sara. They had the same conversation every time he took a business trip or got sick or had a doctor's appointment. "If something happens."

"Nothing's going to happen," Alexia reassured him.

"If," he insisted. "There will never be anyone but your mother, and when the time comes, you and, if you marry, which I know you will, your husband, lying beside me."

She couldn't remember when her father's service ended or how she arrived at Stuart's office. He stood in front of the window, blocking the sun's glare. When he shifted, she was blinded by shards of light. She blinked. She wished she could see his eyes.

As Stuart read Nicolai's will, he kept one hand in his pocket flipping his change just like always. When she was little, she thought he did that because he wanted everyone to know how rich he was. He was a tall, thin man with a high-pitched voice and one of those mouths that seemed to be frozen in a sideways grin. Even though she'd known him as long as she could remember, she could never figure out what he was thinking. He was a quiet man, not one to show his emotions.

Mazda, penthouse apartment, stocks. Hers. He left nothing to Erica or anyone else. She smiled, remembering Erica's words at the funeral home, "We're soul mates." As if. He didn't have soul mates. He had conquests.

Stuart cleared his throat. There was more.

"I'm listening," she said.

Stuart came around the desk to stand in front of her. Alexia wondered when he'd developed all those lines near his eyes and mouth. The skin around his neck buckled and sagged. He was missing Nicolai too. They shouldn't have done this today. She'd insisted. She needed to close this chapter and get on with her life. They were all so damn tired. It would be good to get it over with.

Stuart took off his glasses, wiped them against the front of his jacket, its metal buttons tinkling against the lenses. He put the glasses back on, looked up and met Alexia's gaze. "There's just one more thing," he said. "Your father's final wish. He wants you to go to Greece."

Alexia frowned. Had he known this all along? "But we've buried him here already," she said.

"He wants you to deliver a package to your sister."

"What are you talking about?"

"Your sister, Theodora. You." He stared at her for a moment, then looked away, shaking his head. "I'm sorry, Alexia. I thought he'd told you."

She stood up abruptly, almost knocking into him. "Excuse me?"

His eyes pleaded. "He didn't want to die with this secret hanging between the two of you."

She couldn't look at him. "I thought he was delirious."

Stuart put his arm around her.

She pulled away.

"It can't be true."

"All I know is that he wants you to deliver what's in this box to your half-sister. I mean Theodora." He walked around to the other side of his desk and sat down heavily in his chair.

She stared at him in the same way she'd stared at her father when he used some Greek expression she didn't understand.

"This was hard for him."

"Was it? I think he liked secrets." She crossed her arms against her chest. "He liked to play, and he never minded leaving his messes for others to clean up."

"Alexia, you're not being fair."

"He never told me anything important until it was too late." She felt tears welling up. No way was she going to cry. No damn way. She swallowed hard, blinked and focused on what Stuart had placed on his desk.

She couldn't help the gasp that escaped from her chest. They'd cleared out her mother's things years ago, and yet, here were her ribbons holding the lid of this shoebox in place. Her mother had tied up her hair with these ribbons while she vacuumed the house or weeded the garden. Why had her father used them to tie this box? He could be so clueless sometimes. They were likely hanging around when he needed them so he used them. Never once thinking that maybe she'd like to have them.

Alexia reached out to touch the ribbons, could almost hear her mother's voice again. "We'll clean up, then go to the park."

Sara was standing in front of the mirror in the bathroom. Alexia sat on the closed toilet lid beside the counter, her legs tucked underneath her. "I can help," she said, handing Sara a blue ribbon. She watched her mother loop it around her long, thick hair.

Something cool stroked Alexia's forearm. She looked down at Stuart's hand, at the trail of liver spots.

"You are sisters. This box may make a difference to her. It might help you too."

She turned and walked out of his office, her heels ringing on the hardwood floors. No. No. No. Stuart's pleas dropped behind her. I took care of him my whole life, she fumed as she punched the elevator buttons. I can't remember a time when I didn't. He never trusted me enough to tell me what was going on. Anytime I asked, everything was always great. It wasn't great. He was sick. He had a child with another woman.

Liar.

A few weeks later, on a Saturday afternoon, Stuart showed up at her apartment door, his tie loosened, his jacket slung over his arm. He left his briefcase and a large plastic bag at the front door and followed her into the living room. Alexia ignored the bag. He was still trying to pawn off that box, she thought.

He sat heavily on the couch. She sat stiffly on the loveseat, her hands tucked under her legs.

"I've known you your whole life, Alexia," he said. "I know how hard this is."

"I don't want to have anything to do with that box, Stuart."

She turned her back to him to face Coal Harbour and the flickering lights on the north shore. Why couldn't Stuart have protected her from all this? After all, he'd been a second father to her. And if he couldn't do that, why hadn't he advised her father to tell her about this long ago? This is what lawyers do. At the very least, he should have advised his client to take his stupid secret to the grave.

"Alexia, you're the executor of his estate. Think about your professional responsibilities."

"And what if I don't want to?"

"He trusted you."

She shrugged.

Minutes passed and she didn't move. Finally, she heard the door click closed behind him. Go, she thought. Dad did when things got tough. You might as well too.

Her windows vibrated at the bang of the Stanley Park cannon just as they did every night at nine o'clock. She went to the bathroom and saw the large plastic bag by the front door, saw the shape of the shoebox inside. Forget it, she said out loud. I'm not getting involved. This is not my problem.

She ignored it that night and every night for a week, then two. Each time she kicked it on her way out the door she was reminded of what her father expected. Sometimes she knelt and touched the ribbons and thought about her mother. Finally, she loosened a ribbon from the box, wrapped it around her own long hair and looked at herself in the mirror. She expected to see her mother. Instead, her father's eyes stared back at her.

As a child Alexia had been envious of her friends who had summer vacations with cousins, aunts and uncles. She had vacations with her father or was sent to summer camps. She'd wondered what it would be like to have a big family and asked her father why they didn't visit his. He never gave her an answer that made any sense. More lies.

Alexia had met her aunt Christina only once, when she came to visit in Vancouver a few years before Sara died. She found a picture in her father's desk when she finally got around to clearing it out. A phone number was scratched on the back. As she dialled, she thought, it's the right thing to do: tell a woman her brother is dead.

"You need family now," Christina said. "What is for you in Vancouver?"

If only Christina had brought up the subject of Theodora, Alexia would have sent her the shoebox. Then she could get on with her life. It sat, an undone responsibility, a task she couldn't check off. I don't want to know this half-sister, she thought, or play nice like Dad always told me to do. He'd brag about my honour roll marks, the fact that I was the captain of my undefeated high school basketball team, puffing up my small successes until I didn't know if they were real. When I performed, he loved me. Like some trained seal, I got used to that stupid smirk I could get out of him whenever he liked what I was doing.

After that first call, Christina phoned Alexia every Sunday. At the end of each conversation she said the same thing: "Come home to us, your family."

"Your mother, poor girl, is gone too early, your father too. No husband. You are young. You need to relax, take a break from everything."

"I don't take breaks."

"Time to start, no?"

She ignored her aunt. Work and more of it was the only thing that could keep her mind off what her father had asked her to do. Keep her mind off him. She walked to work and avoided the place on Cordova Street where her father used to meet his sea-wall-strolling buddies every morning for a walk and breakfast. She didn't let herself think about how he'd wave as she went by. She stayed at the office until close to nine. Sometimes when she got home earlier, she'd even forget to anticipate his eight o'clock phone calls, his nightly check-in to see how her day had been. Eventually, she unplugged the phone as soon as she came in the door. She stopped expecting his Saturday morning drop-ins too, warm *galaktoboureko* or some other pastry in a box in one hand, two small bottles of apricot juice from the Greek deli in the other. Instead, she'd go for a run, poke her head in a few shops, pick up a paper, sit on a park bench and read for half an hour, her drying sweat making her cold.

The stack of files lay on the kitchen table. She'd planned to review them, make notes and get ready for the following week's negotiations. Instead, she was sitting on the living room floor and watching one floatplane after another taxi into and out of Coal Harbour. Preoccupied with the sea bus on its treadmill run to the north shore, she blamed the claustrophobic sky for her apathy. Raindrops splattered against her window. She told herself she'd sit for another few minutes and then get on with work.

Damn that shoebox. Why can't I get someone else to take it off my hands? She'd moved it into the front closet because she was sick of tripping over it. What had her father given Theodora? Money? Some old family papers she wasn't allowed to see? Why her and not me? Her stomach ached.

She sat in front of the window until the sky changed from murky to black. She couldn't figure out how to make herself move. The lights from a plane in the harbour disappeared into the sky. Her muscles throbbed. She saw her father's downcast eyes, spotted the quiver in his jaw. He was disappointed in her.

"Don't live like me. You have family," he'd said when he told her about the other daughter.

"What about me?" she said out loud to the blackness beyond the window.

She fell asleep on the floor. When she woke, it was the middle of the night. She felt him standing in front of her, shaking his head. "Why are you sleeping on the floor? Don't you have a bed?"

"I'm not little anymore," she hurled back. "I can do anything I want." The anger in her voice surprised her.

She stumbled to her bedroom. The mirror set lay on her dresser. She'd brought it home after he died. She held the mirror up and heard him say it clearly: "Do this for me."

She pushed the images away. She stared into the mirror at the creases in her face. Her French braid hung loose; frizzy wisps stuck out in all directions. She licked her fingers and stroked her hair to make it lie flat, but the wayward bits refused to weave back into place. She pulled out the elastic and threw it on the dresser.

He wasn't going to let her be until she got rid of that box. She slammed her hand against the dresser so hard her arm went numb. It ached as she typed and revised drafts of her request to the firm. She would send it by email. Once she'd clicked 'Send' she crawled into bed. For the first time in months, she slept until the sun was high in the sky and clawed at her eyelids, untroubled by any dreams.

"We need you here, Alexia. You're one of our finest." Dan stood beside his desk and held onto the piece of paper he'd ripped out of the printer. His tie was cinched tight, his jacket buttoned. The consummate professional, she thought.

"I need to sort some things out." Alexia stood just inside the door to his office. She held his gaze.

Dan, her firm's senior partner, sat down behind his desk, and motioned for her to take a seat. He fingered the edges of her note. "I can't lose you."

"Look, Dan, I know this isn't done, especially by junior partners. But I need to get away for a while. A week, two at the most."

"Is this the best time for you to be taking off?"

Why did he want to be difficult? I've never taken so much as a vacation day, she thought. This is important. Doesn't he get that? And besides, she only wanted enough time to deliver the package to Christina, and convince her to pass it on. He could do without her for that long. The place wasn't going to fall apart.

He picked up the email. She watched him read it again. When he finally spoke, Dan offered more money, flexible hours, and when that didn't work, he said he'd miss her. She sat on her hands, teetered on the hurt one and dug her fingernails into the underside of her thighs. She repeated, "I have to do this," as much to convince herself as to convince him.

"You've got more guts than brains," he said. "I like that." He tugged a short swath of his hair through his fingers; a nervous habit of his she'd gotten used to over the five years they'd worked together. Funny how he could be so formal and businesslike and have this one thing that made him seem so vulnerable.

In the end, he approved her leave on the condition she be available by phone or email.

"I'll be back before you notice."

"I hope so." He grinned, then his mouth returned to its single line. He faced his computer. "Keep in touch. Right?" he said over his shoulder.

The pilot's voice mumbled that they were landing in Athens in twenty minutes and suggested people sitting on the right-hand side of the plane enjoy the view of Vouliagmeni. Alexia looked down on the small boats scattered across the turquoise water and the dots of people on the colourless sand. A perfect postcard scene except for the film of brownish-grey smog. The current temperature: 35 degrees Celsius. She rubbed her hands against the seat and tried not to think about the people she was about to meet.

In the arrival lounge, swarms of passengers elbowed and jostled forward beyond the gate controlled by one short, taciturn security guard. An older couple stopped in front of Alexia. A family of six or seven ducked under the gate and surrounded the couple, preventing her from moving. Shouts, tears, smiles, laughter and words she didn't understand. Alexia tried to get around one side of the group, then the other, but couldn't find a way so she stood and waited, staring up at a ceiling fan.

The guard finally ordered the family to move along. Alexia moved past him and walked into the crowd, into the sea of placards inked with names, a few in English, most in Greek.

Her name, too—ALEXIA—in bold, box letters. The woman who held the sign and a shrub-size clutch of white chrysanthemums was a slightly younger, shorter version of her father. Alexia recognized his high cheekbones and hazel eyes. She stopped, let the wave hit her.

"*Paidi mou*," Christina said. "It is me, your *thia* Christina. You are your father's daughter." She hugged Alexia, her grip pinning Alexia's arms against her sides. The smell of garlic veiled Christina's hair and her dark, too-loose-fitting suit. When she finally let go, Christina reached up towards Alexia's face and pulled her chin towards her. Her aunt's eyes were as clear as her father's had once been.

"I am so happy," Christina said, and before she could finish she sniffled, her face contorted as if holding her emotions in check.

Alexia wasn't sure if she should hug Christina or look away. Christina thrust the flowers under Alexia's nose and whimpered in Greek, pulled out a wrinkled hanky from her purse and dabbed her eyes. The sweet smell of the chrysanthemums made Alexia sneeze. Christina smiled. Alexia rummaged through her bag for a Kleenex.

"*Ella*," Christina shouted and a small mob descended on them. Christina rattled off names and Alexia registered three cousins named Yannis, and one aunt and two cousins with the name Maria. Christina laughed when she saw Alexia's confusion. "Even we have to give them numbers," she said, and as if expecting the family to agree, she turned to them and said to no one in particular, "no?"

"There are differences," one of the Marias said. "You will see."

There were other names: Katarina, Zak and Solon. It was hard to keep them straight. As each of the relatives came forward, Alexia extended her hand. It got crushed against her aunt Maria's plump breasts, ended up inside her uncle Zak's jacket and tapped the cheek of one of the other Marias, who was particularly short and came in too close for a hug. Alexia smiled, and they smiled. She apologized once, and then again, and finally stopped trying to shake anyone's hand. Instead, she let herself be handled.

Alexia's face felt tight, her jaw sore. Maintaining this smile wasn't easy.

"This is just a small part of family," Christina said. She led Alexia towards the exit. The rest followed.

The doors mechanically fanned open and closed again. Alexia caught a glimpse of the brilliant blue sky wavering like a mirage in the heat.

1986

Nicolai parked the rental car around the corner from his parents' house and walked up Vyronos street towards the sea. Houses hadn't changed here since he'd left. Ten or twelve years ago. The old trails in front of the fields were paved now and a village had grown, but the farms remained. A rooster called out. Grasshoppers knocked in the fields. Nicolai glanced up at one open window, then another, and quickly looked away, hoping no one would recognize him. But it was early morning, he told himself. The farmers would already be in the fields. It was just the women at home.

People didn't change here, either. "Why are you back?" he'd be asked as soon as he was recognized. It wouldn't matter how he responded, the gossip would start. They'd say he couldn't make a go of it in Canada or he missed the homeland or he got into trouble. They'd make up some story or another to pass the time. He knew what his family's reaction would be. They'd ignore the stares and whispers. "He's so successful," his mother would brag, "he can afford a holiday like this. You should see the gifts he brought." She'd avoid any mention of his dead wife or the daughter he left behind. All bad luck that reflected badly on the family.

Nicolai passed a tomato field. Stavros was bent over his vines, no doubt checking for worms or whatever ate at tomatoes. Sara would know. He didn't. Someone Nicolai didn't recognize squatted in the field alongside the next house. Chickens pecked aimlessly at the ground beside her. Nicolai picked up his pace and found himself at the end of the road near the channel of water separating Diakofto from northern Greece. He thought he'd left these dead-ends behind.

He turned away from the sea and walked up another side street that led to his old school. Leaning against the chain-link fence, fingers laced through the metal, he stared at the building, the grassy weeds poking through the concrete slab of an outside basketball court where he used to play. Were any of his old friends still in the village?

Back at the car, he got his bag and walked back to his parents' house. Had it always looked so old? Under the whitewash façade, a web of mould clung to the walls. The steps looked like they hadn't been painted since he left. The concrete crumbled, exposing aggregate stone, rusty wire mesh. The peonies beside the steps drooped under the dust.

He'd left his daughter to return to this place? What was he thinking? He'd only wanted escape. From that empty house. Sara's ghost. His anger. He'd become his father. He couldn't do that to Alexia.

And how was he going to face his father? The last time he'd seen him, they'd argued. About his leaving. About who he was. His mother sitting at the table, her head bowed, and her hands over her ears. His father flipping the cupboard doors open and slamming them shut again as he paced.

"Why do you want to go?"

"Canada has opportunities."

"We have the same things. Look here first," his father said, tapping hard on Nicolai's head with his index finger. His father scowled, but his tight-lipped grin stayed in place. "Stop filling your head with useless dreams." He drilled at Nicolai's head again. "Think of someone else."

Nicolai grabbed his father's finger, bent it away from him.

His father didn't flinch.

"You never wanted to be here either."

They stood face to face, his father's pupils large and black, the whites of his eyes streaked with angry red veins, his garlic breath laced with a trace of something else. Something dying. He pushed his father away.

"You are not a son of mine."

"Best news I've heard."

His father didn't come to the ship the day he sailed from Patras. His mother and sisters rode with him in the taxi, took pictures of him in his new suit and waved goodbye from the pier, their hands choking handkerchiefs.

After he arrived in Canada, he wrote to his mother and sisters when he found the time. When Christina wrote, she said, *Father is well. He never changes.*

Nicolai sent his mother and sisters a funeral notice after Sara died, but never told them he was coming home. Once he'd made the decision, there wasn't time to write, and when he thought about phoning them, it was always too early or too late in Greece to call.

A loud yowl made him jump. A striped tomcat with a bloodied eye attacked a larger black one. Nicolai shouted and they ran off, one chasing the other. He rubbed his hands against his pants as if he'd touched the mangy things, smelled himself and caught a whiff of cramped, long-distance travel. Get on with it, he told himself firmly. Get in the house and out of the sun. He heard a noise behind him and turned to the door.

His father opened the screen and stepped forward as if to come out and greet him, but stopped and stood still inside the doorframe, blocking entrance to the house. Nicolai took a step back, dropped his suitcase. They stared at one another.

"The garden looks good," Nicolai said finally, with a nod to the peonies.

His father scoffed. "The narcissus has already wilted." He wore what he always wore: a pair of wool pants, the pressed lines shiny with age; underneath his flannel shirt and thin sweater, a bright white undershirt frayed at the edges. The same cross he'd had since Nicolai was a boy hung around his neck.

"Yes."

"Nicolai!" his mother shouted his name the way she used to when he was a boy. Her face appeared behind his father's shoulder.

She tapped on his back, and when he didn't move she ducked under one of his burly arms, bursting towards her son, wrapping him in her arms. She was shorter than he remembered. Jasmine scented her hair. Nicolai pulled her in closer, held on to her like he used to when he was little, after a nightmare. She patted his back and he tightened his hold briefly, then released her. She led him into the house, her arm around his waist. She told his father to bring Nicolai's suitcase.

His father stood by the sink in the kitchen, gulped his coffee, put his cup down, grabbed his hat and work gloves and headed towards the door. His mother stood beside Nicolai, her arm in his. She took a step towards her husband.

"But why today?" Nicolai's mother asked.

"This woman has a bad memory," his father said. "This is what I do every day."

"Your son is home."

"And this is news?" He shrugged, raised his hands and shook them at her in an exasperated prayer. "*Ella,* what do you want from me? We have to eat."

The door slammed behind him. Nicolai's mother shouted at him through the screen. "One day is too much to ask from you?" She rubbed her hands on her apron.

She smiled at Nicolai without meeting his eyes. "He can't change."

She pushed Nicolai towards one of the kitchen chairs. "Sit, *paidi mou,* please."

It creaked as he sat down. He leaned against the table, cradled his head in his hand, suddenly exhausted. His eyelids closed. He blinked them open. The sleepless night on the plane was catching up with him. If only he could put his head down.

His mother washed grapes in the sink. She found her mother's fine linen napkins in the buffet and rummaged through the drawers for cutlery. As she moved around the kitchen, her black skirt fluttered. She kept talking as if he'd never been away. "Maria's husband was no good, anyway. We knew, but we never said a word. We wonder if Christina will ever marry. She has a nice apartment and a good job at the grocery store, but she's getting old. Solon is a good man. His family is another story. They don't like us. I don't see why not. They're not marrying us." She lowered her voice. "They want money to marry her." The change in her tone made him sit up. He rubbed his eyes and wondered how much he'd missed. This was like one of Sara's mystery novels. Read one, and you've read them all. Different characters, same plot.

"Katarina isn't eating again. She is too skinny. This is why she can't have children." She prepared a coffee as she prattled. "You will remember home when you drink this," she said, placing the cup in front of him.

The coffee smelled burnt. He took a quick gulp. The bitter flavour made his mouth pucker. He squeezed his eyes shut, swallowed once and then again to rid himself of the taste.

She opened the oven door, draped a tea towel over her hands and removed the loaf of bread. She put it on the counter and wiped her forehead with the same cloth. "This is what you need," she said. "Everything will be better soon." A strand of hair escaped the combs she pushed into the waves to keep the hair off her face. It stuck to her wet cheek.

His head drooped and he lurched up. The chair scraped against the stone floor.

"Maybe you should rest, Nicky. Eat later."

She led him down the hall to his old room. He thought about taking a shower, but it was more effort than he could manage. The bed squeaked as he lay down, just as it had when he was a boy. She took off his shoes, put a pillow under his head and covered him with the old comforter. It smelled of mildew. As she bent down to kiss the top of his head her hair fell against his cheek.

He wasn't sure how long he'd slept, but did remember her coming in to see him. His father stood behind her, a hand on her shoulder, his eyes softer. They'd spoken to each other, but he couldn't hear what was said. Nicolai couldn't remember his father ever being tender with his mother and wondered if he had dreamt the whole thing.

In the shower, the spray massaged his neck and shoulders and the hot water surrounded him in a mist he wished he could disappear into. As the water cooled, he turned the cold tap down gradually until there was no hot water left. He got out of the shower, changed and came into the kitchen.

"Water isn't cheap like in your country," his father said. He put his coffee down and dropped the section of the paper he'd been reading on top of the pile on the floor.

"You must be hungry now, Nicky," his mother said and got up. "Sit here."

"He's a man. Stop using his baby name." He picked up another section of the paper and opened it in front of his face.

She shook her head. "Your father doesn't understand." She pushed Nicolai onto the chair. "Your sisters are coming tonight for dinner. They came many times in the last day or so, but I told them to let you rest."

"I've been asleep for a day?"

"Maybe more," his father said. "The young never understand responsibility."

"Your sisters will be happy to see you."

"Maybe they will stop their phone calls. You're back. We know."

Nicolai sat down across from his father, the newspaper between them. Neither said another word. His mother brought him a coffee. "Now you'll feel better."

"I have to go." His father got up and tossed the paper on the floor.

"Is there anything I can help you with?" Nicolai asked. He stood up, leaned against the table for support, looked beyond his father to the back door.

"You can help your mother."

Nicolai sat down on his bed and stared at his feet. His sisters were going to be here soon. They'd want to know his plans. What was he doing here? How long was he staying? Was Alexia going to join him? It tired him to think about questions with no answers. He wasn't going to plan anything again. That much he knew. Life interfered anyway. What was the point?

He told himself he'd lie down for a few minutes until his sisters arrived. The sun jabbed at his eyelids, but he didn't turn his back to the window. Alexia was probably in school right now. She loved school; she loved her godparents. He saw her eager smile. He wished he could bring it on as easily as Sara had. Alexia was fine where she was.

Whispered voices, laughter and the scuff of pans sliding into the oven prodded him awake. Sounds from his childhood. At first, it was just noise. The sky beyond his window was now pinkish blue. He'd slept the afternoon away.

The smell of roasting meat wafted in the air. His stomach growled. He slung his legs over the side of the bed and sat up.

He smoothed his hands over his pants and shirt. The wrinkles refused to give way so he changed and put his clothes into a heap in the corner of the room.

Nicolai came into the kitchen and stood in the archway out of sight. His mother was chopping cucumbers, his sister Christina beside her. Both spoke quickly and raised their voices so they could be heard over the knock of the blade and the static of the radio.

"How is he?" Christina said.

"He's not like he was."

"He'll come around."

She was so like their mother, Nicolai thought. Much taller, but with a similar frame: thin from the waist up, broader through her hips and legs. She wore a dark skirt, a plain white blouse and flat shoes. She was the one who helped their mother manage the house, the one who always thought about everyone else before she thought of herself. He remembered the time their father had beat him with a belt for not coming home right after school. He leaned over the kitchen table and received blow after blow while his sisters huddled in a corner. His mother had shouted, then tried to cajole his father to stop. He pushed her away and she fell. It was Christina who helped her mother up, then grabbed her father's arm. She was sent to her room without supper and wasn't allowed to eat with the family for three days.

"Don't worry so much," he said, moving from the shadows into hissing fluorescent light.

"Nicky," Christina yelled and folded him into her arms.

They stood still like this for several minutes, her bony chest chafing his. He noticed a small man sitting at the table and said, "Hello."

Christina released him and turned around. "This is Solon. I told you about him when I was in Vancouver." She touched Nicolai's cheek. "I'm sorry, Nicky. How is Alexia? Why didn't you bring her?"

Nicolai moved forward and took Solon's hand. "Good to meet you," he said. Solon's eyes were soft, kind. He didn't seem to be the kind of guy who would demand a dowry to marry Christina.

The back door opened and Katarina and Zak walked in. They went immediately to him and kissed him on the cheek. "It is good you came back to us, Nicky," Katarina said. "We have prayed for you and Alexia. Christina told us what a smart daughter you have."

"And this is why I couldn't take her out of school." He swallowed hard and ran his tongue over his lips. If he bit at his lip or the inside of his mouth or if his fingers started tapping, they would know he was nervous and maybe not telling them the truth. They were his sisters. They could always read him.

A singsong greeting came through the front door. Christina and Katarina looked at each other and rolled their eyes.

Maria sashayed in, looking around the room to catch every eye. "The baby of the family is here." She stood back from him when she hugged him as if any contact would wrinkle her dress. She tapped his back and released him, stepped away to get a better look at him, but he knew she wanted him to notice her. She hadn't changed from the little girl he'd known. Whenever she got a new outfit, she'd stand in front of him, a giggle in her eyes, moving side to side and ask, "Do you notice anything different?"

"You look great, Maria," he said.

Maria's high heels clicked against the floor as she sauntered from her mother to her sisters and Solon and Zak, air-kissing each cheek. Christina and Katarina watched her. Christina commented on Maria's expensive tastes.

"She thinks she's better than us," Katarina added.

"Younger," Maria replied and flicked her hair off her shoulder. She laughed and Christina and Katarina shrugged as if this was what they'd come to expect.

The sisters helped their mother arrange the table. The men talked about their crops and Nicolai listened. The static on the radio continued. He turned it off.

"But we need music, Nicolai," Maria said.

Their father came in the door. The talking stopped.

Christina said, "Hello, Papa. How are you?"

"What do you think? I've been working all day." He threw his work gloves on the stool beside the door.

"Have a shower," their mother said. "We're almost ready."

As he walked past, he flipped on the radio and glared at his family. "I want to listen to the news."

When they sat down, chairs scraped against one another, knees bumped and elbows touched. His father stood at the opposite end of the table, gripping the back of the chair with his hands. Christina passed along serving platters of lamb and beef. Once everyone had filled their plates, she removed those dishes and brought others: roasted zucchini, buttered rice and sautéed eggplant.

"Sit down," his father said. "Solon and Zak have already started."

Christina and her mother put the last dishes on the table and sat down, one on either side of Nicolai like sentinels. His father took his seat at the head of the table. "Now we can eat." He nodded at Solon and Zak.

"How is America?" Maria asked.

"Fine." He balled his fists in his lap to stop himself from drumming his fingers.

"You came home to think about things, after Sara, God rest her soul." Maria swallowed a mouthful of rice and patted her mouth with the napkin. "Yes?"

"We're happy you're back," Christina said. She shifted her weight slightly as if kicking at something. "Don't worry about talking about this now."

"What?" Maria asked.

"How are we supposed to explain your return to our friends and neighbours?" his father asked between mouthfuls of meat.

A knife scratched against a plate and everyone turned towards Solon. He met their gaze, then looked back at his plate and put his knife down.

"What is there to explain?" Nicolai asked.

"This is a shame for us," his father said.

Nicolai's fork slipped out of his hand and fell on the floor.

Christina jumped up. "I will get you another one." Her chair knocked against his and he pushed back to let her get out.

"You go to America. You marry someone not of your own blood. You marry outside your church. You have a child."

"We don't have to discuss this now, Papa," Christina said. She placed the fork to the left of Nicolai's plate and squeezed around him and into her chair.

"At least we've never mentioned your marriage and the child to our neighbours," his father said. He put a large piece of meat in his mouth. "You know I don't like lamb. Why did you make it?"

"Nicky loves lamb, don't you remember?" Christina said.

"And I made your beef, too," his mother said. "So we please everyone."

"You didn't tell anyone about my life in Canada?" Nicolai stared at his father.

His mother pulled her chair back, Christina and Katarina stopped eating and Maria shrugged and picked at the zucchini on her plate. Solon's and Zak's eyes were fixed on their plates.

"Your daughter is not of Greek blood. You didn't marry in a church. The child is not legitimate."

"And you wonder why I didn't bring her?" Nicolai said. He pushed his chair back.

"*Ella,*" Nicolai's mother said. "Nicky doesn't have to worry about anything now. There is plenty of time ahead of him." She patted Nicolai's shoulder and smiled. "Eat now, Nicky. Don't worry."

Nicolai picked up his fork and resumed eating, sneaking glances at his father. What made the man so angry? When Nicolai was a boy, his mother used to tell him it was because of what had happened during the war. "After Kalavryta he tried to get away, but we met and fell in love, so he stayed."

"But that was a long time ago," he'd said.

"Nicky, some things are not so easy to forget."

Nicolai knew about Kalavryta. But his father had been just a boy: couldn't he get over whatever it was that happened?

Nicolai's father forked a slice of zucchini. He swallowed without chewing and bit at a hunk of bread. His arm lay heavy on the table, circling his plate as if he expected someone to snatch it away.

His father met Nicolai's gaze.

Nicolai turned towards his mother. "Do you know if Achilles is still here?"

2010

Alexia walked out of the airport towards the parking lot, flanked by Christina and Solon, their arms locked in hers. The rest of the family followed, trying to keep up.

She felt vaguely like a prisoner being pushed and prodded into the streets of a foreign country under the control of strangers, not because of anything she'd done, but because her father couldn't keep his pants zipped. Two aunts nodded in her direction while whispering to each other, hands over their mouths. She could imagine their questions. What was she doing here? Why now? Why didn't she come before, when her father was alive? It's not my fault, she wanted to say. "That's finished for me," her father would say whenever she reminded him of his promise to take her to Greece.

Alexia picked up her pace, tried to wiggle out of her aunt and uncle's grip. Two younger cousins kicked a soccer ball in front of her. She tried to avoid it and accidentally stepped on the back of her cousin's shoe. He stumbled forward, his sock a shock of white against the grimy pavement, his crumpled shoe trapped under her foot.

"Walk a little faster," Christina said to one of the boys. "And put the ball away. This is not a place to play."

One of the boys turned. Solon let Alexia's arm fall. He raised his hand and shook it. The boy nodded as if he'd understood without anything being said. He apologized, slipped into his shoe and picked up his ball, then ran ahead with his cousin. Her relatives had taken her chrysanthemums and her bag. She stuck her hand into her pocket.

Christina leaned into Alexia. She wanted to know if Granville Island was still beautiful. "Such a clean place, no?" She pinched her nose, scrunched up her face. "Nothing smells. And everything you want, they have."

"*Ella,* why you need clean?" Solon shouted. "We are strong because we eat everything, from anywhere. We no sick, never." With his free hand, he thumped his chest. His cough was loud and sudden. It stopped after he spat a bit of phlegm. He wiped his mouth with the back of his hand.

"But if you see it," Christina implored, nodding to Alexia for support, "you like."

"I like nothing. My home is only thing."

"He afraid of airplane." Christina shrugged. "It is true."

"No." Solon raised his chin as if to dismiss her.

"He think if he leave home, bad things happen. I tell him they happen here, too."

"Did leaving help your brother?" Solon asked. "Tell me."

"Solon think if he never leave Greece, he live forever. Death finds us any place."

Solon turned to face Christina. Alexia and Christina stopped. The rest of the family gathered in close around them. "What you know about what I think?" He threw his prayer-clasped hands at Christina.

She shook her head, her mouth opened in a weak smile. "Your uncle is very hard man to live with."

He nodded as though he'd scored a point, linked his arm inside Alexia's again and the three began to walk. One aunt clucked.

Alexia peered down on her uncle's slicked-back hair. Shuttered through his thin strands was a pale patch of skin at his crown. Nicolai used to cover his bald spot by combing his hair back and tying it into a ponytail that hung just under the collar of his shirt. Long hair, wrinkled linen suits, no tie and leather loafers sometimes with, but more often without socks. His style, as he called it, never changed.

When she was a teenager, Alexia's friends used to say, "Your dad is so hot. And the way he dresses is so cool."

"You're crazy," she'd tell them. "At least your dad looks like a dad is supposed to."

"You mean old," they'd say.

"His age."

"Like her father," one of Alexia's aunts said now. She understood a few Greek words she'd heard her father use when he forgot the right English word.

"*Ne.*" She overheard two others agree. "Tall and skinny."

"Only in looks?" another aunt asked.

Alexia looked over her shoulder and the aunts smiled, went back to rapidly swallowed Greek. Their chatter competed with the noises rising around them: the babble of strangers, the screech of a policeman's whistle, the blare of car horns from the queue of impatient drivers and the persistent growl of departing airplanes. They walked through the smog as if through yellowed curtains. Alexia coughed. Her eyes felt itchy, her head ached. None of the others seemed troubled by air they could see. They laughed and talked, their voices raised above the racket.

"I get to sit by the window," one of the cousins said as they approached the van.

Her brother, one of the three Yannises, nudged her and their mother, Maria, slapped the back of his head and glared at him. Alexia caught a smirk on his sister's face.

"*Po po po,* that boy has mischief," Katarina said.

Her father used to use the same expression. When she heard him say it the first time, Alexia had asked him what it meant. "It's just an expression, nonsense words kind of like *tsk-tsk*, something like that, but they are not really words, nothing I can translate."

"He can't sit still," Maria said.

"He is a young man now," Katarina said. "He does not need to act like a child."

"What do you know about children?" Maria said. Her hands were on her hips. She looked up at the sky and muttered a prayer as she crossed herself three times. Unlike the others, who wore shades of black or navy suits, Maria wore an elegant floral print dress cinched tight at the waist. In her shiny black stiletto heels, she loomed over the others. A couple of the older women stood back from the family, shook their heads and whispered to each other, their critical eyes fixed on Maria.

"Someone always finds a reason to fight," Christina said. "Ignore."

Alexia nodded as if she understood. All their antics are hard to ignore, she thought, standing aside from the commotion. She wanted to look at a map, see where Diakofto was, and figure out how much time it would take to get there. Her bag was hanging from her aunt's shoulder. Alexia reached for it and her aunt shook her head. "It is too heavy for a little one like you."

The others began discussing seating arrangements.

"Why did you rent the van?" Alexia asked, interrupting the discussion. "Separate cars might have been easier."

"In America you do this, yes," Christina said. "Everyone goes in a different way. Sometimes, our way is more fun, sometimes no. But we take good with all the bad."

"I will sit beside our guest," Maria said. "I am much younger than Katarina. I would have more to say to our guest." She wrapped an arm inside Alexia's.

"I speak better English," Katarina said.

"I will sit in the back," Yannis said. "When are we going to have lunch?"

"Yes, when will we eat?" another cousin asked.

"Never, if we do not get out of this parking lot," Katarina said. "You will see when we see."

Christina, sweat on her brow and hands on both hips, translated the discussion where she could. The conversation got louder and harder to follow as one person talked over another. Alexia stared at the thin line of mountains in the distance, barely noticeable above the smog. Her eyes stung. She was sure she could taste the smog too. She imagined this was what diesel fuel must taste like.

After several minutes, Christina said, *Ella,* and Alexia's relatives took this as a sign to clamber into the van. Alexia gazed at the cramped space and the vacant spot left for her beside Katarina.

"We are used to being on top of each other," Christina said. "You get used, too."

"I never did," Maria said.

"You special," Katarina said. "You told us all the time."

The rest laughed and Maria feigned a smile.

Alexia crammed herself into the van beside Katarina. Three sat abreast in the back seat, another three in the middle row and now there were three of them in the row behind the front seat. Christina sat in the driver's seat. She'd won the argument with Solon over who would drive. Sweat around her neck had dried into a white line. She pulled out a large hanky from her purse and wiped her face, neck and hands and placed it under her leg.

Solon set Alexia's bag on her lap. "No room in back," he muttered and closed the door. He jumped into the passenger seat. The heavy bag wrinkled her pants and lay against her chest. She smelled her own sweat and the sickly scent of chrysanthemums, even though they'd been stowed into the back with the picnic supplies.

Katarina and Zak were tall like Alexia but fleshier. Their tanned faces and necks furrowed deeply like deflated rubber every time they smiled. Alexia squeezed closer to the window. Katarina's hip lay against her. Alexia slipped closer to the door, but when she moved, her aunt followed. Katarina's hand clutched Zak's hand. How nice for them, Alexia thought. They have each other to hold onto.

She felt their eyes examining her. She suspected that they wanted to ask her something so she turned and said, "Have you been to Canada?"

"We no so adventurous like you or your father," Katarina replied. "He always talk when he was young about seeing the world. He like travel. We." She pointed to herself and Zak. "No." They both shook their heads.

Zak opened his mouth and closed it again. Katarina smiled, patted his thigh. "We don't practise English. We forget the correct word."

"You speak it very well." Alexia said.

"Your *pappou*. He think it important. God rest his soul."

"Grandfather in Greek," someone in the back row said.

"Yes, I know a few words."

"Your father should teach you more," the voice in the back said. "Important to understand your language. Yes or no?"

The others agreed in unison. *"Ne."*

"I blame Nicolai for this. No teach you your language," Maria said.

"He thought it was more important to belong. We lived in Canada." Alexia repeated her father's argument, even though she'd never agreed with him. She asked to go to Greek school when she was a child, but he wouldn't allow it. She never understood why, but he was adamant. Was he embarrassed by where he came from?

"Yes, in America they do not want people different. They melt you in pot so everyone same like everyone."

"I'm from Canada."

"There is a difference?" A male voice from the back seat asked. The van sped forward as if Christina had suddenly jammed her foot on the gas pedal. The engine lurched in protest. The squealing whistle of the wind remained steady.

Alexia turned. Yannis, Maria's oldest son, met her gaze above the rim of his glasses. His pimple-sprinkled forehead gathered up tight as if to challenge her.

Alexia turned to face the front, shifting her bag slightly. She became more aware of the smell of so many bodies stuffed into this claustrophobic space and how it mixed with Maria's pungent perfume and the chrysanthemums. Where were they going?

"America, Canada, they are all the same," Yannis said. "They are capitalist countries where no one cares about anyone. Only money. You are no better than the Germans who are now trying to suck our blood, ruin our country."

What a jerk, Alexia thought. I should put him in his place, tell him that we are not all the same, we have programs to help those who need it. But what the hell is the point? He's a kid. She wondered if she was like that at his age.

"*Ella,* he reads too much," Christina said. "Enough of this. Poor Alexia is tired."

"You are lawyer. You like it?" Katarina asked.

Alexia glanced over at Katarina, unsure for a moment what she'd asked. "Um, not always." She shrugged.

"Why no?" Katarina leaned in closer.

"I like the order, but it feels like I've been doing it for a long time."

"You only have thirty-two years," she said. "What do you know about time?"

Maria said, "This is life. You no supposed to like what you do. You work to live no to enjoy." She laughed at herself and the others laughed, too.

"There are people who are passionate about what they do."

"Yes, we passionate about our food, our family, life, but work is work. This is Greece. We understand what is important."

Christina glanced at the aunts and the cousin in the back row through her rear-view mirror, bit her bottom lip and shook her head so it was barely noticeable. That look was the same one Alexia's father used to give her when she was a child and they were out for dinner or visiting friends. It was his signal to her that she was misbehaving and should settle down. The last time it happened, she'd just finished telling him she was leaving her first job for a start-up firm.

"How come you quit the people who gave you your first chance?"

"This is a better opportunity."

"How do you know these new people will even make a go of it? There are many lawyers out there, some washing dishes because they can't find the kind of job you just threw away." And then he'd given her that look. His head tilted, one side of his lower lip gnawed away by his upper teeth, his eyes fixed on her. There was only the slightest hint that he'd actually shaken his head. He liked to do it this way so if she pushed him on it, he could deny his disapproval.

"I'm not ten anymore," she'd said. "That won't work."

Alexia had left him sitting at his kitchen table, staring out the window, tapping the saucer in front of him with his teaspoon in that nervous way of his. Alexia often wondered if it was the actual beat that calmed him or if he just liked to make noise.

The relatives slipped back into Greek again and Alexia tuned them out. Her younger cousins played a game of slapping hands. They squealed each time with surprise. The family talked louder.

Out Alexia's window, the parched landscape was occasionally dotted with a splash of red or pale pink where someone had planted a bush that looked like a rhododendron. Alexia wondered how the shrubs survived in this heat. Clumps of new houses and building cranes spread over the hills. The highway was brand new, divided and multi-lane. She hadn't imagined so much development, particularly after reading about the financial crisis here, but then she wasn't sure what she expected. Trucks whizzed by, one after the other.

Her father was wrong. He'd told her that Greece had never caught up to the rest of the world and she was lucky he immigrated to Canada when he did. She could do anything she wanted. He was right about the family, though. They were loud and opinionated. Her father was like them. At a party or a crowded restaurant, Alexia heard his voice above the others. He had feelings, as he used to call it, about everything.

Katarina put her arm around Alexia's shoulder. She leaned away.

"This is our new freeway," Christina said, when Alexia poked her head forward.

"It's at least six years old," Solon said. "She exaggerates."

"Alexia, you lucky you don't have husband."

The others laughed and Alexia sat back. Katarina patted her on the shoulder. Alexia nodded and came up with a weak smile in return. A husband? For her? She'd never given marriage much thought. She'd dated briefly in university, but didn't like taking time away from her studies and thought most of the guys she'd met were immature and only interested in getting drunk on weekends. One guy who wasn't like that did come along. He was a political science major interested in a career in politics. They saw each other over several months. She felt comfortable with him, enjoyed their discussions, loved the fact that he was a runner like her. They were having dinner at a pizza joint they went to every Friday night when he called her aloof and distant. "I feel like you're always stage acting. I don't think you're really here with me when we're together."

"It just takes me time," she said, "to get close to people."

"It's been months," he said. "I thought we could have something permanent here if you gave it a shot."

"What's permanent?" she asked. "Not sure there's any such thing."

He started seeing others and stopped calling. She made no effort to pursue him. Let him have his way. She didn't care.

After that, she had a fling with her ethics professor, a man twice her age. He was mature and smart and absent-minded. He liked it when she kept him organized. She got too busy with work after she finished university and eventually moved back to Vancouver. Her longest relationship lasted four years. Joel was older, married and a partner in the firm she worked for right after graduation. It was her affair with Joel that made her realize she liked relationships where the man went home at the end of the night.

"You make this easy," Joel had said to her once as she lay beside him, her head on his chest, his curly black hair tickling her nose. She moved her head slightly, rubbed her nose and still his chest hairs itched. She slid away and grabbed her housecoat. "I beg to differ. It's you and your wife who make it easy on me."

He didn't understand and she didn't explain, but what she meant was that she didn't have to be or do anything. She didn't need to take care of things, look after him. His wife took care of his everyday demands, leaving Alexia the best part of him, the no-hassle part. This perfect situation didn't last. She changed firms and the relationship fizzled. She focused on work. It was the one thing she could count on. Whatever she put into it, she got much more out of it. Clients raved about her work, told their friends about her, and the firm continued to promote her until she became a partner. That gave her control and security. She couldn't say the same thing about her relationships.

Besides, no one was interested in the real her. They only saw the image she'd created for herself: independent, driven, focused, a workaholic. And she wasn't in the market anyway. Her father told her she worked too hard, never raised her eyes from her laptop long enough to notice a man. "No time for that," she'd said to him.

"We're going to stop for lunch at a beach near Loutraki. You hungry, no?"

"A little," Alexia said. "Not really. More tired than anything."

Christina's jaw twitched. Alexia realized she'd disappointed her. These people were trying to engage her, she thought, make her feel like she belonged, and she'd been holding herself back as though she was better than them. They hadn't done anything wrong. She told herself she would try harder, be warmer. Or at least as warm and friendly as she could be. She smiled at Katarina.

Solon rolled down his window and Alexia thought an oven door had opened in her face. Her hair blew across her eyes. The breeze drowned out the conversations in the seats behind her, but she heard Christina and Solon squabble. The others quieted down and didn't interfere.

"*Yati, paidi mou?*" Christina shouted. One hand was on the steering wheel, the other pointed at Solon as if to scold. "We have the air conditioning!" She slapped his arm.

"My neck is sick with the artificial air," Solon replied. He pointed to his neck. His index finger, stained yellow, his hand rough, calloused.

"Thank God you, Alexia, are like your father," she said, and turned briefly to look at her. "Too pretty to settle for one man. Your *thia* have no choice. I had to take Solon."

"Watch what you're doing," Solon said.

Christina had a good sense of humour. Nicolai did too. His voice was always raised and he had a smile behind his hazel eyes just like Christina did now. He liked to get close to people when he talked. His clients saw beyond his boyish grins, his jokes. Every new project became the most rewarding challenge of his career and yet when he decided to retire at sixty-four and sell his business, he walked away from it and told Alexia he wouldn't miss it. "I've worked hard for long enough." His face had grown thinner and his grey whiskers made him look pale. Still, she didn't think to ask him if there was anything wrong. She should have noticed he was sick, confronted him.

"Besides, I can spend time with you, *paidi mou,* and my friends."

He had friends, she had business associates.

The breeze tugged at Alexia's shirt. She held her hair back to keep it off her face. More trucks passed. Christina kept one hand on the steering wheel and tuned the radio with the other. A song she recognized came on and she sang along with the melancholy singer, matching his drones. Solon held his hands over his ears and muttered to himself. Releasing her hold on her hair, Alexia raked her fingers through it. Under her fingernails, a sandy residue remained.

They arrived in Loutraki an hour or so later and Christina shifted into a lower gear, revved the engine as if she was about to take a run at something and drove up over a steep curb and onto the beach. Like nails against a chalkboard, the undercarriage grated until the van bottomed out with a loud bang. Alexia jumped, but everyone else clapped and congratulated Christina. Alexia saw the sign in Greek and below it, in English. *No Parking on Beach*. She pointed it out and Maria responded, "They make the rules so we break them. This is how we do everything."

"We make our own right," Yannis in the back seat said. "Like Socrates and Aristotle."

What a know-it-all twerp, Alexia thought. He'll learn soon enough.

"University teaches them strange things these days." Christina said. The aunts and uncles agreed and that was the end of it.

Nicolai had been as fond of breaking the rules as she was of sticking to them. She paid parking tickets as soon as she got them, but he never bothered. "They don't really expect us to pay those crooks," he used to say after he received the umpteenth letter from a collection agency. She was different from him in all the most important ways. She never accepted social invitations from clients or colleagues. "There could be a conflict of interest," she'd said. "Why would I put myself in that situation?" He allowed his suppliers to wine and dine him. "We're friends. Where's the conflict?" He liked carefree young women and was never faithful to any of them. She liked older married men, but never more than one at a time.

"It's March, *paidi mou.* Water too cold," Christina said when Solon suggested they all go in for a swim. She shrugged her jacket off her shoulders and left it in the van, then slipped out of her shoes and into heavy, old-fashioned sandals.

Solon put his hands together in prayer and looked up at the sky. "At least she makes one concession. She took off her winter jacket. Incredible." He pointed his entwined fingers even higher. "I have to thank God that he took away a little of her stubbornness today. This no happen often."

Alexia left her bag on the floor and tried to leave her purse in the van beside it, but Christina shook her head and gave Alexia that look again so she slung the purse over her shoulder and picked up one of the smaller boxes.

"This is man's work," Solon said and took the box.

Alexia followed along behind them. Even though they were parked on the beach and could have easily had their picnic close to the van, they were in search, Christina said, "of the perfect spot for your come-back-home lunch." Sand filled Alexia's sneakers and rubbed between her toes. She slowed down, got further behind and yet she could still hear the family's chatter. The Gulf of Corinth gurgled quietly onto the shore. Even here, far outside Athens, the smog coloured the air sulphur yellow.

Alexia turned on her cell phone to retrieve her messages. Christina heard the phone's chime. She turned.

"Tired, no?"

"Work never stops," Alexia replied.

"Fresh air and good food will fix," she said. "You will sleep tonight."

Alexia checked the cell phone. Three messages. "I need to return some calls."

"First eat," Christina said. "Calls wait. No?"

"Well, yes, it could." She turned off the phone and dropped it in her purse.

The women layered the shore with multicoloured blankets arranged in a circle. Around the edges, they poked holes in the sand and erected umbrellas that advertised *Mythos* beer and *Metaxas,* the brandy Nicolai used to drink. Casseroles of vine leaves, *moussaka,* and ribs were taken out of the baskets, boxes and coolers, along with several bowls of Greek salad and Tupperware containers of feta cheese, olives and various dips. Five loaves of bread were lifted out of plastic bags and placed in the middle of each blanket on a cardboard cutting board made from the flaps of the boxes that held their supplies.

"*Moussaka* by Katarina," Christina said. Katarina stood up and curtsied. Part of Katarina's three-quarter-length skirt had lodged itself in her buttocks. She picked at the lost material with one hand, waved with the other and said she hoped everyone would enjoy her dish. "*Kalos Orisate*!" She turned and before she plopped down she smiled at Alexia, who looked away.

"*Kalos Sas Vricame,*" the others replied.

Each matriarch presented her signature dish while her family and the rest of the clan looked on and clapped. Alexia ripped at the loaf of bread closest to her. When she realized what she was doing, she glanced around to see if anyone had noticed. Christina handed Alexia a plate and told her to start because she was the guest. Alexia took just a spoonful of everything in front of her.

"No wonder she skinny," someone said. They all laughed.

"No is natural," Christina said.

"Being thin is not a crime," Maria said.

"Having a little meat is good. Think of people who starve in this world. We have to be grateful we have so much."

Katarina agreed.

"Not for me," Maria said.

"You different," another aunt said.

"Who wants to be same?" Maria said.

"That is what I am trying to say," Yannis interjected.

"See the ideas you put in the head of children?"

"I am almost a man."

"You go to university," Christina said. "This does not make you a man."

Plates and forks clanged. The others spoke over each other.

"Ideas are not bad," Maria said.

Alexia had had many of the same discussions with her father, whenever she watched what she ate, bought organic food, drank soy milk rather than cow's milk or switched to gluten-free breads.

"Food is food. It's all good for you. You've just bought into the ads," he'd say.

"I feel better when I'm careful," Alexia responded.

"*Ella, paidi mou,*" he said. "You don't believe everything you read."

"You mean you ad guys lie to make a buck."

"Families are this way," Maria said, the food in her mouth muffling her voice.

"We take good with bad," Christina said and avoided Maria's eyes.

"Not all families wild like yours, Maria," Katarina said.

"At least we are alive," Maria said. "Have a pulse."

Everyone began to talk at once. Alexia remembered how she used to get excited and talk with her mouth full. As she'd gotten older, she'd hated the way her father talked with his mouth full, bits of food spewing out with the words. It was raw and undignified. I'd never let anyone see that much of me, she thought. As she sat watching these people, her father's family, she remembered how, when she got older, it became her turn to chide her father for talking with his mouth full.

One night, he'd been helping her with her homework, as he did whether she wanted him to or not. "Your paper doesn't support its conclusion," Nicolai said. Alexia was in high school, she knew full well what she was doing. She didn't need his help. He shrugged and smiled out of one side of his mouth as if he'd won a point. A bit of spinach from their dinner of *spanikopita* was stuck in his teeth.

"I can't understand what you're saying," Alexia said. She hoped to finish dinner before they got into it. She really wanted this to be the time he didn't tell her what he thought. Just let the paper be, or better yet, tell me how great it is and leave it at that.

"I'm sick and tired of the problems with the natives you write about in your paper, *paidi mou*. When do they take responsibility? Why is it always someone else's fault? And why do the rest of us have to take care of these people?"

Alexia stood up, took the plates away and washed them. He continued arguing. When she turned around, she saw he had her paper in front of him, an oily stain colouring one corner. He was scratching notes on her pages with his ballpoint pen. She listened as he went over his comments because she knew if she didn't, she'd be up all night.

"But I'm making that point on the next page. Don't you see?" Alexia said, though when it got even later, she stopped challenging him too. Instead, she let him ramble on and ignored most of it, submitting the paper the way she wanted it. That was the last time she showed him her homework. She got an A and never mentioned it.

"*Ella*," Christina said. "Kids are kids. No? We were young once. We old and sometimes we forget."

They quieted down as if pondering what she'd said and later hummed agreement. Alexia's younger cousins finished eating and kicked a soccer ball around. The men lay down to nap and the women cleaned up. Alexia picked up a few plates to help.

"You will have plenty of time to ruin your hands when you have husband," Christina said, gently slapped Alexia's hands and took the plates from her.

"If you are lucky, you won't find one," Katarina said. "Too much work." They laughed and flung rolled-up napkins at each other.

Alexia lay back on a blanket and listened to their chatter and laughter as they filled garbage bags and stuffed their empty containers back into their baskets, boxes and coolers. She'd never really understood she was part of such a big family even though her father talked about them, and when he received letters from Christina he'd give Alexia updates. She used to hear his translations of those letters and imagine what these people were like. Tall like Nicolai, funny and loud. Different. In her mind, they were exotic, and when she was a kid, Alexia missed them without ever knowing who they were. Maybe it was a good thing she hadn't met them then. Not having a family made her more self-sufficient. Perhaps all the noise would have scared her or repulsed her in some way. Or maybe she would have rejected them altogether.

He told me Greece was a paradise, she thought, but never bothered to take me. The first time he called, a month after he left, I didn't recognize his voice. Someone had taken my sad, unable-to-get-out-of-bed dad and turned him into a cheerful, happy one I didn't know. I accused him of not being my father, cried and threw the phone. What an idiot. Mavis tried to make things better. "You have to be a good girl," she said, "while he's away." That's all I've ever been. I knew if I didn't behave, he wasn't going to come back.

Alexia watched her aunts finish packing the containers. Their world was so different than hers. It didn't matter. She was here to do a job. That's why she was here. Nothing more. She rummaged through her purse for her cell.

5

1986

Nicolai ran towards the swing, waving his arms. Her little hands clutched the chains, her knuckles white. The man gave the swing another push. She rocked even higher.

"That's high enough, Alexia." He meant to shout, but his voice came out a cracked whisper. Could she hear him? She tried to smile, wanting to please.

She tilted her head and met his eyes. Her smile disappeared.

"Hey, you. Stop that." He yanked the man's arm.

The stranger turned.

Nicolai recognized his hazel eyes, his own lopsided smirk.

The man stared at Nicolai, daring him to do something, anything. The other Nicolai pushed Alexia again, his hands hard against her back.

"It's going too high, Daddy."

"It's okay, you know what you're doing," both men said in one voice.

"No," she said and let go.

"Alexia!" he screamed, grasping for her. His hands fell to the side of the bed.

He bolted awake. His eyes darted around the room. He heard the groan of pipes and a flush down the hall. He lay back into the sag of his boyhood bed, staring at the ceiling, willing the dream out of his head. A spider lowered itself from the beam, bobbed along a thin line caught in the shimmer of the early morning sun. Nicolai rolled over, pushed himself to the edge of the mattress, then sank back into the middle. He pulled the covers over his head. Alexia was with Stuart and Mavis. She was safe.

He heard a door slam. The radio in the kitchen came on, the male announcer's tone loud and insistent. Nicolai understood every word and none of it was English. It was his native tongue, the language he spoke with his parents, his sisters. Greek. He was back to where he'd started, in the home he thought he'd never return to.

There was a crash. The radio must have been knocked over. A whispered mutter. Then static. The announcer's persistent voice replaced by a cheerful tune that echoed off the walls, a clear sign that his father was gone for the day. Above the clatter of dishes and the rush of water in the sink was his mother's voice. What did she have to sing about? He walked down the hall to the bathroom and turned up the hot water.

"Ah, Nicky, did you sleep well?" she asked as he came into the kitchen.

"Yes, okay." He sat at the table and his mother poured him coffee. A bowl of cling peaches, another filled with yogurt and a small plate with two soft-boiled eggs was placed in front of him. Thick slices of his mother's warm bread sat in a basket.

"You have to eat, build your strength." She hovered beside him.

He picked at the fruit, sipped the coffee and reminded himself he had to call Alexia. His mother turned towards the counter to knead another ball of dough. "Wasn't Maria's skirt short? What did you think of Solon? He will make a good husband. Did you see how little meat and vegetables Katarina took? And she didn't finish that."

Midmorning he went with his mother to the market. He carried her bags as they walked from one stall to another. She laced her arm in his. "You remember Nicolai, don't you?" she asked the friends she met. "He's a successful businessman in America now, but he didn't forget his family. Yes, he's here for a visit."

"Ah, even the owl thinks her baby is the most beautiful," the tomato seller said. She put her hand on Nicolai's shoulder and leaned into him. "Your mother is proud of you. She talks about you all the time."

They had lunch in the café across from the railroad station. The wood floor was as faded and cracked as it had always been; the metal chairs and uneven tables still had bits of napkin stuffed under the legs to keep them level. "I never go out for lunch," his mother said, "except if one of your sisters comes." She waved at people she recognized, pointed at Nicolai and mouthed, "My son."

Nicolai picked at his calamari, his gaze on his plate.

Someone slapped him on the back. He dropped his fork.

"You're here," the man said. "It has been too long."

Nicolai looked up at Achilles. "You haven't changed one bit," he said, taking his friend's hand.

Achilles kissed him on both cheeks.

He smelled of the same stale cologne they used to slap on their faces when they were teenagers. His hair was as long as it had been in high school. His pants were tight; his shiny shirt unbuttoned to where a growing belly stuck out. He wore sandals and that same silly, almost hopeful grin he'd had as a boy.

Nicolai's mother looked up briefly, but went back to her salad. "This onion is sour," she said.

"What are you doing here?" Achilles asked.

"He comes to visit us," his mother said, edging her chair away.

"Hello." A woman stood behind Achilles. She ducked around him and leaned down to kiss Nicolai's mother on each cheek.

Nicolai stood up and his chair fell backwards. "Hello," he said, letting the chair drop as he took her hand.

"You don't remember me?" Her face grew red.

"Should I?"

"Dimitria. Your cousin. You used to tease me and pull my hair."

"But you were a kid with braces the last time I saw you." He righted the chair. "Please, sit. I'll find more." An image came to him. A time when they were kids playing alone in her bedroom. They were barely teenagers.

"We are at the bar," Achilles said. "You enjoy your lunch. But we should get together soon." Achilles put his arm around Dimitria's waist. "Right?"

"Yes." Nicolai shook Achilles's hand. Dimitria offered hers. He took it in his. She had a strong grip, a man's hand. Sara's hands were small. They were the first things he noticed about her. Even in this place, far from home, he couldn't get away from Sara. He was sure there were moments when he didn't think of her, but he couldn't say when.

He watched Achilles and Dimitria move to the other end of the café before he sat down. "You have to be careful with that one," his mother said. "He has big ideas for this and that and no money. He is all talk."

Nicolai tore at his bread, then dropped it, uneaten, on his plate.

"Dimitria thinks she'll get Achilles to settle down, but he's not the type. You can knock on a deaf person's door forever. He will never answer."

"He had all the girls following him in school." Nicolai gazed over at the bar. Achilles sat close to Dimitria, whispering in her ear. She nodded. "I guess he's got whatever it takes to make a woman happy."

"He feeds women lies and they believe him." His mother glanced over at the bar and shrugged. "She'll never find a good man."

"Maybe his way is better."

Her head tilted towards the bar. "He has nothing. You have a daughter."

"Yes, the one my parents refuse to acknowledge." He folded his hands, clutched them together in his lap.

The lines around her mouth deepened. "Your father is old-fashioned," she said at last. "He thinks we shouldn't mix cultures." She patted her mouth with her napkin. "Differences or no differences, family is all we have."

He leaned back in his chair. A group of men squeezed around the table beside them were arguing. One man smacked the newspaper. "Athens can't understand what we need."

"But we put them there," one man said. Others shouted in agreement and they all started talking at once.

"Someone is always mad," Nicolai said. "What kind of family is that?"

His mother picked at the last bits of salad and threw her fork into the bowl. "Nothing left here to worry about." She looked around the café and beckoned the waiter. "We need a good cup of coffee."

Nicolai glanced again at Achilles and Dimitria, wondered what they were talking about. His mother put her hand over his, stopping him from tapping his spoon against the table. "It's a good thing some things stay the same."

He faced the café rather than her. "He's ashamed of me."

"It has nothing to do with you." She moved her hand up to his forearm. Her skin looked dry, flaking. It was so thin he could see the blood pumping in the dark, swollen veins. He wanted to hold her delicate hand, make things better, but how could he take away the years of washing dishes, cleaning up after him and his sisters? His father? "We have to understand," she said. "Life was not so easy for him."

"The war ruined him." He said it like a catechism. His fingers drummed on the table. "I've heard it all before. That's no excuse."

She picked up her napkin and folded it once, then shook it out and folded it a second time along different lines. "He wanted to go to America or Australia or England, anywhere, just to get away." She shrugged and snapped the napkin. It drooped open.

"I know the story. He met you in Patras and fell in love."

"We have you, Christina, Katarina and Maria." She threw the napkin down on the table. "They will clean this. I don't have to do it for them." She swallowed her coffee in one mouthful. "Bitter," she said, her face scrunched up. "I don't know why I'm surprised."

"He didn't want any of us." Nicolai leaned toward her.

"Something very bad happened to him. None of us can understand." She moved her chair back and snapped her fingers at the waiter. "Stop passing off your dirty water as coffee."

Back at the house, he stood at the kitchen table and watched her wash potatoes in the sink. He was never quite sure what to do with himself in the kitchen. It had been the same with Sara. She commanded the kitchen, had her system and knew what she was doing. His mother put a peeler in his hand and said, "You can help, you know."

When his father came in, he continued to the bathroom without greeting them. He returned to the kitchen a half hour later and turned on the radio. "Is dinner ready?" he asked, sitting down in his chair at the head of the table. Nicolai sat at the opposite end.

"What did you do today?" His father wiped his fork and knife against his sleeve.

"He helped me," his mother said before Nicolai could respond.

"Good."

"And your day?" Nicolai leaned towards his father. Was it possible that they might finally have a real conversation?

"My days don't change. One day is the same as another."

"Yes, I suppose that's true."

"If you hang around women, you'll become like them."

They ate. In the background, the news anchor's voice droned the day's events and catastrophes. When his mother said something, his father silenced her. "I'm trying to listen. I can't hear you and the radio at the same time."

She would stop talking, then start again. "That coffee was awful today. Dish water couldn't taste worse than what they tried to sell us."

Nicolai smiled and nodded. "No one can make a cup of coffee as good as yours."

His father got up, walked over to the radio and turned up the volume.

His mother shook her head. When she turned to glance at Nicolai, he averted his gaze.

He finished dinner and went to his room, leaving his parents at the table, the weatherman's voice now in the background, warning about the high temperatures, dry conditions and wind gusts. The day had passed and now it was too late to call Alexia. He calculated the time difference. She'd be in school. He'd make sure to call her tomorrow.

The phone woke him. He hadn't heard his father leave. This was the first time since he'd arrived that he'd slept without dreaming of Alexia. Sara. His mother called out his name from the kitchen, came to his door and knocked quietly. "Telephone," she said.

"Give me a minute," he said, slipped into his pants and went to the phone.

"How's the sleeping beauty?"

Nicolai recognized Achilles's voice right away and smiled.

"Does he want to get a coffee this morning?" Achilles asked.

Nicolai arrived at the same small café where he and his mother had had lunch the day before. Achilles was already there, reading the newspaper and sucking on an ice cube. His iced coffee was a milky brown.

Achilles stroked the tuft of hair on his chin and nodded towards the train outside. "It brings tourists to see the gorge and Kalavryta. They stay for a night or two in our village before and then again after they come back from that place. There are many ways to make money here."

Nicolai ordered a coffee.

"I want to show you my project. Do you have the time?" Except for the hint of a beard, Achilles's face was as smooth as when they were children. His smile was mischievous, as if he knew a secret about you that you hadn't told anyone else. Achilles hadn't followed the usual path of families around here, farming his father's land, or at least Nicolai could see no signs of it. His fingernails were not stained like those who had worked the fields. Despite their best efforts, they could never wash away the dirt rooted day after day beneath their nails.

They walked across the railroad tracks, past the school and down to the narrow pebbled beach. A slice of crumbling blacktop ran between the beach and a large, empty field. Remnants of a newspaper blew across the road and flapped against a twisted and decaying olive tree.

"Can you imagine what someone could do here?" Achilles placed his arm around Nicolai's shoulders. "Think of restaurants and cafés. We could build a boardwalk all along the beach with lights. Tourists could stroll anytime they wanted. It could be beautiful."

"I suppose so." Nicolai walked ahead.

Achilles caught up. "This could be ours. Together we could make our little village special. If it doesn't change, it will die."

"It's been the same way for hundreds of years. They can't kill us off so easily."

"But we could do better, don't you think?" He laced his arm through Nicolai's. "I think about settling down sometimes. Doing better. Maybe this is what I need."

"I won't be staying. I have a daughter in Canada."

Achilles stopped and tugged at Nicolai's arm to make him stop. "Is she with your wife? Are you divorced? This is what is said about your return to the village. And this is not the only thing." He shook his head. "I tell you this as your friend."

Nicolai kicked at a stone. "My wife died," Nicolai said. He picked up the stone and threw it into the water. The breeze blew sand into his eyes. He blinked once, and then again. The tiny grains remained, grating.

"I never heard you had a daughter," Achilles said.

"I didn't marry a Greek girl."

Achilles nodded. "Come out with your cousin and me tonight."

"I don't know." He rubbed his eyes and blinked again. "I'm not much in the mood." He was barely functioning. Couldn't Achilles see that? Nicolai couldn't handle going out and trying to make conversation, pretend to take an interest in what they were doing. He tapped his thigh, stood staring at the distant mountains beyond the bay.

Achilles put his arm around Nicolai again. "It would do you good to get out of that house."

He met Achilles and Dimitria at the old *bouzouki* in the centre of town. Achilles ordered a large platter of *barboni,* a couple of bowls of olives and several plates of grilled vegetables and potatoes. He waved and more baskets of bread came.

"This is too much," Dimitria said.

"*Ella.* How often do we have a special guest from America? We have to celebrate. Isn't that right, Nicolai?"

"I'm with my cousin on this one. This is too much."

Achilles shrugged. "So, as I was saying, I have spoken to a few people about this project and they're as excited as I am."

Nicolai put a couple of potatoes on his plate. He felt Dimitria's eyes on him. He looked up. She smiled and looked away. She leaned back into her chair and tilted her head towards Achilles. She wore a light green turtleneck. Nothing unusual or special about it. Why had he noticed?

"It'll be an exciting project. You need to get your mind off things."

"What things?" Dimitria asked.

"I don't think I was supposed to say anything," Achilles said.

"My wife passed away a little while ago. My daughter is with her godparents," Nicolai said. He suddenly felt tired. He leaned his head against his hand.

The music started. Achilles raised his voice. "I have big plans for us."

"I don't make plans anymore," Nicolai said. It was nice that she didn't ask him anything about Sara, whether she was Greek or not. All those silly questions.

Dimitria wiped her mouth, dropped her napkin on her lap and patted his hand. That image again. Her father found them asleep, her head on his chest. They were scolded. He was told to go home and tell his father what he'd done. He hadn't done anything so he said nothing. He didn't see much of her after that.

Nicolai picked up his napkin and wiped his mouth. Her hand fell away.

After dinner, they listened to the music for a while, then Nicolai said he was tired and was going home. "We'll come with you. Let me get this," Achilles said, pointing at the check in the middle of the table. He opened his wallet and flipped through the bills, counting under his breath. Setting the bills down, he took his change purse from his jacket pocket, opened it and picked out a few coins. He shook the purse as if looking for more, then emptied it onto the table. He looked at the check again. "Interesting."

"I can help." Dimitria pulled her purse from the back of the chair.

"No woman of mine has to pay."

Nicolai reached for the check. "I'll handle it."

Achilles picked up the bills, put them back in his wallet and leaned forward to tuck it into his back pocket. Dimitria elbowed him. He smiled and said, "You Americans are very fortunate. Yes?"

He scooped up the change and dropped it into his change purse, clicking it closed.

Nicolai ignored the comment and paid the waiter.

"How is it living with your parents again?" Achilles asked.

"My father hasn't changed."

"Kalavryta was hard on that generation," Dimitria said.

"My father got over it," Achilles said, "but he was young. Yours was older."

"What do you mean?"

Dimitria squeezed Achilles's hand and shook her head.

"What did I say?" Achilles asked. Smiling at Dimitria, he said, "People react to things differently, that's all I wanted to say."

Achilles walked a little ahead of Nicolai and Dimitria along the dark streets. He whistled. The breeze pressed against them, cool and persistent. Dimitria pulled her jacket off her shoulders, Nicolai held it up for her, and she slipped her arms through the sleeves. Had she leaned back against him? Or was he imagining things? He hadn't been close to a woman since Sara died. He pulled away.

They dropped Dimitria off at her house and Nicolai recognized it as the one he'd walked past the day he'd arrived. She must have been the woman he'd seen working in the field. He'd forgotten a lot about this place.

At the next corner, Achilles veered down one street, Nicolai took the other. "I'll call you," Achilles said. "To talk about a few things."

He could still hear Achilles's whistling long after he rounded the corner for home.

The next day, Nicolai ran into Dimitria on the street on his way to the butcher to buy a roast for his mother. Four bags of groceries were inching their way down her arms, just as she tried to hook another one on.

"These are bigger than you are," he said, taking her bags. Her forearms were scored red. "Look at your arms," he said.

She pushed the sleeves of her sweater down. "This will pass."

Nicolai chatted about the food they'd had at last night's *bouzouki*, how he couldn't get Greek food like that in Canada.

"You're not happy to be home, though."

"Why does everyone have to read more into what I say?" He was tired of watching what he said around his father. And if he wasn't careful with his mother, he knew she'd put words in his mouth. And now Dimitria was doing it too? He was so sick of all of this. He picked up his pace without really intending to.

She pulled his arm and stopped him. "I only meant these aren't the best circumstances for your return."

He nodded. They continued walking towards her house in silence. When they arrived, her mother opened the door. "And who is this?"

"Don't you remember Nicolai?" Dimitria said.

The woman was dressed in black from head to toe. She squinted. "Why can't you carry your own bags? It is not a man's job to do this."

"I'm a relative, *Thia.* It's okay for me to help my cousin."

The woman grabbed the bags from Nicolai and shook her head. "Young people today don't know what to do." She disappeared somewhere in the house. Nicolai and Dimitria stood on the front step.

"My mother is suspicious of all men," Dimitria said. "She wonders why I haven't married and had children like all my friends."

"How about Achilles?"

Dimitria put her finger over her mouth. "Don't let her hear you."

"I don't expect many mothers like him."

She shrugged. "We pass the time together. We're just friends. There is nothing more to it than that."

I guess everyone needs a friend, he thought. "I suppose asking you out to lunch is out of the question."

The eagerness he saw in her eyes scared him. Why the hell had he opened his mouth?

"Yes, but you should do it anyway," she said.

He looked away. "Okay, so how about it?"

Dimitria opened the front door. "I'm going to the café for lunch, Mamma. I will return soon." She slammed the door behind her.

Her mother came from the back of the house and hurtled out the front door behind them. "Why not have lunch here?" she asked. "We have food at home. Why waste your money?"

"Thank you, that is very nice of you, *Thia.* I could take the two of you out."

"Look at me." She pointed to herself. "I'm not dressed. Stay with us and tell us about your life in America." She kissed him on both cheeks, put her arm in his and led him up the walkway and through the front door. Nicolai heard Dimitria scuff her feet behind them. As a child she used to do the same thing when she didn't want to play with him or his sisters.

His aunt arranged cold cuts on a platter, made a salad and cut some bread. Nicolai sat at the kitchen table and watched while Dimitria set the table and filled the glasses with water.

"You are missing a fork here," her mother said, pointing to one place setting. She shook her hands at the sky in mock frustration and winked at Nicolai.

Dimitria got another fork.

"She's a dreamer, my daughter. I have to watch her all the time."

"She thinks I'm this way because I'm an artist." Dimitria sat down. She put some salad on her plate and took a piece of bread.

"Offer our guest something first." Her mother pulled at her own hair in an exaggerated way. "She won't find a husband because she doesn't know what it means to be a wife." She laughed.

"I won't spoil anyone," Dimitria said, "especially a man."

"Isn't this the way women are in America, Nicolai?" her mother asked. She passed the platter to him. "Please have more. You've taken so little."

Nicolai put another slice of cold roast beef on his plate. "Yes." He could never tell Sara what to do. She'd put him in his place. He loved that about her.

"And look at all the problems they have."

"You watch too many soap operas, Mamma."

Nicolai laughed and passed the platter of cold cuts to Dimitria. She placed it on the table in front of her mother without helping herself.

"Eat," her mother said.

"No, thank you."

"God put animals on the earth for food." Her mother's hands were on her hips.

"And we treat these creatures badly."

"This one has funny ideas." She pointed at her own head as if to say her daughter was not altogether there. "Ignore her."

He liked watching the sparring between Dimitria and his *thia*. He wished he could be this comfortable with his own family. Sometimes when he was alone with his sisters and his mother, sitting around the kitchen table, he could be. But he was a kid the last time he remembered that happening.

Later, his *thia* told Dimitria to show him her sketches. "If you like boats, you will like what she draws. If you don't, well, I guess you won't."

A small studio had been set up at the back of the house. Nicolai banged his head on the doorway as they entered. Dimitria turned on the light and he ducked under the archway. The room opened up to a drafting table her father had built for her.

Scanning each print on the wall, he studied the details, and then stood back to get a different perspective. "You're good."

"I just play with this and sometimes a tourist buys one." She stood beside him, her hands behind her back.

He moved to see one ofher other sketches and brushed up against her. Both apologized and moved away. He walked over to the sketch she had on her table. "I should probably get back. I haven't bought that roast yet and my mother must be wondering where I got to."

Dimitria nodded. "How long will you be staying?"

"I don't know."

She stood a few feet away. "Take your time," she said.

"I'll thank your mother before I leave."

"She'd like that. Her daughter is apparently too ungrateful for that kind of thing."

He smiled.

As soon as he entered the house, his mother snatched the roast from him. "I've been waiting for this, but I guess you were too busy having lunch with your cousin and her mother to worry about that."

"How did you know?"

Her back was turned to him. "My dead brother's wife called and said she didn't realize you were back, why hadn't anyone told her?"

"So what's the big deal?"

"We have our life. They have theirs. We don't mix and disturb each other."

"If family is all we have, as you always say, why don't we?"

She turned to face him. "I suppose you told them your whole life story."

"What do you mean?" he asked.

"You need to keep some things to yourself." She put her hands on her hips like she used to when he was a boy and she was annoyed with him.

"You don't want me to tell anyone about Sara? About Alexia?"

She met his eyes. "It's only that we have to invite them here now." She turned towards the counter again. "This is difficult."

"You don't have to if you don't want to. We had lunch. So what? It just happened. There are no expectations."

"There are always expectations," his mother said. She rinsed the roast. Watery drops of blood leaked onto the counter and floor as she settled the lump of meat into the old dented roaster.

2010

Diakofto was a cluster of houses huddled together on a spit of land dangling into the Corinthian Sea. Alexia first saw her father's village from the highway.

At this distance, the village looked like the postcards her father used to Scotch-tape to the wall above his desk. The tape would give way in a corner and the pictures would bend forward. When he bothered to notice, he'd add more tape. The images became smaller and smaller as the border of tape grew wider. Dust settled and darkened the tape. No way he'd take those postcards down and throw them out. No way. She'd dreamt about going to Diakofto so many times when she was a child. But he'd waited too long. Don't, she told herself. You're here. He's dead. She shook her head.

"What's wrong?" Katarina said.

No one had said a word for the last while. Strange for them to be so quiet. They must be tired. "Nothing," she said. "I was thinking about my father's postcards."

"Strangers do not see our village is special." She patted Alexia's leg. "You will."

The relatives in the row behind her came to life, briefly to drone their agreement.

So far it didn't look very special to Alexia.

She peered at the village through the van's grimy window. She wished she could wash the window, so she could see more clearly.

The van veered off the highway onto a steep, narrow road, then onto another. Alexia noticed a gas station that seemed to be an old hardware store too. On the opposite side of the road, a highway was under construction: rebar sticking up like a skeletal spine, workers climbing its back, trucks milling back and forth kicking up dust. Where was the recession she'd read about in the news back home? Surely the construction she saw in Athens and in the towns along the highway could not have reached this tiny place. She'd imagined Diakofto like the idyllic villages in the Greek travel ads: captured once and forever unchanged. She liked the sound of that. She smiled, and at the same time gulped down hard, then again. Where had they come from, these ridiculous tears? Get a grip, she told herself, staring out the window. She swallowed, opened her eyes wide, bent forward slightly and wiped them against her shoulder. I need some sleep. That's all.

Two rocky peaks loomed above the highway construction, blackened and disconnected. She hadn't expected mountains. She'd intended to research this place before she came, but in the end, she did what she always did. She updated her colleagues, prepared a transition plan, met with her clients, wrote instructions about how and when to reach her, given the ten-hour time difference, and spent time cajoling Dan into believing the office would survive without her. Her personal agenda got lost somewhere in her professional obligations.

She squinted up at the mountains.

"This is where our town gets its name," Christina said, "*dia* means through and *kofto* means to cut." She met Alexia's eyes in the rear-view mirror. "Many years ago, the mountain cut in two."

"How?"

"Nobody knows. An earthquake, maybe." Christina shrugged. "An act of God. One minute it was a mountain like all the rest. Then, everything changed."

Christina turned and drove down what looked like the town's main street. Cars, tractors and mopeds were double-parked with the street vendors' miniature trucks, which were weighed down with fruit and vegetables, fish and meat, copper pots and pans. Men sat at small tables outside cafés. Women with shopping bags slung over their arms and lists gripped in their hands stood in line in darkened bakeries and butcher shops. Small groups of young people milled about on the sidewalk. Solon rolled down his window. Alexia could smell the sea but couldn't see it. A copperware vendor shouted and women pushed at each other to gather around him. A donkey brayed.

Solon yelled to someone sitting at the corner café opposite the railroad station. The man turned and waved. A car horn blasted.

"*Ella*," Solon shouted, then rolled his window up. "No one has any patience."

This was Greece, Alexia thought. Loud and in your face, just like her father. She relaxed a little. Her father had told her that there was always noise, people would stop to chat and gossip, that everyone knew everyone. It looked like he'd been right about that.

The van crossed the railroad tracks and turned down a residential road. In the schoolyard, a teenager shot a basketball at a naked hoop. Modern houses with dull aluminum shutters lined the streets. In front of the houses, goats sniffed at the ground behind lopsided wire fencing, bleating their protests. Vegetable gardens ran alongside each house. Lilacs were in full bloom. The roads here, like the main road, were paved. "These houses are so new," Alexia said.

"You wanted something old and falling down?" Christina eyed her in the rear-view mirror.

"We modern, too," Maria said. "It is not only in America."

"It's just that my dad said things never change here."

"He thinks everything stay like he left it," Christina said. "Life changes here like it does for other people in other places. Those who leave forget."

Alexia had expected to spend her days poking around quaint ruins and meandering through cobbled streets. But viewed up close, it didn't look at all like a postcard. That was a trick of the light and all this white aluminum siding and stucco. In fact, except for the fields and animals, Diakofto didn't look much different from one of Vancouver's suburbs. "What do people do here?"

"Live," Christina said.

"We enjoy what we can," Maria said. "Not too much."

"Do you get bored?"

Christina slapped the steering wheel. "Boring is for people with nothing."

Katarina nodded, the rest agreed and Alexia gazed down at her watch, feeling as though she'd been told off. She was still on Vancouver time. Nine a.m. Normally, she'd be in a meeting at this time. Her days started at five a.m. with a shower. Then, she'd eat her dry cereal, make a list of things she had to do. At the office by six, she'd get through emails, then review her files before others came in.

The van crept along narrow lanes. Alexia peered into the windows of the houses they passed. Through the lace curtains she could see tidy kitchens, messy living rooms, someone reading at a table, and in the last house, a silhouette behind a shower curtain.

They lurched to a stop. An old goat meandered across the road.

A man's hand reached out and groped the glass shelf beside the shower. He flicked back the curtain and snatched the plastic bottle on the sill. A streak of bright white shot though his thin beard. His mouth opened in a grin. She blinked and turned away.

The van inched forward.

At the end of a dead-end street they pulled up to a narrow, three-storey house. "Thanks be to God," Solon said, jumping out first. The others tumbled out onto the sidewalk, stretching and groaning. Solon took Alexia's bag and Christina walked ahead through the door. Alexia stared at the plain lines of the house, aluminum siding, shingled roof. Where was the village she'd imagined? Where were the whitewashed stone houses, the blue wooden shutters, the labyrinth of pathways? Where was the past?

Christina took Alexia's hand and pulled her into the doorway of the first room they passed. It had two loveseats covered in bright wool blankets. A television with twisted rabbit ears sat in one corner. Family pictures hung on the wall, some in tiny ornate frames, others in large ones. They were scattered about as if set there the moment they came into the house, wherever a spot could be found, no thought given to any order.

Christina pointed to a miniature Acropolis near the television. "A gift from a relative in Athens. And the vases are for the roses Solon brings to me each day from the garden," Christina said.

"*Ella.*" Solon said. "No one cares about this."

Maria and Katarina smiled, winked.

They were so proud of how little they had, Alexia thought. "It's very homey," she said, nodding.

Down the hall, the kitchen held a chrome table and four wooden chairs. High cupboards hovered over a tiny fridge and stove. At one end stood a fireplace encased by blackened walls. "You like it. No?" Christina asked. "Homely? No?"

"Um, homey means comfortable. Warm. Homely is another thing."

"This is problem with English. So many words are the same." Christina shrugged.

"Greeks invented the alphabet," Solon said. "What can anyone show us?"

The entourage cheered. Solon patted Zak on the shoulder. "Yes or no?"

"I didn't mean to criticize," Alexia said. "I'm sorry."

"He has to argue." Christina hugged Alexia to her. "Come. See the rest."

Doors opened and banged shut behind her as Alexia was shown the next floor, which had a bathroom and two closet-sized bedrooms. They all shuffled up another flight of stairs to the attic. Maria pushed ahead of Katarina. This started some of the younger cousins shoving. The acrid scent of sweat made Alexia light-headed. Did they all have to go on this tour? Hadn't these people seen this house about a million times before this?

Christina said she had made up a room in the attic in preparation for Alexia's arrival. The white walls were freshly painted. There was a twin-sized bed, an armoire, a desk and a wooden chair. Heavy dark beams outlined the low ceiling. She could stand fully upright only in the centre of the room. Alexia thought about princesses imprisoned in towers.

"Christina did very nice job," Katarina said.

Christina smiled, put her hands behind her back and looked away as if waiting for confirmation from Alexia.

"*Ne,*" Alexia said.

"*Bravo,*" the rest cheered. "You one of us."

The sudden outburst made Alexia jump.

Maria slid her arm inside Alexia's. "Don't worry. Soon, you get used to us."

"Come see." Christina pointed at the double doors at the opposite end.

Maria pushed Alexia towards them. Christina whispered to Solon and Katarina held her hand over her mouth. The others formed a semi-circle around Alexia. She reached for the handles and opened the doors.

A terrace strung with bougainvillea and grape vines stretched before them. Christina pointed to her small pots of rosemary, thyme, basil and marjoram. "Very nice for cooking. No?"

"I don't cook much." Alexia thought about the baking she used to do with her mother, then Mavis. Why had she stopped? It used to be so much fun.

"And look, lemons," Christina said. "Juice in morning. Every day you want."

More herbs surrounded the old lemon tree rooted in a clay tub.

Alexia nodded.

Long rectangular planters filled with bright red geraniums hung from every corner. Maria pointed to the royal blue, pink and bright yellow pillows and throws that covered the weathered chairs and benches. "Christina make these."

"They are beautiful." Alexia picked up one of the pillows and held it to her chest.

Christina smiled. "*Ella,*" she said. "Let her rest now. She's tired from the long trip." She herded everyone off the terrace. Each aunt, uncle and cousin hugged Alexia or touched her shoulder or arm as they walked past. She tried to acknowledge them with a smile or a returned hug. Christina waited until last. She held Alexia at arm's length. "I am so glad."

"You've done so much."

"Nothing." Christina left.

Alexia closed her door. It had been a long day. She needed sleep. The trip had finally caught up with her. She heard the clink of glasses downstairs and walked back onto the terrace. From here, it looked idyllic. You couldn't see the highway or the new construction. Olive groves stretched to the mountains. She smelled basil and leaned down, clipped a leaf and brought it to her nose. She inhaled deeply.

The next day she woke in the dark, got dressed and tiptoed down the stairs, runners in hand. She sat on the floor in the front hall and laced them up. The front door scraped against the floor as she opened it. She winced. Another door creaked open upstairs. She hurried outside, pulled the door up slightly and closed it behind her, then ran up the deserted street. She didn't know and didn't care where she was headed. She just wanted to exercise her travel-stiff body.

She followed one street, then another, down to the edge of the water where fishermen lined a concrete overhang, poles in hand or propped between piles of rocks. The sky over the mountains blushed pink. The breeze echoed in her ears. Her lungs ached in a good way. She needed this.

The group of men fishing on the shore turned as she got near. The scent of the sea hung over them like a net. Leaning into the others, one man said, "*Amerikanithia.*"

No, I'm Canadian, she thought. But who really cares? They don't know the difference. "Good morning," she called as she passed.

Alexia ran up another side street and out onto the main road where the bakery and the butcher shop were now lit, their doors propped open. Coming towards her, an old lady no more than five feet tall dragged a cart behind her. The woman waved at Alexia, forcing her to stop.

The old woman's voice was calm, but her stare fiery, her face creased into an angry scowl. Alexia leaned in closer to see what she could do to help.

The woman's hair was pinned into a black scarf. Grey whiskers grew out of a mole on her cheek. Her breath was stale. She pointed at Alexia and crossed herself, muttering in Greek. Alexia shook her head. "I'm sorry. I don't speak Greek."

"You want to know where I got these?" Alexia said, pointing to her shorts.

"No good." The woman shook her head vigorously and muttered once more under her breath, crossed herself again.

"Have a good day." Alexia kept her voice light, continued to smile. Of course she wouldn't wear her shorts to the office, she thought, but she was out for a run. No one was supposed to see her. She set off at a jog. After half a block, she turned. The woman was still there, staring at her.

"Where have you been?" Solon's voice came from the direction of the kitchen, shadowed by the flutter of newspaper, a crackle of static and running water.

She pulled off her running shoes and walked into the kitchen, the floor cool against her feet. "Out for a run," she said. "Did I wake you?"

Christina turned from the sink. Her smile disappeared. She bit at the bottom of her lip, crossed herself. "We go upstairs now and talk." She quickly wiped her hands on her apron and placed them firmly on Alexia's shoulders.

"I could use a shower first," Alexia said.

Solon dropped his newspaper.

"Too late now," Christina muttered.

"You went outside like this?" Solon asked. "I do not understand."

"Like what?"

"Our neighbours." He clasped his hands and shook them in her direction, refusing to look at her.

"In America, they dress like this," Christina said. "I saw this when I was there."

"This is not America. We do not bring talk to us." Solon got up from the table, walked past Christina and Alexia and out the front door. "I go to work, now. Fix this, Christina."

Alexia stared at her aunt.

In the week since her arrival, Alexia had settled into a routine. She woke to the static of the radio, got dressed, went downstairs and adjusted the station, tuning the announcer back into the kitchen, clear as a stream, though it never stayed that way for long.

Solon looked up from his coffee. "It is this way."

"Does it move by itself?" Alexia asked. Did he do it to annoy her or was it to give her a chore to do each day so she'd stop going for runs? She wore sweat pants and baggy shirts despite the heat. Still, it didn't seem to satisfy him.

"*Ne*." He shrugged, picked up the paper, fanned it out and hid behind its pages.

She wanted to ask him about the radio, but her cell phone rang. She took the stairs two at a time and caught the phone before it went to voice mail.

"When are you getting back?" Dan said when she picked up.

"What are you doing there so late?" she asked.

"Someone's got to do it," he said, the accusation sharp in his voice.

"I'm sorry. I'm trying to get to know my father's family. I need to do this."

"I need you."

"What do you need? I'll find some Internet café. I can do the work and do what I have to do here too."

"That's not what I meant."

"What's wrong? What is it?" she asked. There was silence at the other end. "Hey, still there?"

She moved around the terrace, into the corners where she thought she might get a signal, then leaned over the side, but found nothing but dead air. No connection with the outside world. She slumped in one of the chairs. Bougainvillea petals stuck to her shirt like crumpled tissue paper. She picked them off and held them close. They were so brilliant. So damn fragile, despite the thorns sticking out from each branch. Thankfully, they hadn't scratched her. She let the petals drop to the ground.

She picked up her bag, threw in her cell phone and went downstairs.

"Where you go now, *paidi mou?*" Christina asked.

"For a walk, fresh air." She opened her arms as if for inspection. "Is this okay? Am I covered up enough?"

"Do not get lost." Christina pretended to push Alexia out the door.

Not a walk, a mission. Alexia walked up one side street after another searching for a high point where the phone would work, but every street seemed to end either at the front door of someone's house or in an empty field of wildflowers. She walked up the unfinished sidewalk along the rocky beachfront. Wires hung from the streetlights, a few missing light bulbs. It was a beautiful spot, though. She saw how someone had put some effort into the place. Bags of cement were strewn about, most of them burst open.

No signal here either.

She raised her phone over her head, walked out into the field of overgrown grass and wheat and God knows what. Candy wrappers, bits of newspaper and squashed cans rustled underfoot. A man was ambling around, kicking at the ground as if searching for something he'd lost. She recognized him: it was the man she'd seen in the shower when the family had first driven into town. The shock of white in his beard was unmistakeable.

The man waved and headed towards her. Was she trespassing on private property? She didn't wait to find out. She hurried off in the opposite direction.

"You back so soon?" Christina said.

Alexia nodded and climbed the stairs to her room. She'd try again tomorrow. If she could just find a way to connect once or twice a day with the office, she could do what she had to do for Dan and get on with what she had to do here. It can't be this damn difficult. It's the twenty-first century. Even here. She dropped her bag, picked up her book, found a comfortable chair on the terrace and tried to read, though the question kept nagging at her: how do I make this work?

One afternoon while Christina was out at the market, Alexia found an Internet café not far from the house.

"Line no work," the clerk said. She had heavy eyebrows and her hair was dyed purple black as if to match her tiny miniskirt and tank top. Her fishnet stockings had a Band-Aid on one knee as if this was meant to fix the hole and stop the stitching from running. She can get away with the Goth outfit, Alexia thought, and I can't wear my shorts when I run? "Maybe tomorrow in afternoon," the girl said. There was no one else in the place. Still, she wiped down the clean tables.

"Does this happen often?"

The girl smiled and shrugged. "I only tell what they tell me."

Alexia came back again and again. The Internet was hit and miss. The cell phone was hopeless. She thought about asking Christina if there was a larger town nearby, but then the scent of lilac would hit her, or she'd see the way the sun touched the tip of the olive groves, notice the shimmer of the mountains and she'd feel the tension drain from her legs. Maybe hit and miss with the technology wasn't bad. She could make that work.

Alexia put her laptop in the bottom drawer of the armoire under her running shorts, a pile of tank tops and jeans. The loose skirts and pants and baggy shirts she'd bought at a small store in the village were better for this climate and more acceptable to these people. She could do without their stares and lectures. It was bad enough having to be here without feeling like some kind of freak.

A breeze kicked up and blew strands of her hair across her face. She tucked them behind her ear. No connection today. Okay, she'd try tomorrow. But the cell phone. She wasn't giving up on it, just yet. It sat beside her. She checked it from time to time to make sure it had a connection. On her lap, the weight of Rohinton Mistry's *A Fine Balance*, Theodora's picture stuck between the pages as a bookmark.

She thought about her half-sister every day. She'd come all this way and hadn't yet talked to Christina about taking the package off her hands. It was still hidden in her room. She held the picture up. She'd found it taped to an inside corner of her father's desk. She would have missed it if the edge of the picture poking up hadn't scratched her hand. *Theodora. 19 years old.* A round-faced girl on a beach towel spread out over peach-coloured sand. A set of legs, hairy and masculine, stood over her. Whoever took the photograph had cut that person's body off at the waist.

The girl had smooth olive skin; her hair was light brown or blonde. It was hard to tell. The strap of her bikini top drooped off her shoulder, the one closest to the camera, as if to tease the photographer. But, it was the eyes that drew Alexia back to the picture, again and again: one hazel, the other a rich brown.

Christina walked out onto the terrace.

Alexia jammed the photograph back into her book.

"Ah, you're reading," she said. "You like being here. No?"

Christina's apron was stained with spots that looked to Alexia like egg yolk. Close to her waist, the tiny seeds of a tomato were crushed against the fabric. A trace of flour lingered on her large hands.

"Catching up," Alexia said. "I don't get a chance to read. Work gets in the way."

"You get this reading from your mother. Your father didn't like the books."

Alexia nodded and remembered how her mother used to go to bed early. "I need to know what happens," she'd say, as she slipped her latest novel under her arm and padded in her baby-blue fleece pyjamas to her bedroom.

"Why?" Alexia had asked.

"We all have to run away once in awhile," she'd call over her shoulder, before closing the door. When would she be old enough to do those kinds of things, Alexia remembered thinking.

"You think about her. No? And your father?" Christina sat down on the bench, wiped her hands on her apron and put one hand over Alexia's.

"I don't know," Alexia said.

"You not alone. We help with everything."

Christina's hand was wrinkled and spotted. Sara's had never aged. Stop thinking about Mom, she told herself. The package. It was a perfect time to bring it up.

"Christina ..."

Christina turned towards Alexia, keen for whatever would come next.

The cell phone interrupted. Alexia jumped up and walked over to the edge of the terrace. "Hello? Hello?" She heard a muffled voice and leaned out as far as she could in hopes of capturing a signal. Christina grasped her from behind.

"What's wrong?" Alexia asked. The phone was dead.

"You crazy. Three floors down. You hurt yourself. For what? If they don't find you, maybe it good for you and them. No?"

"I should check my messages."

Christina stood in front of her, blocking her way. "Why no take a look at what is around you?" Christina pointed to the olive groves. "What is messages when you have this?" She put her arm around Alexia's shoulders, and together they looked at the view. "We were talking about your mother and family. Nice talk. You wanted to tell me something. No?" She turned to face Alexia again.

Her smile was tired, yet keen. Alexia didn't want to hurt this woman, take away what little smile she could manage. "It is beautiful here," Alexia admitted.

"Yes, we like it, but we do not see people from here. Your *thio* Solon and your *thia* sit on our stoop in the front instead. Better place to see. The neighbours across are fighting again with those on other side. They funny people. Not right in their heads. We see what happens. Interesting. No?"

"I've lived in the same building for six years and have no idea what my neighbours do." Nor was Alexia all that interested.

Christina stood close. Her breath smelled of fresh pastry. "Being in each other's lives brings spice to our life."

Christina's hands weighed on her shoulders. "It is like a soap opera."

Alexia walked away and again Christina followed.

"No, not like television," she said. "This real life."

"Sounds like gossip to me."

"It only talk. We need some fun. We do not know what happens tomorrow."

Alexia shrugged. "I don't know."

"Maybe we need change scenery?" Christina said.

Alexia pointed at the cell phone. "I should make this call."

Christina told Alexia to get dressed because they were going out. "You will like it." She hurried towards the double doors. "When you have to make call, you will."

Fifteen minutes later, Christina called up to Alexia. She finished brushing her hair, and shrugged when she saw herself in the mirror as if admitting this was the best she could do. She took the steps two at a time, her skirt billowing and falling, and billowing again.

Christina told Alexia that the train, which followed the river from the Vouraikos Gorge all the way to Kalavryta, a village high in the mountains, was the most amazing ride in the world.

"People come from all over for the views."

"So why aren't we taking it?" Alexia asked as they drove in Christina's car over the tracks and past the station.

"*Ah*," Christina said. "They work on it now."

"If it's a matter of a couple of days, why don't we wait?"

"Since two years they work. And they tell us it take another two."

"What are they doing?" Alexia asked. "Rebuilding the tracks?"

"We don't know. They do not tell us too much."

"It must be hard on the economy, losing all those tourists."

"Money comes and goes like water through hands. Do you not see our politicians in Athens? They say they make mistakes. It is not their fault. They are *kleftis*. You know this word? No? And we pay. We always pay." Christina shrugged. "We see what we see from the car. It not the same but is interesting for you."

They drove along a narrow road and crossed under the national highway. On their right, trucks entered and exited Diakofto's industrial zone. Dust and exhaust fumes yellowed the air. The road tapered upward as Christina's car drove towards the turquoise sky ahead. "Upper Diakofto is there," Christina pointed towards a village tucked in the hills. "It burn in big fires of 2007."

Naked trees leaned against one another, littering the tattooed ground. Shells of houses stood beside others untouched by the fire. How could one be completely ruined, the one beside it left standing? "I read about it on the Internet. It was big news for days in Canada when it happened," she said. "Did they ever catch anybody?"

Christina shook her head. "Bad things happen. We have learned to expect this."

"Well, what do the police say?"

"People here know who did this, but no one talks. You don't know who you are talking to. Maybe a friend of one of these people who do this. You have to be careful."

They travelled further up the road, leaving the burned land, the forest and the houses behind. Serrated mountains crouched close to the road, forming an impenetrable wall of rock. Beyond Alexia's window, the few guardrails still standing gave peek-a-boo views of unforgiving drops into the gorge. Alexia forced herself to look down. A forest of different shades of green hid anything that might lie underneath.

"You can only see things the right way from train. Believe me, it beautiful. One day you see. Waterfalls, cliffs, everything."

Christina flipped on the car radio and sang along. The lines on her face softened. She had a nice voice, Alexia thought. Dad liked to sing too, although he never knew I overheard him on those Sundays when I got up early and found him lying on the living room floor, listening to his Greek music.

An hour later they turned off the road and parked at the bottom of a long driveway that led to the Holy Mega Spileo monastery. Like a child leaning against its mother, the building with its many balconies seemed to be cradled within the arms of the mountain.

"This is oldest monastery in Greece. Built in front of special cave." Christina picked up her jacket out of the back seat and thrust her arms through the sleeves. It was the same jacket she'd worn to the airport the day Alexia arrived. The dark skirt and blouse were also the same. She pulled the strap of her purse over her shoulder and wedged it high under her arm.

They walked up the steep driveway. Kids skipped past them, laughing and joking, school bags swinging from their backs. A lone teacher struggled to herd them.

"They don't understand the hardships others have had."

"Kids should have fun," Alexia said. "It's the only time you're not supposed to have worries and responsibilities." Though when she thought about it, she couldn't remember a time when she was truly carefree, not even when she was in school.

"Yes, it is true. One day they learn that life doesn't stay the same. Look at this monastery. It burned four times and Germans in war killed all monks and others who work here and threw them over the cliffs."

"What?" Alexia stopped. "Why?"

"We are a country that has been invaded many times. We have no reasons for why. Things happen and we manage." Christina continued towards the entrance as if she hadn't noticed Alexia was no longer beside her.

Christina was certainly her father's sister, Alexia thought. Cheerful on the outside, defeatist on the inside.

Alexia hurried to catch up to her aunt. "But the monastery is still here."

"Yes, people build again. We Greeks maybe not smart. But we stubborn."

They entered the building and walked its empty corridors, looked out the prison-cell windows towards the valley beyond the road below. Puffy, low clouds stretched across the sky. The walls of the hallway were lined with black and white photos of what the monastery used to look like, and alongside these, portraits of former priests. Their solemn stares fixed on Alexia as if blaming her for their fate. She looked out a window. She focused on the bit of horizon she could see beyond the bars.

They walked out another door and stood in front of the cave. Water seeped from the rocks, forming a pool at their feet. Light trickled in from above them, giving the algae on the stone a bright green sheen.

"Look at him." Christina pointed her head in the direction of an older man just ahead. He touched his companion's cheek and kissed her hand. The woman turned away as if annoyed. Neither took notice of Christina and Alexia.

The man grinned and for a few seconds, Alexia saw why the young woman beside him was attracted to him. The young woman grabbed at his beard so he was now looking only at her and moved them on.

Christina leaned into Alexia. "We call them *yoes.* Playboys, you say in English."

"Dad was like that."

"Nicolai is brother, husband, father," Christina said. "He was not like this."

"He liked young women and his fun." Alexia crossed her arms. I like you, Christina, and you've been very good to me, but I can't help it, she thought. I lived with him. I know what he was like, what he really cared about. You have no idea. Wait until you hear about Theodora. Then you'll know.

"He had reason."

"You mean excuses," Alexia said.

Christina's jaw tightened. "How can you understand? You are so young."

The mountains were the first thing Alexia noticed as they drove into Kalavryta. They hovered close around the tiny village, their snow-covered tips reminding her of Vancouver's north-shore mountains. She liked mountains. They made her feel comfortable most of the time even though they sometimes scared her, too. It was gorgeous here and so peaceful. This might be the place she could tell Christina about the package, maybe over lunch. After they'd taken in the sights. It might be the perfect time.

They parked the car near the railroad station. A train with two passenger cars stood in front, its paint chipped and faded, rust creeping up its flank, poppies growing underneath its undercarriage and around its iron wheels. "While they fix the tracks, they leave the train to fall apart," Christina said. "I never understand."

Christina and Alexia crossed the quiet main street and walked up a cobblestone path. Train tracks were painted onto the stone. Alexia wondered if the train had once come this way. Christina slipped her arm inside Alexia's. She pointed out the whitewashed houses, with their square wooden bay windows jutting forward. Alexia feigned interest and slid her arm out to take a closer look.

She knew Christina was trying to make this a special day for the two of them, but it just made her think back to the special days she used to have with her mother, "when Daddy isn't allowed to come and we can go anywhere you want. It's our time." They'd held hands and giggled their way through museums, plays, Granville Island, restaurants, art galleries and the library. Later, Sara told Nicolai he wasn't allowed to ask them what they'd been doing because it was girls' stuff. She'd smiled when she'd said that and winked at Alexia.

After her mother died, her father had tried. She had to give him that. He had set aside some time each week just for the two of them, but they both got busy, him with his work, her with school. She didn't care. Why should she? He didn't.

"Revolution of 1821 started in this province," Christina said, bringing Alexia out of her daydreams. "Independence from the Ottomans." Christina puffed, out of breath.

"I'm afraid I don't know much about Greek history."

"Your father teaches you. No?"

"Maybe he tried. I don't remember." An image flashed in her mind of sitting beside her father at the kitchen table, books in front of them.

Her neck was stiff, had been since she woke up. Christina's feather pillows were lovely to look at, but not very comfortable.

"In 1943, the Germans burn the village and kill all men and all boys more than thirteen years," Christina said calmly, as if sharing a bit of family history with a friend. "This building is museum now, it was school before, where Germans tried, but did not succeed to kill women and children too."

"That's horrible," Alexia said. "Why didn't someone stop them?"

"You are young," Christina said. "You still believe you can make things better."

Alexia touched Christina's forearm. "But you can."

"I do not know this."

The building looked more like a government office than a school or museum. Christina said it had been a concentration camp run by the Italians from 1941 to April 1943. "Better the Italians than the Germans."

They entered the first large room. Laid out under glass was a child's notebook, the letters smeared and fading. Televisions and video equipment sat in various spots around the room, the murmur of voices echoed. They went over to the first television and listened to the testimonials of survivors. Alexia read the subtitles. *There was no escape.*

"Your grandfather was here," Christina said.

Alexia turned to face her. "And survived?"

"His mother refuse to let him go."

I knew it, Alexia thought. It was possible to change the course of events if you really wanted to.

The next room had a high ceiling and tall bolted doors on one side. On the walls were black and white pictures, the faces of those who died the day of the massacre. A light would illuminate one picture, then switch to another. Christina crossed herself. Alexia closed her eyes. There was too much suffering in the strangers' stares. Too many young faces.

Christina stroked Alexia's arm. "That is your great-grandfather over there in the top corner. He died with the others that day."

Alexia waited for the light to find her great-grandfather's face. She stared at the shadow of him, her neck aching with the strain of holding her head in one position. Her father had never told her about any of this.

When the light found him at last, Christina bowed her head in prayer. Alexia stared at the photograph in shock. It looked just like her father. It's not him, she told herself. You never even knew this man. Still, she had to look away. She swallowed hard, her hands together behind her back. Squeezed tight. Her neck throbbed.

The light moved on to another photo, another set of features, another pair of staring eyes. Had any of them known what was going to happen? Why couldn't they get away?

Behind the fenced grounds of the museum stood a life-sized sculpture. A life-like scene. Alexia moved closer, knotted her fingers through the mesh. Exposure to the elements had turned the sculpture green, but still the four bronze figures seemed so real. A dead man in a suit lay on a blanket, his eyes open to the sky. A woman tugged at the blanket where his body lay. A young boy no more than six pulled at her sleeve as if to persuade her to let go, leave the dead man behind. Another figure stood apart from the rest. A girl, slightly older than the boy, her arms limp by her sides. *There is no victory in war,* was scratched in various languages on the slab in front of the figures.

Alexia searched the girl's vacant gaze and tightened her grip on the fence. The bronze girl looked to be the same age she had been when her mother died.

Alexia was eight. A bright yellow glow crawled under her closed bedroom door and woke her. Her eyes were dry and itchy as she stood at the top of the stairs outside her room. She rubbed at them and focused. Her mother lay on a grey gurney downstairs, her soft and worry-free face vacant and pasty. Mavis tried to hold onto Alexia when she ran downstairs, but she'd ripped herself out of the embrace, reached for her mother's hand. She'd always had warm hands. This icy skin wasn't hers. Alexia drew back at first, then took Sara's hand and stroked it gently so as not to damage the delicate skin. She rubbed harder and still no warmth returned. Mavis tried to encourage Alexia away. Stuart was standing beside Nicolai, an arm around Nicolai's shoulders. Her father had said, "Leave her. It's okay." Stuart nodded to Mavis, who stepped back. Alexia knew nothing was going to be okay again. Still she couldn't give up. Her eyes throbbed and her hands ached. Time passed and no one moved. Alexia kissed the cold hand, and let it drop.

Alexia ran past her father, past Stuart and Mavis, and past the two paramedics who stood, one with his head down and hands behind his back, the other with his pinkie in his mouth gnawing like an animal caught in a trap. Locking herself in the bathroom, she turned the lights out and lay on the floor in the dark, her own hands frozen, the smell of her mother's vomit still on the clean tiles and in the air. She shivered out of control, but she couldn't get off the floor.

Alexia couldn't think of this right now. Not now.

Christina put her arm around Alexia. "One day everything okay. The next all is wrong. The hands stop at 2:34 that afternoon, the moment the killing started." Christina pointed to the clock at the corner of the tiny church in the square, then to the cypress-covered hill. "The big white cross at top of hill is for dead." Christina crossed herself as all Alexia's relatives did when they passed a church, a cross, a holy place. "We don't like the Germans."

"Things have changed since then."

"People no change," Christina said. "First the Germans tried to kill us all. Then we tried to kill each other because they left us to starve. Even now they try to cut the bread from our mouths. They say they are helping us with our debts. They are only helping themselves to the interest on the loans. And don't forget German companies did work in Greece and were paid for that work. And they sold their products here too. They are not doing this for us. They are doing it for themselves. And if we cannot pay anymore, they will take our land, which is what they want. They have new ways but it comes to the same thing. Our destruction." She shook her head. "And we Greeks are no better. You saw the burn land before. Some of the farmers do not like the development, the new highway. They do not like that our prices cannot compete with the prices protected by other European countries. They burn their land rather than let the government take it. And they burn the land so not to sell their crops for nothing. Fires do not stay in one place. Other land burns."

She walked ahead of Alexia into the church. Gold icons covered the dark walls. Even with the heat outside, this small space felt cool and clammy. Beads of moisture trickled down the walls. A few short rows of wooden chairs ran the length of the room. It would be difficult to fit fifty people in here. Candelabras squatted in a base of sand in each corner; the light of flickering candles warmed and lit the church. One old woman swept the floor and a few others knelt with their heads bowed over their clasped hands. Alexia listened to their murmured prayers. Christina prayed in the front row. Alexia sat in the back and watched, removed but curious about their demonstration of blind faith.

Christina walked over to a group of candles in one corner, lit seven and crossed herself after each one.

The sudden ring of a cell phone was amplified in the stone chapel. Alexia snatched her purse. The elderly women turned and stared. Alexia fumbled. The ringing continued. The woman cleaning dropped her broom and put her hands over her ears. Christina placed her index finger over her mouth and made a sign to switch it off. Alexia dumped the contents of her purse onto the chair, groped through the mess, but still couldn't find the phone. She sat on all her junk. The ringing finally stopped. The two old women stared at her, shook their heads and pointed to the crucifix at the front of the church. She mouthed the words, *I'm sorry,* but they turned away. One leaned into the other and whispered, and then glared back at Alexia as if to warn her she was being watched. She got up, stuffed everything back into her purse and made her way quickly out of the church.

The sudden heat and brightness made Alexia reel. This place was too much. First the museum, then this church, Christina's stories, the old women in black. The harsh light. And those statues, that scene. Why couldn't she get that little girl out of her head? The girl just stood there watching her mother struggling with the dead body. It was the girl's father. It had to be. He lay on the ground like Alexia's father had lain in his bed when she found him that morning. Tucked under the blanket as if he were still asleep, as if nothing was wrong. Except everything was. His room was freezing. Had she turned down the heat the night before? She couldn't breathe. Where had the air gone?

The sun burned into the top of her head. She raised her arm to shade her eyes. She should have worn a hat today. Why hadn't she?

She shook her head, stuck on her sunglasses, and took a deep breath. Stop it now, she said to herself sternly. It'll be okay. She repeated the same words she used to say to herself when she was a child, soothing herself to sleep. It worked then. It would work now.

Christina came out of the church, wiped her face and put on her sunglasses. "Please turn off the phone."

"I didn't know it was on."

"This is a holy place," Christina said. "It is to respect."

"I know."

"If you know, you do not act this way. It is a shame for me and for you."

Christina walked towards one of the three cafés in the square. Alexia watched her take a seat first, before she sat down beside her. An umbrella shaded them from the sun. Out of the dark building, an old waiter shuffled to their table. Christina ordered orange juice for the two of them without asking Alexia what she wanted.

"I'm sorry, *Thia*," she said. And she was.

Christina met her gaze and smiled. "This is first time."

"Excuse me?"

"First time you call me *Thia*."

"I'm trying to learn a few words." She smiled weakly.

"You make us proud, Alexia, if you learn your language."

Alexia nodded and sat back. She took a deep breath. The images were already waning. It was just this place that made her think of things she didn't like to think about. She had to refocus.

She was curious about why Christina had lit seven candles. Her father used to light candles in the church at home. When she asked him about it, he said, "I light one for your mother, one for my family and one for you, *paidi mou*, so God watches over you."

"Why seven candles?" Alexia asked Christina.

"One for your mother, one for your father, one for people who die here, God rest their souls, one for your *thio* so he no make me mad all the time, one is for the family so they find way and one is for you. The last one is for someone you do not know."

"Theodora?" Alexia spoke her name before she'd had the thought.

Christina didn't move. Perhaps she hadn't heard.

The waiter appeared with dessert menus and two glasses of water. Christina dismissed him with a dark look.

"It is good he told you," Christina said.

"Did everyone know but me?" Alexia stared at Christina.

"It was never easy for him."

"It's not easy for me. I'm left to make a delivery for a *yoes.*"

"Do not talk about dead father this way." Christina pointed her finger. "It no right."

"He fathered a child with another woman and left her to bring it up. He never even bothered to see that child. What would you call that?" Alexia turned to face the church. Two girls sat in front, holding hands. They watched the boys and cheered. One of the boys kicked a soccer ball down the street and they scattered and ran after it. The girls skipped along behind them. Alexia wished she could follow.

"No his idea." Christina touched her forearm.

Alexia turned in her chair. "Things happen." She shook her head. "Is that it?"

"What is delivery?"

"He left a package for Theodora. He wanted me to give it to her in person."

"What it is?"

"I don't know. Why should I care?"

"You with family now. Take time. We look in package together." Christina took a sip of her water, licked a drop that ran down the side of the glass.

Alexia wondered what else Christina knew.

"I was hoping I could leave it with you so I can go back to Vancouver and forget about it."

"Vancouver again. Why? You stay here and not see her. She lives in Aigio, has husband and son and life. You do not have to run away from her."

Alexia leaned in toward Christina. "So you're saying I shouldn't see her?"

"It complicated. No?"

Christina swallowed a bit of water and coughed. Alexia patted her back and signalled to the waiter for another glass of water. Christina's eyes glistened and tears marked her cheeks.

"What does Theodora know about me?"

"She know nothing about you and nothing about Nicolai, God rest his soul."

7

2010

Christina and Alexia wandered through the back streets of Kalavryta, heading for the path that led them to Kappi hill where the cross stood towering over the cypress and pine trees. Neither had said more than a few words to each other since they left the café. Christina said this was a place of sacrifice and Alexia wondered if she was talking about Nicolai rather than Kalavyrta and the war.

"Dad would have loved it here," Alexia said. Perhaps he had been, she thought. Not that he told her anything about it.

"It is sad place," Christina said. "There is nothing to love."

"Yes." She'd put her foot in it again. How could she talk to her aunt about her father? About Theodora? She needed to know.

The road came to an end and a stone pathway began. On one side, a pristine lawn surrounded by pine, cypress and oleander trees. It looked peaceful, Alexia thought. You could lie here in the shade and read a book, forget yourself. On the opposite side, a low stone fence separated them from the twisting road that led to a parking lot at the top of the memorial.

"The ones who died here walked this hill," Christina said. "Out of respect for their sacrifice, we no drive. We walk."

Christina's back was stooped as she trudged up the steep path. She crossed herself and muttered under her breath. Alexia kept her eyes on the cross ahead and the tall concrete slabs keeping vigil at its foot.

The manicured grounds near the top of the hill were punctured with metal crosses leaning into the grass. From each cross hung a chain necklace bearing a tiny wood plaque with a name and date. She couldn't read the Greek letters. The numbers were the same: 13 – 12 – 43.

Christina stopped in front of each cross and prayed. Alexia stood behind her, waiting. Stay focused, Alexia told herself. She pushed the thought of that awful statue at the museum out of her mind. Clouds drifted over the sun, obliterating its bright light. She wrapped her sweater around herself, crossed her arms.

Beyond the crosses, the lawn disappeared into a forest. They found a path through the trees and walked up to the cross and the three lofty concrete slabs. Alexia held her skirt down against the wind. Etched into the concrete was a list of names and beside each name, the age the person died. 13. 15. 17. 14. Christina wept. Alexia stood to one side and poked at a pine cone with the toe of her shoe.

Alexia stood waiting for what seemed like hours. She reread the numbers over and over as if reviewing a spreadsheet of figures for a potential merger she was negotiating. Except there was no making sense of these numbers. She gazed out over the mountains, the way they cradled the valley below. Groups of mourners lingered on the grounds. What am I doing here with these people? I don't understand them or what they've been through. I'm not Greek. Christina should have brought Theodora. She'd get these walls, this place. She'd know what to do, how to act.

Christina dried her eyes and led Alexia down into the small bunker dug into the hill. Medallions lined the walls and dangled from the ceiling, tributes from the families of the dead. They glinted in the light of hundreds of candles burning inside the tiny space. Christina lit one more.

Back in the village, Alexia followed Christina into a *taverna* and sat at the bar out of the sun's reach. The stone walls were garlanded with white and yellow plastic daisies sprouting from dusty green foliage. B*ouzouki* guitar replicas stood silent on the shelves beside motionless ceramic dancers in traditional dress. Sorrowful music wailed from speakers. It was the kind of music Nicolai had listened to every Sunday morning just before dawn, his eyes closed as if in a dream, his hands, like those of a mime, moving in time with the beat. Alexia was about ten the first time his music woke her. She'd crept out of bed and found him lying on the living room floor. He smiled as he sang and hummed. For a long time, this was their Sunday morning ritual. She listened and watched, then slipped back into bed before he noticed her. Though the language and the sounds were foreign, she felt safe. He was there. They were together. When she was older, she'd stay in bed, a pillow over her head, willing herself back to sleep. Just when she thought she couldn't stand another Sunday, he started bringing his girlfriends home. That was the end of the Greek music.

Her father would have loved everything about this *taverna*, she thought, from the old men who smoked and gossiped as they nursed coal-black, thimble-sized coffees, to the chatty bartender who talked with his hands, poured drinks and served food, unperturbed by the soup and coffee he spattered on his pants. If her father were here, he'd watch the bustle of people eating and visiting, and find a way to insert himself, make friends. He'd introduce her to everyone, "This is my daughter, the lawyer."

Alexia preferred to keep her distance. She didn't want to be beholden to anyone.

She pulled her sweater off and draped it over her shoulders, as Christina said the cave lakes and the *Agia Lavra* monastery were close by. She pointed over her shoulder as she swallowed another bite of her chocolate crepe. Alexia nodded. She needed to talk to Christina about Theodora. Alexia had to decide what she was going to do about her. Chocolate dripped onto Christina's chin. Alexia touched her own face and mumbled, "There's something."

"An insect?" Christina asked.

When Alexia shook her head, Christina swallowed another mouthful. "Then nothing to worry about."

"Do you know Theodora? What's she like?"

"Again with this?" Christina threw up her hands. "Think about the history so close to you. The monastery of *Agia Lavra* is in the trees, only five kilometres away."

"You talk about people all the time," Alexia said. "Why don't you want to talk about Theodora? She's part of my history too."

"Yes, but you have time. No rush. First you think of bigger history."

Alexia picked the olives out of her salad and dropped them onto a side plate.

Christina bit down on her lip, shook her head. Her eyes burrowed into Alexia. "What kind of Greek you are?" Christina asked.

"I've never liked them."

An olive rolled off her fork and onto the floor. She ripped her paper napkin in two, scooped up the olive, scrunched up the package tight and stuck it in the ashtray.

"*Paidi mou,* you smart girl. No?"

Alexia wondered what might come next, because her father used to say the same thing just before he made a condescending remark. "I like the oil, not the actual olives."

"But you Greek. No?"

The smell of fried batter and stale grease in the air made her queasy. Alexia sniffed at her sweater to see if the odour had settled. To anyone watching, it would look like she was wiping her nose on her shoulder. No one was paying attention.

"Our banner with real bullet holes is in monastery." Christina leaned into Alexia, touched her arm. "You should see."

"Shouldn't I want to deal with these family things first?"

Alexia's cell phone rang.

Dan got to the point. "What's the status on the Springs and Gordon merger? I've had several messages. Anything I should know?"

"What happened to 'how are you doing? Are you having a nice time?'"

Christina took the phone out of her hand and stared at it as if to see which end she should speak into. "We have lunch now," she said while holding it out in front of her. "She calls you back. Later. Late, later." Christina poked at several buttons. "Where is off?" Without waiting for a reply, she said, "Did I tell you cave lakes are 827 metres?"

Alexia snatched the phone back and listened to dead air. "Hello, hello. Hello?" She shook the phone. "That was my office, my work. It was important."

"You on vacation." She took a mouthful of chocolate. "No?"

"If there's a problem, I need to deal with it."

"Problems wait. Never worry about this. Lakes inside cave more interesting. How you say, unique. Do you know about them? You study in school these things?"

"I don't know." Alexia rolled another olive to the side of her plate.

"Spend time looking, instead on phone. It better than worry about your father and sister, all those things. You learn about your history. Think about things first and the answers come. This history. It is who you are." She pointed her gooey fork in Alexia's direction. "Who we are." Christina made a circle with her fork and aimed it back at herself. Her eyes were clear, her voice strong and firm, and her hands punctuated her points. She would have made a convincing lawyer, Alexia thought.

"Oh, *paidi mou*," Christina said, and pointed to Alexia's chest.

Chocolate speckled Alexia's white linen blouse. Christina spit on her napkin and rubbed at the stains. Alexia sat still, unable to move. Her face felt warm. Christina didn't look up from her task. Her hand was heavy against Alexia's chest.

"Everything is fine." Christina tucked her napkin away on her lap.

"I'll take care of it." Alexia pressed her napkin against the wet spots.

"You worry too much." Christina garbled through a full mouth.

"Excuse me?"

"Stains clean. Broken things fix." Christina swallowed, patted her mouth with her napkin and dropped it on the table beside her. "Only time, you no bring back. You exactly like your father. He worry about too many things."

Alexia shook her head. "He wasn't the type."

"He no show, but he worry," Christina said and swallowed her last bite of crepe. "When we children, he worry about the anger in your *pappou* and he protect me, all his sisters and our mother. I try to keep the peace in the house, but he would fight our father if he tried to hurt us."

Alexia didn't know who Christina was talking about. It sure didn't sound like her father. "He had friends and went to parties.

He didn't like problems, refused to deal with stuff. His answer to any question was, 'it's too complicated'. He left me when Mom died." She shook her head. I took care of him and he still left. And when he came back, I took care of him again, well, at least until he started dating all those women. Then he had no time for me. You just didn't know him. "He wasn't someone who worried."

"Parents protect their children. This is why you no see."

Maybe some parents do, Alexia thought. That's what you're doing for Theodora right now. I can see that. I can't figure out why. But I will.

Alexia excused herself and went to the bathroom. In the privacy of the stall, she patted each dribble of chocolate with pieces of wet toilet paper. She rubbed harder and elongated the marks. Her shirt was now spotted in faded brown dots and frayed toilet paper. Flicking away the paper, she took off her shirt, squirted some of the pink dispenser soap hanging above the sink onto it, and washed it, making sure she didn't touch the grimy sides of the sink. She rinsed her shirt, squeezed every drop of water out of it and rolled it up in some paper towels. She put on her sweater and buttoned it up, knowing she'd be hot when they left the restaurant. She thought about what Christina had said. Anything could be cleaned. Really, how do you wipe away Theodora? A child was not like a shirt or a napkin or underwear you could wash out.

The image came clearly. She'd locked the bathroom door at school. She was in grade seven. She took off her panties and tried to wash the sticky gore away. When she couldn't, she stuffed her panties with toilet paper, put them back on, felt cold wetness against her thighs, the clump between her legs, took a breath to steel herself, unlocked the door and went home without telling anyone. Nicolai looked up from his desk as she walked in. He put his pen down. "What are you doing home so early?" he asked.

"Wasn't feeling well." Standing in the hallway, pack on her back, she couldn't move. She hadn't expected him to be there.

He quickly slipped the file into his desk and came to her. "What is it?"

"Bleeding." She couldn't come up with anything else.

He removed her pack, checked her arms, hands, face and legs. "Did you fall?" He stood in front of her. "I don't see anything."

Why did he have to ask questions? She pointed to the area below her stomach. He stood still like he didn't know what to do either. Maybe she shouldn't have told him. He was her dad. He wouldn't know about this stuff. She should have called Mavis.

"*Paidi mou*, I'm so happy for you," he said. "You are becoming a woman." He hugged her. The familiar scent of forest on his shirt reassured her. His ponytail dangled over his shoulder. She smiled in spite of all that had happened.

"Your mother, God rest her soul, would be so excited if she were here." He took his handkerchief out of his pocket and blew his nose, patted his eyes. "This is a good day. Nothing to be ashamed of." He kissed the top of her head.

Later he'd bought her books, took her to the store to buy pads, and answered questions she'd thought about asking but couldn't find the courage. He talked, she listened and eventually she became comfortable enough to respond, ask a few questions.

She remembered other times when he'd surprised her with his thoughtfulness. At her first concert, she saw him in the audience, leaning into the people around him, talking and pointing at her. His eyes glistened and he pulled out that handkerchief her mother had given him before she died. They had been close then. After he came home from Greece, it was just the two of them gossiping into the night about what they did during the day until she said, "I think I should go to bed now, Daddy." Later, when she went to high school, Nicolai started to bring women to her basketball games. He used to call them "my friends." They were much younger, the same age as Mom when she died, but showy like him, nothing like Mom. Alexia heard them in his room, laughing and talking. What had she done to make things change?

They were back in the car. Alexia sat quietly, watching the scenery dash by.

"Do not think too much." Christina had a tight grip on the steering wheel and manoeuvred the narrow road back towards Diakofto.

"I'm looking at the scenery."

Christina patted Alexia's thigh. "You think about her. But the past is done."

Alexia leaned back in her seat and closed her eyes. The voice in her head would not stop. There's no point discussing Theodora with you. You won't tell me anything anyway. He wanted me to deliver that stupid shoebox, don't you get it? He didn't ask me how I felt about it. He forced me into this. And now you're not going to help me either. Alexia tucked her hands underneath her. I don't want to deal with it either. But I have to. I knew I'd end up doing this on my own.

Christina was calling up to her. "We go to the market. Katarina is here already. And we can have lunch after we finish shopping. You come, yes?"

"No!" Alexia said, more emphatically than she intended. She pictured Christina standing at the bottom of the stairs, her liver-spotted hand on the handrail peering up the staircase in the direction of the attic. "Thanks," Alexia called down. "But I have to work." It sounded like a growl even to her. They'll probably talk about me, she thought.

Alexia peeked out the attic window. Katarina was pacing in front of the house, her shopping cart rattling behind her. Finally, Christina joined her. Alexia heard Katarina mutter and point in the direction of the window. Christina shrugged. Alexia moved from view.

She lay on her stomach on the floor, Theodora's picture propped against her book. She stared at those two different-coloured eyes—innocent, happy, hinting at mischief—and tried to imagine how this girl would react to having a sister. What would she do with Nicolai's letters? That's what was in the box. When she'd returned from Kalavryta, she went straight to her closet and flipped the lid of the shoebox only to find stacks of envelopes, each addressed to Theodora Christopoulou from Nicolai Sarinopoulos. He'd used his full name even though he'd gone by the name of Sarino ever since he'd immigrated to Canada.

"We have to fit in," he'd told Alexia when she asked him why they didn't use their full name. "This is easier."

A few of those envelopes lay beside her book. She picked up the first one, flipped it forward and backward, examining it to see if there was a slight tear or opening she could pry. She'd convinced herself she needed to know. It might help her figure out how to approach Theodora. The envelope was sealed. She pictured Nicolai licking the envelopes and then stamping each with his company seal, his beloved Greek flag. She picked up a handful of envelopes, looked outside her window to make sure Christina and Katarina were gone and went down the stairs into the kitchen. She put the kettle on the burner, lit the flame and stood watching it, her hands behind her back, the envelopes on the counter beside her. She waved the first over the screaming kettle. The envelope became damp. She wiped it against her shirt quickly, turned off the gas and ran back upstairs. She unfolded the letter and found it was written in Greek. All that effort and she couldn't read it. She put the letter back in the envelope and put the envelopes back in the box in the same order she'd found them. Theodora could have the letters and the old shoebox, Alexia thought, but not Mom's ribbons. He'd probably used them when he ran out of tape. He was thoughtless that way. She hid the ribbons under her pillow.

Nicolai sometimes made her funny cards for her birthday, but he'd never written her a letter, not even when he left her. What did he write about in those letters to Theodora? And why her? What was so special about her? Alexia flung the picture towards the wall. It floated and fell short. Don't be so childish, she told herself, and picked it up. The floorboards groaned as she paced. She pressed the pointy end of the picture against her temple, leaving tiny needle-size impressions on her skin.

A bus pulled up in front of the roadside shelter where Alexia stood with five others. She'd decided that just laying eyes on Theodora might help her figure out what to do. But now that she was about to get on the bus to Aigio, she wasn't so sure. Her stomach felt hollow, her throat tight.

A white-bearded Greek Orthodox priest—in a black square hat, floor-length black tunic and scuffed loafers—stood with his back to her. In front of him were four young, stocky women in navy skirts and pastel blouses, their babies slung on their hips. Each stood with her legs slightly apart, in flat, practical shoes. One child screeched. Alexia jumped. The baby's mother raised the child over her shoulder and patted its behind, then adjusted her hair band and bags. Gurgles replaced gasped protests. Calm down, Alexia told herself. Start worrying when you arrive.

The women nodded to the priest and he stepped onto the bus first. He touched their heads and those of their babies as he passed and they kissed his hand. Alexia waited well out of his reach, smelling diesel fumes.

She got on board and stopped to count out the fare. She flipped each coin back and forth to make sure she knew what it was worth. The bus driver clucked his impatience. He took what he wanted from her outstretched hand and nodded for her to move to the back.

Walking up the aisle, she received guarded smiles and nods from a few passengers. Did they know what she was up to? She had no reason to feel guilty. She was simply doing what her father wanted, fulfilling his last wish. Still, she couldn't shake the image of Christina's smile or the feel of her hand on hers when they were in Kalavryta. Christina had said, "We help. You not alone with this."

She took a seat next to the window. Stop thinking, she told herself. It's too late to turn around. You're committed now. And besides, Christina's not telling you everything she knows, so she's not being very helpful, is she? And she had suggested not seeing Theodora at all, hadn't she?

Unlike the cramped buses in Vancouver, this one had reclining seats, leg room and air conditioning. There was no scent of damp sweat as there was on rainy days she rode the buses in Vancouver where soaked passengers stood sandwiched. She would never get used to that dank stench.

Every few minutes, the bus jolted to a stop. She tried to distract herself by watching the passengers who got on and off with shopping carts, packs and farm tools. She focused on these people, looking at what they were wearing, imagining who they were.

When the bus arrived in Aigio, Alexia left the station and walked to the first main square with a water fountain. She cupped water into her hand and slurped away her thirst, then splashed her face and the back of her neck. Benches flanked the triangular sides of the square. She'd read about this place in her guidebook. It was an embarrassment to the community because the renegade planner had designed the square as a triangle. Squares were supposed to be square. Why hadn't there been simple, easy-to-follow rules like this for her life?

She wandered among the village streets and through some of the parks beyond the main shopping area. The guidebook said Aigio had a population of about 30,000. Who would notice her? If she didn't manage to track Theodora down, she'd at least see another Greek town. Be a tourist. And she might be able to find an Internet café here that actually worked so she could update Dan, deal with whatever he and the office needed.

She walked into an open market and as she turned a corner she saw a short, husky woman fondling and sniffing a large cantaloupe. She was holding a child who had his legs wrapped around the woman's hips. The woman's long hair, her tiny shoulders—reminded Alexia of Theodora, although the woman's hair was dark, not light, and she was heavier than she'd been in the picture. But who knew when the picture was taken? Her hair could be dyed now. And she could have put on weight. Christina had said Theodora had a son. She'd at least given her that much information.

Alexia moved around the stack of tomatoes, stumbled over a crate of oranges and fell against the stranger. Oranges crashed into tomatoes and rolled in all directions. The woman pushed her away. Alexia caught her balance and stood still. The child whimpered. The woman stared at her the way opposing lawyers did whenever they suspected her motives. The woman's eyes were different than Theodora's, her face chubbier and older. It wasn't Theodora at all. The woman turned and disappeared into the crowd.

The clerk ran out from behind his stand, kicked at the mess on the ground and waved his hands. He shouted but she didn't understand what he was saying. She shrugged. A few women stood around, no doubt wondering what would happen next. Alexia's face felt warm, her armpits damp. She calmly picked up the tomatoes and bagged them. "Here," she said, sticking out her hand. The clerk snatched the Euros he wanted. "I'm sorry." He didn't respond. She walked away, ignoring his grumbles.

Get on with it, she told herself as she stood outside the market trying to control her breathing. You didn't come here to dilly-dally. Go see where she lives. Maybe you'll figure out why Christina doesn't want you to meet Theodora. That was true, wasn't it?

She'd made it pretty clear. She wouldn't bother to answer a few simple questions. "We help," Christina had said. Then answer my questions, for God's sake.

Alexia pulled the crumpled piece of paper with Theodora's address out of her bag along with the small map in the guidebook. The address looked to be a few blocks away. She could walk there. She didn't have to find the right bus or flag a taxi.

The number was on the fence. She checked it against the one in her hand. It was the right house. Alexia glanced briefly at Theodora's house as she walked past, careful not to stare. She went around the block and came back. She found a spot in front of a boarded-up shop where she thought she'd go unnoticed and stuck the guidebook in front of her face. She moved it down slowly for a better look and held her breath. The house looked more like an oversized garden shed with one window out front and a door to the side. Just behind the front façade, there seemed to be a second storey with a couple of windows. The curtains were drawn. Clumps of sunflowers and other wild flowers lined the white picket fence and gave peek-a-boo views of the vegetable garden. Two plastic lawn chairs leaned against the house as if done for the season.

Something moved. She saw the sunhat first. A young woman in jeans and a T-shirt stood up just behind one corner of the fence and stretched. The woman gazed down at the garden, wiped her face with the back of her hand, then kneeled down again. Oh, God. Now what? Alexia heard her heart pounding in her ears, and forced herself to calmly stick her book in her bag, turn around and walk away from the house. When she rounded the corner, she picked up her pace, heading toward the bus depot.

All the way back to Diakofto, Alexia had one thought: what now?

As soon as she got to her room, she tucked Theodora's picture into her laptop bag and placed it in the bottom drawer of the armoire.

She hid the brown paper bag that read *Aigio Market* under her laptop and placed the tomatoes in Christina's hanging basket.

"Some stores have no good quality," Christina said, when she saw the tomatoes. "Where you get these? I can take back to *kleftis* who sold them to you."

"A small shop," Alexia said, and picked up her book, gripped it tightly.

"Where you go today? Why you no come with us if you want to buy tomatoes?" They were on the terrace. The parched sun dipped behind the mountains. Christina stood very close to Alexia, her hands on her hips.

"Exploring," Alexia said.

"You find what you look for?"

"I wasn't looking for anything in particular."

She turned her mind away from the problem of Theodora and focused on routine. It was the only way she was ever going to make a rational decision. She ran most mornings. No one stared at her anymore. They were used to seeing her. After her run, she did push-ups and sit-ups, then a series of squats and lunges as she lifted large cans of cling peaches and other fruit she found in Christina's pantry. She went to the market with Christina and Katarina or took walks along the path leading to the beach. Another week or so passed. And again the questions forced themselves to the front of her mind—when am I going home? should I meet Theodora or leave things as they are? how do I get this package to her? what is Christina hiding from me? That day, she doubled up on her run, then sat with the fishermen a little longer listening to their chatter, trying to decipher all the Greek words. They put bait on her line, placed the rod in her hands. The line wiggled and jumped; she screamed and almost dropped the rod. Laughing, a fisherman took it off her line and offered her the slimy body. She shook her head, pushed it back in his direction. "*Efcharisto. Oxi.*"

She called Dan from the government telephone centre, the OTE.

"You said it would only take a week or so," he grumbled. "It's already been more than three weeks."

"I know," she said, "but I haven't figured things out yet."

"What's to figure?" he asked. "You've had a nice visit, eaten all the Greek food you're probably ever going to want and now it's time to come home."

You have no idea, she thought. "It's not that straightforward."

"I don't like not having you around."

"What are you talking about? You've got a whole office full of people. My being gone for a little while isn't going to make much difference."

"It does. To me."

"What's going on?"

"I don't know what I have to do."

She wanted to ask what he meant. It wasn't like she hadn't been available to answer his silly questions, listen to him go on and on about a problem with one of the accounts. Before she could get the words out, he passed the phone to one of the lawyers who was looking after her cases. Dan was frustrated. She got that. But, he only cared about what she could do for the firm and the precious clients. At least she'd found a way to deliver when the Internet was working at the café, calling him at the OTE. Why couldn't he just be happy with that? Wasn't that enough?

Katarina and Zak came over for dinner that night. Along with the discussion about when to pick the olives, who they'd sell them to now that no one in the country had any money to buy things, and what the politicians would do next, Zak mentioned a man he worked with he thought Alexia should meet. "He is no good," Katarina said, and nudged Zak. "The young baker is a different story. I know is perfect for you."

"I'm not looking for a boyfriend," Alexia said.

"You have friend in Vancouver?"

"Work keeps me busy." She put a small piece of lamb in her mouth.

"It good to marry someone your own kind," Katarina said. "You be happy this way."

"I thought you discouraged marriage."

"They complain," Solon said, "but they know they have good life."

Christina slapped his shoulder. "Better than some."

"*Po po po,* how she can put up with that son, I don't know," Katarina said.

"They have hard life." Christina nodded, chewing her meat.

Alexia noticed that blood and meat juice was already beginning to congeal on Christina's plate.

"She deserves this."

"Who are you talking about?" Alexia asked.

Christina and Katarina exchanged a glance. Christina shrugged. "Maria. Who else?"

"Her son born bad," Katarina said. "Hard to change."

"It not his fault," Christina said. "She took care of herself. Travelled, had fun, men. Never give him what he need. Now she has problems."

Katarina nodded and added, "She this way from birth."

"She thinks only of herself and what she wants."

Alexia had heard it all before. *Selfish. Unloving. Only cares about what she wears. Finally Maria remarried. It took long enough. This husband at least better. He put some sense into her.* Their eyes flashed with anger and a kind of satisfaction she'd seen in her father's eyes. Why did they only see fault? They seemed to enjoy it. But why would they enjoy someone else's struggles? And why did they want to convince her to join them in this gossip? She didn't want to be part of their club. It was mean and petty.

Alexia liked Maria. At least that aunt didn't talk behind your back the way Katarina and Christina did. If you couldn't say something directly to a person, you had no business saying it at all. Then again, Alexia had seen more of Katarina and Christina than she had of Maria.

Nicolai used to call one of their neighbours Tarzan because he was always climbing the trees in his yard to trim them. When she called the neighbour Tarzan, he laughed and asked her why. "That's what my dad calls you," she said.

Later, Nicolai scolded her. "Some things we don't have to share. Understand?"

"That's not very honest," Alexia had said. "Mom said we should tell the truth."

"Yes, but there are some things you keep to yourself, things that stay in the family."

She couldn't describe the look he gave her that day, but she never forgot it. There was nastiness in it she didn't understand. "Why say anything at all?"

"To pass the time," Nicolai had said. He smiled in that same way he did with his friends and clients. It didn't make any sense.

Did he like these people, or hate them? Which was it? No, it didn't make any sense then, and it didn't make any sense now.

"What do you say about me when I'm not here?" Alexia asked Christina.

"Maria has problem," Katarina said. "We help." She shrugged.

"Why not talk to her?"

"You people do this. Say what you feel and think. We no hurt people the way you do in America. This is better."

"How does it help?" Alexia asked.

"We talk, we find solution," Christina said. "Then we guide in nice way."

She couldn't help herself. "And you call this nice?"

"Women," Solon said. "They like their secrets."

Over the next few days, Alexia dreamt of meeting Theodora, imagined conversations. Each time she stopped herself by studying the Greek book and the elementary notes Solon had given her.

One day, nothing seemed to work. She wandered out to the field to ask Solon a question about a Greek word she'd written down, but now could not read. He'd distract her.

"*Paidi mou,* you put the accent here," he said. "Don't say it like the English. Say it like a Greek, from your heart."

"And with a lot of spit."

"*Ne*. Exactly." He smiled for her.

Alexia walked the olive groves with Solon, listening to his history lessons. The next day she helped her aunt shop, weed the pots on the terrace and dust Christina's collection of ceramic knickknacks. But the distractions were not doing the trick. She couldn't stay in limbo forever. Nicolai had given her a responsibility. She needed to get it done and go home. It didn't matter what he had written in those letters to Theodora. He had left his belongings for her, not his thoughts and musings.

At the end of the week, Alexia took the bus again to Aigio. This time, she put the letters in her pack, intent on getting rid of them once and for all. She sat on her hands and looked out the window, the pack on her lap. The land was more scorched than ever. Did it ever rain in this country? She thought about the letters. How was she going to explain why she had them? She'd figure it out as she went.

The bus came to a stop. Three young girls got on, laughing and talking over each other. They squeezed into one seat across from Alexia, their spindly arms around one another's shoulders. Alexia glanced over at them. One of the girls noticed and whispered to the others. They giggled. Alexia turned to face the window. It had been a long time since she was a kid at school, laughing with her friends, worried about all the silly things that girls worried about when they were teenagers. As an adult she had work friends she got together with on a Friday night for a drink, and Mavis and Stuart, who she saw some Sundays when she and Nicolai went over for dinner.

When Alexia arrived in Aigio she went directly to Theodora's house. She had no trouble finding it: she remembered every turn. She watched the house for two hours, walking up and down the side streets that ran parallel. The straps of the pack etched themselves into her shoulders. She tried pushing her shoulders back, but it didn't help. It was easier to carry than her briefcase or even her purse, but her shoulders hadn't gotten used to carrying things this way.

Finally, Theodora came out, a child on her hip bunching up her floral skirt and grabbing at her pink blouse. Christina had told her Theodora had a son. And here he was. Theodora too. Close enough to say hello.

The child was dressed in a blue sailor outfit and wore a ball cap. She guessed he was maybe two or three years old. That woman is my sister, that kid is my nephew, she thought. How could this be? Here was something else this woman had given Nicolai, a grandchild. Alexia's jaw tightened. Nicolai was a grandfather. He would have liked that. "You know the kind of schedule I keep," she'd say when her father asked her if she had someone special in her life.

Theodora slung a large canvas bag over her shoulder and carried a wallet in her right hand. She couldn't have been more than five feet tall. She was striking, handsome more than pretty, with high cheekbones, long sandy-blonde hair, full lips and olive skin. Alexia couldn't see her eyes, but she was sure they had the contrasting tinge so clear in the picture. Theodora looked quite a bit younger than Alexia had expected.

Theodora walked down the street and disappeared beyond the next corner. Alexia followed. Theodora peered in every store window and dawdled. Alexia stopped when Theodora stopped, glanced away, but kept Theodora in her sights. She was not good at this game. Why not come clean and tell her? I tell her the story, give her the letters, get the hell out. Part of her couldn't wait to put an end to all this nonsense. The other part liked that she had a secret her father had shared only with her.

In the market Theodora went to a stall near the back. She chose a bunch of bananas, a carton of strawberries, some apples and a vine of bright, red tomatoes. Garlic, a couple of cucumbers and three large green peppers were also bagged for her by a rotund clerk in a crisp, white apron. Theodora sniffed everything she selected. Her hands were like Nicolai's and Alexia's: meant for holding delicate things very carefully, as her father used to say when she complained her hands were too small for her to be good at basketball.

As she left the market, Theodora stopped to talk to a woman who had her hand extended and her head bent low. Alexia had passed this woman in the market when she was here before. She remembered the woman's stale grease scent. She'd walked past her without making eye contact.

Theodora spoke to the woman, smiled, then handed her a package she'd dug out of her bag. The woman hugged Theodora.

She's a better person than me, Alexia thought.

Alexia followed Theodora to the butcher shop. She waited outside, watching her through the shop's front window. Four chairs stood in a row inside. Three women and a man sat in the chairs, waiting their turn. Theodora made her way to the front. She talked to the butcher for several minutes and he stroked her arm when she leaned against the glass case displaying all forms of dressed meat. The butcher kissed the child's cheek.

Theodora had a few words with each of the women and the man, then blew a kiss in the direction of the butcher as she walked out. She had a nice smile.

Outside, Theodora's son leaned his head into her leg, then pushed himself away from her and whimpered. She bent down, picked him up and whispered in his ear. He rubbed at his eyes.

Theodora carried on down the street to a park, where she dropped her bag and slipped out of her shoes. Holding her son, she climbed the slide, sat with him in her lap and slid down. She held him tight around his waist. His hands were above his head, holding her face. Both laughed.

The breeze kicked a few dry leaves towards Alexia. She stepped out of the way, allowing them to gust past.

Theodora sat at the bottom of the slide, dug out a hanky from her pocket and wiped the boy's nose. She kissed the back of his neck and he giggled. She made circles in the sand with her feet and her son was transfixed.

Theodora brought her arm up and over her son's head to look at her watch. Her smile disappeared. She slipped her high heels into her bag and put on a pair of black ballerina flats. With her bag draped over one arm and her son in the other, she rushed across the street, turned up at the next corner and into a café. Now what? Alexia wondered. I should go home. I should. Or maybe go to that Internet café I saw earlier and do some work. I should.

Alexia found a seat at a table near where Theodora was sitting across from an older woman. She plunked her pack on the floor. The sun slanting through the floor to ceiling windows made her squint. A waiter pulled down the blinds. She nodded.

The older woman looked at her watch. Alexia recognized the Greek word for late. She called Theodora "my dear." But the words seemed wrong coming from her mouth. Her jaw was rigid, her smile plastered in place with heavy makeup. As she spoke, fine lines turned into crevices.

"Elena, I'm so sorry. We stopped at the park," Theodora said. "To play."

Alexia understood what was going on between these women by the tone of their voices, the expressions she saw when she stole the odd glance. The language lessons with her uncle had helped too. She picked up fragments of sentences: "don't worry about me. I am only worried for your son. He is like his father, gets ear infections."

Theodora grinned helplessly.

"I'm sure you don't want your son to get sick. You want to be a good mother. And of course, I know you are," the old woman said.

The boy shimmied to the floor, searched through Theodora's bags. The older woman scolded him for being on the floor.

Theodora picked him up. He had one of her high heels in his hand.

The older woman shook her head. "*Xanthoula.*"

Little blonde one. Solon always made note of anyone with fair hair.

What the hell was wrong with that old bag? Alexia wondered.

Alexia sat on a bench in a park and picked at her *souvlaki* thinking about Theodora. From what she had glimpsed of Theodora's world, her life was already complicated. She didn't need anything else. Nicolai had wanted her to have those letters, but this was likely more for his benefit than for this poor girl. It was a way to deal with his guilt. Nothing more. She watched people walk by and left her half-eaten *souvlaki* to a crow too bold to worry about her feeble attempts to shoo him away.

The sky darkened. She felt a chill and a couple of drops of rain. Now it decides to rain, she thought, looking up at the sky. It could have waited until I got home.

Heading to the bus depot, she took a couple of turns, but didn't recognize the street she walked up. Finally she came around another corner and found herself in the park where she'd watched Theodora play with her son.

Theodora sat on a bench while her son dug around in the sandbox. She blew her nose and dabbed at her eyes. Her high heels were beside her, her feet bare.

That old bag wasn't worth crying over, Alexia thought. I don't know a thing about you, but there's no way you deserved what that bat dished out. Nice in one breath, mean in the next. Okay. I can't get involved here. I don't even know this mystery sister. She's the sister Nicolai pulled out of a hat. She has her life and she has to deal with it herself.

Alexia walked towards the road she now knew would lead her back to the bus stop. But she couldn't stop thinking about the older woman. She was a bully even though she was trying to be subtle about it. Alexia had seen enough of that type at the negotiation table to last a lifetime. Theodora was clearly unable to defend herself. Alexia slowed down. She retraced her steps and got back to the park. Okay, I guess I'm doing this, she told herself. I just want to make sure she's all right. Nothing more. Not just yet, anyway. Alexia shifted the pack.

She walked towards the bench where Theodora sat. "*Kalimera,*" she said. She raised her eyebrows, tried to fasten a casual, friendly smile in place. She dropped the pack on the bench.

Theodora smiled. "Good afternoon."

"Yes, you're right, it is the afternoon," Alexia said. "I'm still learning Greek."

"It is very difficult language," Theodora said. The bright hazel of one eye contrasted against the dark brown of the other. Her cheeks were red and the skin at the edges of her nose was raw. She twisted a Kleenex between her fingers.

"Nice shoes," Alexia said, avoiding Theodora's eyes. "You're the first person, besides my aunt Maria, who wears anything but black flats and dark skirts." Why am I blabbing like an idiot? She pushed the pack to one side, sat down and tucked her hands underneath her. She took a deep breath and tried to steady her voice. A chill caught her and her shoulders shook.

"Where are you from?" Theodora blew her nose. "You have family here?"

"Aunts and uncles and cousins."

"I have no family but my husband's. My mother dead since five years."

"And your father?" Here I am talking to her as if I'm talking to any other stranger I meet on the street, Alexia thought. This is my half-sister. Be careful.

"My mother had a good friend who was like my stepfather. He retired to his island after she died. My real father died before they could marry," she said. "This is the shame of my family, according to my mother-in-law, who doesn't let me forget I have no father. My mother never married and she never wore black, like widows must."

Alexia shook her head. Her hands ached against the wooden slats of the bench. She pulled them out, looked at the angry slices imprinted across her hands.

"What is wrong?"

"Um, nothing, I'm just listening." Your real father didn't die, she wanted to say. Your mother lied to you. Will the time ever come when I might say these things to you?

"I am sorry," Theodora said. "We normally keep these things to ourselves. I am upset. I do not know what I am saying. Forgive me."

"You're talking to a Canadian. We're used to airing our dirty laundry."

Theodora stared at her. "We hang clothes after we wash them. Not when dirty."

Alexia laughed and turned. "It's just a silly expression. Hard to explain."

Theodora's son waddled over, pointing to a place on his arm. Theodora examined his chin and pudgy arm. She dabbed at his eyes with her sleeve, found a wet cloth in her bag and wiped his face. "You be the death of me, Nicolai."

"That was my father's name," Alexia whispered. A strand of hair fell out of its braid and flew across her eyes. She pushed the hair away. It tumbled across her eyes again. She folded her hands in her lap, gazed out towards the swings.

"This is a common name here. It was my mother's favourite name," Theodora said. "I call him Nicky to make it shorter."

"It's a very good name," Alexia said. "Not so common in Canada."

"Would you like to come back to my house for coffee? It looks like the rain will get worse. Or you prefer tea? I live very close to this park."

Alexia fiddled with the strap on her pack. I can't come to your house, she wanted to say. I barely know you. And what are we going to talk about? The truth might slip out. I might end up leaving this pack with you. Then what do we do? It's too soon for all that. She stood up to leave, slung the pack over both shoulders and lurched backwards slightly under its weight.

Theodora turned away. "This is our Greek hospitality," she said. "We are too friendly. It is how we do things. That is all."

Alexia saw the curve of Theodora's back, her narrow shoulders. She told herself she should leave right this minute while she had a chance. Instead, she said, "Why not?"

2010

Theodora jumped. The angry rattling caught her off guard every time. She glanced at the back door. Andreas was shaking the handle and twisting it back and forth. His special touch, as he liked to call it, wasn't working. One day that door wouldn't open at all, but there was no talking to him about fixing it. Like everything else, he had to do it in his own time.

The latch clicked into place. He was standing just inside the doorway.

The kitchen with its pale blue cupboards looked like a child's dollhouse when Andreas was standing in it. Even the cypress trees in the yard behind him shrank.

They stared at each other for a moment, as strangers sometimes do when they realize they are in the wrong place. Theodora finally smiled. His jacket was buttoned to hide most of the bloodstains, but he couldn't cover up everything about his work. "Your apron is dirty again," she said.

"I wipe my hands. That's what it's for."

"And the rags I made?" she asked in a mothering tone.

"I couldn't find one."

Theodora shook her head. "I told you to keep them close. Where you work." Last night as she did laundry, she cursed him when the bleach she used to soak his apron burned her hands and stung her eyes.

But, today, she couldn't be mad at him. Her eyes softened.

"I dropped the lamb." His shoulders were rounded; his arms like large unmoveable tree trunks by his sides.

He was tired. The circles under his eyes were darker.

"Then, it sprayed back when I tried to carve away the fat," he said.

"You have no pity for me, the work I have to do in this house."

Yesterday, when they'd had the same conversation, his arms were behind his back. He smiled as if he couldn't wait to share his surprise. "What is it?" she asked and tugged at his arms until he produced the box of *galaktoboureko.* The custard-filled pastry was her favourite. He brought them home once or twice a week and never took one unless she offered it to him. "Go on," she said.

He pushed the box away. "They're for you."

"For us. Come on, take one."

Today, he stood empty-handed by the door. His high cheekbones and large hooked nose jutted forward as if trying to escape. His deep, brown eyes usually moistened whenever he saw her. It had been that way since they were children playing behind the school or in her mother's yard.

Theodora got up and the chair fell to the floor behind her. "And I call you clumsy." She laughed. She walked over to him in that slow way she knew he liked. He looked away. She was glad that she could still do this to him.

Whenever she reached out for him, he would pick her up and bring her close so her head fell into the crook of his neck. He teased her. "I have my own little princess."

This time, he crossed his arms. She stood in front of him until he looked at her. She held his gaze until he finally nodded, grinned slightly and dropped his arms. She cuddled into him, her head against his chest. He squeezed her shoulder, his other arm by his side. His jacket reeked of meat. Still she hung on.

"I've never heard my mother complain," he said. "Housewives have to take care of their houses, their men, their children."

She pretended to scratch her nose and kept her fingers close to her face, using her own familiar scent to diminish his. Complaining, digging at me in that mean-spirited way of hers is the only thing your mother ever does, she thought. She breathed through her mouth, told herself to let his comment go. It wasn't worth fighting over.

As children, Theodora and Andreas played in her mother's backyard or roamed the fields by the inlet. They kicked his soccer ball up and down the schoolyard and when they had a match, he played goalkeeper, letting in her feebly kicked balls.

"Stop cheating," Theodora said.

"I'm trying to help," he said, holding the ball to his chest.

"With this help of yours, I won't get any better. Stop it." She punched his arm and the ball dropped. Her feet kicked the ball out of his reach. She lined up the ball and booted it as hard as she could. He dived for it and missed.

The other children ignored Theodora or whispered things behind her back. "What do they say?" she asked Andreas. They sat with their backs against the spreading oak tree behind the school, shoulder touching shoulder, lunch pails on their laps.

"Stupid things," he said. "I don't know." He threw his sandwich into his pail.

"What's wrong?"

"Nothing." He stood up and looked out into the distance. Theodora followed his gaze to the chain link fence.

"I can't wait until we get out of this place," he said.

Theodora brushed the dirt from her skirt as she got up off the ground.

"Can I come over to your house after school?" he asked.

"We never go to your house anymore."

"I know," he said. "I don't..."

"Your mom doesn't like me either."

Andreas wrestled his arm around her throat, held her head close to his chest and messed up her hair as he would with one of his male friends. "Stop feeling sorry for yourself."

As they got older, Andreas would bloody the mouths of the boys who teased Theodora.

"Why were you in another fight?" Theodora asked him.

"I just get mad sometimes."

"Did that boy say something?"

"About what?" Andreas asked.

"I don't know."

"No, nothing." He shrugged.

"You're lying."

"It's not worth it," he said. "You have to keep things to yourself. You know."

He didn't have to tell her, Theodora knew what was said about her and her mother. She heard the whispers. Was Andreas defending her? She could fight her own battles. She'd do what she had always done. Ignore what they said and after a long time, they would leave her alone.

On her sixteenth birthday, he gave her a gold necklace. A diamond that looked like a tiny sliver of glass sat encased in a pendant the shape of a miniature hand. He kissed her neck. She turned to meet his gaze. He looked away.

"I want to," she said, and kissed him.

When they graduated from high school, Theodora's mother insisted she go to university. Andreas worked in his father's butcher shop. "You go," he said to Theodora when she complained she didn't want to go to Athens. "One day I'll have my own shop and you will come back and help me with the books, everything."

"Won't you miss me?" she asked.

He smiled. "Maybe."

Home after the first year of university, they met by the beach. She stood in front of him. His hands were in his pockets and he looked at his feet. "So I suppose you like living in the big city," Andreas said. "You've made lots of friends. The village is boring to you now."

"It's the same as here," she said, and touched his arm. She hadn't made friends in university either and wondered if people could see her mother's shame even when they didn't know anything about her. "I don't want to go back."

"Marry me," he said. "And you won't have to."

"My mother would kill me."

"No, she won't. You're being dramatic."

"She wants me to have a better life, get out of this place."

"What's wrong with this place?" he asked. "I'm here."

"I remember when you wanted to get away."

"This is our home," he said. "It's different. We're not in school anymore."

"Not different. Your mother still hates me."

"She doesn't."

"I haven't been to your house since we were children."

"Come next Sunday."

They sat on Elena's straw-covered chairs at her wooden table in her oversized kitchen the following Sunday. Platters of marbled roast beef, roasted chicken, fried sausage and rare lamb lay like sacrificial offerings. Theodora tried to look away, but her eyes would somehow skirt back to the platters. She had to be polite. Her mother had taught her well. But how could she eat any of this?

Andreas's brothers and their wives, aunts, uncles and cousins all came that day. She wasn't used to so many people. They seemed nice. They asked her where she'd bought her red dress and the high heels with the splash of red at the toe.

"My mother got me this dress in Athens," she said. "We go there once a month."

Andreas's sisters-in-law shared a glance and smiled tightly. One nodded, the other winked. Theodora's face felt warm.

"My mother's friend George bought the shoes for me in Corfu," Theodora said.

A cousin at the opposite end of the table said, "Some are lucky," then swallowed hard as if what was in her mouth had gone down her throat the wrong way. "Marriage will change all this."

"It doesn't have to," Andreas said.

"He opens a shop," his sister-in-law said, "and he thinks he's a millionaire."

His mother smiled slightly, but didn't look up from her plate, while the others nodded. "It's good to have dreams," she said. "Better still to have family who can help make your dreams come true."

Andreas shot his mother an angry look.

Now what? Theodora wondered. What had she done to upset Andreas or his mother? Elena had been very sweet to her, kissing and hugging her when she came in, walking her to the kitchen, her arm laced in Theodora's. She didn't know why she'd worried herself sick about coming here today.

Plates of roasted zucchini, eggplant, peppers, garlic and tomatoes were passed around first. Then the heavy platters of meat.

Theodora took only vegetables and a few spoons of beans. The meat was passed to her again. "You must eat. You have nothing on your plate," Andreas's brother Petros said.

"I don't like meat," she said over the loud chatter. "I haven't eaten it since I was a child."

The multiple conversations sputtered. Petros rolled his eyes; his wife readjusted her napkin on her lap. A few others stared at Theodora.

Theodora looked at Andreas, wondered what he was thinking. He glanced over at Elena. Sitting at the head of the table, she finished chewing, wiped her mouth, folded her napkin and put it beside her plate. "You know," she said slowly, her eyes dark as coal, "it's nice to be an intellectual. My son tells me you went to university for, what was it? A year or so?"

Theodora nodded. So they've talked about me. That's good, she thought.

"But they don't teach you everything in those places." She shook her head. "God gave us this meat to enjoy. Yes or no?" Elena said.

Theodora reached for Andreas's hand. His head was bowed; both hands were clasped together on the table. She turned to face his mother alone.

"There was no such thing as we can't eat this or that when I was a child," Elena said. "It's good that children have so much these days. You are all very lucky."

"Mamma, things change," Andreas said. "Theodora grew up this way."

"Yes, we can't blame our little *xanthoula*," Elena said.

"At least she likes the butcher." Andreas hugged Theodora.

Everyone laughed. When Elena smiled, her eyetooth peeked out between her lips spiking her bottom lip. She patted her mouth with a napkin. The tooth disappeared.

The conversation went back to how Andreas's new shop was going, which led to why cousin Anna was getting a divorce, what was going on with Uncle Yanni and his girlfriend, a young woman from Athens who kept him away from the family, and how Cousin Dmitri was so smart, he'd been accepted into the London School of Economics. "His mother should be thankful,"

Elena said. "But she complains. He is too far from home. She'll never see him. Those English girls are wild. That woman is never happy." Theodora listened, glad the conversation was no longer about her.

Andreas stroked her hand under the table.

"You could do anything," Theodora's mother said when she told her she was getting married. "Finish university first. Then see if you still feel the same way."

"I don't want to go back to Athens."

Theodora married Andreas on a rainy day in June. "Rain brings good luck," Theodora told her mother, who sat with her friend George on one side of the church. George had lived with them since Theodora was a child.

"You're so young," her mother said, wiping a tear away.

George put his arm around her mother's shoulders. "She's emotional. Don't worry." Her mother looked away.

She hoped things would change with Elena after she married Andreas. But the name Elena gave her, *xanthoula*, 'the little blonde', stuck to Theodora.

"This is a term of endearment," Elena said.

"My name is who I am," Theodora had said.

"Yes and no," Elena had said. "Besides, this suits me. It is easy for an old woman like me to remember."

Life didn't get any easier with her mother-in-law. "Oh, I don't want you to go to any trouble just for me," Elena said when Theodora made some meatless dishes she hoped Elena would try. "Who am I, after all? I'm only your husband's mother."

"I thought to try a different dish," Theodora said.

"Different can be good, but this is your husband's work. Are you ashamed of him?"

"If he picked up garbage for a living, would I have to like garbage?" Stop being angry, she told herself. The woman is just trying to be helpful.

"He's a butcher," Elena had replied. "A good one. Or don't you think so?"

"Why do you think I don't?"

"You didn't have a father to take care of you and teach you things," Elena said. "You have a good husband now. You take care of him. I know you already know this. But you don't want to be alone when you are old, like your mother. Do you?"

It wasn't her fault that her father had died before her parents could marry. It wasn't her fault that her mother never married George. But none of this mattered to her mother-in-law or anyone else. She had understood this from the time she was a child. All the other kids had teased her that she was a bastard.

The day Theodora told Elena she was pregnant, Elena squeezed Theodora's arm until it hurt. Theodora pulled away. "Eating a little meat is good for my grandchild. You are going to be a mother. That comes with many responsibilities. I'm sure you will manage. But it won't be easy. A child is not a toy you play with and discard like some people throw away their men."

Andreas encouraged her to ignore Elena. "She wants the best for us."

She argued with him at first, but started to put a few pieces of meat on her plate. She hated the texture, but shredded each slice into thin, very fine bits so she could swallow the pieces whole without allowing them to linger in her mouth. When she was alone, she packaged her leftovers, hid them in a brown bag at the back of the fridge and later dropped them off outside the market to the beggar woman who gave her a toothless smile and a sincere embrace.

Theodora released Andreas. "I have to tell you about my day."

"Let me clean up," he said. "I'm tired."

"What's wrong?"

"There's always one thing or another."

He gave her hand a peck.

Nicky ran his cars into Andreas's foot over and over again, making crashing sounds. "Is there no other place he can play?" Andreas said.

"He's happy you're home," Theodora said. "That's all."

Andreas tsked as if he didn't believe her. Holding onto her shoulder to support himself, he took off his shoes and then left her in the kitchen. His gamey odour hung in the air. A few minutes later she heard the familiar whistle and groan of the pipes protesting the demand for hot water.

She'd tossed her high heels into the corner by the door when she came in earlier with Alexia. Theodora liked being in her bare feet when she was in the house, even though Elena called her a *chorikos* whenever she saw her this way. "You are no better than a peasant, my dear *xanthoula*, when your feet are naked. Perhaps you don't know this. I'm so sorry I'm the one who must tell you these things."

She picked up her shoes again and, this time, put them into the closet, beside Andreas's work shoes. She looked around the small kitchen for anything else she needed to tidy up. Like his mother, Andreas disapproved if things were not put away. "But I like clutter, I like our home to have that lived-in feel," she said to him whenever he complained.

"That's just an excuse for a messy house."

"Just because things are hidden away doesn't mean everything is in order."

Theodora shook her head and reached into the closet to neatly line up her shoes. She didn't like it when she lost control and got angry with him. He'd always been her best friend. But now it seemed that her agitation with him and with Elena grew each day. Again, she thought about the conversation she'd had with her mother-in-law a few hours earlier. One day she'd win her over. Or maybe her son would put her in her place.

Theodora always knew when Andreas had had a bad day. The time he spent cleaning up helped him shed the grime, and sometimes the stress too. She promised herself she would listen to his grievances—perhaps a shipment hadn't come in, or an employee hadn't shown up, or Mrs. Makarios had yet again brought back a few scraps of beef and complained it was too tough even after she'd cooked it for several hours. Whatever it was, she would reassure him, knead his neck and shoulders, then hold him as long as he needed. She'd make sure he was fed and she'd wait her turn to tell him about Alexia. She would put Andreas first. She had made that decision long ago, shortly after one of the last times she saw her mother.

During that visit, Theodora burned the roof of her mouth on the tea she tried to sip slowly. She paced, unable to sit down. "And she has the nerve to call me *xanthoula.*"

"She won't be around forever," her mother said. "He's her son. She loves him."

"I'm his wife," Theodora said. "I should come first. George does that with you."

"Don't put Andreas in the position where he has to choose. It never works."

Theodora banged her hand on the kitchen counter. "I want to stay home sometimes on a Sunday or visit you."

"Talk to him." Her mother sat in her oversized chair and sipped her tea.

"He doesn't listen to what I want. He tells me to get ready so we can be on time as though we're late every Sunday. His mother must have complained to him about it like she does with everything."

"You've told me yourself how he defends you in front of her. He's a good man. Take care of him, your relationship. You shouldn't let a good man go."

She turned. Was her mother a little paler than usual? The chair seemed about to swallow her. "My father died. You didn't let him go," Theodora said, sitting cross-legged at her mother's feet, resting her head on her lap. "This is not your fault."

"I pressured him." Her mother took another sip of tea and ran her fingers through Theodora's hair.

"What do you mean?" She looked up into her mother's eyes.

"This is all in the past." Her mother stared out the window. "There is no point."

"You've always blamed yourself, Mamma. And I have never understood."

Her mother had told her that her father had died on the ship he crewed in the Aegean, a few months before they were to be married and six months before Theodora was born. Kids at school whispered that her mother never wore black like other women did who had lost their husbands. "Your father ran away," they said. She ignored these taunts, believed her mother, even though her mother didn't like to talk about him and gave her only a few details about him, said he'd been away a great deal, and died too young for her to really know him.

When she was a child, Theodora hated him for dying and leaving her alone. George became her friend. She hinted to him, more than once, that he should marry her mother. "I'm the willing one," George said.

Her mother poured Theodora some more tea and showed her the new outfit she'd bought for her in Athens. She seemed tired, but Theodora was too preoccupied to ask her how the doctor's visit had gone.

Theodora received the call from George early one Saturday morning as she was getting ready to go to the market. He'd found her mother on the kitchen floor, a glass shattered beside her. He knew she was already dead. "I didn't hear her get out of bed," he said. "I might have helped. Why didn't I hear anything?"

The telephone was pressed hard against her ear. Her hand shook.

Theodora helped George organize the funeral and when that was over and done with she stayed in bed for more than two weeks. What would she do without her mother? What would life be like now?

Elena moved in with them to take care of Nicky. One night, on her way to the bathroom, Theodora overheard Elena and Andreas talking.

"Maybe she should be in a hospital. She needs more care than I can give her. I can help pay for this too. It's not a problem. I will do anything for my son's happiness."

"She'll be fine soon," Andreas said.

"I will take care of you and the baby," Elena said. "Until she gets better. If she gets better."

She heard her mother's voice again. "You shouldn't let a good man go."

Shortly afterwards, George told Theodora he was returning to his island.

"I can't live in this place where everything reminds me of her," he said.

"What about me?"

"You are like my own. I will come whenever you need me."

Her mother had cousins, but she said they never liked her. "Forget about them," she told Theodora once. "It can only bring bad feelings."

Theodora would tolerate Elena, would take care of Andreas and Nicky. They were the only family she had.

Theodora leaned against the kitchen counter; her arms behind her, her hands folded one over the other. She tightened her buttocks as her mother had always told her to do. "Men like something firm to hold onto." Her thighs twitched and the muscles contracted. She held her legs slightly apart, then wiggled her toes and pressed her weight down onto the floor as though trying to imprint herself on the stone.

"Alexia was nice," Theodora said, "wasn't she, Nicky?" He lay on his stomach at her feet. Distracted by the tinny sound of smashing metal cars, he seemed not to notice her. "You too?" she said. "Go ahead, ignore your mother. Just like your father." She bent down and moved his bangs away from his eyes. His forehead felt warm.

She scanned the small kitchen and wondered if this space would ever be what she wanted it to be. After her mother died, she'd talked to Andreas about building an extension so she could hang her mother's drawings. They were wrapped in plastic and sat in the shed.

"We don't have the money for all your fancy plans," Andreas said. "I'm a butcher. We don't have enough bread to eat, but you still ask for a radish to open our appetites."

"You talk to me like your mother does." She threw her chin up defiantly.

"What she says sometimes fits. Make sure your blanket always covers your feet. Remember that old saying?"

"We're not exposed, if that's what you mean. We have the shop. We sell some crops, too. And eggs. Don't forget. We have some money saved."

He smiled then, and stroked her hair. "You'll always be a dreamer."

"One day we will have the best house on the street. I'll have a space for my mother's drawings and for my own photographs. Maybe even sell a few."

"You want people to notice us," he said. "There's no need to bring the evil eye over our heads or people's tongues to our door."

"I don't care about these old superstitions."

"In spite of this, I love you," he said. "Isn't that enough?" He held her at arm's length, patted her back. "Be humble," Andreas whispered. "It's better. Safer too."

She wondered now if her life might have been different if her real father had lived. There was no point in thinking about these things. Even she realized the futility.

Theodora slid open a drawer. She took out the photographs she'd taken, put them on the counter and flipped through the first few. She loved the one of the old man cutting and preparing his fishing line, the stern concentration on his face, sweat on his brow. And the one of the women huddled together in the square, hands around their creased faces listening to gossip, their eyes small, droopy and resigned. Her preoccupations were about having the right light, capturing honest expressions, the smallest detail, and getting it all just so. In her photography she wanted to capture people as they were. It was fine when their anger or disgust wasn't directed at her.

Theodora rubbed her eyes. Late afternoon sunshine seeped through the undersized window above the back door, reflected off the old stove and lit the cramped space as if the electric lights were on. This was her house. Her mother had bought it for her. It was the dowry Elena had insisted her son had to have before she would allow him to marry. This was the kitchen where her new friend from Canada had been only a few hours ago. A hint of Alexia's perfume lingered and reminded Theodora of the brief conversation they had over chilled apricot juice.

"That is a nice perfume," Theodora said. She kicked off her shoes when she walked in the house and was in her stocking feet. She poured the apricot juice, brought it to the table and sat down beside Alexia.

"It is fresh, like grass after rain." Theodora sipped her juice and looked over at Nicky, who sat on the floor, his toys spread out around him. He played with a small box.

"I don't know how you stand this heat," Alexia said. "I miss Vancouver's rain."

"We get rain too, but not too much. A little in the spring, like now. Mostly in the winter. You smell like that."

Alexia grinned. "Thanks. I'll remember that the next time I put this stuff on."

Theodora had tried to apologize and Alexia had reassured her she was teasing. She did that sometimes, she said. "My father liked kidding people too. Blame him."

"My husband's family is the serious type."

"Are you like that?" Alexia leaned forward slightly in her chair.

"No. I didn't used to be." Theodora shrugged. "Maybe now."

"What were you like? I mean, when you were a child."

"Happier, I believe. My mother supported all I did and my stepfather was good."

"So what happened?"

"My mother died. I do not know, I thought things might be different."

"I think you make your own opportunities."

"What do you do with a mother-in-law who never thinks you are good enough? I always hear the negative—how do you say in English?—implied even when she says nice things. Perhaps I am seeing things that are not really there."

Alexia looked away then and Theodora wondered if she had shared too much, had been too eager to push herself onto Alexia. "I am sorry to be saying all these things," Theodora said. "Usually I am not so talkative. What must you think of me? Here everyone talks." She gulped hard. "And so it is hard to make friends and tell them what you really think and feel. I feel comfortable with you, maybe because you don't come from here. Greeks have a saying: if you share a confidence, it spreads like olive oil."

They watched Nicky play. Theodora offered Alexia more juice.

Alexia declined but agreed to meet for lunch the following week.

Nicky had his catcher's mitt on now and was pestering her to throw the ball. She didn't know when he had handed it to her.

"Daydreaming?" Andreas asked when he walked into the kitchen. She hadn't heard the water turn off or his heavy footsteps on the stairs.

"Feeling better?" She tucked her photographs back into the drawer, handed Nicky the ball and turned around to face Andreas.

"I'm clean," he said.

She kissed his cheek and grabbed some plates to set the table. He smelled of the lye soap he used to scrub his hands. She'd bought him perfumed soaps and hand cream, but after they sat unopened on the bathroom counter for months she used them herself. "I'm not a woman," he said when she asked him about it. "I want to smell like a man."

They ate and talked to Nicky. Theodora asked Andreas about the shop, but he said, "You know it never changes from one day to the next." After dinner, she washed the dishes while Andreas watched the news and Nicky played beside her on the floor. Later, she bathed her son, got him into his pyjamas and brought him to his father for a goodnight kiss. Andreas turned his head to the side to kiss Nicky, moving both her and his son so he could keep his eyes on the screen. Theodora teased him and stood for a moment in front of his view. "Come on," he said.

When she heard Nicky's deep, abandoned breathing, she shut the bedroom door and went down to the living room, where she found Andreas lying on the couch staring at the ceiling. She leaned against the archway, her hands working in a dollop of hand cream. "How about a massage?" she asked. "Or one of my back rubs?"

"Why do I always have to hear my mother's complaints?" He sat up and swung his legs around. His face was worn, his eyes vacant.

"Why do you listen?" She told herself she'd try to understand him. Why was she making things worse?

"The boy was dirty, he didn't have his hat, you wear high heels, they're not appropriate when you're meeting her, you know that. She is old-fashioned. She has her ways. Good or bad."

"So her big complaint has to do with my shoes?" She threw her hands up. "If only the problems of the world were this small."

"Don't make light of this." He rubbed his temple.

"It's silly, don't you think?" She sighed. How could she stay mad at him? He couldn't stand up to his mother either. She went over to him. He turned away.

"Elena would begrudge my very breath if we allowed it," she said. "You know."

"You're exaggerating. She's old. She's always helped us. Can't you just try?"

Theodora inhaled. What do you mean, helped us? Since when? Theodora wanted to say. Elena hadn't helped her one bit. She stood above him with her arms crossed. But his watery eyes and his defeated back, the sideways pleading grin made her sit down beside him. She shook her head. She had to be strong for both of them. "I'll try."

He stretched out and laid his head down on her lap. He rolled over to his right side, held onto her thighs as if afraid to fall. He fell asleep holding onto her. Even when she couldn't feel her legs, she didn't move.

1986

Nicolai laid his jacket on top of the pebbles, then sat down. The small stones poked at his backside. He shifted, but it was no use. He had thought this stretch of beach had more sand. Or at least that's how he remembered it whenever he thought of the place. Water gurgled onto the shore. The sea raised its caps. Seagulls bounded, shrieking and fighting over scraps of fish. Nicolai listened to the short, quick scratches Dimitria made against the canvas.

"Where do you get your ideas?" he asked.

"The images come when my hand starts its work. My father told me this would happen but I didn't believe him. He was right, of course." She sat in a rickety chair low to the ground, the canvas propped up in the pebbles. Her hair was pushed inside a scarf. As she drew, her bare feet moved back and forth until her heels were buried. "When our fathers are alive, we don't appreciate them."

This answer, like all the others, started in one place and wound around to another. He tried to focus. "My father is a hard man." Nicolai gazed at the shoreline across the way. The trees looked brittle, the land dried out.

The rocks under her chair grated as she moved.

He could feel her stare, but his eyes were fixed on the sea.

"We can't possibly understand what they went through." She tapped the canvas lightly with her pencil as if to get his attention.

"Does that give him an excuse?" He stood up, kicking up pebbles and sand. Why was everyone so keen to defend his father? His mother. His sisters. And now Dimitria. His father could have talked himself into forgetting about the war, gotten on with his life.

"You don't know how you would have reacted," Dimitria said.

"I'll never be that kind of father. I'm sure of that." He had left rather than take the chance that his anger and grief would hurt Alexia. He'd done that much.

He picked up his jacket. A gust came up and blew sand back towards Dimitria. "I should go," he said.

"Okay," she said.

"I'll see you around."

Nicolai's mother asked him where he was going. "A coffee with Dimitria."

"You're going out with her again? I have work to do here. You could help me."

Each day his mother made lists of things she needed done. He washed the outside walls of the house, watered the vegetable patch at the back and painted the chipped cement stairs at the front door. Some of these chores kept him home for a few days. He checked off all the things on her list. Still, she added more. "I need some fresh air," he said finally. "I'm going for a drive." He was glad he'd kept the rental car. It gave him the means to escape the claustrophobic confines of his father's house.

"Have you spoken to your daughter lately?" She stood with her hands on her hips blocking the back door.

"I called her last week. She didn't believe it was me." He laughed. "She threw the phone down, accused me of not being her father."

"Ah, this is a sign," she said. "She needs you."

He wanted to tell his mother that he could barely take care of himself, let alone Alexia, that at least here, he had distractions that didn't remind him of his old life, of the world that had fallen apart when Sara died. Achilles. Dimitria. When he was talking to Dimitria or having a coffee with Achilles or watering his mother's vegetable patch there were times when he didn't think of Sara. Was he feeling better? Would he forget her altogether? He would never allow that to happen. Never.

His mother grabbed him by his arms as if she meant to shake him. Instead, she took hold of his chin, pulled him down so she looked him in the eye. "No child is better off without her father."

"She's in school," he said. "Mavis and Stuart are her godparents. They love her like she's theirs." He kissed the top of his mother's head. "Don't worry so much. Everything is under control." In fact, Stuart had told him the same thing when he called his office a few days ago. "We're fine. Alexia is doing well. Nothing to worry about."

Nicolai drove down the deserted strip of land by the water's edge where Dimitria sketched most days and Achilles had taken him a few weeks before. Achilles had grand plans for a boardwalk with restaurants and bars. Nicolai had listened politely. He didn't encourage him or ask too many questions. A big project was not what he needed. He wasn't sure what he needed, but he knew he didn't want anything to complicate his life.

He saw Dimitria up ahead walking on the side of the road, her easel under one arm, a box under the other. The back of her shawl was pulled tightly around her, the tips flung over her shoulder and waving in the breeze. He drove up behind her slowly until finally she turned. He rolled down his window.

"How about a ride somewhere?"

She stowed her things in the back seat and jumped in beside him. "Aigio is not so far," she said. There was that eager smile again. Was this a good idea? He glanced over at her and grinned. These doubts were not his, they were his mother's. Dimitria was his cousin and a friend. Where was the harm?

"I have done all the talking," she said. They sat across from one another in an outdoor café, the ocean crashing against the rocks below them. "You must be bored."

"Not in the slightest." He gulped his coffee.

"How is your daughter?" She placed her hand on his.

"She is well. It is good for her to be with her godparents right now." He pulled his hand away.

"You must miss her."

"Yes."

She stared at him. He suspected she was waiting for him to say more, but what could he say? It was true that he missed Alexia, but he was relieved as well. He needed time to sort things out before he could go back and be the father she deserved. "We should go," he said, and threw some bills on the table. He pushed his chair back.

She looked up at him and didn't move.

"I can't explain it right now," he said.

He dropped Dimitria off at the same place he picked her up. They made no plans. Still, whenever he could, he'd show up, always in the same spot, and she'd be there waiting for him. They'd go to some other village for lunch or a coffee. Their meetings were a secret: that much was understood even though neither one of them said it.

When his mother asked him where he'd been, his answer was always the same: "Just out exploring. There's a lot to see."

"Have you been to Kalavryta?" Dimitria asked when they couldn't decide where to go one afternoon. They sat in the car by the beach. She faced him. His fingers drummed the steering wheel.

"No, my father wouldn't let me go when I was a kid. He wouldn't sign the consent form at school. According to him, this was not a place for anyone to visit."

"Let's go." She stopped the relentless patter he made with his fingers by cupping her hand over his. "Stop. I thought you'd outgrown that old habit of yours. You used to do it when you were a child."

"You remember that?"

"It made me crazy," she said.

He started the car. "Old habits are hard to break."

At the memorial on top of the hill in Kalavryta, they stopped at the crosses. They murmured prayers. This is what Greeks do. He remembered explaining this to Sara in Vancouver the first time she saw him cross himself and whisper under his breath when they passed a cemetery. "But why?" she asked.

"I was raised this way," he said. "You watch your parents, you do what they do."

"But you don't know any of the people buried here," Sara said.

"I know it's strange. It's our way to honour them," he said. "We show more respect for the dead than we do for the living."

Nicolai stared at the name on the cross, strokes of black angry lines. He thought of his grandfather, who had died here. He wished he could have known him. Maybe if he had lived, his own father would have been better to him, played basketball with him, listened to him and supported him like the other fathers supported their sons. Nicolai was about ten years old the first time he came running into the house late after a game. He wanted to tell his father how many baskets he'd made, how he saved the game. His father sat at the kitchen table. His belt lay on the table beside him. No words were said. With a look, his father directed him and Nicolai leaned over the chair. He didn't cry out.

"It wasn't your fault," he whispered now, gazing at his grandfather's name on the plaque. "You died. How could you stop him? Maybe my father just never liked me. Who's to know?"

"Pardon?" Dimitria said, lacing her arm in his.

He stepped back and took in the scattering of tiny crosses. Someone had tried to plant grass on the grounds, but it grew only in ragged patches here and there. The names blurred. "It's hard to imagine such tragedy."

"Especially since we didn't live it."

"But we've never escaped. I see that now."

"You speak about your father again," she said.

He shrugged. "Not really."

"When you're ready." She tightened her grip around his arm.

He stroked her hand. "I know."

They entered the Kalavryta museum. In the first cavernous room there was old farm equipment, mannequins dressed in period clothing, bullet casings, guns too old to be used again. There were glass cases, but most of them were empty. A sign indicated they were still in the process of setting up the display. Three televisions sat one on top of the other in the corner, their screens blank.

A woman about his mother's age dressed in black with a kerchief over her head greeted them. "We are still adding to the museum," she said. She pointed to the televisions. "These will show the survivor testimonials. We have government money for students to conduct the interviews this summer."

Nicolai nodded.

"Do you have family here?" she asked.

"My grandfather was Nicolai Sarinopoulos," Nicolai said.

She stood back slightly and looked at him intently. "A picture of him will be in the next room," she said finally, then turned and went back into her office.

Nicolai and Dimitria entered a room that looked as if it had once been a gymnasium. At one end was a set of double wooden doors bolted by long metal bars, meant never to be used again. Even with its bright lights, the room felt creepy to Nicolai. He tried not to imagine the basketballs being thrown, the cheers from the low bleachers against the wall. Now, hundreds of pictures lined the walls. The faces stared at him.

"There's Achilles's grandfather," Dimitria said.

Nicolai stood close beside her, their shoulders touching.

Nicolai startled at the touch of a hand on his back. He turned and saw the woman who had greeted them.

"How is he?" she said.

"Who?"

"We were just children then. Your father and me. You have his eyes," she went on. "I've never forgotten him. He was my best friend."

"Why didn't you mention it before?" His father had a best friend? He couldn't imagine it.

"I wasn't sure I should," the woman said. "How is he?"

Nicolai shrugged. It was too much of a coincidence, like a dream, or a plot out of one of Sara's novels. "He's an angry man," he blurted.

She nodded, as if she'd expected as much. She turned her back to Nicolai and gazed up at the pictures. "You young people don't understand what they did to us. I was here in this gymnasium that day, with all the other children. Four hundred and ninety-eight died in our village. The Germans killed others. Twenty-six other villages in our province were burned and the people murdered."

Nicolai touched her arm. She stared at him as if she wasn't sure who he was.

"Your father tried to save us," the woman said. "He thought he'd convinced the Germans. He was such a charmer; he could make anyone do anything. He got food for us when the soldiers first occupied the village. Everyone liked him because he was a generous boy, would do anything for a friend or his family. Is he still like this?"

Nicolai shook his head. "No. Not at all."

"This surprises me. Maybe he blames himself? But it wasn't his fault. His mother tried to tell him to... Ah, what is the point of these old stories?" She jammed her hands into the pockets of her skirt and turned away.

"How did he try to help?" Nicolai asked, putting out a hand as if to hold her back. He'd known her for five minutes and she'd already become the most important person in his world. He didn't even know her name.

"I've said too much," she said. "You should ask him. It's his story to tell."

"I'm just trying to understand."

She turned to face him. "The mothers had a sense. They wanted to protect their sons. All mothers are the same."

"So what did he do?"

The woman shook her head. "Speak to your father. He was a good boy. I know they couldn't beat that out of him."

Nicolai stared at her. "I'm sorry, I didn't get your name."

"It's not important."

"Look, I know he must have done something that's made him the way he is. What did he do?"

"At least listen before you pass judgment," Dimitria said.

He shrugged off Dimitria's hand. "You've never lived with him," Nicolai said, the words like slivers in his throat.

"The Germans asked the young boys their age. No one knew why at first."

"And?" Nicolai said.

"He wanted to help us," the woman said. "He was like that. He didn't know what would happen. None of us did. Even the night before it happened, he told me that everything would be all right." She stared up at the wall of pictures. "He wasn't even scared when they separated us into two groups. He thought he understood. The deaths of his father, my father, my brother and the other men hit him very hard."

Nicolai scanned the faces in the photographs, then the information under each picture. "They were all over thirteen years old." Nicolai said. His father was sixteen then.

Nicolai felt his legs weaken. He reached for the wall; Dimitria caught his arm.

The woman turned away. "Only survivors know the truth."

Nicolai drove down the mountain, hardly seeing the road in front of him. He forgot Dimitria was in the car until he felt her touch on his hand. "Are you okay?"

"I'm sorry," he said. "Just when I think I understand what he might have gone through, I find out another bit of information that makes me think even less of him." He glanced over at her. "He lied about his age. I'm sure of it now. That's what that woman didn't want to tell me. He knew that if he told them he wasn't thirteen yet, it would save him. He must have been small for his age, like I was."

"I'm not so sure."

"He must have."

"What would you have done in his place?" Dimitria asked.

He shrugged. "I hope I'd be brave. But I'm his son, so I probably would have done the same thing. Lied to save my own skin. We're both cowards."

"It doesn't matter anymore."

"He never was someone I could admire. You probably don't know the story, but after he left Kalavryta, he tried to leave Greece, too. But he fell in love with my mother. Instead of leaving together, I guess he stayed to please her."

She nodded. "That's not so unusual."

"No wonder he's so bloody angry. He survived that slaughter and when he tried to escape, he couldn't even do that. Staying in Greece was like having his nose rubbed in it every day of his life. When she talks about it, my mother makes his staying sound like some kind of love story. It's a lie."

She gazed out her window, her hands clasped tight on her lap.

"What? Am I wrong?"

"You can't undo what has been done."

"I'm not trying to. I'm trying to make sense of it. Don't you see?"

She turned toward him. "That woman in the museum hinted, but wouldn't tell you the whole story. I understand that. She has suffered too much and can't talk about it. Okay. But it leaves you assuming the worst about your father."

"So?" He shrugged. "It *is* his fault. It must be. Otherwise, why not tell me about it? He's never said a word about the war."

"That's the problem. The person who holds a secret cannot live with it and the people who don't know the secret assume the worst. It's horrible for everyone."

"I have no idea what you're talking about."

"You torture yourself with all these small bits and pieces. It's not good. Why can't you accept there are many things you will never know and leave it at that?"

"I blamed myself every time he got angry," he said. He couldn't stop talking, didn't want to. If he talked from now until he died, it wouldn't be enough to make up for the drought of words in the house he grew up in. "I tried to be a better son, do whatever he asked. But nothing satisfied him."

"Look, I'm going to tell you what I know and you're not going to like it. Maybe it will help you, maybe it won't. But secrets don't serve anybody except those who want to feel smug and pass them around when it's convenient.

"He was trying to escape, but she kept him here," she went on, not waiting for him to respond, to tell her he didn't want to know any more about his father. He'd had enough for one day. "They had you. That's why your father couldn't get away after the war. Your mother got pregnant to keep him in Greece. In the family, this is what has always been said about your mother and father."

"Me? I'm the cause of all of this?" Nicolai looked at her. The car veered onto the gravel shoulder. He yanked it back, let up on the accelerator. He wanted to stop, face her, tell her she was the one lying now. There was no place on the winding road to pull over.

"I'm sorry," she said. "I thought you should know."

"Is this why you thought I should drop all of this? Because you didn't want to have to tell me or have me find out through Achilles or someone else?"

"I wanted you to know so you would stop blaming yourself. It wasn't your fault. At least, not in the way you think."

He turned up the radio.

"Say something," she said.

"Right now I've got a ton of things on my mind," he said. He clicked off the radio. He became perfectly silent, as cold as the voiceless radio.

"Tell me what you're thinking." Dimitria said.

He stared out at the road in front of him.

He went to bed that night before his father got home.

"I'm not hungry," he lied.

"Are you sick, Nicolai?" His mother put her hand on his forehead.

He jerked away. "No, just tired." He stared into her eyes, hating their softness. Why did you do it? he wanted to ask. Because of you, he's resented me my whole life.

"What?"

He turned. "I'm tired."

He heard his father come in and listened to their whispered conversation. "It's probably just a cold. You worry about him too much," his father said.

"And you don't worry enough," she said. "He's your son."

"He's a man. He has to learn to take care of himself."

Nicolai pulled the pillow over his head. Sleep, when it finally came, was empty of dreams.

"Your mother tells me you haven't come out of that room," his father said when they met in the hallway, both of them on the way to the bathroom. Nicolai thought he'd heard the kitchen door slam, his father leaving for the day. His bladder had ached for some release, but he'd held on, waiting for that sound of his father's departure. His gaze moved beyond his father to the kitchen. The room was dark, the sky the deep blue of a dawn that promised another sunny day.

"Are you sick?" His father stood in his overalls and heavy flannel shirt, an empty glass in his hand. "Should we call the doctor?"

"I'm just tired."

"You're not going to get over that sitting around this house. Things don't get better by themselves." He threw his arms out at Nicolai in exasperation and sprinkled him with the few drops of water still left at the bottom of the glass. "You young people only make excuses." He jabbed Nicolai's shoulder with his finger.

The hallway seemed to narrow. Nicolai suddenly found it hard to breathe, as if the oxygen had been sucked out. He wiped his face with the back of his hand. He heard the tap drip in the bathroom down the hall. And rustling behind him. He pushed his father's hand away. "I'm not a boy."

"You're not a man either."

"I will do things in my own way, in my own time."

"Such a luxury!"

"I know."

"What do you know?"

"Everything."

His father shook his head and smiled in that way of his that used to terrify Nicolai. "You know nothing." He walked to the kitchen, filled his glass with water and guzzled it as he stood at the sink, his back to Nicolai.

Nicolai followed. He wasn't going to let this go. Not this time. "You stayed in Greece because you had to. Otherwise you'd have left long ago. That's what makes you so bloody angry."

"I would never run away from my family."

"Maybe you should have," Nicolai said. "We'd be better off."

"You don't know what you're talking about."

"If you hadn't fooled around and got her pregnant, you would have left."

He heard a sigh and spun around. His mother stood there, her grey hair down and around her face, her housecoat loosely tied around her, her feet bare.

"It wasn't love at all," Nicolai said, meeting her gaze, "like your little romantic story."

"Why do you say such things, Nicky?" She tightened the belt of her housecoat, pushed her hair off her face.

"Now I understand." He pointed his finger at her. "He's angry because you kept him from leaving. Because you had me and he never wanted any part of a child."

His mother walked into the kitchen and sat down heavily on the chair, her head in her hands. "You don't understand."

He followed, stood over her. "Because no one bothered to tell me."

"What would we have said?" his mother asked. "Have you always told your daughter everything? You would protect her. Wouldn't you? That's all we did. We wanted to protect you."

"I would never lie to her," Nicolai said. "Never." His hands trembled.

Nicolai's father stood staring out the kitchen window, his large hands gripping the counter as if he was afraid that if he let go he would fall.

"You think people don't talk? Where do you think I heard about this?" He shouted at his father. "How do you think I found out about what you did to get out of being killed in Kalavryta?"

"You've been listening to your cousin with the big mouth." His father spit into the sink. "We don't mix with your mother's family. And this is why. They think they know everything. They know nothing. I will not allow you to see her again."

"You don't have a say."

"I sacrificed everything for you."

"And you've held it over me every day of my life."

His father turned, brushed past Nicolai and walked down the hall.

His mother had begun to weep, but he didn't move to comfort her. Why should he? They were both to blame.

His father came back into the kitchen, a suitcase in one hand, a pile of clothes in the other. He threw the suitcase and Nicolai's clothes out the back door. "I want you out."

"What are you doing?" His mother was sobbing, running to him, tugging at his arms.

He thrust her off, went back into the bedroom, got the rest of Nicolai's things and flung them out onto the pile at the bottom of the steps. He shouted at someone next door, "What are you looking at? Mind your own business."

He turned to face Nicolai and pointed. "I don't want you here when I get back," he said and stomped out of the house, kicking at the suitcase as he passed.

Nicolai went outside, picked everything up in one scoop and shoved it into the suitcase. His mother followed, picking up the sock and T-shirt that fell out of his grasp. He banged the suitcase shut. The clasp wouldn't close. He threw the suitcase in the car anyway. She touched his shoulder and he grabbed the sock and shirt from her outstretched hand.

"Please stay, Nicky. You know him. He gets angry, but I will talk to him. We'll work it out. Things will pass. You'll see. Your mother has always worked miracles with your father."

"It turns out I didn't know the half of it."

"You know your mother," she said. "That won't change."

2010

Alexia had seen an ad for a moped in the grocery store and called. She agreed to meet the seller in a *taverna*.

"It's you," he said.

"Yes, the person who peeks in windows."

He laughed and she grinned. "It's a small place."

"Coffee?" As he leaned towards her his peasant-style shirt fell open. A gold cross lay against the grey hairs of his chest. An old hippie, Alexia thought. She looked away and towards the door. "Thanks, no."

"Let's sit then and talk."

"I have to get back. Could I have a look at the moped?" She pointed to the door.

He took her hand in his. "My name is Achilles."

She shook it firmly. "As in the heel?"

"Yes, exactly. You know our old Greek stories."

"Some."

"And yours?"

His handshake was weak; still,he held on until she pulled her hand away. "Alexia."

"You visit your relatives here. Yes? And do you like our village?"

He laced his arm through hers as they walked out into the parking lot. She let him. She was getting used to this closeness

Greeks seemed to need. His flared pants covered his sandalled feet and swept against her leg as they walked.

"How old is it?" Alexia asked as they stood outside in front of the moped.

"Like new." He patted the seat. "Maybe it has ten years. No more."

"Yeah, one owner, low miles, driven by an old lady."

"No, only Achilles and my friends."

She laughed.

"Did I say it wrong?"

"Just funny."

"I am glad I do this for you. It is nice laugh," he said. "Like it comes from the angels."

She smiled. He was a flirt, and she didn't feel like resisting. It probably made him feel good too. His cologne smelled stale. Still, he was charming.

"It's hot. Yes?"

He was old enough to be her father, but he was handsome in that strong-nosed, dark-eyed, silver-haired Greek sort of way. He reminded her of that Greek singer her father liked so much, Georges Moustaki, who seemed to get better looking the older he got. Or at least his image on CD covers was airbrushed well. Even though she didn't understand the words, his voice enticed her. She still sang a few of the words she had heard Moustaki sing without knowing what they meant.

Achilles ran his tongue over his lips. Get the moped and get out, she told herself. She unlatched her arm from his and kicked the bald tires. She didn't need to be another one of his conquests.

"Shall we go for ride?" he asked. "I show you the village. Work I do on promenade by sea."

"If you say the bike is okay, I believe you."

He asked her out to dinner then.

"I can't. Sorry." I don't want to hurt your feelings, she thought, but I've got other things to think about right now. And none of those things include you.

"Yes, it is difficult with relatives," he said. "You be with them all times."

She paid for the moped in cash and put on her helmet. He stood in front of her, pulled the helmet down on her head and fiddled with the straps. The scent of mint drifted on his breath. She held herself away, fought a sudden urge to stroke his beard. His laughing eyes goaded her until she shifted her gaze to the sky. When he had tightened the straps to his satisfaction, he smiled. She pulled away and got on the moped. He kissed her hand.

She started the moped and puttered away.

"These things very dangerous," Christina said when Alexia got back to the house. "Tourists get hurt. Be careful, no? I do not think this for you, *paidi mou*."

Alexia grinned. She was thinking of Achilles. His lips on her hand, his head bent in front of her, the tiny bald spot at the crown of his head. Why? She couldn't say. She liked older men, or at least that was her history. And he was certainly that. "I can explore more places, see more things," Alexia said. "Get to know my roots."

Christina grinned. Alexia retreated to her room, threw the keys on the bed, and sat down beside them. Lying seems to come easily to me all of a sudden, she thought. First I don't tell Christina I went to Aigio. Okay, the first time didn't really count because I didn't even talk to Theodora. But the second time I talked to her, made a plan to have lunch. I bought that stupid moped to make it easier to get around. To go back to Aigio. She pulled the pillow over her head.

"Little *manikos,*" Solon said. "Where you go?"

Alexia met his gaze. "Scatterbrain? No one's accused me of that before."

They sat across from one another at the kitchen table. This had been her and her uncle's routine for six weeks now. Solon scratched out another short sentence. He held up the chalkboard he'd borrowed from a neighbour. Lime-green dust puffed out under each of his strokes and settled on his hand, the table, his pants and shirt. Christina faced the sink, her hands submerged in frothy suds. The squeak of clean glasses and plates punctuated the sound of dishes tumbling about in the sink.

"This chalk is no good," Christina said. "My lungs weak since a long time."

Solon shook his head and smirked at Alexia. His eyes flickered playfully. "She will outlive us all. You wait to see."

Christina picked up a tea towel and patted her hands dry. She swatted his broad shoulders with the towel and made Alexia smile, too. "*Ella, paidi mou,* we try to study here," he said. Alexia had come to expect it, count on it. She enjoyed the way Christina and Solon were together. Would she ever have that? She knew what her parents had had was very special, but it had been so long ago. She wasn't sure if she had just made up what she thought of as good memories.

"A sacrifice for me is okay if you learn your language," Christina said. She pinched Alexia's narrow chin and grumbled she was no more than a skeleton. Christina's smile was sincere, but her left eye drooped slightly and glistened. A single tear marked her cheek.

"Are you tired?" Alexia asked Christina.

"I am on my feet all day and not young now. My lungs no good, my blood no good. Things no good. I know death is not far." She groaned, but her smile stayed intact. "We have to accept we begin to die the day we born."

"*Ella,* more talk about death," Solon said. "There are other things to talk about."

Alexia quizzed her about what the doctor had said and Christina reported, "With all his book learning, he knows nothing. He gives me no answers."

"But what does he say?"

"I do not know," Christina said. "Iron. Low iron."

"Did the doctor give you medication to take for your blood?"

Christina shrugged. "Some pills."

"But you're not taking them."

"I eat good," Christina said. "What more I need?"

"Do what the doctor tells you to do," Alexia said. "Let's get that iron right now. Where is it? I'll get it for you."

Alexia started to stand up, but Christina put a hand on her shoulder. "Do not bother yourself with this now."

"I used to tell my father all the time: do what the doctors tell you. Ask questions when you don't understand what they say." Alexia shook her head. "We're responsible for our own health, happiness, our lives."

"But he dead. No?"

Solon muttered and finished writing the sentence.

"Okay, I am going, I am going." Christina slipped out of her apron, grabbed her jacket and purse, and left.

Alexia felt exhausted. Learning a new language was humbling. Solon shook his head. His dark gaze chided her and she dropped her eyes to her notebook. The page was blank, except for a couple of sentences.

She still hadn't told Theodora the truth, but since she'd spoken to her, she was more motivated to improve her Greek. What would Theodora think of her? How could she tell her? Alexia turned the page and pressed down hard. The spine of her book cracked. The blank page was more evidence she hadn't been paying attention or taking notes as Solon had encouraged her to do: "Write down. Is important."

Solon tapped the board. "Are you ready?"

"*Sygnomi*." Alexia made sure she pronounced each syllable.

"Sorry," he said. "This is important word to know."

"Where did Christina go today?" Alexia asked.

"You worry about this?" He raised his voice, grinned.

Was he mad? Alexia wondered.

"Women. Who knows where they go or what they do?" Solon threw his hands in Alexia's direction as if ridding himself of them and her. "*Ah*."

"I'm a little preoccupied. Work. You know."

"You will not learn this way," he said. "*Sin Athena ke hira kini*."

"In other words, pay attention."

"Ah, you understood. Good. Now understand one more thing. Holiday is for fun."

"They expect this of me." She shrugged.

"They or you?" He walked over to the stove where the one-cup coffee maker stood. The tar he called coffee oozed into his cup, blackening its white sides. Christina bleached the cup every night. "You no think anyway. *Ella, paidi mou*. Maybe next time."

He wandered out of the kitchen and Alexia heard the front door open, then shut with an ill-fitted thud. Grabbing her phone, she went upstairs to the terrace. She had to check in, do her duty, but she felt less and less obliged to do so.

She was going to see Theodora today. She saw Solon sitting on a boulder in the field below, sipping his coffee. He seemed to be talking to himself. She shifted so she could no longer see him. She stared at the phone. It took her a moment to remember what she had wanted to do with it.

After his usual, "How are you doing, kiddo?" Dan's tone changed. "When are you coming back?"

"Not sure." She fingered the bougainvillea, sneaking a quick look at Solon. He hadn't moved.

"Aren't you bored yet?"

"I'm getting Greek lessons from my uncle, running every day, fishing with the locals, listening to the village gossip, hanging out with my crazy relatives, and of course still working and getting grief from my family for doing it."

"I need you back."

"What do you mean?" She pushed her bangs off her face.

"I'd like you back."

"Okay, what's going on?"

"You know."

"Tell me."

He cleared his throat and she heard the squeal of his chair move. "These assistants of yours are screwing up. Can't think past their textbooks."

"How are they going to learn?"

The line went quiet. Had it dropped again? "Are you there? Hello?"

"Yup."

"Tell me."

"I miss you. It's not the same."

"Maybe this is a good time to ask for a raise?" She laughed.

Dan didn't. "For such a smart gal, you don't grasp much. What do I need to do?"

"Look, I sent the instructions on the Brown Mayer merger yesterday when I had a connection. Got back some questions and sent back answers. What else do you need?"

"Why did I let you leave?"

Alexia pictured him at his large desk, files piled on the floor beside him. His hand twisting, then releasing short tufts of his hair through his index finger. He only did it in meetings with her. She hadn't noticed him doing it around anyone else. Maybe he did. She didn't know. All she knew was that it softened his all-business-like exterior. When she thought of it, she smiled.

A sigh, then more silence. What did he want? She wasn't going to be gone forever. Why couldn't he just understand? She'd never asked him for anything before.

"I should go," Alexia said. She hung up. The phone rang again a few minutes later. When she answered it, Dan said he'd send an email with some questions about another merger. "They're interested in the provisions dealing with staff and severance packages. They want to know costs and ramifications."

She said, "I'll get to it as soon as I can," and clicked off again, looking over the edge of the terrace. Solon's stained cup sat empty on the rock. She couldn't see where he'd gone. Thank God, she thought. Still, she wished she could have talked to him about Theodora. Somehow she thought he might understand.

She turned off the phone, got her pack and her helmet and the keys to the moped.

Alexia ran into Ziizika's tavern out of breath and slightly dizzy. The moped had been slower than she'd anticipated. It whined and begrudged every attempt to accelerate. Cars sped by. A driver gave her the finger. Faster, sleeker mopeds overtook her. Bus drivers honked their horns. The traffic fumes burned her eyes and irritated her lungs, forcing her to stop on the shoulder as far off the freeway as possible. Slower vehicles drove in the shoulder lane to allow faster ones to pass. She knew it wasn't safe for her to stop there, but there was nowhere else.

She got off the bike and stood behind it, her hands over her ears. Her chest heaved as cars whizzed by. The moped was her only shield. She thought about what might happen if a car careened towards her. She cursed Achilles. He'd used his charm to get her to buy this stupid old thing. She hadn't asked many questions, hadn't even test-ridden the damn thing. Beware of hand-kissing Greeks bearing mopeds, she thought.

She took off her helmet and dropped it by the front wheel. A few minutes later, it tipped and rolled down the short, sandy embankment. The wind pushed at her. Like a spoiled child, she refused to move. She kicked at the gravel at her feet. She thought about returning to Diakofto.

Her frustration wasn't getting her anywhere. She knew that. Sliding into the ditch, she retrieved her helmet, got back on the moped and drove on the shoulder until she finally found an exit. She decided to take a chance. The back road looked like it was heading in the direction of Aigio. Her hunch paid off.

She arrived twenty minutes late. Although she could see the sign for the restaurant, she couldn't reach it, trapped as she was in a maze of one-way streets. She went around once, then two more times before she found a parking spot five blocks away. She ran as fast as she could, the sound of her heart pounding in her ears.

Alexia spotted Theodora sitting in the corner, bouncing a fidgeting Nicky on her knee. Her stomach felt empty and nervous, as if she was about to throw up. Theodora waved her over. Theodora's hair was pulled back in a ponytail. "I did not think you would come," Theodora said, and gazed at the back of her son's head. She didn't look at Alexia and seemed to be using her son as a shield.

Alexia felt sweaty and spent. She wouldn't have bought the moped, wouldn't have come, if it wasn't for having to meet Theodora here for lunch. And she wouldn't be in this country either if it weren't for their father. Their father. He fathered both of them. How did things get so out of control?

Alexia shrugged.

"Do not worry." Theodora laughed, putting Nicky down beside her. "Sit down."

"What?" Alexia couldn't control the irritation in her voice. She threw her gloves on the table and they fell onto the floor. "Nothing's going my way today." She bent down and picked up her gloves.

Theodora pointed at Alexia's head.

She gingerly touched her head, then rolled her eyes. She'd run the entire way with her helmet strapped onto her head.

"I'm such an idiot," she said and laughed. She took off the helmet, released her ponytail and ran her fingers through her damp, tangled hair. Her face felt caked with dirt. A fine layer of dust covered her blue pants and tiny insect bodies speckled her shirt.

Nicky stared at Alexia and whimpered. Theodora tried to comfort him with whispers and a stuffed frog. Its chest croaked when she pushed it. Nicky turned away from Alexia and lay down beside his mother on the bench. "He is not even two," Theodora said. "He is shy."

"I scare small children," Alexia said. "I'm a mess." She signalled towards the bathroom and went to wash her face and hands, fix her hair. People stared as she walked by. She smiled. What else could she do?

When she returned to the table, the waiter plopped a glass of water in front of her and stood above her, tapping the bottom of his tray. He asked what Alexia wanted. Theodora answered, her eyes slightly tipped down. "She's just arrived." Her olive skin was radiant against her orange sweater. She had one of those open, trusting faces. How can I sit here and be dishonest with her, Alexia asked herself, not tell her who I am and what I'm doing here?

Theodora's bare legs were crossed and slanted to one side of the table as if she wanted someone to notice them. Dressed in a snake-covered stiletto heel, one foot bobbed persistently. The other shoe lay on the floor like discarded skin. Her son watched her swinging foot, sucking his thumb, his frog tucked into his chest. The toy's murmur seemed to comfort him.

"You look great," Alexia said. "I feel like a hag."

"What is hag?"

"Hag means a woman who is old, dirty, more like a witch." Alexia pointed to herself. "The complete opposite of what you look like. I'm jealous."

Theodora looked away, a blush rising.

"I don't know why I bought that stupid moped. I let a good-looking Greek charm me." Alexia spotted another smear, this one on her pants, and dunked her napkin into the glass of water and rubbed at the mark. "I thought I got all these bugs off when I was in the bathroom."

"My husband had a motorbike once. We used to go on many trips. I like the air, the roar, being on the road. Away. The sound drowns things."

"I don't know how I'm going to get home on that thing."

"Eat now," Theodora said. "Later we think."

Alexia nodded and glanced at the menu. She couldn't figure out what she wanted, didn't know what half of things on the menu were. She peered over at Theodora, who hummed quietly to her son. Liking Theodora wasn't going to be difficult. Telling her the truth was another matter. Theodora would surely feel betrayed and that was going to be the end of it. "I don't know what I want."

"You are not the only one," Theodora said. "I marry butcher and I don't know what to make for supper most times. I never know. This happens."

"And that's okay for you?"

"Okay or no. What can I do? Nothing. Yes or no?"

Alexia nodded. "I like to control things."

"Yes, I see."

"How?"

"I can see the worry on your face."

"Are you talking about my wrinkles?" Alexia teased.

Theodora furrowed her brow, stared at Alexia with intent. "Your eyes look like this," she said. "Like you think all the time. Never stop."

Alexia laughed at the face Theodora made.

"You like I order for us?" Theodora asked.

"Please."

Theodora ordered grilled vegetables, a salad, bread and olives. "Calamari?"

"No thanks." Alexia listened and understood a good part of the conversation between Theodora and the waiter. The Greek lessons were helping.

Without the distraction of the waiter, Alexia stared at her cutlery, then began talking quickly. She found herself going on about the highway, the cars and trucks and buses, how people used the shoulder as another driving lane, how frightened she'd been on the moped. As she talked, she ripped at the bread on her side plate and shoved small bits into her mouth. Theodora looked down at Nicky.

Alexia put the bread down, swallowed what was in her mouth. Stop it, she told herself. She had no reason to be nervous. She ducked down to see what Nicky was up to. He was tracing the dark lines of his mother's shoe with his index finger, the thumb of his other hand in his mouth. They both watched him for several seconds. "Nicky plays somewhere else, another world."

"When I'm nervous, I talk too much."

Theodora said, "I am more quiet when I am nervous."

The waiter arrived with a bowl of salad, a plate of grilled vegetables and a small bowl of mixed olives, and placed them in the middle of the table. He asked whether he should bring side plates.

"*Ne,*" Alexia said.

"*Oxi,* we have forks. Do we need anything else?"

"*Piato,*" Alexia said.

Theodora speared a slice of zucchini, made several dainty cuts in the oily flesh. She gave Nicky a few pieces, then took one small mouthful for herself.

Alexia wondered if Theodora had heard her ask for another plate.

"Andreas liked eating like this," she said. "One plate, two forks. Before we marry." Theodora's smile waned slightly, her shoulders rounded. She sat up straight again as if someone had rapped her shoulder, warning her to fix her posture. "He is a very good man. We are friends since childhood."

"Maybe he's concerned about germs."

Nicky sneezed. She brought him to her lap. "*Kalo yia mena, kalo yia sena,*" she said and kissed his stomach. He giggled, his head thrown back, pushing her face away.

"Excuse me?"

"When a person sneezes, it means someone is thinking about them."

"Everyone talks about everyone else in this country, so it's no wonder."

"If they think about us, then we hope they think good thoughts."

"That's nice. Highly unlikely, but nice."

"Yes, yes, you are right. So we Greeks have solution for this, too. If they think badly of us, then we wish the bad thoughts go back on them instead."

"Get them before they get you. Is that it?"

Theodora nodded. Alexia thought about her father's many girlfriends and how she had once wished bad thoughts on them, hoping they would die or move or leave her and her father alone.

She had really tried with his first "friend." It had been a long time since her mother died and she wanted him to find someone. She was a teenager, after all; she understood. But that first woman didn't have much interest in Alexia's copy of *Moby Dick* or any of the other books she showed her. Instead, the bimbo said, "We should go find your father, see what he's doing." She couldn't remember her name, but she remembered her fake smile. Later, Alexia overheard her say to Nicolai, "Can you get a sitter next Saturday so we can spend some quiet time alone?"

"Sure," he said. "Why not? My friends Mavis and Stuart are always eager to have Alexia over for a weekend."

After that, Alexia made no effort with his women. She sulked and her father ignored her. Sometimes she got angry with him and he said, "You have your friends. Doesn't your old dad deserve a few, too?"

"But they don't like me," Alexia said.

"You don't try."

The more she hated them and closed herself off, the more he insisted they attend her basketball games, come over for supper, go to the movies.

Loud shouts erupted at the bar. Theodora and Alexia turned towards the squabbling group of men. When they realized everyone in the restaurant was staring at them, the men shrugged. The women at the table beside Theodora and Alexia shook their heads and returned to their conversation.

"Men," Alexia said. "They have to better one another."

"Do you have husband?"

"Too much responsibility. No."

"There is someone at the bar who looks at you." Theodora tilted her head.

Alexia didn't turn. "My life is complicated enough."

"How is it complicated?"

Alexia shook her head. "Losing my father, getting to know his family. Well, my family, too. It's all complicated." Was she really using Nicolai's throwaway word to describe what she was facing?

She glanced over at the bar and caught a glimpse of the man's confident smile. "No, I don't need any more complications."

"Life is this way." Theodora passed the bowl of olives.

"No thanks."

"You don't like olives?"

"I know. I know. People have bugged me about it my whole life. My father used to shake his finger at me." She mimicked his finger wagging and Theodora laughed. "And give me one of his looks, supposedly to force me to give them another try."

Theodora laughed again.

Alexia grinned. She liked Theodora's laugh. "He said I was stubborn. I guess I am. But I hate olives for real." Alexia scrunched up her face and pulled her cheeks inward. "They're just too sour for me. I don't get why anyone would want to eat them."

"My stepfather told me tree-ripened olives were the best. I believed him and tried one. I guess it was a joke. I did not understand. This was the end for me."

"Why did you order them?"

"I thought you might like them. I should ask you first. Yes?"

"Do you see your stepfather often?"

The waiter hovered and asked if they wanted coffee. They both shook their heads.

"We talk on the telephone once per week," Theodora said.

"Do you go to see him?"

"Elena doesn't believe married women should travel without their husbands. Andreas is busy in his shop. But I want to one day. He is the only father I have."

As they talked about Theodora's stepfather, her husband and Alexia's career, Theodora's smile remained fixed, but now and again her mouth twisted as if forcing herself to maintain it against her own wishes. Her plump lips hinted at what she was feeling and reminded Alexia of her father. He'd say one thing, but his jittery mouth said something different. And his eyes, the way he sometimes looked away, betrayed his thoughts.

"You remind me of someone."

Alexia wondered what might come next. Had Theodora seen pictures of Nicolai? Or might Nicolai have sent pictures of Alexia to Theodora's mother?

"A girl from my school," Theodora said.

"You go to school?"

"Not now. When I was child."

"This is my first time in Greece."

"And I have never been outside of Greece."

"Do you have any memory of your father?" Alexia jabbed her fingernails into the bottom of her thighs, a habit she'd developed after her mother died.

"He worked on a ship and died in an accident before I was born."

"Your mother told you that?" Alexia blurted out. "Um, I mean, did she tell you about him? What he was like?"

"My mother told me a little, but she did not like to talk about him. I had a stepfather who was good to me my whole life."

The waiter stepped in to see if they wanted anything else. They hadn't finished the salad and were only partway through the vegetables. Theodora asked the waiter to remove the olives and to bring back a tray of the day's selected desserts.

Alexia stared at her. They had both been lied to by parents who should have told them the truth. And now, Alexia was caught up in these lies. How was she going to get herself out of this thing? How could there ever be a happy ending to this?

"The *bougatsa* is good. Save room." Theodora's smile was so innocent.

"Dessert should always come first." Alexia edged her hands out from underneath her. They felt stiff.

"Elena says sweets are the devil. *She* is the devil." Theodora put her hand over her mouth. "Oh. I should not say these things."

"It's only between us."

"I do not want anything bad to happen to her. I just wish she lived somewhere else or..." She patted her mouth with her napkin, shook her head.

"Or liked you more?"

"*Ne.*" Theodora looked directly into Alexia's eyes for a moment, then quickly away. I bet you're shy, Alexia thought. Like your son. Maybe you got that from your mother. You sure didn't get it from your father.

"She's probably a bitter old woman."

Theodora nodded, then laughed. "I wish I could say these things."

"You could. It feels good to say what you think."

Theodora shook her head.

"You think it, though. Right?"

"When I do I must pray or invite her to our house when I do not really want to, or I call her to see if she wants me to help her in her house.

"You know, she is not all bad. She is nice sometimes," Theodora continued. "Then I let my guard down just a little. Maybe I only misunderstand her. She does say and do nice things, but I always feel there is another thing behind."

She's right, Alexia thought. It's never as simple as that. Alexia thought of her father again. He didn't listen to anything when he had his mind made up. Still, she knew he loved her. She didn't believe it sometimes, but she could be a brat too. A spoiled brat. Now that he was gone, she missed him. When the phone rang, even here, she thought he'd be on the other end. She swallowed hard. Don't, she told herself.

He tried to send letters to Theodora, but never did. Why didn't he? Didn't he love her, too? What was he afraid of?

After they finished their salad, Alexia and Theodora shared the *bougatsa* in the same way they'd shared lunch, two forks, one plate. It didn't occur to Alexia to protest.

Theodora fed Nicky one mouthful of the custard for every half-mouthful she took herself. He sat on her lap, his lips smudged in creamy yellow. When a dollop or a crumb fell on his lap, he became agitated, screeched and pointed. Alexia wondered if this was how he demanded to be cleaned up. Theodora accommodated, but she seemed less fastidious. He pushed her hand away, took the napkin himself and wiped away what she left behind.

"You become more obsessed, Nicky," Theodora said. "Like others in the family."

"I'm a bit like that myself," Alexia said. "Dan would say I was more than a bit. He teases me about it."

"Who is Dan?"

"Kind of my boss. One of the senior partners. And a friend. I guess." She smiled and wasn't sure why.

"Your partner?"

"No, no. One of the owners of the firm, the business."

"But he is a boyfriend too?"

"No. Just a friend." Alexia felt herself blushing.

"Maybe more. Yes?"

"I don't think so." Alexia turned to the window. A woman walked in front of the stores across the street. She had a kind of walk that was familiar to Alexia, an outfit maybe she'd seen before. She shrugged.

"Something?"

"No, nothing."

The waiter brought the bill and Alexia picked it up.

"This is for me to take care of," Theodora said, reaching to take it from Alexia.

"Next time," Alexia said.

"But you are a guest in my country. It is my duty."

"There will be another time," Alexia said. "Not to worry."

Theodora smiled. "Thank you. This is very kind."

After lunch, Alexia walked with Theodora to the park.

Theodora picked Nicky up and placed him on the swing. Alexia pushed him. Her high heels discarded, Theodora belly-flopped over the swing beside them and rocked back and forth. The tips of her toes kicked up the red dust.

"Do you work?"

"I take pictures," Theodora said.

"Oh, a photographer." So Theodora turned out to be the creative one. Nicolai would have liked that.

Theodora stopped swinging. "It is only a dream now."

"I'd like to see your photographs sometime."

After a long while, they left the park and walked back towards where Alexia had parked the moped. Theodora ambled and glanced into every store window and Alexia had to slow down not to lose her.

"You do not see when you walk fast."

"It's getting late," Alexia said. It was around four. "I had a good time, though."

Theodora brightened. "I thought you did not because of your rush."

"I worry about things. I worry about that moped, about the dark, about how I'll get home, about everything."

"Andreas says I should be more like this."

"I have never told anyone this," Alexia said, "but I don't like being like me. Nothing I can do about it, though. Next time I will have more time." Alexia uttered the commitment before she realized what she'd done.

When they arrived at the moped twenty minutes later, Theodora hugged Alexia. At first, Alexia didn't know what to do with her arms. She held her body away, but Theodora drew closer and held on until Alexia hugged her, patted her back. They stood still like this for a few seconds and then unlocked. Alexia looked away. This girl deserved to know the truth.

She watched Theodora walk down the street, Nicky bouncing and fidgeting in her arms. She put on her helmet and turned the key in the ignition. She saw Christina then, leaning against the door of a small shop on the corner. Alexia sat very still on the puttering moped. They looked directly into each other's eyes.

2010

Oregano, onion, garlic and beef bubbled in a pan on the stove. Nicky lay on his stomach at Theodora's feet, colouring over the lines of one of the simple drawings in the book she'd made for him. His foot lay against her leg. She reached for a cucumber on the opposite counter, tripped over him and caught herself before she fell.

"Ella, paidi mou," she said. He shuffled a little closer. She chopped the cucumber in half and hacked at it in the same way she'd done the tomatoes, green peppers and onions, already mingled in a pool of murky red in the glass bowl. Slow down, she said to herself. It can't be done any faster.

Nicky's hair was flaked with tiny cucumber peel shavings. If he noticed, he would fuss until she cleaned him up. She didn't have time for this. She grabbed the last half of the cucumber. She'd spent too long over lunch, played in the park, gone for a walk. It had been so much fun talking to Alexia, getting to know her. She could have spent the evening with her too, but they both had to get home. Family. Commitments.

She heard the tick of the blade against her fingernail. She threw the knife down, certain she'd sliced through skin. The knife bounced off the cutting board and onto the counter. She held it still. A faint bruise was building under the nail. Her skin hadn't been pierced. She rubbed her finger, took a deep breath. Everything had to be on time for Andreas.

She threw the watery cucumber into the bowl and gave the salad a quick toss. Later, she'd add the olive oil and lemon. Nicky sat still while she picked cucumber out of his hair. She wiped up tomato and green pepper seeds from the floor, washed her hands and got the bowls. Nicky followed her every step. "*Ella, paidi mou,*" she said. "I'm busy. Can you see?"

She slung him onto her hip. He clutched at her blouse and whimpered as she finished setting the table and wiped down the counter. "What's wrong now?"

"He thinks he's going to fall," Andreas said from the door. "He doesn't need to be held all the time." The door slammed shut behind him. "You can put him down when you're cleaning. He's almost two." He draped his jacket over the kitchen chair and leaned against its spindly back. The chair creaked. He let go, stood away from it. "I have to fix this one of these days."

"We have closets," she said, pointing to his jacket.

"Yes, but I don't want to take the pleasure away from you." He went to her, slipped his arm around her waist, kissed Nicky's head, then Theodora's cheek and walked over to the stairs. "I'll be a few minutes. I'm starving."

"I'm behind."

"This is new?" Andreas smiled.

He'd had a good day, she thought. Thank God for small mercies. She had, too. His supper was late. So what? It happens. She pulled a chair close and sat down heavily, sliding Nicky to the floor. He picked up the colouring book and his crayons. He scratched black, then red, and finally yellow across the drawing she'd made of all three of them at the beach. "You'll be an artist, Nicky." He put his head on her foot and moved his crayons back and forth until only the faintest outline of their family could be seen. "You are getting heavy." She bent and rubbed his back. "But you won't let me go. Will you?"

Theodora went through the list of things she had to do. The stew was simmering, the salad done, and the potatoes on. A bottle of Andreas's homemade wine was in the fridge. Water glasses were filled and on the table along with a cold bottle of water for refills. Andreas was usually dehydrated when he got home. Too busy to take breaks during the day, he brought back the bottle of water she packed for him, half full. She stuck it in the fridge for the next day.

Everything was ready. Once they started eating, everything would be fine. She hated being rushed.

Gently, she shifted Nicky's head off her foot, stepped around him. She hoped he wouldn't follow. She poked a fork into one of the potatoes. Still hard. She picked up the pot and stuck it in the fridge. They'd be good tomorrow.

Making sure dinner was on time night after night required a precision she didn't have. It was one more boring thing she had to think about, then do. "Why don't we go to the *taverna* sometime?" she'd asked Andreas one night.

"I've been working all day," he said. "We're lucky. I have work. You should read a newspaper, listen to the news. See how many people are on the street with nothing. The country is in trouble." He had stared at her sternly then, as if she were a little girl who had just asked for an impossibly expensive treat. They didn't have a lot of money. She knew that. God knew she hadn't had a new outfit or shoes in such a long time, since her mother died. She took good care of her things, all the things her mother bought for her. They were expensive, she knew that, and they would last. She'd make them last. Hadn't Alexia told her how good she looked? She'd never suspect how old that outfit was she wore today.

But what harm was there in going out once in a while? How much could they spend? And why did everything have to be on his time? When had she stopped telling him what she needed, what she wanted? "I want to spend my life making you happy," he used to tell her. "It's the only thing I care about."

"Where's the bread?" Andreas said as he walked into the kitchen and surveyed the table. His hands were on his hips. Theodora was reminded of the old women in the market, nagging about the price and condition of the lettuce.

"It smells good."

She grabbed the basket of bread and sat down.

"No potato?"

"We'll have it tomorrow."

"If one day you remember everything, I will think aliens have kidnapped you and put someone else in your place." He pinched Nicky's cheeks lightly. The boy giggled and pushed his father's hands away. "Your mother has a bad memory. Hey, Nicky."

"This is not funny." Theodora picked at her stew.

Andreas tore a piece of bread in two and swiped a piece across his bowl. "I'm only joking." He touched her hand with the back of his. "You know that."

"I felt rushed," she said. "I don't like it."

"Did you get home late?"

"I met a friend for lunch," she said. Would the chunks of meat on her plate never finish? "Things carried on."

"What friend?"

"You don't listen." She put her fork down. She had picked out all the vegetables. Only the meat remained like a big fat lump in the middle of her brown-stained bowl. "The girl I met last week. She is visiting her family. She's from Canada. I told you."

"I don't remember." He ate like a starving man.

Why didn't he look at her anymore? She tucked her hair behind her ear, shuffled in her chair, pulling at her skirt. "You don't listen when I talk."

"You believe you tell me things, but I know you don't."

"I told you this morning. I was trying to think about what to make for dinner because I wanted a meal I could put on early and leave. I wasn't going to be home. I needed dinner to be easy. Remember?"

He shrugged. "I guess potatoes didn't fit into your plan."

Theodora rubbed at Nicky's mouth. He squealed, pushed her hands away and forked a small bit of meat into his mouth, smearing his cheek.

"And you were too busy talking to come home." Andreas dabbed at his chin with a piece of bread. "What do you need with strangers?"

"I need." She wiped her son's face again and his head rocked back and away. He kicked his feet and tried to grab the cloth. "I'll do it," she said. She picked him up and plopped him straight back down. This time he sat still and she ran the wet cloth over his face. "Try to get some in your mouth. Your mother's job is difficult enough."

"I only asked a question," Andreas said. "You are too nervous these days."

"It's the way you ask, the way you expect." She pitched the cloth on the table.

"I work." Andreas mopped up his bowl with the bread, then ate the bread. He took another, ripped it in two, patted one side of his mouth with half, ate that, patted the other side with the other half and swallowed that piece too. She pushed the napkin towards him. He fingered it, but didn't pick it up.

"Did you eat too much at lunch?" Andreas asked.

Theodora shrugged.

"We can't let food go to waste. Not now. Not in these times when so many have nothing." He picked at her bowl. She moved his to the side and put hers in front of him. He nodded. "It's very good," he said. "You should try it."

"Maybe if there is anything left."

She made it because it was his favourite. Couldn't he see that? *"All I ever want to do is make you happy."* When was the last time he'd said that to her?

She knew she loved him. She hadn't always known, but she'd come to realize it that year before she went to university. He liked her photographs so much that he saved his allowance to buy her a fancy camera the year she went to Athens. Over lunch with Alexia, she was again reminded how lucky she was to have Andreas, Nicky, her own family. There was an obvious loneliness in Alexia's voice. "I'm busy," Alexia had said. "I don't have time for that." Even Theodora, who didn't know Alexia very well yet, knew this was just an excuse.

Theodora's own life was different. Better. Maybe she'd been too smug in that thought. When she'd left Alexia by her moped, she picked up Nicky and practically ran all the way home. She usually let him walk, but he moved too slowly for that today. She wondered what Alexia's life was really like. Maybe a little loneliness was not a bad price for a bit of freedom.

"Maybe I shouldn't make dinner every night." She stared out the window.

"I support this family. I'm the one who worries about tomorrow. Money. Where it will come from. How we will pay for things."

"And I do nothing?"

"It's different." He placed his hand on her shoulder.

She shrugged his hand away. "The way you say that, you mean easier."

Nicky threw his bowl at them, splattering the table.

They stared at him.

Theodora rushed to him, kissing his cheek. Andreas stood close and mussed his hair. "You're right, little one," Andreas said. "We're being silly. Hey, Nicky?"

"I guess the rush of making dinner, being here at a certain time," Theodora said. "Next time I won't worry so much."

"You know you don't have to rush for me. Dinner even an hour late is fine. Don't make yourself like this. It's not good for us." He ran his finger over the last bit of sauce in the bowl.

She reached for his hand. He lightly stroked hers with the back of his and leaned over to peck her on the lips. How was it that she'd fallen in love with this man, his meaty breath? She smiled.

"I don't know why I get so crazy." She folded her napkin and put it on her lap.

"If the foreigner does this to you, don't see her," Andreas said. He shuffled his chair back, scuffing the floor.

"She probably won't be here long," Theodora said, and picked up their bowls. When she stood up, the napkin fell. She stepped on it, leaving it crushed on the floor. "And besides, I like spending time with her."

When she turned, Andreas was already gone. She wiped Nicky's mouth with the cloth again, picked up his bowl and heard the crackling sound of the television going on in the living room. The familiar newscaster's monotone voice followed. Nicky took his book and walked towards the sound. Theodora turned on the hot water.

She already felt close to Alexia. She was easy to be with and she didn't judge her. She could talk to her, trust her.

Theodora grabbed the first bowl and scrubbed it, the bruise under her nail aching in the soapy water.

12

2010

Alexia leaned forward on the moped. The wind pressed against her, whistled inside her helmet. She followed a half-ton truck, maintaining her speed and staying a comfortable distance behind. Her fingers tightened on the handlebars. Her legs pressed together, tender at the spot where her knees ground against each other. As cars made quick lane changes and trucks passed without warning, her eyes remained fixed on the truck's fender and the wobbly load of hay strung together with rope. She only had to follow it until she got to her exit. She'd be off the freeway, and close to home. But then what?

The bale at the top suddenly shifted and fell, bouncing towards her, scattering bits of hay and a cloud of dust as it hit the ground. She swerved into the opposite lane, cutting off a car that was already trying to pass her. A horn blared. She passed the truck and swung back into the lane. A scowling driver shook his fist at her as he sped by, his Volvo trailing diesel fumes. She stifled a cough, allowed herself to blink. Stay focused, she repeated. Her arms were spent, like the moped that sputtered when she tried to accelerate again. Finally, it kicked into gear. Another exit sign hovered above her head.

A few minutes later, Alexia left the freeway. She glanced into her rear-view mirror once and then again. Nothing behind. Olive groves on one side, the sea on the other. The moped whined over the hollow boom of the breeze, the echo of cars, trucks just behind her. She glanced into the mirror again. Nothing. The noise persisted.

She wondered how she'd made it back this far. Catching herself in the mirror, she saw Christina's hazel eyes. Christina had all but forbidden her to meet Theodora. Still she had gone. What would Christina say?

I could deny the whole thing, she thought. Say I was out exploring. It wasn't me you saw, Christina. It wasn't.

Alexia lurched around the parked cars that clogged Diakofto's narrow lanes. A man stood on the sidewalk ahead, his back turned. Don't cross that damn road. These tight turns are bad enough. I don't need any more surprises. Pay attention.

He dashed out into the street. Alexia squeezed the brakes and closed her eyes. The moped pitched and stalled. She put her feet down, felt ground. She was still upright, thank God. She clenched down on the brakes again. She opened her eyes, then slowly unlocked her fingers. She shook them out, rubbed her hands and remembered the pedestrian. She tried to get off the moped, see to him, but her legs refused to move.

He stood curled away from her. As he uncoiled, he patted himself down checking for injury, then charged towards her, shouting words and waving his hands. She recognized the streak in his whiskers. His beard had been trimmed close, but the white stripe was still there, like a scar.

He stroked the tuft on his chin with the back of his hand. Behind him, the late-day sun tinged the tips of his silver hair, giving it a fiery glow. His olive skin seemed to darken. His eyes crinkled and he grinned.

Like he doesn't have a care in the world, she thought. "What is wrong with you?" She pulled the moped up onto its kickstand, took off her helmet and pushed it into his chest. "What are you, blind? Can't you see?"

"I see you try to kill me. Yes?" He shrugged. "But I forgive." He held her helmet in one hand and extended his other arm to pull her close.

Alexia pushed him away.

A horn blared behind her. She jumped. Achilles held her in his arms, tossing the driver a hand gesture. He smelled of lavender. Grey curls teased the narrow opening of his shirt.

She pulled away. He laced her helmet through his arm, grabbed the handlebars and pushed the moped off the road. She followed. His back and shoulders flexed underneath his shirt.

"I could have done that," she said, as he parked the moped.

"Yes," he said. "You strong. I like this."

"You sold me a lemon."

"*Oxi,*" he said. "I sell moped. Not lemon." He opened his arms towards the moped like a salesman presenting his latest prize. "Perhaps I give you lessons. Yes?"

"It's a death trap. It can't keep up. It's junk and you know it."

"It needs special touch." He put his arm around her shoulders. "Like a woman."

Alexia ducked away from his arm. She pointed to her helmet. He passed it to her.

"You need drink. Yes? We talk and everything is okay." He pointed to the crowd gathered around them. "We do not give show here."

"You're lucky I don't sue you."

"If your mind change, I be in *taverna* where before I give you my moped."

"You mean where you pawned this piece of junk off on me, junk I paid for."

"Achilles and his fine moped, we no junk. You see."

The moped started on the first try. She shifted into gear. Alexia ignored his grin and ready wave. "Choke on my fumes," she said, hoping he'd heard her and actually understood.

Normally at this hour, Christina would be in the kitchen preparing dinner. Alexia found a pot of steaming water on the stove and smelled a roast in the oven so she knew her aunt couldn't be far away. The kitchen seemed big and empty without Christina in it, fussing over dinner, or the dishes.

Alexia went upstairs, dropped her pack, helmet and keys on the bed and stepped out onto the terrace. She could see Christina in the distance, bent low in the field, picking beans. Solon stood beside her, holding a bowl as Christina filled it. Alexia rubbed her palms against her pants. Why am I so worried about what she thinks? It's not like she's going to ground me.

"I'm not a baby," she'd said to her mother. They'd been arguing about what Alexia was wearing. It was a week before Sara died. Just one week.

"I don't want to wear those pants." Alexia slapped her mother's hand and the pants fell to the floor. They both looked at each other. Alexia tucked her hands behind her back, looked away.

"The ones you've got on aren't clean," her mother said.

"I'm not going to take them off."

"Why won't you do this?" she said. "I'm tired. Don't you understand?"

"I'll wear what I want," Alexia said and stormed out of her room, grabbed her pack and went to school without saying good-bye.

She'd hit her mother with her own hands. How could she? Her mother was sick. Alexia couldn't concentrate all day and when the last bell rang, she ran home as fast as she could. She snuck into her mother's room and stood at the door, holding her breath, listening. She pushed the old chair closer to the bed, plopped herself on top of her hands and watched her mother's face, logging each tiny detail: the freckles on her nose, the pale pink of her lips, the narrow face. She'd practised what she would say. *I'm sorry, Mommy. I'm a brat. I didn't mean to.*

Her mother moaned and Alexia stroked her forehead. Her mother smiled. "You're so independent. It's a good thing." When Sara touched Alexia's cheek, her hand felt cold. It didn't matter. She wanted her mother's hand to stay there forever. It fell away. Alexia held her mother's hand close to her cheek. Sara was asleep again. Over and over, Alexia pictured her mother's face. What shade of grey were her eyes? Get it right. She started it as a game to help make the time go faster until her mother woke up.

Alexia stayed with her until her father came home. Nicolai made dinner, fed Alexia, cleaned up, and put her to bed. She heard them talking later, then Nicolai humming. Alexia had fallen asleep to that sound, still trying to figure out the right word to describe the colour of her mother's eyes.

"*Thia,*" Alexia called out. Christina would like that, but so did she, the feel of the soft syllables in her mouth.

"I make supper soon," Christina called back without looking up.

What's she thinking? There was only one way out. "We should talk," she said, hating to say this out loud.

"After. We come in soon." Christina stayed bent, her back to Alexia. Her apron seemed to be cinched too tight, little bits of pudginess spilled over the bow.

Alexia stepped back into the room, threw herself on the bed. Stop worrying, she told herself. It doesn't help. She sat up against a pillow and waited for the scrape of the front door, their voices in the kitchen. Christina knew. She'd probably told Solon. He was so proud of her when she started to speak Greek, put basic sentences together, his morning lessons finally paying off. She shook her head. What would he think of her now?

Alexia punched at the numbers on her cell phone as if playing a video game. She heard his voice. Surprised, she dropped the phone and lost the connection. She picked up the phone and redialled.

"Hey, kiddo. Don't hang up on me again."

"Dan?"

"Who else have you been calling?"

"I don't usually have any reception here. Um, I'm waiting for my aunt," Alexia said. "I need to resolve something."

"You don't sound too happy about it."

"I pissed her off."

"Hard to imagine." He laughed, but it sounded forced.

She had probably interrupted him in the middle of reviewing a file. She could picture the concentration on his face as he leaned into his computer screen for some kind of direction. He's probably anxious to get back to whatever he's doing. Get off the phone, she told herself. "How's everything?"

"Not the same."

Alexia heard the scratch of wood on wood at the front door downstairs. Over the rush of water in the kitchen sink, their voices rose, quieter than usual. "They're back. I should go face the music."

He cleared his throat. "You want to talk?"

"I have to deal with it." She got off the bed. She wished he could help. But no one really could.

"You don't have to do everything on your own."

"It's the only way I know." She paced.

"Cheer up. This may mean I'll get you back here faster."

"And how will that help?"

"It'd make me happy."

"I better go," Alexia said, shaking her head.

In the kitchen, Christina stood hunched over the sink, washing beans. She leaned to one side as if she needed support. Solon sat in his spot at the table, reading the paper, his glasses part way down his nose.

"Can I help, *Thia*?"

"I fine."

"Is your back okay?"

"It okay."

"I'm happy to help."

"No."

Alexia stood in the doorway. Now what? she wondered, staring at her bare feet.

Solon put down his paper. "What go wrong with you two?"

"You know," Alexia said.

"No."

"She didn't tell you I had lunch with Theodora today?"

"Who?" Solon asked. "Christina, what goes on?"

Christina rubbed her hands on her apron and turned. There was a dark puffiness under her eyes.

"You didn't tell him."

Christina shook her head. "This between us."

"Why you look for troubles?" Solon said.

"I'm not," Alexia said.

"Christina, did you tell her?"

Again Christina shook her head.

"Tell me what?" Alexia said.

"Why bring problems on our head?" Solon said. "We keep things separate. It works better. No one is bothered."

"I'm the only one who has to decide what to do. Not you. And why do you care anyway? This has nothing to do with you. She's my sister."

"You lie to me," Christina said finally. "You see her and no tell me. Not right."

"You didn't want me to see her," Alexia said. "Don't you remember?"

"I did not say this. I said we think about this together. Do you remember? We only want your happiness."

"And meeting Theodora won't make me happy?" Alexia said. "Why?"

Christina turned and leaned into the counter. She muttered, but Alexia didn't catch what Christina said.

"I can't talk to you if you won't be honest with me. You're hiding something. What is it?" Alexia said, shaking her head. "You're exactly like my father. He never trusted me either." They want to keep their dirty little secrets to themselves, lord them over me. Tell me when I don't expect it, and watch me squirm. Then I'll be left holding the bag, dealing with one more bloody surprise. I was an idiot to let my guard down.

Alexia stalked out of the kitchen and flung open the front door. It jammed against the floor. She pulled it hard. Nothing. She yanked at it with both hands, heaving it up slightly. The door finally opened. She walked out of the yard and started up the street with no idea of where she was going. She just had to get away from the secrets, the lies, the betrayals. Before she knew it, she'd broken into a run. She told herself to slow down. Instead, she sped up. She heard the knock in her ears and ran faster.

When she couldn't catch her breath, she jogged, eventually slowing down to a walk. She felt like her legs were about to give way beneath her. She bent over and clutched her knees, gulping air. Her sides ached. When she finally stood up, she walked back and forth, massaging the spot just below her ribs. She pictured Christina bent in the field, hunched over the sink. Christina's lip-bitten smile after Alexia had blurted Theodora's name to Solon, accusing him of knowing when he didn't. Alexia shook her head. They'd been so good to her. But that didn't give them the right to tell her what to do. And it didn't give them the right to keep things from her either.

He was where he said he'd be. Dimly lit, the small *taverna* reeked of cigarette smoke. A couple sat at the table in the corner, their tongues slithering in and out of each other's mouths. Three women were crowded into the booth closest to the bar. Grinning, he tilted his head towards the three women and raised his glass in a toast, nodded as if inviting himself to their table. Alexia stood at the door. The bartender elbowed Achilles. He turned, slid off his stool, ambled towards her, as deliberate as a runway model.

Achilles ran his hands up and down her arms, then hugged her. Her arms stayed by her side.

"Yes?" The buttons of his shirt bored into her chest.

She pushed herself away. "How about that drink?"

"Anything for you."

She ordered a glass of white wine and the bartender brought her a bottle of *retsina* and a glass and placed both in front of her. Achilles poured. Sipping his beer, he straddled the stool beside her. He stroked her hand and gently pressed his knee against hers. She didn't shift away. She watched the outline of his stomach, the way it moved under his shirt as he breathed, wondered what it would feel like against her. He'd be a distraction. No different than the married lovers she'd been with. He was charming. She had to give him that. And a free spirit. She could stand to be around a bit of that right now.

"You no happy. Yes?"

Alexia laughed. "You could say that."

"Tell me," he said. His black pupils burrowed into hers, until she turned away. "You mad at Achilles. Yes?"

"It's family stuff," she said. "This would not interest you."

"How you know what interests Achilles?"

"Those women back there." Alexia nodded towards their table.

"Women like when men see."

The raw, smoky pine flavour of the wine burned her throat, making her wince. She put the glass down, pushed it away, sat on her hands, feeling the cold through her pants. He rubbed her back. Goose bumps lifted on her arms. She sneezed. It was his cologne. She sneezed again. He grabbed a napkin from the pile on the bar and offered it to her. She turned to him and took the napkin from him.

"My family isn't happy with me right now," she said and faced her glass. She took another sip, and again pushed it away. The bartender refilled it, even though she shook her head and tried to put her hand over the glass.

"Then I be family for you. We work on my promenade by the sea."

"It doesn't look like much has been done for a long time."

"We run out of money," he said. "One day it will be beautiful."

He told her about his vision for Diakofto, how it would be a destination for tourists, even without the train. The town could be so much more.

We could all be so much more, she thought. I'm always pissing someone off, doing things someone doesn't like.

He kissed her. She liked the sweet smell of his mouth and the way his lips covered hers. What was she doing? She didn't need this right now. It wouldn't solve a thing. She pulled away.

"We go to the beach now," he asked. "Or you prefer privacy?" He pointed to the ceiling. "There are rooms upstairs also."

He moved in and tried to kiss her again.

This was crazy. She had to get home. As much as she craved something that would blast apart these damn thoughts, a Greek lover was not what she needed right now. And particularly someone like him. He was a taker and she was too tired to give anything of herself right now. She left a peck on his cheek, felt his stubbles against her lips.

Christina and Solon were pacing in the living room when she walked in. Alexia peered down at her watch. It was after ten. "I'm sorry I'm so late." And I'm sorry I hurt you, she thought. My father asked me to do a job. I've met Theodora. I have to follow through and decide what I'm going to do now. I don't have a choice.

"We talk when you go out. Solon and me think it is you to decide what you do." Christina held Solon's forearm. "No?"

Solon shrugged. "I do not want to bother her or her family." He didn't look at Alexia. "You have to think of her, too. What is best for her."

"But why would it be a bother?" Alexia asked. "Aren't we all family?"

"You hungry, no?" Christina said. "Eat." She opened her arms to direct her towards the kitchen.

"Yes, we family," Solon said. "But everyone has his own life. We live this way, each to his own side. Do you understand? This is how we do things."

"When I was little," Alexia said, "I wanted to meet you all more than anything in the world. You were my family. Why would it be any different for her?"

"She might not want to know about us," Christina said.

"Why not?"

"If she does not know we are here, it could be like a shock to her."

"But then we'd get to know each other and in time..."

"In time," Christina said. "We say this, no? Things will change, be better in time. But life is not so simple. There are many things you do not understand."

And I never will if you don't tell me, Alexia thought.

Solon pointed to the stairs. "I go to bed now," he said. "I am too tired for this." He shuffled up the stairs.

"Come eat," Christina said.

She'd find out what they were hiding and why and once she knew, she'd decide what to do about Theodora. Someone had to put a stop to these stupid secrets. Alexia followed Christina into the kitchen. "Just a small plate, please, *Thia*," Alexia said.

1986

Nicolai lurched out onto the freeway, his foot hard on the gas pedal. The tires kicked up gravel. A horn boomed. He glared into his rear-view mirror and saw the front grille of a semi bearing down on him. He hunched his shoulders and tightened his hands on the steering wheel.

The semi barrelled past, cut back in front of Nicolai's car, and hit the brakes. Nicolai pumped his, punching the horn. The truck driver sped off.

"Asshole," Nicolai yelled. He thought about chasing the driver, doing the same goddamn thing to him. Instead, he slowed down. You're one to talk. You screw up everything you touch. Who's the asshole?

He thought about Alexia, the day they moved out of their house. When she asked him what's next, why didn't he say, "I don't know, sweetie, we'll work it out, together."

He should have stayed in Vancouver, with her. Here he was homeless, his clothes all over the back seat and nowhere to go. Nicolai drove into Aigio and down the main street. The bakeries were busy. Women stood inside, talking. He slowed down and thought about getting a dozen chocolate éclairs for his mother. When he was a kid and she got mad at him for not finishing his chores, he'd spend the last of the money he saved from his part-time job on two éclairs for her. After that, she'd forgive him anything. But he wasn't a kid anymore.

There was nothing for him in Aigio. He turned around and drove back to Diakofto. He needed time to think. What would he do next? He passed his favourite café, but when he saw some of the men he'd gotten to know in the last few weeks sitting outside, smoking and gossiping, he knew he didn't want to stop.

At the next corner, a man flagged him down. Nicolai slammed on his brakes. The seat belt tightened, cinching him against the back of the seat.

Achilles jumped into the car.

Before Achilles could close the door, Nicolai drove on.

"What's wrong with you?"

"You want a ride or not?"

"I'm headed home. I don't know why I go to that *taverna*. Those farmers don't have a clue about what I'm trying to do for this town. They are not like you. You are a man of the world, someone who understands what the boardwalk development could bring." Achilles slapped him on the shoulder, turned on the radio.

Nicolai took the next left. Achilles said he had a cousin in Athens who had committed to partnering with him on the development.

Nicolai turned up the radio.

Achilles raised his voice. "He knows what an opportunity looks like."

Nicolai turned the volume up again.

Achilles clicked the radio off. "What's with you?"

He lurched to a stop in front of Achilles's house.

Nicolai stared into his side mirror at the narrow, deserted road behind him. Achilles turned to face him.

"Why are your clothes in the back seat?"

"I've got to get going."

Achilles gripped Nicolai's shoulder. "Did the old man kick you out?"

"It wasn't exactly the best place for me."

Achilles got out of the car, closed the door and leaned in the window. "So now what?"

"I'll think of something."

"If I didn't live with my parents, you could stay with me," Achilles said. "But I don't think they'd approve. You know how people talk."

"I said, I'll think of something."

"You will." Achilles tapped the roof of the car. He slipped into the house without glancing back.

Nicolai drove to the stretch of beach where he used to meet Dimitria. He checked his watch. She wasn't there, though she usually was at this time of the morning. A woman and her two children tossed a ball around. He parked the car and watched them. Thank God he hadn't brought Alexia to Greece. She didn't need to see his father's rage, all this family drama. At least he'd saved her that much. She was probably having dinner with Mavis and Stuart right now, her homework done, maybe getting ready to watch TV.

He checked his rear-view mirror and his side mirrors. Dimitria had always been here before. He could talk to her. She'd encouraged him to do more of it. He couldn't. And now that he needed someone to talk to, he'd pissed her off. She might never speak to him again. He wasn't sure why he'd done it, except that day in Kalavryta she'd become like the old woman in the museum, like all the rest of the small-minded villagers. He didn't want to hear any of their gossip. There are some things that people should keep to themselves. It made life easier for everybody. She was supposed to be a friend. She said she didn't like secrets either, she just wanted to help. Maybe. He checked his mirrors again.

The woman and her children were walking back towards their car. If only he could find Dimitria. She'd help him sort out what to do next.

He drove to the bakery and picked up a sandwich and some water. He returned to that spot on the beach and ate, then walked up and down the beach. He waited in his car, listening to music and dozing off. His head drooped and yanked him awake. The sun made the car into an oven, leaving the sky hazy. He rubbed his eyes. This was ridiculous. She wasn't going to show. He turned the key in the ignition and drove back to Aigio.

He found a motel on the beach that rented rooms by the week. It had a double bed that sagged in the middle with an ugly floral bedspread, a kitchen with a hot plate, a bar fridge and a spartan bathroom. He didn't need much. There was a postcard view of the ocean out the stamp-sized window. This would be home for now. The room smelled of disinfectant, but at least it was his. He wouldn't have to wait for his father to leave the house before he got up in the morning or look at his mother and think about what she'd done.

He got up each day with a plan to go out and explore, get some exercise and call Alexia. Instead, he went to the café a few blocks away, bought a coffee and read the four newspapers he picked up at the stand across the street. This took most of the morning. Lunch and a long walk through the shops ate up the rest of the day. When he finally connected with Alexia days later she asked him how his work was going.

"It's not easy right now." Sitting at the kitchen table in the motel room, he tugged at the cord and wondered how far it might stretch. He leaned his elbow on the table, holding the phone. Her voice sounded so close, it was as if she was just outside the door.

"Things get better," she said. "You told me that."

"How is school?" He jerked at the cord harder than he intended.

She didn't say anything. Had he pulled the thing out of the wall? "Are you still there, *paidi mou*?"

She cleared her throat. "You must be working too hard, Daddy. It's summer now. I'm going to camp for ten days. Auntie Mavis signed me up. You won't be able to call me."

"Okay." She wasn't close at all, he thought. She was far away and had already started with things, left him behind. That was what he'd wanted. Wasn't it?

"Um, you're busy anyway, right? I mean, I don't have to go. I could stay home. We could talk on the phone. Or maybe you're almost done. When are you coming home?"

Even now, after all he'd done to her, she was worried about him. "The camp sounds like fun. Go. Don't worry about anything. How about if I talk to Mavis now?"

"Okay, see you soon, Daddy."

She was so eager to please him.

He heard the knock of the phone being put down, the muffled voices. She hadn't heard him say it, but the word slipped out anyway. "Maybe."

Mavis reassured him that Alexia had brought home an excellent report card and was excited about the camp. They'd picked it out together. "She misses you."

"I'm still sorting through stuff."

"She never complains." There it was. Mavis's friendly and accepting tone, as if it was perfectly natural for a father to abandon his little girl. Goddamn you, Mavis. Get mad at me. Tell me I'm a shit. You know it and I know it. Let's not pretend. Next time, I'll call Stuart. He'd tell me the truth. I'm a shit.

"I'm so glad you're not alone with all this," Mavis said. "Being with family helps."

"It's supposed to."

He told Mavis he'd call again, gave her his number if she needed to reach him.

After she had hung up, he kept the phone against his ear, listening to the hum. It became a nagging beep and then, a recorded message ordered him to hang up. He smacked his temple with the phone and punched the wall. He was no better than his father. He shook his head. How could he be like him? He wasn't. He rubbed his hand. His knuckles were scraped and dotted with tiny pinpricks of blood where skin had torn away.

He hung up the phone, dropped onto the bed, curled up against the pillow and wrapped himself in the bedspread. *Sara.*

She gave him an exasperated look. She was trying to explain, but he refused to see her point. "You're not being rational," he said. "Stop being so emotional."

"I feel it. Why don't you?" She turned away as if she'd heard enough. "I can't talk to you."

"I'll do better," he said and woke up. Against his cheek, his pillow was wet. The room was dark, and the light through his window was fading. "Don't know if I know how to do any better."

Nicolai wiped his face against the bedspread, got up and brushed his teeth. The mint flavour masked the foul taste in his mouth. He pressed the wrinkles out of his shirt and pants with a damp face cloth, then wiped his armpits with the same cloth. He threw it into the sink and left his room. He had to get out of here, go for a walk, find a quiet café. Get a drink. Eat. Get away.

He peered through the front window of the candle-lit café. Two men sat at a table by the cash register and smoked. One was reading the paper and the other was picking at his plate between drags on his cigarette. A bell clanged as Nicolai entered. The man in a waiter's uniform jumped up, leaving his cigarette in the ashtray. He welcomed Nicolai with a wide-toothed grin, slipped one arm into Nicolai's and swept his hand across the room. "The best seat in the house for you, my friend. You have your pick."

Nicolai chose a table at the back near the kitchen.

"Good choice, my friend. Close to the kitchen. Please come with me and you can choose what you want yourself."

The other man butted his cigarette, put on a hair net and followed.

In the kitchen, the men raised one lid, then another. Nicolai leaned in to smell each pot. Garlic, rosemary, oregano. The place smelled like his mother's kitchen. Why wouldn't they just let him order from a lousy menu?

They opened the oven, lifted the tin foil from the pans of *moussaka* and *pasticcio*. Nicolai pointed at the *pasticcio*. "Come see the rest," the cook said.

"I can see." Soup spilled down the sides of one of the large pots on the stove, the walls were stained with red and brown spots, and the floor felt slippery under his feet. His mother's kitchen was clean all the time. She'd insisted on it. "We're not pigs," his mother would say whenever he tracked dirt into the kitchen. Stop thinking about her, Nicolai told himself. It doesn't solve a thing. Stop thinking. Period.

Nicolai returned to his table and found a full jug of white wine. A glass had been poured for him. The waiter grinned.

He ate half the *pasticcio* and sat back to sip the wine. Despite the many business trips he'd taken for clients, he'd never gotten used to eating alone. "Take a book," Sara had said, but he'd forget her advice until he was sitting at a table, the only one in the place sitting alone.

The bell clanged over the door. Dimitria and Achilles walked in. Damn it. I don't need any company tonight, he thought. There had to be a back door, another way out of this place. Maybe through the kitchen. He stood, then thought better of it and sat down. Maybe they'd leave. Achilles liked places that were fancy, had more noise and people he could charm.

Achilles pulled the chair out for Dimitria and when she sat down, he kissed the back of her neck. She slouched forward, pointed to the chair across from her.

Great! A perfect view. He tapped his fingers against his wine glass. He heard the faint sound and stopped. He held the glass with both hands.

Achilles stroked Dimitria's cheek, then pulled in closer and kissed her. She turned her head. His lips met her cheek.

Nicolai bit at the skin around his thumb.

Dimitria turned towards the window.

"What's wrong?" Achilles said. "We're alone."

"You know I don't like to do this in front of other people," she said.

Achilles looked around the café. "But there is no one here."

Thank God, he was sitting close to the kitchen. He could see the entire place, but no one could see him, hidden behind a jut in the wall.

As though he'd been summoned, the waiter stood at their table. "Would you like to see what we have tonight, my friend?"

Nicolai threw some money on the table, started to get up.

"Tonight, you choose for us," Achilles said.

Nicolai sat down, took a sip of wine. He could outwait them.

Achilles stroked Dimitria's face, then her hand. She smiled without looking at him and picked up her glass, forcing his hand to drop. Nicolai caught most of the conversation. It wasn't anything he hadn't heard before. Achilles talked about the boardwalk. Wasn't she tired of all that? he wondered. Dimitria sipped wine, didn't say much. When their salad, *moussaka* and fish came, she thanked the waiter. "More wine," Achilles said. "My lady needs more."

She shook her head. "I'm fine."

Achilles held his hand up when the waiter asked whether he should bring anything else. "We're very good," he said.

Dimitria's smile was timid, but it was different than the ones she gave Nicolai. When she smiled at him, her eyes came alive, her face softened, relaxed. There was no shyness.

"And where is the money going to come from?" she asked.

"These are just details." Achilles shrugged. "The dream makes things happen."

"To start with, yes, but then you need money." She wiped her mouth with the napkin, then the corner of her cheek where Achilles left a peck.

"You worry too much." He brought her hand to his mouth and kissed it.

"I have some money I can lend you, but it is not enough."

"A start is all I need, my love, and of course, someone who believes in me."

Nicolai pushed his chair back. It squealed against the floor. He waited for Achilles to shout hello, come over and slap him on the back.

They continued talking as if they hadn't noticed.

In the kitchen, the cook told him the back door had been jammed shut years ago.

He wasn't going to stick around until Achilles and Dimitria left. He walked past them, staring straight ahead. They wouldn't notice. Lovers only had eyes for each another.

"And where did you come from?" Achilles asked as Nicolai passed their table.

Dimitria dropped Achilles's hand, picked up her napkin. She folded it into an impossibly small square and put it back on her lap. She didn't look at him.

"What a surprise," Nicolai said.

"For us, too," Dimitria said. As she stood up, her napkin fell. She bent to pick it up.

"My love. What is the matter?" Achilles said. "Join us, Nicolai. Please."

"Yes, please do," Dimitria said. Her olive skin turned pink, her lips pressed shut.

"I don't want to impose."

"We have plenty of time." Achilles hugged Dimitria. "Don't we, my love?"

She shrugged out of Achilles's embrace and took Nicolai's hand. "Please stay."

Nicolai thought: she seems to be pleading. "Okay," he said. She smiled then, just like the time he told her she had a ton of talent.

They pulled up a chair for him. Sitting between them meant that while he listened or talked to Achilles, he had his back to Dimitria.

Achilles ordered more wine. He picked at the *moussaka,* pushing bits of eggplant and potatoes into a small mound as if building a sand castle. He didn't take a bite of any of it. "We've just been talking about business."

"Yes," Dimitria said. "That's all."

Her perfume lingered. He couldn't tell what it was, but it was the same one she'd worn the last time he'd seen her. He adjusted his chair to face her. Their legs touched. He moved his away. Or had she moved hers first? He looked into her eyes and wondered why he hadn't noticed the copper speck in her pupils before tonight. Well, why would he? He was a married man. Yes, she was dead, but Sara would always be his wife.

"What happened to your hand?" Dimitria said.

Nicolai looked down at his knuckle. "A little accident. It's nothing." He adjusted his chair, turned to face Achilles.

"...people walking, eating, partying on our waterfront," Achilles was saying.

"It could be good." Nicolai nodded.

When they stepped out of the café, the rain was coming down like a steady stream of pebbles. Achilles ran to his moped, grabbed the plastic sheet he had secured on the back and covered the seat. Nicolai and Dimitria waited under the large awning in front of the café, watching Achilles. I should say something to her, Nicolai thought. But what? I disappoint all the women in my life.

"I can give you a ride to Diakofto if you want," Nicolai said, finally. "Achilles could pick up the moped tomorrow."

"You know him," she said. "He's stubborn."

Achilles ran back. He flicked water from his hair and shirt, spraying Nicolai and Dimitria. "Maybe we can wait it out," Achilles said. The plastic sheet he'd placed on his moped flipped up in the wind and blew across the parking lot. They watched it tear in two. The bits were caught in the gust and flew in different directions. No one gave chase.

"I could give you a ride," Nicolai said over the growling rain.

"We had some plans for tonight, didn't we, my love?" Achilles put his arm around Dimitria's waist. Her back stiffened.

"If you're going home anyway," Dimitria said, "I think it would be good."

"I live here now."

"What?" She turned.

Nicolai shrugged.

"His father threw him out."

She put her hand on Nicolai's shoulder. Lightning exploded and lit her face. There it was again. The copper flicker in her eyes.

In the car, Achilles sat in the back and Dimitria in the front. The rain turned to hail. Nicolai's hands gripped the steering wheel. Achilles poked his head between the two front seats. He commented about the unpredictable weather. His damp hair and clothes smelled of sour cologne. Nicolai kept his eyes on the asphalt, lit up with hailstones.

When they finally entered Diakofto, Achilles sat back. In the rear-view mirror, Nicolai caught a glimpse of Achilles crossing himself. "You might as well drop me off."

"Good driving," Dimitria said.

He nodded, but didn't look at her.

"Make sure you take my love home safely," Achilles said. He held Nicolai's shoulder firmly, then touched Dimitria's face. "This wasn't exactly what we had planned."

The rain stopped and she suggested they go to the beach. "It's still early."

The light at the front door of her house was on when he drove by. The living room was dark except for the blue light of a television. "Your mother is up."

"Probably."

"Won't she wonder where you are?"

"I'm a big girl."

They drove in silence. Nicolai parked at the end of the beach where they used to meet. He turned off the ignition. He didn't know what to say to her. Should he apologize for the other day? Tell her what happened with his father? Where would he start?

She turned to face him. She took his damaged hand in hers, kissed each knuckle.

He met her eyes. She smiled. He cupped her face in his hands and kissed her. When he pulled away, her eyes were closed, her lips still puckered as if she hadn't realized he was no longer there.

"I'm sorry," he said. "I'm not ready for anything." He turned away. "I'm not sure I'll ever be. I don't even know what's going on with me. I'm all over the place, lonely, stupid, can't cope. I don't want to drag you into anything. I don't know."

She took his hands in hers. "It will pass."

"I'm not so sure."

She gently touched his face and he leaned towards her hand. It felt so long since he'd been caressed. He kissed her temple, then her hands and neck, squeezed her breast. She moaned and he kissed her.

"Ouch." She pulled away and held her breast.

"I'm so sorry. I don't know what I'm doing."

"We have to get used to each other," she said, guiding his hand back.

"No." He turned away. "I'm a mess. I don't know what I want or what I'm going to do. I'm married. I'm bad news."

She held him. He tried to pull away, but eventually he put his arms around her waist and lay his head against her chest, listened to her heartbeat. He wanted to fall asleep to this steady sound. They held onto each other until she whispered his name.

"I should get back," she said.

"I'm sorry to make such a mess of things," he said.

She kissed him. "There will be another time," she said.

"But there can't be."

"We need each other, Nicolai," she said. "You can see this, can't you? Don't you remember when we were children? How we were together all the time? Playing, talking. We couldn't do anything about it then. Now it's different. We can do what we want."

"What about Achilles?" he asked.

She kissed him.

He pulled away. "We're cousins. I haven't resolved anything. I'm..."

Her mouth covered his.

1986

The lights skimmed over his eyelids and woke him. He heard the car pass. It was dark again. Nicolai curled up closer, lay his head on her chest, as he had before. Something hard prodded at his back and he shifted away from it, closer to her. "I've missed you," he whispered. Her breathing remained steady. He blinked the sleep out of his eyes. Her wrinkled skirt had crawled up as she slept and exposed her sunbaked thighs. He squeezed his eyes closed and held his breath. They were in his rental car and pinched together into the passenger seat. He slid into the driver's seat and sat staring out the windshield. What had he done?

Dimitria moaned and stretched out her arms. Her hands struck the inside of the car's roof. She smiled as if she had just realized where she was. She turned towards him and stroked his arm.

He started the car. "We have to go." He stomped on the gas pedal. Dimitria lurched upright, threw her hands against the dash. He stared at the road, though he could feel her glare. She buttoned her blouse, smoothed her skirt, ran her fingers through her hair. Her seat belt clicked.

Nicolai stopped the car a block from her house and left it running. She reached over and stroked his cheek. He turned away.

"Don't do this," she said.

He rubbed his nose. Her smell hung on his fingers. He wiped his hands on his pants. "I shouldn't have done..."

"Turn it off. Please."

He leaned across to open her door. His arm grazed her breasts and he apologized, nodded for her to leave. "I have to go," he said. "It's not your fault. I just can't."

"Why act this way?" she asked.

He drummed the steering wheel and stared straight ahead. She got out and slammed the door. That's good, he thought. Be mad at me. I deserve it.

He pulled away. Half a block down the road, he slowed down at the yield sign and glanced into the rear-view mirror. The squall of dust he'd kicked up hadn't yet settled, but he could see her standing alone as if unsure which way to turn.

Nicolai weaved in and out of his lane, jerking through the gears and gunning the engine. He heard the muffled sound of a horn somewhere behind him. So what? We've all got problems. Get over it. The road took a long, steady bend. What if he just let go? He relaxed his hold on the steering wheel. Guardrails flashed by, a blur. He pressed his foot down. He'd fly, land somewhere, anywhere. He'd stop hurting everyone. *Alexia. Mamma. Dimitria.* He shut his eyes, tightened his grip. His hands ached. Let go. Go on.

He took his foot off the pedal, and the car slowed down. He opened his eyes. The barrier rushed to meet him. He yanked the steering wheel left, and moved smoothly through the curve.

He banged the steering wheel. *Coward.*

Driving past Aigio to Patras, he followed the road that led to the docks. It didn't matter where the next ferry was going. He'd get on and with any luck end up in a small Italian town where no one knew him. Forklifts scraped across the concrete, picking up cargo and hauling it onto ships. A sign at the gate to the terminal read, *Closed. Open at 7 a.m.*

He could wait. It was only a few hours. He'd sleep in his car. There was nothing special he'd left behind in Aigio. He had his wallet and passport. What else did he need?

A uniformed guard approached the car, tapped at the window with a baton.

Nicolai shrugged as if he didn't understand.

The man gestured for Nicolai to roll down his window.

"You cannot stay here," the man said.

"I have nowhere else to go."

Raising his baton, the man pointed to a turn-around exit lane. "Come back in the morning. We open soon enough."

Nicolai stared at the man. The man waited. His eyes were dark and hard. He reminded Nicolai of his father.

He turned the car around and drove down the road. Five hours until the first ferry sailed. Time enough. He'd go back to Aigio, take a shower, pack up.

A loud and intermittent ring nagged him awake. Maybe it would go away if he lay still, ignored it. The light annoyed him. Why had he left it on? He'd fallen asleep as soon as he'd put his head down, but then woke every hour or so to look at his watch. The last time he checked, it was a couple of minutes after four. He pulled the covers over his head. He had another hour or so before he had to get up.

The ringing persisted. He reached out and slapped at what he thought was his alarm. The ringing stopped for a few seconds, then started up again.

He shoved off the bedspread and crawled over to the kitchen for the telephone. The alarm clock fell to the floor behind him. Finally he picked up the phone. "Yes?"

"Daddy, is that you?"

Nicolai sat, his back against the cupboard and rubbed at his eyes, grinding the small crusty specks in the corners.

"Were you sleeping? What time is it over there?"

"I don't know." He reached down for the clock. Shit. The ferry had left more than an hour ago.

"What did you say, Daddy?"

"Nothing, *paidi mou*."

"Auntie Mavis let me stay up so I could call you."

He propped himself on one elbow and stacked two pillows behind him, lay his head against his hand.

"...did this big hike in Pemberton, and had to spend the night all by myself." She took a deep breath. He knew she was waiting for him to say something. Wake up, he told himself. This is your daughter, for God's sake.

"I wasn't really by myself," she said, finally. "I could always see a tent a few feet away on both sides of me. But it was really cool and kind of spooky, too."

"And I guess you made lots of friends," Nicolai said. He scratched his chin.

"They came from all over," she said. "But we promised we'd write and come back next year. I mean, if that's okay with you."

"That's good."

"You're working too hard, Daddy. Right?'

"I guess so," he said. "Can I call you another time?"

"I just wanted to tell you about my hike," she said. Her voice was quieter, distant. "I didn't want you to worry."

"Glad you did." Really? He wasn't acting like it. And no wonder. She just reminded him of how badly he'd betrayed her and made a mess of everything else.

At the ferry terminal, he watched the ships come and go, had lunch and drove back to his motel. "The ferry I wanted was full," Nicolai said when the clerk asked. He checked in for a single night and unpacked the things he'd packed that morning. He left early the next day and returned in the afternoon. The same guy greeted him. "It is hard to leave us."

"I know which room it is," Nicolai said, ignoring the clerk's ready smile.

After three or four days of hanging out at the docks, scanning the ferry schedule, he realized there was no place he wanted to go. He took out an open-ended lease on the room. The clerk flashed a condescending grin, making Nicolai feel like a child again. Mocked and tolerated, but only just.

Late one morning, he drove into the mountains. As the ground-hugging fog began to dissipate, narrow fingers of light poked through the clouds. The road ahead steamed as it dried in the heat. He noticed a lookout on the left. "Let's stop up there and take a look," he said, and turned to find Dimitria wasn't sitting beside him. These drives were the kinds of things he'd done with her. She would touch his arm, then point to something in the distance. "Look at that shade of red on the mountain. The sun is hitting it perfectly. I wish I could capture these things."

He parked and got out of the car. Villages peeked from folds of the forest below. "How about we find our way down and have lunch?" he said. He cupped his hand at his forehead to shield his eyes from the sun. No reply.

Nicolai stared down at the valley. He saw her as clearly as if she were standing there in front of him. Her blouse was open, the crease of her breasts teasing. He ran his fingers through his hair. He definitely needed to find new places to go.

"I heard you have the best food," he said to the man who greeted him as he walked into the café. The man smiled, brought Nicolai the speciality of the house. This became his way of greeting all café owners he met. There was nothing unique about any of these places. But if his comments made them feel good, why not?

He drove to Kalavryta on a hot day because he thought it would be cooler in the mountains. On one side of the road, rocks hung above him and on the other, cliffs dropped away. It took all his focus to drive. Still, in the few short straight stretches, he remembered the conversation he'd had with Dimitria when they'd been here.

"Don't you wonder how all of this was created, what our grandfathers and great-grandfathers had to do to settle here?" she said.

"Not really." Why would he?

"These hills were the beginning of our independence in 1821. They protected so many people before the Germans came." She talked about the history of the monastery and guided him around Kalavryta, her arm in his.

He felt her hand on his forearm. He swiped at it. Her touch would not be wiped away. How could he blame his parents for what they'd done? He was no better. How the hell had he ended up with his cousin? And worse still, he couldn't get her out of his mind. It was too soon for someone else. He knew that. He should go home, get on with taking care of Alexia. Except, right now he wasn't sure he could ever go back. Who would he be when he got back? I'm just another idiot who let his wife down, he thought. Alexia knows it, too. She might not be able to admit it to herself yet, but she knows. One day, that's all I'll see in her eyes. Disappointment.

He lay in bed, wondering where he'd go today. He could go back to Patras or further north for a few days. He'd already done these things so many times.

In the kitchen, he glanced at the map spread open on the kitchen table. He flicked the coffee machine on, paced up and down in the small kitchen and went back into the bedroom to get dressed. He turned off the coffee machine before it was done and slammed the door behind him.

He drove to the beach in Diakofto and parked.

Her chair and easel weren't lodged in the rock. He looked for her down the beach. There was no one. He'd wait. He had nothing better to do, anyway. If she didn't come today, maybe he'd come back tomorrow. We'll see, he told himself. He might find other things to do tomorrow and he wouldn't have to come back here. He might call Stuart. Talking to him might help, but while they were friends, he wasn't sure he could tell him all of this. Not over the phone, anyway. Stuart would think he'd gone crazy. And maybe he had.

A light tap startled him. He looked around. She stood outside the passenger door. He leaned over, opened it. "I was just looking at the view."

"You came back," she said.

"I need us to be friends," he said.

She got in the car, held the door ajar with her foot. "I broke up with Achilles."

He stared at her. "Did you tell him?"

She pushed the door back and forth with her foot, didn't look at him. "He didn't want to know the reasons. He turned it around and made it his idea."

"What we have can't be anything more than friendship."

"I know," she said.

"Let's get a drink," he said.

She closed the door.

The restaurant overlooking the beach was noisy. They ate and didn't say much. The racket was a distraction. As he glanced across the crowded room, he felt Dimitria's hand on his. He looked at her, saw the question in her eyes.

"Sorry," he said. "I like watching people."

She nodded. Her smile reassured him, made him feel comfortable.

"Have you spoken with your daughter?" Dimitria asked.

"Briefly," he said. "She just got back from a hike. She's off to a summer camp next."

"You must miss her."

"She's having a great time. She makes friends easily. She slept out in a tent by herself. She said it was cool." He used the English word because he couldn't think of how to say it in Greek.

"Yes, it would be cold."

Nicolai laughed. "Cool means fun, good."

"Yes, of course." Her cheeks turned rosy pink. She smiled, bowing her head as if she didn't want him to notice.

But how couldn't he notice? She had a beautiful smile. "We're just about done here," he said.

She folded her napkin and put it on the table.

"Would you like to see where I live?" he asked. "I think I have a bottle of wine."

She nodded. "If it's okay."

He knew it wasn't a good idea. But he didn't want to take her home just yet, go to that awful room by himself. He just needed a little company.

As she walked past him into his room, her arm grazed his chest. He took in the curve of her neck, the outline of her spine under her blouse, the sway of her hips. He kicked the door shut. Moving in close, he put his arms around her. She leaned into him. He breathed in her perfume and smiled for the first time in days, since the last time they'd been together. She turned to face him, her lips parted.

"I'm not sure I can ever be what you need," he whispered into her hair.

She pulled away and he tugged her close. He stroked her back, clipped off her bra and pushed her towards the bed.

She cuddled into him, straddled one leg over his. She traced his nipples, then the hair on his chest with her fingers. Her head lay on his shoulder, pinning him down. "You wanted this. You came back to me after all these years away," she said. "Yes?"

"I came back because I couldn't cope after my wife died." He put his hand over hers. His shoulder felt numb. "I need a friend more than anything else."

"I want this, too."

He held her close. Still, it didn't feel right. Her touch bothered him somehow. Like it was too much, more than he could ever repay. She was gentle, beautiful, and she wanted him.

He pulled Dimitria on top of him, and buried his head in her long hair. Shifting, she took him inside.

Nicolai woke to a banging at the door. He sat up quickly, knocking Dimitria away. Half awake, she whispered, "What's wrong?" He put his finger to his mouth.

"It's Christina. Let me in."

He heard the slap of her hands against the door and didn't move. Dimitria pulled the covers up over her breasts. Her head fell back against the headboard. He shook his head, whispered to her to be quiet. She sat still.

The noise stopped. Christina must have gone. He threw off the covers, intending to go and check, then stopped.

"Are you in there?" Christina kicked at the door. "Please, Nicky."

Sitting on the edge of the bed, he held his breath.

"I know you're here. Your car is in the parking lot."

Moments passed. He heard Christina pace on the narrow sidewalk in front of his door, stopping every few minutes to jiggle the handle. He bit at his lip and held his breath. Could he outlast her? As a kid, she'd always been good at finding him when they played hide and seek. Once, he'd hidden in a small cupboard in the kitchen. He'd found it by accident. He was sure she hadn't seen it, but she didn't give up. Twenty minutes, half an hour passed. He was ready to come out. His legs and arms were sore. Finally, she flipped open the door. "Got you," she said. She had more patience than all the rest of the family put together.

"You can't hide forever." Christina thrust herself against the door.

"How did she find me?" he whispered to Dimitria.

"It's a small place. Achilles might have talked."

He tiptoed to the window, peeked through a crack in the curtain. "I think she's gone." He turned. "I've got to get you home."

"There's no rush," she said, reaching to pull him back to her.

"We can't keep doing this." He held himself away. "I can't add more craziness to my life right now."

But she was beyond listening. He saw it in her eyes. She was pulling him on top of her, nuzzling his neck, making everything so damn difficult.

They sat in a crowded café, surrounded by men standing at the bar. "Why don't you come back?" Christina asked, her eyes pleading, rather than angry now.

The conversation the men were having at the bar flared in anger, quickly doused by nervous laughter, a slap on the back. Nicolai grasped bits of their talk. "The government is driving us to ruin. We have to starve before they're happy. Why do they keep the prices of our olives so high? We can't compete." They all nodded, clinked their glasses one against the other. Nicolai sat facing the men and the bar, his shoulder pointed towards Christina.

"Why are you doing this?" she asked. "It's not right."

"You know why."

"Mamma is heartbroken." She shook her head.

"I can't do anything." He sipped his coffee slowly.

Christina leaned back in her chair. "She's made you this way."

He turned to face her. She looked so much like their mother. Her eyes drooped slightly as if a weight was pulling at each corner, slanting them.

"What are you talking about?" Nicolai asked.

"I know about Dimitria."

"She has nothing to do with this." He slammed his fist against the table and the men at the bar turned. Christina hunched over, her hands covering her ears. Nicolai shrugged. "This is my sister," he said.

The men nodded as though they understood, then went back to their conversation.

"She's your cousin." She stole glances across the room and kept her voice low. "This is a big shame for us."

"Have you been following me? How do you know what I'm doing?"

"People talk."

"People talk about many things. They are not all true."

"But this is," she said.

She glared at him the way she used to when they were kids, silently commanding him not to argue with their father yet again. "We are the oldest. We have to keep the peace."

"And what our mother did to keep our father wasn't shameful?" Nicolai shot back.

She shook her head.

"He always felt trapped."

"He made choices during the war. Choices he still can't accept."

"I'm so sick and tired of hearing about how the war made him what he is. There were lots of men who suffered in the war. How many turned out like him?"

"Maybe they didn't give as much as he did." She looked at the cup in front of her. She raised it to take a sip of the coffee she hadn't yet touched, then changed her mind. She put her hands around her cup.

"They lost their parents, they saw the massacre, and many starved to death. Then, the civil war. They nearly killed each other off. They all went through the same thing." He flicked his open hands at her as if to rid himself of her. "I know what happened to them."

"No. He did more." Her knuckles were white.

"Like what?"

"We shouldn't be talking about this." She looked beyond him, towards the front window of the café. "It's not good for any of us."

"If you're going to play these games, I don't want to know." He ran his tongue over the roof of his mouth. It felt raw. He must have burned it with the coffee. He took another small sip and swallowed hard, making things worse.

"He became friendly with the Germans." Her voice dropped to a whisper.

"So?"

She dabbed at her eyes with the crumpled napkin and blew her nose.

"What? For Christ's sake. What the hell is it?" He growled the words, his hand clutching at her shoulder.

She jerked away.

He turned his chair, his back now to the men at the bar. He wished he could be part of that group, talking about politics and crop prices rather than watching his sister weep.

"I went to the village, talked to people. He told them he'd fix things and scrounged food for them when he could."

"Great, he was a hero."

"I thought if I knew, things would be easier."

"And is it?" I know he lied about his age, he thought. You're not going to tell me anything I don't already know. Spare yourself. It's not worth it. I know.

"What else could they have done?"

"He lied about his age to get out of being killed. There, I said it. That's what you couldn't get out. Right. Now I've said it. Stop crying."

Christina cleared her throat. "You'll never understand, will you?"

"He made his choices. I can't do anything about that."

"Then do it for me." She placed her hand on his arm. "Solon's family is pushing him not to marry me. If they hear you've been fighting with our father or someone sees you and our cousin, I will lose him," she said, reaching for his hand. "We need to show we are a good family."

"So that's what this is all about." He got up, threw some bills down and left Christina at the table, alone.

Achilles walked into the café as Nicolai was leaving. He spun around, put his arm in Nicolai's. "Where are you going in such a hurry? Let's have a coffee."

"I'm busy."

Christina pushed her chair back, threw the napkin on the table and left.

Achilles watched her departure. "Family trouble?"

Nicolai returned to the same table he'd shared with his sister, ordered himself and Achilles a coffee. Why was Achilles being friendly? He knew what had happened with Dimitria. Punch me out or yell, he thought. Let's get it over with. "So how's it going with the boardwalk?" Nicolai asked.

"Still waiting for people to come through with the money they promised." Achilles waved to the men at the bar and nodded.

"I'll invest." Nicolai shrugged. "It's as safe as anything else."

Achilles turned to face him. "So, first you steal my woman and now you think your money will make things better."

"The boardwalk is more important to you." He pointed his spoon at Achilles. "You know it and I know it. Let's not dick around."

"Sometimes I wish I could have more," Achilles said. "Just once. Just to experience what it's like." He stared straight through Nicolai. The grin gone. Then just as quickly, Achilles tilted back in his chair, stroked his beard. "You'd better be careful. She's not interested in just having a little fun."

"We're friends. We both understand that."

Achilles shook his head, then brought all four legs of his chair to the floor. He extended his hand. "Should we seal our new arrangement? It's a small sacrifice for me to make to guarantee my dream."

Nicolai wasn't sure why, but Dimitria's hopeful smile came to him just then. How was he any different than Achilles?

Nicolai sat at the kitchen table in his room with the phone to his ear. The line rang busy again and he put the phone down. A few seconds later, he picked it up again. Still busy. He wondered if Alexia was talking to one of her friends or if Stuart or Mavis were on the line. He tapped the receiver against his head.

A knock rattled his door. "Yes," he said.

Nothing. He hung up the phone, opened the door. The black shawl over his mother's head made her seem older, smaller.

"What are you doing here?"

"Are you going to let me in?" She pushed the shawl down around her shoulders. She stared at him in that determined way of hers and he stepped back to let her in. Nicolai looked out into the parking lot. His father was sitting in the car, staring straight ahead. The engine was running.

"He brought you?"

"This was important to me."

Nicolai pulled out a chair. She shook her head. He walked to the other side of the table. They stood, the table between them.

"We said some stupid things," his mother said. "It's time for you to come home."

"I can't live under the same roof. Too much has happened."

"We'll forget everything and go on like every other family." Her arms were crossed as if she was prepared to wait until she persuaded him to see things her way. She had to be strong to handle his father, keep their family together.

"I can't."

"You have to think of others more than yourself," she said. "This is important to your sister, too. You know the problem Solon's family has given her."

"You can't change him. Or the decisions the two of you made."

"Your father was right. Your cousin fills your head with stupidity." Her eyes scolded him as if he was a boy again and she was mad at him for not having fed the chickens before he went to school. "You can't see that now. But you will."

"It's not her fault. What you did has nothing to do with Dimitria."

"Do not use that name in front of me." She threw her hands, then her chin at him. "She is to be blamed for all of this."

"It's your fault, yours and Pappa's." He jabbed the air with his finger. His voice cracked. "It's always easier to blame someone else."

"Your father brought me here. He's a good man."

"You've convinced yourself of that. Good for you." He walked over to the door, opened it. "He came because he wants to avoid any more talk, any shame I might bring to him. You know it and I know it. There's nothing else."

He looked over at the car. His father glared at him.

"Why do you do this, Nicky?"

She reached to touch his cheek. He moved away. "It's too late."

She walked through the door. He kicked it closed behind her.

Dimitria lay beside him, her leg and arm against him. "My mother is giving me trouble," she said. She squeezed in closer. "I'm bringing shame. If I don't stop seeing you, she wants me to move out of the house."

He stroked her hair. There were moments when they were together, having sex, when he forgot about his family, all these problems. Even so, he hadn't been able to completely let go, not the way he had with Sara. Dimitria's perfume tickled his throat and he coughed. "Sorry."

"We're adults. I don't know why they don't see this." She kissed his chest. "They're treating us like children. Like the time my father found us sleeping."

"Your father was pissed off," Nicolai said, leaning against the headboard. "He said I had to tell my father what I had done. I didn't. Why would I? I didn't do anything. We were kids playing and we fell asleep."

"Was that all it was?"

"Nothing happened," he said. "I never told my father a thing."

She sat up and faced him. "Your father knew. That's why the two families stopped seeing each other. Why your sisters hate me."

"Come on," he said. "How did he know?"

"They always know," Dimitria said.

He fingered her hair. "They made the mistakes." He pulled her against him. "You could move in here. With me, if you want. There's lots of room."

She shrugged.

She wants to know if I mean it, he thought. I don't know. It will fix the problem we have right now. I can't think past that.

"You could for a little while just until we see what happens."

"Just a little while?"

He covered his eyes with his arm. "I've told you. This isn't an easy time for me."

"You're not the only one." She kissed his arm. He brought his arm down, held her.

15

2010

Alexia and Maria sat across from one another at the kitchen table, talking about Maria's new sweater. The low-cut cashmere hugged Maria's curves. "It's the best store in the village," Maria said. "You'd like it."

Alexia thought about the tailor she used to go to in Vancouver, the suits she had custom made. You're a professional, you need to look the part, she had told herself. She hadn't missed those suits one bit.

Alexia heard what sounded like a book fall in the living room. "Can we help?" she called.

"Don't worry about Christina," Maria said, leaning closer. "She likes to do things her way."

A few minutes later, Christina came into the kitchen, a stack of photo albums in her arms, her face flushed.

Alexia stood up quickly to help.

Christina hugged the albums to her chest and waited while Maria cleared the cups, creamer and sugar bowl, then she dropped them on the table with a sigh.

"I thought you were going to call us to come in there," Alexia said. "Wouldn't that have been easier?" She fingered the velvet cover of one of the albums and caught a whiff of something old.

"In the kitchen we are comfortable. No?"

"You don't like to use the other room, do you?"

"She keeps it for important guests." Maria rolled her eyes, smirked. "We are family. Not so special."

"My heart is in the kitchen," Christina said. "This is where I live."

"The rest of house is a museum," Maria said.

"What do you know? You do not come very much."

"The children, husband," Maria said. "You know."

They'd been speaking to Alexia in Greek for more than a week. She didn't understand everything and often had to reply in English, but she'd learned enough in the six weeks she'd been with them to have a basic conversation. Had it really been six weeks? She'd learned a language. At least, she'd done that.

Christina picked up one of the chairs, placed it beside hers and patted it for Alexia to sit down. Christina's leg was warm against hers. It made her think of her mother, and the Saturday mornings they spent at the kitchen table sitting side by side eating the cookies they'd just baked. "Are you ready for another one?" Sara asked as she touched Alexia's leg.

"*Ella,* Christina. You're almost on top of the poor girl. It's enough," Maria said. "Give her some air to breathe."

Alexia crossed her leg, detaching herself from Christina.

Christina picked up the first photo album. She pointed to the chair across, directing Maria to sit down. She grinned.

Maria tsked. "And she's supposed to be the oldest, the most mature of all of us."

Christina reached across the table and patted Maria's hand. "And the smart one."

Maria shook her head. They laughed like young girls sharing a secret.

"We laugh when we can," Christina said. "We have to because nothing lasts. You see this with the riots in Athens. The money problems. There is always problems."

No kidding, Alexia thought. When her father finally came home from Greece, her life should have been easier. They settled into a brand new condo and she started in a new school. He went back to work and the only thing he said about his trip was, "Everything was okay." She knew he could leave her behind again anytime. Sometimes he picked her up after school, sometimes she walked home. He went to all her concerts, came to parent-teacher interviews, and they had special nights once a week, just the two of them. That first time they had one of those special outings, she stared at her burger, the ketchup she slopped on her fries and she thought she was going to be sick.

"We'll take it home if you're not hungry," he said, then he gulped her fries one after the other, talked about what he was doing with the new account.

She smiled the way he liked her to and waited for that break in his voice. If it came, she knew what would happen next. He was going to tell her he was leaving again, explain it away as another business trip.

That night, she listened for his snoring. When she couldn't hear it from her room, she got up, quietly opened his bedroom door, and watched him while he slept, his body curled away from her. That was when she began to save her allowance. She wanted to be prepared in case he left again.

The day her father discovered her jar of coins he said, "Money is to be enjoyed. You can't take it with you." He towered in front of her, his hands on his hips, waiting for an explanation.

"I might need it." She met his gaze. "That's all."

"For what?"

"I don't know right now," she said. "But one day..."

He laughed that deep belly laugh of his. "I will take care of you. Don't worry so much, *paidi mou*."

Christina cracked an album. A spider scuttled out. She swatted it with the tea towel tucked into the waistband of her apron. She threw the carcass into her cup. "I will put it down the sink later."

Maria scrunched up her face, grabbed the cup and put it in the sink.

"Your father." Christina pointed to a black and white picture of a baby leaning against a stack of pillows. He held a rattle in his fist. His knuckles were dimpled. Below one eye, a single tear. Alexia saw herself. "Like your father since the day you were born," her mother had said when Alexia asked who she looked like. "I wanted another me, got another him. I'm happy with that. Don't get me wrong."

"Beautiful baby, your father. No?"

His face was slightly bony even then.

"He has a small tear under his eye. Do you see?" Maria pointed.

"Even as a baby, he knew life was not going to be easy," Christina said.

"What do you mean, Christina?" Maria asked. "He went to America to live like a king."

"*Ella,* he was the only boy in the family. You know how our father was," Christina said. "You know the things he said. Why are you only a B student? You're not working hard enough. Come home after school, stop fooling around with your friends. Playing is for babies. It was always the same thing, over and over again."

Maria shrugged her shoulders, thrust her chin forward, closing her eyes in that way Alexia had come to see Greeks do when they didn't agree with what was being said. "He did this to all of us, don't you remember?"

"He used the belt on him for stupid things," Christina said. "He was always in trouble. And when Nicolai had enough and left us, our father did not even see him off at the ship when he went to America. He didn't write to Nicolai and when Nicolai married your mother, *po po po*." Christina bit at the bottom of her lip. "He didn't send a gift, a card, nothing. It was as if Nicolai had died, just because he didn't marry a Greek girl." Christina shook her head and wiped at her eyes with her apron. "Our father, your *pappou,* was from a different time. He saw many things to make him like that. It was not only his fault."

"He was this way with all of us," Maria said. "He asked Katarina what was wrong with her after her fourth miscarriage. She still blames herself for not having a child. And look at you, you refused to have children. You know Solon wanted them, but you refused."

"*Ella,* the right time never came." Christina shrugged.

"You were afraid to be like him or maybe like our mother. Admit it."

Christina shook her head. "This is what she thinks." She placed her hand on Alexia's leg. "She only has strange ideas. No one pays attention to her."

Maria shrugged. "Believe what you want. You know it's true."

Christina turned the page. A girl dressed in white lace sat stiffly on a wooden chair. A boy stood behind, his hands on her shoulders. The rims of the girl's eyes were creased as if to stifle a giggle. His were focused and stern, angry with the photographer maybe for wasting his time. “Our parents,” Christina said. She crossed herself. “God rest their souls.”

“But they are just kids,” Alexia said.

“Yes, they were very young, teenagers only,” Christina said. “Maybe too young.”

Alexia thought about her father. He never told her much, never complained, but during one of their last conversations, he’d hinted about his own father.

“I didn’t want to be a dad at first,” Nicolai said.

“You didn’t want me.” Alexia said.

He shook his head and hugged her. “You don’t understand.” He kissed her head. “I was afraid I’d be like my father. But I think you made me a better father. Not that I didn’t make mistakes.”

“Your *pappou and yiayia,*” Christina said. “On their wedding day.”

“They don’t look happy,” Alexia said.

“Happy? No one thought about this then,” Maria said. “She held us together.”

“My father used to say the same thing.”

“He wasn’t a bad man, our father,” Christina said. “He made us learn English, helped us buy houses, and did things to help. He helped Nicolai, too.”

“How?” Alexia turned.

Christina shook her head. “One day, God willing, you will understand.”

“He didn’t help Nicolai after he came home when your mother died,” Maria said. She reached over and touched Alexia’s hand. “He was a stubborn man.”

“He thought Nicolai brought his own trouble when he married someone outside our church and culture. This is what he told us, but I think he always wanted the best for Nicolai. He wanted him to do better with his life.”

“Christina forgets many things.” Maria laced her fingers around her cup. “You didn’t agree at first with Nicolai and his marriage either.”

“I listened to our father, then,” Christina said. “But when I met Sara, I changed.”

"How can you say that?" Maria glared at Christina. "You didn't like how she kept her house. You told us that Alexia's toys were all over the place, there was no discipline because they played all the time, there was dust and I don't know what else."

"*Ah,* did I say this?" Christina stared down at the picture.

"After you came back from America."

"But I went," Christina said and shrugged as if what Maria was saying was information she hadn't heard before. "None of you did."

"Maybe if our father helped Nicolai after your mother died," Maria said, "life might have been different. We might have stayed close."

Alexia caught Christina eyeing Maria severely.

"It was a different time. Solon's family was demanding. Our father thought that Nicolai might hurt Christina's chances of getting married. Christina thought so, too."

"Why?" Alexia asked.

"Gossip, talk, who knows." Christina sighed. "They have funny ideas in those days."

"You had those same ideas, don't forget," Maria said. "You still do."

Christina shook her head and rolled her eyes. She turned another page. Nicolai was older in this picture, in his early twenties. The collar of his shirt drooped around his neck even though his tie looked like it was bound as tight as a noose. He'd rolled up the sleeves of his suit jacket. Still, he looked like a little boy lost in his father's clothes. That suit had been in her father's closet since she was a child. "I bought the best I could afford," he said, when she asked him about it. "I keep it to remember where I came from." After he died, Alexia found it at the back of the closet. She'd cleared out most of his stuff, but kept this suit.

"Maybe if your father had brought you with him to Greece," Christina said, "after your mother died. We might have been together."

"It's hard to know," Alexia said.

She felt Christina's stare and looked down at his picture.

His eyes seemed to be laughing as if he'd gotten a joke no one else could. He had that same silly grin most of his life, Alexia thought as she stared at the picture. Except maybe for the time after Sara got sick.

"He couldn't manage," Christina said. "And he probably thought our father would not accept you. We don't know why we do things until much time has passed."

"Your father told us you were very brave," Maria said. "You took care of him after your mother died."

An image came to mind. One of the lists she'd made to help her clean the house. The cleaning ladies had helped her make that list.

"You didn't like to help your father. No?"

"I wasn't given a choice." Alexia shrugged.

Maria ran her hand through her hair and sighed. Christina turned to the album, outlined Nicolai's face with her finger. "He had hopes for himself and for you, too, Alexia. You were the most important person to him. The most important. He made many choices to make sure you had a good life."

"Like what?"

"One day." Christina dabbed at her eyes with her apron.

"You haven't seen these pictures before?" Maria asked.

"*Oxi,*" Alexia said.

"This is Christina's fault."

"Our history has to be in one place," Christina said. "How else can we find what we need when we need it?" She dropped her apron, wiped her hands over it.

"Christina is the keeper of the pictures," Maria said. "I beg and still she won't give me any."

"You still don't know how to take care of things." Christina pointed to the oven. "Get the buns, will you?" She shut the album and reached for the next one.

Using a tea cloth, Maria slid the buns out of the oven, placed them on the counter, turned off the element and opened one cupboard door after another, moved things around as she searched.

Christina put her hands over her ears and shook her head. "Stop!"

"Where is a platter for these?"

"Leave them to cool first," Christina said. "We'll eat soon."

Maria stood with her back to the counter facing them. Christina turned pages. Each picture had an accompanying story and as she listened, Alexia wondered how often and in how many ways these stories had been told. There were pictures of Katarina, Maria and Christina when they were children, a few more of Nicolai, then pictures of husbands and children, cousins and older relatives now gone. She had missed all of this growing up. Why did he keep them from her? She swallowed hard. He should be here sharing all this with her.

Christina and Maria grinned when they talked about cousins who had done well. "Vassilis owns a restaurant in Athens, and his wife is an engineer." They laughed when they told stories about skipping school to go to the beach to meet friends. When they spoke about a dead relative, they crossed themselves. "Life is cruel. No?"

A picture fell out onto the table. A round-faced teenager sat alone on a bench, the beach in the background. Dark with a slight curl to it, her hair was pulled back off her face. Her head was tilted away from the camera, staring into the distance. Christina grabbed the picture and shoved it into the last page of the album, glanced over at Maria. "She's dead now," Christina said. "God rest her soul."

"If God allows it." Maria turned and put her cup in the sink.

"What do you mean?"

"She didn't always do the right thing, so we don't talk about her in this family."

"Who is she?" Alexia asked.

"A dead cousin," Christina said. "We've seen enough for today."

"*Dimitria*." Maria turned. "The name means 'of earth.' Because we didn't like her, we said she was of dirt. *Eh,* she's not part of the family," Maria said when Christina gave her one of her looks and crossed herself. "What's the difference now?"

Christina flipped the page to a photograph of a man hunched over, his arms wrapped around a young boy's shoulders. The boy stood in front of the man, clutching the man's pant legs in his tiny hands. They were laughing. This is the way it's supposed to be, Alexia thought.

"This is your *pappou* when he was a little boy. He is with his father."

"I saw the picture of my great-grandfather when we went to Kalavryta." There was something they didn't want her to know. She hadn't found it yet, but she would. Maybe Kalavryta would be a good starting point.

Christina closed the album, stacked it on top of the others at one end of the table. She walked over to the counter. "We eat now and look at more pictures later."

"There is more to the story," Alexia said. You know it and I know it, she thought.

"Not much. He married our mother and had a family." Christina pulled out a platter from the cupboard above the stove. A bowl sitting on top tumbled down and she caught it. She shook her head. "Life isn't always good, but with God's help, we manage."

She handed the platter and the bowl to Maria. "Get the cheese, too," she said. "We need it to help the buns go down."

2010

The clicking sound echoed off the pavement, bouncing against the houses and the squat stone walls. Maria's high heels. There was no getting away. All Alexia wanted was some fresh air and to be alone to think and figure out what was in the stories they told, the pictures she'd seen, that they didn't want her to know. Christina bit her lip, shook her head just enough so Maria would notice, but she didn't want me to see. How could I miss it? Or the angry looks Christina gave Maria.

An albatross whined somewhere above their heads. Alexia looked for it, but the sun pierced her eyes. She turned away.

Maria prattled. "Solon is a good man. He adores Christina. Why doesn't she see that? And not to give him children. So selfish. She thought she'd turn out as angry as our father or maybe a bit conniving like our mother. Impossible. She'd never be like that. Ah, but maybe she was afraid too. Maybe she didn't want to bring a child into a world like this. I don't know. She doesn't tell me. She keeps things inside."

"Yes," Alexia said. Now we're getting somewhere. Keep going.

"Christina told me you are very busy and never relax."

"And what else does she say?" Alexia pointed them towards a bench. When they sat down, Maria took off her shoes, stretched her long, slender feet and rubbed her heels against the top of her shoes as if scratching an itch. Her toenails, long and filed, were a flawless cherry red.

"We know Nicolai told you about your sister. This is why you came."

Alexia turned to face Maria, who was admiring her bare feet, moving them in one direction, then another. So they all knew about Theodora.

A couple walked by and the man tipped his hat and nodded. Maria wished them a good afternoon. Alexia managed a quick nod. She'd forgotten her sunglasses and the sun made her eyes tear. She sniffled, dabbed at her eyes with the cuff of her sweater. "Is this all you people do?" Alexia asked. "Gossip about other people behind their backs?"

"You get used to it."

"Ladies."

Achilles stood in front of them, Greek sailor hat in hand, his lips parted. His buttery teeth had a moist sheen.

Alexia couldn't see his eyes through his dark, over-sized sunglasses, but she noticed a couple of smudged fingerprints at one edge of the reflective lens. He's stuck in a time warp, she thought. The breeze picked up. She pulled her sweater over her shoulders. The albatross screamed.

Achilles stroked his beard. "Nice day," he said. "Yes?" His smile flashed easily as if he kept it always at the ready.

"We are talking," Maria said. She put her hand on Alexia's shoulder.

Alexia nodded, but couldn't make herself turn away. Her face felt warm again. She pushed the sweater off her shoulders. It fell behind her onto the bench.

"So perhaps an interruption is good."

Maria turned her back to him, making herself into a shield.

"Or perhaps not."

He walked away. Alexia sat so she could watch him and hold Maria's gaze at the same time. He turned and winked. Alexia shifted, using Maria to block any further view of him.

"You like him?"

"Who?"

"That man." Maria pointed her head in the direction where Achilles had gone.

"He's not my type." She leaned against the back of the bench and watched the clouds shift across the sky. Well, actually if she looked at her record honestly, she could see that most of the men she'd been with had been older. They were mature and interesting, she told herself. Achilles was interesting in his own way. More like playing with fire. Nothing more serious than a diversion. Maybe for a couple of nights.

Alexia could feel Maria watching her. She closed her eyes. No sound, except the light breeze. "What was my grandfather like?"

"You don't like this talk."

"I'm interested in the family." She sat up and looked at Maria. "That's all."

"You be careful with that one."

"What happened to my grandfather in Kalavryta?"

"No one knows. Except he was supposed to die, but instead he lived."

"They only killed those thirteen and over. I read about it in the museum."

"Yes, it is true, but he had more years. When we were young, kids at school said he lied to save himself. I don't know what is true."

"This is more gossip."

"He worked to save his money, leave Greece. But then he met my mother."

"That's it?"

Maria shrugged. She got up. "What more do you want?"

Alexia stood alone in the museum in Kalavryta, watching the video interviews with the survivors of the 1943 massacre. Some boomed their versions, looked steadily into the camera, resolute, like reporters informing everyone about the latest catastrophe. Others murmured, heads bent. English words scrolled along the bottom of the screen. She read the translation, listening to their voices. As she watched the screen, the woman came on with her story. As Alexia listened, the woman in the video looked away as if she'd realized someone was staring. The camera followed. In her lap, a handkerchief. Her knuckles white from wringing it.

We shared everything we had with our neighbours back then. It was a good life. When the Germans came, everything changed. My mother kept us inside. We couldn't play. They took over our church. We weren't allowed to go to pray.

The woman pushed herself forward on her chair and stared into the camera. Her pupils grew larger and darker. She raised her voice as if she wanted to make sure she was being heard.

They came through the door and told us to get out, their guns in our faces. Every house was cleared. We were a large group, walking toward the school with no idea about what was going to happen. It was a parade like the ones we have on Good Friday. We didn't know. We were separated. We were on one side with other women and children. We couldn't see our fathers or husbands. They asked each of the boys their age and then directed some of them to where we stood. Others were taken away.

The woman shook her head. The video flashed to another man. As he spoke about the last time he saw his father, he wept. Alexia turned. She couldn't watch anymore.

"It is very sad."

A woman stood beside her. "You speak English," Alexia said.

"A little."

Alexia smiled. That's what they all said and then they'd go ahead and speak perfect English. The young woman was shorter than Alexia. She wore jeans and a T-shirt. Her nametag read Zoë.

"I have seen you here before."

"My great-grandfather died here." Alexia nodded. "My grandfather was just a boy. I don't know much."

"Would you like to?" Zoë put her hand on Alexia's shoulder.

Alexia nodded only slightly. She didn't know what she'd find here, but for some reason she felt her family's secrets were somehow tied to this place.

"Maybe I have information in our archives."

They sat in Zoë's office in two newly upholstered chairs, facing each other across an old wooden desk. Logbooks were stuffed into an entire wall of shelves that bent under the weight. Through the barred window, dust motes swam upstream in the bits of filtered sunlight. The room was freshly painted but smelled of rot. You can't hide that, Alexia thought.

Zoë turned the computer screen around so they could both see. Alexia told her her grandfather's name. Names and dates flipped by as Zoë searched the list. Slow down, Alexia wanted to say. She couldn't read a thing. The screen's bright light and the foreign letters moving so quickly made her dizzy. Alexia sat back in her chair.

"Many people moved away after this day because it was too difficult to stay. They didn't want their names to be recorded. They disappeared."

Alexia leaned her elbows on the desk. "Are there any other records?" What was she really looking for?

"I have nothing on your grandfather. No."

Alexia thanked Zoë. A dead end. Now what? She lingered.

"My grandmother was one of those children," Zoë said. "You could talk to her."

"I don't want to be a bother." Alexia pushed her chair back and stood. "It's okay. I can ask my family." It had started because she was sure Christina was keeping secrets from her about Theodora and the family. But what did Theodora and her father have to do with this massacre? She knew she was just stalling because she didn't know how she was going to tell Theodora who she was.

Zoë motioned for her to sit down. "I will call her. It is no trouble."

Alexia followed Zoë to a souvenir shop. They entered the unlit store. The bell over the door sounded weakly, as though it had been stuffed with a cloth to silence it.

The old woman in the store walked out from behind the counter, a cane in her hand supporting each step. Her smile came slowly, deepening the wrinkles in her face. She hugged Zoë, asked her who her friend was. But when Zoë told her why she'd brought Alexia to see her, she shook her head.

"No," she said. "I don't talk about these things." The shawl she wore over her black dress seemed like a weight she was forced to carry, a load that might break her bent back in two. "When you called, you said you were coming for a visit. Not this."

"But she looks for her family," Zoë said. One hand was on the counter, the other raised as though she was pleading.

"Everyone leaves after that day." She shuffled behind the counter, stood at the cash register and tapped the old-fashioned keys. They made a dull, broken sound.

"Her great-grandfather died here. Her grandfather disappeared."

"Many people did." She sat down on the stool and rested her arms on the counter. She picked at the grime under one fingernail, scraping the dirt out with another fingernail. Tiny black bits fell onto the counter. "My friends all go."

"His name was Nicolai Sarinopoulos," Alexia said, moving closer to the counter. "He was the second Nicolai. His father was the first and my father, the third."

The old woman's cheeks collapsed into themselves, shrinking her face.

"Did they take him away?" Alexia persisted. "Do you remember?"

"Why must I talk about this?" She spoke to Zoë, but stared at Alexia.

"It might help me understand," Alexia said. "Please."

The woman closed her eyes as if in prayer, said nothing for several minutes. Alexia waited. Zoë rubbed her grandmother's shoulder, whispered in her ear. "How will people understand, if we don't tell them?"

"He was a neighbour who walked me to school every day. Our parents teased us. They told us that when we married, we would give them many grandchildren. He was a good boy." She continued to pick at her fingernails as she told the story.

"They came in the early morning and ordered everyone out of their fields and back into their houses. No one was allowed to wander, go to school or work. This lasted several days. Nicolai was bored. He snuck out his bedroom window the first night, after his parents fell asleep. It was a test, to see if he could do it. There couldn't be as many Germans as the rumours had it. He walked as far as the end of the lane and ran back, climbed up the tree and slipped through my window. He told me all about it. I remember how proud he was. He was smarter than they were.

"Every night he went a little further, until eventually he was returning only a few hours before sunrise. It started as a game, but then he brought back food. He told me he had found the storage containers the Germans hid in the cellar of an old farmhouse they were using as their supply base. Nicolai shared whatever he had. 'They take so much from us,' he said. 'They won't miss a few crumbs.'

"He was my best friend and I tried to warn him. 'Let's do what they tell us for now and when they leave, life will go back to normal.'

"'Don't worry,' he said. 'They aren't smarter than me.'"

The old woman shook her head, stared at her cracking nails and took another laboured breath. "I followed him one night. I don't know why. But I did. God, forgive me.

"I could see Nicolai standing to one side of the kitchen window, hidden but watching. He didn't see me. It was colder than usual. I could see his breath. I held mine. Inside the farmhouse, I heard the Germans talking and playing cards around the old wooden table. All of us kids had been in that kitchen at one time or another. The boy who lived there was one of our friends. We were all friends before the Germans. Music drifted in and out. I thought it must be a radio. I don't know if he could see much through the grimy film on the window, and I couldn't see anything in there, but I thought it must be a radio.

"Someone walked past the window and Nicolai ducked. He was probably holding his breath like I was. I'm sure he told himself to get the food and get home. Maybe he even thought about what I told him. Do what they tell us to do. That's what I said. But I knew he wouldn't. He said my way would never fill our stomachs. Maybe he was right. I don't know.

"I could see he was nervous. He shifted from one foot to the other, like he did sometimes when he was excited. Maybe he even thought he shouldn't have come out that night. Maybe he was mad at me for warning him. He probably told himself to stop listening to other people, just do what he knew was right. I could almost hear him. 'Girls, what do they know? What good are they? They scare you so you do what they want.'

"I heard a crack nearby. Nicolai saw me then. I was in the bushes."

Dirt lay on the counter in front of her. Alexia's hands were behind her back, clenched tight. Her breath was shallow. Do I really want to know? she asked herself.

"You don't have to say anymore," Zoë said. "It's okay."

The old woman stared at Zoë, then at Alexia. "It is time to get this off my conscience. I can go to my grave in peace."

Zoë looked at Alexia as if to ask, "Are you all right?"

Alexia wasn't sure. She nodded.

"We looked at each other," the old woman said. "He shook his head, told me with his eyes to get home, leave him alone. Before I could do anything, a soldier came around the corner of the house and before Nicolai could run away, he'd caught him by his shirt. The mud made a sucking sound as it freed his feet. I will never forget that sound. Even if I live one hundred years. The soldier pushed him forward. Nicolai stumbled. The soldier caught him and carried him along. A door creaked open. He was in the barn. I snuck into one of the stalls. They didn't hear me. There was moonlight coming through a small opening near the ceiling. I saw everything.

"The soldier pushed Nicolai onto his hands and knees and dragged his pants down. He must have felt the tear of skin, a sharp pain or something threw him forward. He turned, saw the man's long, thin fingers holding his hips. He tried to pull himself away, but the German held him, thrusting himself harder into Nicolai. I closed my eyes. I didn't know such things could happen. I didn't know anything. My jaw hurt. I didn't realize how tight I held it. All I could hear was my grinding teeth and a few gasped breaths from that German.

"When I opened my eyes again, I saw the man pulling his trousers back on. Nicolai was curled up on the barn floor, covering his head with his hands.

"'It's not the end of the world,' the soldier said, in perfect Greek. The enemy knew our language. We were lost.

"Nicolai didn't move. I couldn't move.

"'I want to show you something. A boy like you will find it interesting.' The man pulled him to his feet, asked him if he wanted a cigarette.

"Nicolai shook his head, buttoned his fly.

"The man deposited a couple of cigarettes and a lighter in Nicolai's shirt pocket. 'Maybe later, hey?' He tousled Nicolai's hair. 'Come. You'll learn.' The man pointed to a heap of dirt in one of the stalls. 'Just dig a little with your hands. It's fun. You'll see. It's like you're looking for buried treasure.'

"Nicolai stood still. I could smell it now. I couldn't before. Or maybe I did, but I was too afraid to notice at first. It was worse than any other barn I'd been in. How could that man stand it? I wanted to throw up and I knew Nicolai thought the same thing. He wouldn't though. He wouldn't give that German pig the satisfaction.

"'No?' The man put his arm around Nicolai's shoulders. He pushed the dirt away with his foot.

"I saw the bloodied face of the farmer who used to live in the house. A delicate, mud-caked hand lay on his shrunken cheek as though caressing his face. The farmer's wife maybe or his son. I put my hand over my mouth so I wouldn't scream. I wanted to run away, but I couldn't leave Nicolai behind.

"The man held Nicolai by the shoulder. 'You do what you're told, and this doesn't need to happen to you. Don't go thinking you are like those independence fighters you Greeks are so proud of. This is a different time. We are different conquerors. You are not them. Remember.' He ran his fingers through Nicolai's hair. 'I will take care of things.'

"Nicolai looked the soldier in the eye. 'And my family?'

"'Your family, friends, everyone will be safe.' He snickered then. 'And to think, our commandant thinks this is the most dangerous centre of resistance, a place that must be wiped out. You don't look too dangerous to me.'

"I ran home as fast as I could," the old woman said. "I waited for him. His lip was bleeding, his shirt and pants were dirty. I pretended I didn't know. I had a few candies he'd stolen from them before. I tried to give them to him. He yelled at me, told me to leave him alone. He'd never done that before. We were best friends." Her eyes were dry.

The old woman leaned into the counter. "He went out every night after that and brought us cans of meat, many different things. We never talked like we used to. He thought he'd saved us. He was so young, so proud. When they came to the door and dragged us to the school, he still believed. I remember his smile. He trusted them.

"Nicolai stood in line with the rest of the men. The women and young girls were in another line. They were being herded into the school along with some of the younger boys. He heard the question being asked of the boys in front, nodded to me and mouthed, 'It's okay.'

"'How old?' one German asked.

The soldier from the barn pulled him aside before Nicolai could answer the question. 'I'll take him.' He pushed Nicolai into the gymnasium. 'I keep my promises.'

"The gymnasium was full of women and children. We all wondered what would happen next, but no one was brave enough to ask. Except Nicolai, of course. He went looking for the man he knew. One of the soldiers pushed him back in the room, snickered at him. 'You should be with the rest of them. Not here with the women and babies.'

"'Let me go with the men,' Nicolai said.

"'This is the place for boys,' the solider said. 'Your place.'

"His mother and sister held him back, told him to stay with them. 'You are the man of the house now,' his mother said in a tone I'd never heard before. 'We need you.'

"'Maybe I can find out what's going on.'

"'I can't lose you too,' his mother said.

"The doors were locked. He pushed himself out of his mother's arms. He ran to the window along with the others. The men were marched up Kappi hill, the Germans beside them pushing them on with their rifles. He told me that he should be with them. He was old enough. He could do any work the men could do. At the top of the hill, they disappeared.

"We heard popping sounds, over and over again, but we didn't know what they were. I saw Nicolai kneel down beside his mother and pat his sister's head. 'We're going to be fine.'

"I smelled the smoke, but didn't think anything of it right away. Maybe they were burning some trees. I didn't know.

"Then a woman screamed. 'They are burning us alive.'

"Some of the mothers huddled around their children, covered their faces with anything they could find. Others kicked and scratched at the door.

"Nicolai threw himself against the door until it gave way. We saw the flames eating the walls of the school. We all ran out and into the fields. The two German soldiers left to guard us ran off in the direction of the forest. No one chased after them. The stronger women helped the ones with children on their hips, the young boys helped the older women climb up the hill to find the men. The fields were vacant.

"Nicolai ran ahead. I could see him pumping his arms. How his lungs must have ached.

"He reached the top of the hill before any of us. When we made it up the hill ourselves we saw the lifeless, twisted bodies lying across the backside of the hill. Blood seeped into the cracks in the ground like rainwater.

"I was separated from my mother and my father was among these men on the ground. I didn't know what to do so I followed Nicolai. I couldn't look at those dead faces around me. He searched through the bodies, stepped on a hand. He made the sign of the cross. All the women were wailing. I don't know how he did it, but he seemed to ignore them. He found his father leaning against a tree, a gaping hole in his chest, his eyes open. He held him close, rocked him back and forth as you would a baby.

"His mother and sister found him like that and knelt down beside him. His mother moaned and crossed herself. His sister stared, her eyes blank and tearless.

"'Why did you hold me back? I could have stopped them,' he shouted at his mother. He stood up and pushed her away.

"She fell. His sister helped her up.

"'I could have helped.' As he paced, he punched his legs with his fists. His mother's hair was grey at the temples, her face without colour. He kept hurling insults. She refused to turn her eyes away or let go of his sister's hand. He slapped his mother. Others pulled him away, beat at him with their hands. He wouldn't stop. He fought them until his fists were bloody and he was out of breath. On her hands and knees, his mother pleaded with them to leave him alone. Blood dried on her lip. He pulled himself off the ground, spit at all of us and ran down the hill.

"I never saw him again," the old woman said. She wiped her forehead with a hanky. "His mother died a few months later. His sister disappeared. The rest of us were too busy burying our dead."

Alexia felt dizzy. She swallowed hard to keep everything inside.

"We found that German too. The one who hurt Nicolai. Dead in one of our fields, stabbed to death with a pitchfork. Someone got him maybe before he got back to the rest of his group of murderers. We don't know where they all went. They disappeared as fast as they came to our village." The old woman swiped her shawl over the counter. Dirt fell to the floor at Alexia's feet.

My grandfather, Alexia thought.

"It comes back every day," the old woman said. "The smell of the mud of so many graves, which we dug with our hands. This is in my nose even up to today. I hear women and children screaming and crying when there are none around. They took our husbands, fathers and brothers, and they left us without compassion. Our village changed. Now, we keep to ourselves. Don't help each other, like before. We are not the same."

Alexia stared at the woman. She couldn't think of anything to say.

Zoë stood beside her grandmother, an arm around her shoulders.

"Your father was here many years ago," the old woman said.

"When?"

"I don't remember. But I spoke to him in the museum. And his sister was here before him. You look like them."

"Did you tell him about my grandfather?"

"He didn't ask. I didn't tell."

"And my aunt. Did you tell her?"

"She wanted to know," the woman said. "She came back over and over, but I never told her the whole story. Not like I told you. She put two and two together. I know, because she hasn't visited me in a very long time."

The woman shook her head. "War does many things. One day, it stops. But what it leaves never does. It stays like a disease with no cure." She placed her hand on Alexia's shoulder. "This is not a way to live. At some point, we have to forgive. It is the only way to survive."

Alexia heard children shouting and laughing outside and looked around. A man peered through the window, his nose squashed against the glass. The camera around his neck swung back and forth, thudding against the window. Zoë and her grandmother turned. The tourist moved back quickly. He walked away.

Alexia had felt on the verge of throwing up the entire time the old woman had been telling her story, and when she got to the moped, she couldn't keep it down. She wiped her mouth with her father's old handkerchief and leaned against the moped for a long time to settle her stomach. She gazed at the looming cross on the hill and shook her head, trying to separate the image of her father from the image of her grandfather in Christina's photo albums from the image of her great-grandfather in the museum. So much sadness. So many sacrifices. All for what? She didn't know.

Alexia kicked the stand and started the moped. The motor wheezed as she took the corners. She'd thought getting at the truth would help, but she didn't feel any better. This was worse than those stupid rumours about her grandfather lying about his age. Gossip was easier to live with. That's why her aunts spent their time doing it. Christina knew the truth, but didn't tell anyone. She'd held onto this secret for God knows how long. Maybe that was her way of sparing the rest of them.

The breeze smacked Alexia in the face, kept her focused on the road. What good would it do to tell them this stuff? It had nothing to do with Theodora. It explained a lot about why Christina was so secretive, why her aunts were afraid that good things never lasted, but it didn't tell her anything more about Theodora or her father. Maybe there was no more.

1986

Nicolai eyed Achilles.

"So you're sticking around," Achilles said. He sat across from Nicolai, rocking back on the chair's hind legs. Stop already, Nicolai wanted to say. The creaking sound continued. Was he that oblivious? Achilles smiled innocently. You can't fool me. You know exactly what you're doing, Nicolai thought. And you know it's bugging me.

Nicolai looked down at the hardcover book in his lap. The glossy pictures were meant to persuade tourists of the wonders of Greece. A few pages were torn out. He flipped through what was there, tried to ignore the noise and imagine the kind of Greece captured in the pictures. It wasn't the Greece he'd grown up in, but it was the one he'd somehow remembered after he moved to Canada. He covered his ear by putting his head against his hand.

Achilles's chair came down with a bump. He grinned at both Nicolai and the young secretary behind the front desk. "I'm a kid at heart," he said.

"Not sure I should be partnering with you," Nicolai said.

"Who will guide you through, make sure no one cheats you?"

"I want to be involved in every aspect." Nicolai put the book down and turned to catch Achilles's eye. "We understand each other. Yes?"

Leaning back in his chair, Achilles teetered against the wall. "You say this because you have a woman and everything is rosy like Easter Sunday. But not every day is Easter. One day you will return to Canada and where will that leave poor Achilles?"

"I have no plans." Nicolai picked up the book and put it down again. There was nothing in the book that interested him.

They left the lawyer's office after signing the papers. The stretch of land on the beach was now his. Nicolai had put down the money. Achilles agreed to raise the money for any future development. Once he had it, Achilles would steer the development of the land. Nicolai would oversee the project. It felt good to have work again.

"The only money I make is the little I get from my father when I help him on the farm," Achilles said. "But I have some very good friends who believe in this."

"I'm counting on it."

"This land will pass down to your daughter one day. She will come back to Greece and enjoy the investment you made. You will see."

"I doubt it."

"We can't predict the future," Achilles said. "Let's celebrate what we have."

"I should get back."

"I don't see a ring through your nose. Does she have that much power over you? It's only been a few weeks."

There was that silly grin again, that oh, come on, let's-go-have-some-fun grin, the same one that had talked Nicolai into staying late after school to play basketball when he was a kid. Nicolai could still feel his father's belt across his backside. There was always trouble when you got involved with Achilles. But what the hell. What did he have to lose? Nicolai would always own a small part of Greece even if Achilles never came up with other investors and the development didn't take place.

Nicolai bought a bottle of cheap champagne, a package of plastic cups and a case of beer. They parked on Nicolai's narrow strip of beachfront, cracked open the champagne, finished it quickly and started on the beer.

"People will come here for their evening stroll," Achilles said. "They will buy a coffee or a beer and watch the sunset. Young people will dance until morning."

"Let's hope."

The beach was deserted. A small wave kicked up onto the shore. When it subsided, a light film of slime coated the rocks. Nicolai tried to imagine the boardwalk, the restaurants and cafés they planned, the string of lights weaving from one place to the other, the people pouring out from the open doors. Another wave hit, spraying his windshield.

"We're two men in our prime. We don't need hope. We have what we need," Achilles said. He tapped Nicolai's head. "We have our brains." He pounded his own chest with a closed fist. "And we have passion and strength."

They finished the beer as the sky turned pink. Lights flickered on the opposite shore and Nicolai fell asleep. Achilles was talking about the type of light standards he wanted along the promenade. "What do you think?" Achilles asked.

Nicolai's head flopped back against the headrest. "I can't right now."

Nicolai pushed the hand away. "Let me sleep," he said. He tried to turn, but felt trapped. He leaned back and fell asleep. The hand prodded him again.

"You're in for it now," Achilles said.

Nicolai sat up and hit his chest against the steering wheel.

"She won't be happy." Achilles grinned.

Condensation had built up on the inside of the windshield. Nicolai flicked on his wipers. The dewy film remained. He wiped it off with his shirtsleeve. It felt cold against his skin. He heard the waves crashing against the shore, but could no longer see the beach in the dark.

"No one tells me what to do," Nicolai said.

"Women want someone they can rely on." Achilles sighed. "They like dependability. I know."

So he was late. We were celebrating. He would explain what happened. Dimitria would understand or she wouldn't. That was up to her. He wasn't going to sweat it.

The sun peeked out from behind the motel in Aigio. Nicolai parked the car. He leaned his head against the headrest. Did he really want to go inside? He came to Greece to get away. How had he fallen back into so much responsibility: a piece of land, Dimitria? My fault, he thought. I let it happen. I should have left Dimitria alone, told her that after Sara there wouldn't be anyone else. It was true. He should tell Dimitria again. Remind her. Convince her that this couldn't be anything more than what it was. Temporary. He had told her. And she heard him, too. "Time will pass, you will see," she said. A million years could go by. Nothing would change. He knew that. And he had to think of Alexia, too. No one would replace her mother. He wouldn't allow it.

Dimitria stepped out the front door of their room, her easel under one arm and a suitcase in the other. He watched her struggle with the door. The easel dropped to the ground. She threw her suitcase down and kicked it. She pulled the door shut behind her and looked around to see if anyone was looking.

Nicolai thought about ducking.

They stared at each other. Neither smiled. Several seconds passed. Go, he told himself. Try to explain.

He got out of the car. "Where are you going?" he said, walking towards her.

"What do you care?" She grabbed the suitcase and jammed the easel under her arm. She walked past the front of the building, out of the parking lot and onto the main street, clearly headed to the bus stop a block away.

He should let her go. It would be better for her that way. Instead, he took a deep breath and followed.

He caught up with her, put his hand on her shoulder. Maybe if he explained, she'd understand. And that would be better for both of them. "What's going on?"

She picked up her pace, ignoring him.

"I guess you're mad." He walked beside her, keeping up. She didn't turn to look at him. Finally, he stepped in front of her. "Let me take this," he said and reached for her suitcase. She pulled it away.

"What's with you?" he asked.

"If things are going to be this way, I'd rather be alone," Dimitria said. She dropped her suitcase and held the easel against her chest.

"You know what Achilles is like. You know him better than I do."

"Are you going to throw that in my face for the rest of our lives?"

The copper in her eyes had turned fiery and challenging.

"I'm sorry. Achilles wanted to celebrate. I went. I didn't think I'd be out that long." Nicolai stroked her face. "That's all I meant."

She tilted away, hugged the easel tighter. "I thought something had happened to you."

"No, I'm still here," he said. He put his arm around her shoulders.

She shrugged it away.

"I don't know what you want from me," he said.

"Respect what we have. This is important."

"I can't give anyone very much." He lowered his eyes, shuffled. He couldn't help himself.

"Then why are we here?" She held his chin up with her finger. Their eyes met.

"I don't know the answer to that." They felt like the most honest words he'd ever said. He grabbed her suitcase. "Let's go home."

"I won't be treated badly," she said. "Not by you or anyone."

"I know."

A smile skipped through her eyes, stayed fixed on her lips. It was proud and smug as if she'd won a long-fought debate. She passed him her easel. "Take this, too."

Nicolai and Achilles met at the café every day over the next two weeks to lay out plans for the boardwalk. They interviewed architects and builders. "I don't know why we're doing this," Nicolai said after they finished speaking to a father and son construction team. "We don't have all the money we need."

"It's coming," Achilles said. He sipped his coffee, scanning a magazine.

"I'm not going further into debt," Nicolai said. They sat in a café in Diakofto.

"Take a look at these lights," Achilles said and pointed to three ornate light standards in the magazine. "Nice?"

"I was thinking of more rustic lights, more typical of the islands or Plaka. Strings of lights, nothing fancy."

"The ocean can be hard on things."

Nicolai looked at the picture again and shook his head. "They look like they're out of the streets of London. That's not what we want."

"Our small place in this world could use a little class," Achilles said, leaning back in his chair. He grinned as he turned the pages, nodding to himself.

Nicolai squeezed Achilles's forearm. "Listen. We're not buying anything until more investors come on board. Understand?"

Achilles flipped another page. "Suit yourself."

"You think otherwise?"

Achilles put the magazine down, scooted his chair a little closer.

Shit, Nicolai thought. Here comes another sales pitch.

"If we do some things now, we will be ready when the money comes." The smell of coffee was stagnant on his breath. "Can you advance the money yourself to get us started so we're not waiting for something to happen?"

Nicolai edged his chair back. "Not a good idea."

"Take a risk for once in your life," Achilles said. "It won't kill you."

Nicolai stood to leave. He walked towards the door. A hand touched his arm. He turned.

"Come sit with us, Nicky." Katarina sat across from Christina who was warming her hands around a cup of coffee and staring out the window. Katarina pointed to the empty chair at the table.

"I really can't," he said.

"You can spend time with him and not with us?" Christina asked.

"*Ella, paidi mou,*" Katarina said. "We are family."

Her clothes hung on her as if from a hanger. He hated himself for making Katarina worry. Whenever she couldn't cope, she'd stop eating. She'd done it since she was a child. They all teased her about it, scolded her for it, but she wouldn't stop. "I can't bring it to my mouth. I can't," she'd say.

Maybe he should sit down. They were his sisters. He could talk to them. He'd always been able to before. Why not now? Try, he told himself. Just try.

"That man will cheat you out of everything," Christina said. She had their father's stern, unforgiving stare.

"As if my family is any better," he said.

"Our father is right," Christina said. "You've lost your head."

"He doesn't know anything."

"Let's sit and talk, Nicky," Katarina said. "Please." She held onto his arm. Her long fingers were like talons.

He needed a new beginning. "It's too late." He walked back to where Achilles sat. "Set up a time with the bank," he said. "Let's get this thing rolling."

He walked into the motel room, threw his briefcase on the kitchen table. Dimitria rinsed out her cup, put it on the counter and turned. "Your daughter called," she said. "She sounds like a nice little girl. Very smart."

"What?" Nicolai tried not to shout.

"We had a chat." Dimitria leaned against the counter.

"What did you tell her?" He stood in front of her, held her shoulders.

She pulled away. "Nicolai, you're hurting me."

"What did you talk about?"

"I guess you don't trust me to know what to say?"

"It's too soon to say anything," he said and grabbed one of the chairs. He sat down. "Don't you understand?" She's just a little girl, my little girl, he thought. I don't want to tell her about all of this. You. The family. This stupid boardwalk project. Greece. It's too much for her to understand. She's never going to forgive me.

Dimitria rubbed his back. "I said I was a friend." She kissed the top of his head. "You have to tell her when you are ready."

"Yes." He shut his eyes tight. Thank God, he said to himself. Thank God.

"Why don't you call her?"

"Not right now. She's probably in school. Maybe tomorrow."

She grabbed his arms, pulling him up. She held him close and stroked his back. He was tired. Just so tired. Her hair smelled of jasmine. A trace of cooking grease mingled with the scent. He moved his face slightly, but didn't pull away.

Nicolai listened to the phone ring, hoping no one was home. He hadn't spoken to Alexia since she'd talked to Dimitria. How was he going to explain? Maybe he could avoid talking about his living arrangements altogether. The phone rang a sixth, then a seventh time.

"Hello," she said.

"Um, Alexia?"

"Daddy," she said, elongating the *y*.

He rolled his eyes. "Are you there by yourself?" He paced back and forth in the short space the telephone cord allowed him.

"No, we're making cookies. I said I'd answer the phone."

He heard a crash in the background. "Oh, damn."

He smiled, but felt a knot in the centre of his chest. "What's going on there?"

"I guess I was pulling on the phone too hard. It fell. It's okay now."

"So, *paidi mou,* how have you been? What are you up to?"

"It's my turn to bring something to school. I'm bringing cookies," she said breathlessly. He heard a knock and scraping. "Oh, damn. Aunty Mavis is helping me."

He kneaded the spot on his chest.

"It's been a long time since you called."

He heard a thud.

"Okay, I'm sitting down. The phone is on the table beside me."

"So what else have you been doing?" He pulled at his telephone cord, but it refused to stretch any further.

"I talked to your friend the other day."

Nicolai stopped yanking the cord. He picked up a spoon, drummed it. "Yup, she told me."

"Where did you meet her?"

"Here."

"What does she do?"

"Um, she's an artist."

"Cool," she said. "Hey, what's that noise?"

Nicolai slid the spoon out of his reach, propped his elbow on the counter and supported his head.

"So does she paint or draw or what?"

"Yup, stuff like that."

"I'd like to see it."

"How's school?"

"Good," Alexia said. "She said her name was Dimitria. That's a nice name."

"Yup."

"Will you bring her back when you come back?"

"No. She's like… I don't know," Nicolai said. "She's no one. No one you need to worry about."

"I'm not worried," Alexia said. "Are you?"

Nicolai heard a noise behind him. He turned, becoming entangled in the telephone cord. Dimitria stood just inside the door, two bags of groceries in her hands.

"Are you coming home soon, Daddy?"

"I've got to go," he said. "Sorry."

"Wait."

"I'll call you back. Promise." He clicked the button hard with his finger.

Dimitria turned her back to him, dropped the bags on the table.

He unknotted the telephone cord. "I was wondering where you went." He banged the phone down. "Shit."

Dimitria looked up towards the ceiling like she was trying to find an answer in the heavens. She shook her head. "You told your daughter I was no one. You didn't even tell her, did you? That I'm at least a friend."

"It's too soon. She just lost her mother. And I'm not there." He put his hand on her shoulder. "This is too much."

She pulled herself away, rummaged in one of the bags. She tossed apples, an eggplant, a zucchini, cheese and bread on the table. Jars of olives and artichoke, a tub of yogurt and a carton of milk were plopped beside the rest. She creased and folded each bag into a tiny rectangle and threw them on the table. The bags opened up, refused to remain folded. She swore under her breath, snatched one of the bags and hit the milk carton with her elbow. It wobbled on the edge of the table. She let it drop. Milk sprayed against his legs when it hit the floor.

Nicolai grabbed a cloth out of the sink and wiped his pants. "I don't need this bullshit."

"You think I do?" She threw the bag at him.

"Hey." He yanked at her arm. "I thought I explained everything to you."

Dimitria pushed him off, slammed the door behind her as she left.

Nicolai sat at the kitchen table, taking sips from the bottle of Canadian Club Dimitria had bought for him more than a week ago. "Something special for my Canadian," she'd said. He couldn't tell her he didn't drink whiskey. "You haven't touched it," she said. "Don't you like it?" He made an excuse. "It tastes best when you're in the right mood," he said.

He took a swig, pushed everything off the table into the pool of milk on the floor. The crashing sound of broken glass calmed him. He kicked at the apples, the eggplant. They rolled away. He put his head down on the ceramic tiles of the table. They felt cold against his cheek.

He heard a light tap at the door. She'd come back. He got up and slipped on the slime of milk, yogurt and broken glass. He caught himself on the counter, rubbed his hands against his pants and threw the door open. "Thank God you're," he started to say.

His father broke the silence. "Are you going to let me in, or do we have to talk at the door so all the neighbours can hear?"

"What are you doing here?" Nicolai said, shoving his hands deep into his pockets.

His father walked past him into the cramped kitchen. "What happened?"

Nicolai shut the door, stood in front of it. "Nothing."

His father bent to pick up the milk container, put it in the sink.

"Leave it."

"Please yourself." His father said. He leaned against a chair.

"Why are you here?"

"I don't want you to make the same mistakes."

"Yes, I know all about it."

"My mistake was getting involved with someone in the first place."

"I know this story."

"You think you know," his father said. "No one can tell you anything. You've always known all the answers." His leathery hands turned white as he gripped the back of the chair.

"I've heard this before, too." Nicolai drummed his fingers against his thighs. His father was here to berate him again, tell him what to do. He didn't need to listen to any of his bullshit, not anymore.

"I'm not here to argue with you," his father said.

"Since when?"

"You're right to blame me," his father said. "I went after your mother. I wanted her. I'm the one who started it even though I knew I was going to leave. This is my regret. Not you or your sisters or your mother," he said and poked at his own chest. "I'm the one to be blamed for everything."

"Isn't it a little too late to tell me all of this?"

"Don't play with this girl's feelings."

"Oh, now you care about her feelings." He pointed at him. "Since when?"

"Since the two of you were children. And got caught."

"What do you mean?"

"In her room."

"How did you know?" Nicolai asked

"Her father. Your mother's brother came to me, asked me if you'd said anything about it to me. He'd asked you to tell me. He blamed you for what happened. You were the boy. Like father, like son. That's what he said—to my face."

"We were kids, playing a stupid game of house," Nicolai said. "We fell asleep. Nothing happened."

"I don't know if it did or it didn't. But I wouldn't allow him to blame my son." He stared at Nicolai. He looked so much older, even frail. The skin around his neck hung loose.

"I'm not you."

"That's good," his father said. He pushed himself away from the chair. "You have a daughter. She needs you."

"You don't have to tell me."

"When children are young they admire their parents, love them without any questions," he said. "That feeling they have doesn't last."

He's trying to tell me how to be a parent, Nicolai thought. What the hell did he ever know about being one?

"Life is the same way," he said. "Everything new is good. But time interferes. New becomes old and worn, and no good."

Nicolai stepped aside. His father put his hand on Nicolai's shoulder as he walked to the door. Nicolai flinched. The hand dropped away. They looked at each other. You can't fool me, Nicolai thought. You only want things your way. This is just a new tack.

His father held the door handle, but didn't open the door.

Go, Nicolai thought. You've said what you wanted to say. Get out.

His father gazed at Nicolai again. His father's eyes were bloodshot, his mouth open like he was about to speak. But he didn't.

Nicolai quickly closed the door behind his father, locked it. He picked up the broken glass, the fruit and vegetables, and threw everything in the bin under the sink. He scrubbed the floor with a wet tea towel, rinsing it out and wiping the floor again. Something sharp stabbed him. He pulled his hand back. A sliver of glass was lodged beneath the skin of his thumb. He sat on the floor, rubbed at the glass. It cut in deeper. He could tell himself that was what made him weep.

Later that night, Dimitria came in and crawled into bed beside him. "I'm not myself," she said. "It's all happening so fast."

"Yes," he said.

"There's plenty of time to talk," she said and kissed him. "We'll work everything out together." Dimitria pulled herself on top of him.

When he woke, Dimitria's head was on his chest, a leg draped over his. He stared at the ceiling. A memory of Alexia came to him. Sara hadn't been feeling well and he'd decided to take Alexia out skating. She was a kid. She needed to have some fun, a bit of fresh air. But, once he had his skates on, he sat on the bench moving his feet back and forth, listening to the sound of metal scraping against ice. He was torn. What was he doing here? Sara taught him how to skate. She should be here. But she wasn't. And he had no business being here without her. They didn't have much time left.

"Come on, Daddy," Alexia said. But still he couldn't move. He shouldn't have come. She stood in front of him. She pulled at him. He shook his head. "I'm not going to go either then," she said. He looked at Alexia as she balanced on her skates, her head bent.

He held out his hands. Her eyes questioned him. "Okay, let's try." he said. She took his hand. They'd skated together for two hours that day, neither one prepared to let the other go.

He stroked Dimitria's hair. She had comforted him when he didn't think that would ever be possible. He had to tell her that. He would thank her. They'd stay friends.

Dimitria cuddled up closer. "Why didn't you wake me?" She stretched out.

He rolled his legs off the side of the bed and sat up.

She leaned towards him and touched his back. "We have to talk."

"I have to go home." He didn't turn to face her.

The sheets rustled as she shimmied closer to him. "Is something wrong?"

"I have to go back."

"Will you bring Alexia with you when you return?" Dimitria asked.

"She's a child. I have to take care of her."

"And us?"

"I'm sorry."

"We can be a family," she said. "Have a bigger family."

"It's not possible for me to love anyone else," he said. "Sara will always be my wife. I'm sorry. I didn't mean for this to happen. "

"You don't know."

"I wish it could be different," Nicolai said.

"Then make it so." Dimitria put her arms around him. "We can do it together."

She held him. He held her. His arms were numb. They sat this way until he finally got up and went into the bathroom.

"You can run with things," he said to Achilles. "Do it your way." They were walking along Nicolai's section of the beach. Nicolai had listened to Achilles talk, said nothing at first.

Achilles put his arm around Nicolai's shoulder. "But you wanted to be involved. This is as much your dream as it is mine." He shook Nicolai as if to wake him. "It's your land. Don't you want to see what happens to it?"

"I have been away from my daughter too long."

"Dimitria can be demanding," Achilles said. "I understand this. We men do. But she's not the only fish in the sea. Next time don't get too close."

"It has nothing to do with her. She understands. I have a responsibility."

Nicolai recognized his father up ahead by the curve of his back. He stood with an octopus in his hand. His arm went up and he flung the octopus against the rocks once, and then picked it up and threw it down again. Its eyes popped out when it hit the ground with a fleshy splatter. Nicolai hated this way of killing and tenderizing octopus.

"Let's go this way," Nicolai said, trying to steer them in another direction.

But Achilles continued ahead. "Hello! I thought I recognized you."

Nicolai's father turned.

"Nice size, that one," Achilles said.

Nicolai's father didn't respond.

"A good fisherman like you should be able to talk some sense into his son."

"Can't you see I have work to do?" Nicolai's father said.

"He's leaving us. Don't you understand? Tell him to stay."

"If this is true, it is a good thing." He picked up the octopus, and again threw it against the rock.

2010

Alexia followed her aunt through the market. Christina had a bag slung over her arm, and her shoulders were rounded. "Let me carry that for you," Alexia said.

Christina turned. "I'm not too old yet," she said. "I can carry many things."

"I want to help," Alexia said.

"You are good," Christina said, and patted her face. "You are here with us."

You know what happened in Kalavryta, Alexia thought. You gossip about everything. But you kept this one secret.

"You have good walk with Maria?" Christina said, sniffing a melon.

"Yes, fine."

"She has young thoughts. No?"

"You told her about Theodora."

"Yes," Christina said. "My sisters have always known you came to find her."

"But you didn't say anything to Solon. Why not him, too?"

"You have to choose what to say," Christina said, "and when to say it." She reached for Alexia's hand. "No?"

Alexia squeezed Christina's hand. "I am going to see her again, *Thia*. I'm sorry you don't approve. But I have to see Theodora."

"You have to choose what is right for you," Christina said, and moved along to the vegetable stand.

Alexia pulled off her helmet and attached it to the handlebars of the moped, then ran her fingers through her damp hair. Her shirt was stuck to her back. She pinched the material, billowing it back and forth. She let go and the shirt fell limp again, fixing itself to her skin. She sniffed at her armpits. The body spray only lightly masked the smell of her sweat. She saw Theodora kneeling on the pebbly sand, a two-storey sand castle in front of her. Nicky was shovelling sand into a pail. A few feet away, their blanket lay under the shade of a beach umbrella.

"How is the moped now?" Theodora stood and hugged Alexia.

"I'm getting used to it." Alexia patted Theodora's back. Today she was going to tell Theodora who she was and what she was doing in Greece. She couldn't keep this charade going.

Theodora released her. Alexia sat down on the blanket under the umbrella.

Theodora sat beside Nicky shaping another wing on the castle. Their feet and legs were coated in fine pink sand.

"Do you have your costume for bathing?"

Alexia slipped out of her pants and dug a tube of sunscreen out of her pack. She put a few dollops on her cheeks and nose and slathered the thick cream on her legs, arms and chest. She rubbed hard, but the pasty film remained. The light breeze kicked up sand.

"The sun is good," Theodora said.

"Too much of anything is never good."

"You worry so much."

"That's what my father used to say," Alexia said. "I'm careful, that's all." Alexia stared out into the distance at the shadow of land on the opposite shore, then at Nicky's sand castle. "You two are experts at this castle-building."

Sand fell away from Theodora's legs as she got up. "Nicky and me like building. Right, Nicky?"

He poured another pail on top of the new corner of the castle.

"One day we will have a nice house."

"Your home is so cute," Alexia said.

"No place for my pictures."

"A studio?"

Theodora clapped her hands together. Sand fell away. She brushed more off her legs. Catching it, the wind blew the sand back at Alexia. Her eyes stung. She rubbed them. When Theodora plopped herself on the blanket, sand drizzled like spring rain.

"I brought pictures," Theodora said. She opened the large portfolio embossed with her initials. "My mother gave me this." One by one, Theodora flipped the first few pages: Andreas smiling at a customer, another one with him in his meat locker, still others at home, at the park and in the kitchen. Alexia knew she would like him. He had a gentleness about him that Theodora had captured time and again. There were pictures of Nicky playing at the beach and other pictures of old women standing in line at the bakery, gazing at what they wanted as if it was still out of reach.

Theodora showed her a picture of the market at the end of the day, garbage bins bursting. Bruised fruit and rotten vegetables littered the ground. "I love this," Alexia said. "It says so much about what we don't see."

"You have a good eye," Theodora said.

"Only opinions."

Theodora turned the page to the last photograph. A woman hugged Theodora from behind, resting her chin on Theodora's shoulder. The woman's eyes crinkled. Her olive skin was tanned brown and her long hair hugged her face. She had Theodora's shy smile.

"My mother. Ten years since I took this. She was beautiful."

"What was her name?"

"Dimitria. It means…"

"Yes, I know what it means." Alexia felt the bile in her stomach rise. How could this be? Maria had told her Dimitria was a cousin. "Because we do not like her, we used to say she was of dirt," Maria said. Alexia took a deep breath. "It means 'of the earth.'" She croaked, and cleared her throat. She coughed, swallowed hard. What the hell had he done? His cousin.

"It is a strong name for a strong person." Theodora smiled.

Alexia got up off the blanket, stood out in the sun and stared at the ocean. You bastard, she thought. Why did you do this to us? We don't deserve this. Theodora doesn't deserve this. Alexia rubbed at her legs to get rid of the sand, managing only to coat her hands.

"What is wrong?"

"Nothing. No."

"What is it?" Theodora said. She grabbed Alexia's hand and pulled her back to the blanket.

"I don't know. Family. Stuff." She tried to smile. Don't let on, she told herself. This isn't fair, Dad. It's not fair.

Theodora put her hand on Alexia's thigh. "Do not worry so much."

Alexia nodded. "You are quite the photographer."

"You like them?" Theodora touched Alexia's shoulder as though she wanted to make sure she'd heard correctly.

"Very much." If and when she finally told Theodora the truth, it would surely destroy what they were building between them. And there was nothing she could do to stop that. Her father and his family had made sure of that. Christina, Maria, all of them knew but none of them had bothered to tell her. She squeezed her eyes shut and reached out for Theodora's hand. "You're very good."

When Alexia pulled up to the house, Christina was sitting on the stoop, elbows propped on top of her legs, hands clutched together. Alexia parked the moped, ripped off her helmet. She strode over to Christina. "Why didn't you tell me?"

"We go inside. No?" Christina stood up and looked around to see if anyone was about. A neighbour hung out the window across the street. "Hey, Christina, everything okay?" Christina waved at the neighbour, put an arm around Alexia's shoulders. "This is no place."

"Why not tell the whole world?"

Christina pushed her inside the house, slammed the door behind them. "I will make tea. We will talk. Everything will be fine. No?"

Alexia pulled away, turned to face her. Christina opened her arms up as if to show she had nothing in her hands. "What is it?"

"Dimitria is your cousin." She jabbed at the air with her finger, heard her voice rise, tried to control it and gave up. "My father and Dimitria. Theodora is my..." She slammed her hand on the table. "I can't even say it."

"Maria said things?"

"Theodora showed me her mother's picture. The woman was older, but I recognized her from your pictures."

"Yes, she is our cousin." Christina said and turned, picked up a few crumbs on the kitchen counter and threw them into the sink. She wiped her hands on her apron. "But she had other men before."

"I'm sure she didn't. And you are, too, or you wouldn't try to hide it." Alexia paced.

"How can I tell you this? It is a shame for me."

"How could he have had an affair with his cousin?"

"It was not exactly an affair." She turned away from the sink and caught Alexia's gaze. "It was only for a few months when he was here, after your mother, God rest her soul, died. It was small, nothing important. We stay away and it passes."

"Pretend like nothing happened?"

"Why not? Your father did for so many years."

"What do you mean?"

"He never called her or visited or talked about her. Why should we?"

"Theodora has no one else."

"Her mother chose this when she went after Nicolai. He did not want this, I am sure, but he always had a big heart," Christina said. "It is her fault. Not your father. He only loves those who know how to take things from him."

"It takes two."

"If we accept your sister now, shame comes on all our heads."

"Then we live with it," Alexia said.

"And what about her? Do you think she wants to know or to tell her husband and his family the story of her life, that her mother and father were cousins?"

"I'd want to know."

Christina shook her head. "You do not live like we live."

"I know everything," she said, staring at Christina.

Christina shook her head.

"Everything." Alexia held Christina's gaze.

Christina sat down hard in the chair, covered her face with her apron.

Alexia slammed the door. "Don't wait for me. I don't know when I'll be back."

She rode along the side streets and out onto the back roads. A memory came back to her. A woman she'd spoken to when she'd called her father once while he was in Greece. Was that her? Theodora's mother? He said she was nothing to worry about or some such thing. He never talked about her again. She never thought to ask. What had she talked about with that woman? She couldn't remember.

She called Dan from a field. He was the only one she could think of to call. How had she ended up like this? No one to talk to or confide in.

She asked him how things were going at the office, but Dan cut her off.

"Something's wrong," he said. "What's going on with you? Are you all right?"

"I'll work it out." She kicked at the stones on the side of the road.

"Want to talk it through? Maybe I can help."

"I should go." I can't even make sense of it, she thought. How could you?

"I want to help," he said. "Not everyone thinks like you do, you know. There's no shame in asking for help once in a while."

"I'll call you in the next few days," she said and hung up.

She found herself at Maria's door.

"Come in," Maria said. "You have fight with Christina?"

"I know about Dimitria."

"Come, we talk in the kitchen. Everyone is out tonight anyway."

Alexia followed her into the cluttered kitchen.

"I make tea."

"How did it happen?"

Alexia sat down at the table. Maria sat across from her, the tea forgotten.

"Our father made life difficult for Nicolai when he came home after your mother died, God rest her soul. And we listened to our father; we didn't help Nicolai. We are ashamed of what we did. He needed us then. If he had our support, this unnatural thing could not have happened. Our brother went to his cousin's open arms. They had been close when they were children. They got in trouble once because our uncle found them asleep together. But it was nothing. They weren't even teenagers."

Alexia sat back. Maybe Mom was just a sorry second to him, she thought. When Mom died, he went back to Dimitria, the woman he really loved. "He left me to come back to find Dimitria. He'd been in love with her all along," Alexia said. "Is that what you're saying?"

"No. They were just kids playing house, if it was even that. More likely they were talking, got tired and fell asleep as kids do sometimes, nothing more. Her father reacted for no reason. His dirty imagination."

It must have been more than that, Alexia thought.

"I think it was easy for him to go to her because she made it easy for him, loved him when we turned our backs on him. And we only did this because people talk."

"Yes."

"And there are many sides to this story."

"Christina was the last of us to marry, but she was the oldest of the girls. Solon's family didn't like her. They were looking for any excuse to stop the wedding. I do not think Solon would have allowed it, but Christina was scared. We were all scared for her."

"And what does that have to do with my father?" Alexia touched Maria's forearm.

"We hid this thing between Dimitria and Nicolai. Christina married and Nicolai went back to Canada and everything was fine again."

"But Solon's parents are dead and he didn't have anyone else. Who cares now?"

"Solon is different than his family. You are right. But he is still a proud man."

"My father wanted me to find Theodora. Maybe he cared about her more than he cared about me."

Maria leaned over and cupped Alexia's face. "He went back to Canada for you."

Alexia sat back, her hands open on her lap. "He wanted me to give her the letters he wrote to her. He wanted us to meet, for some reason."

"She has family now. Maybe she doesn't want to know."

"Maybe he wanted to put an end to all this secrecy." Or he wanted to rub Theodora, his love child, in her face. Alexia didn't know what he wanted.

"He want or you want?" Maria took Alexia's hands in hers. "You have to understand us," Maria said. "I get divorce a long time ago. I know you know this because Christina and Katarina talk about it to this day. They say my son is not good because he went through a bad time after the divorce. I have a new husband now. The divorce, as I said, happened many years ago. But it is fresh in their minds like it happen yesterday. There is no happy ending like in the books. You live with us long enough and you will learn this."

1986

"Why didn't you tell us you were coming?" Mavis said. She told him to come in, but he hesitated. He stood at the front door, his hand on the handle, his other arm wedged against the doorframe. His head hung to one side. She looked at him, waiting for an answer. He felt like the wooden sculpture of Christ on the cross in the church in Kalavryta. The lines of resignation carved into the wooden face had made Nicolai weep.

"It's been weeks since we heard from you."

"I know. I'm sorry," Nicolai said. On the plane, he'd tried to imagine what it would be like. He pictured himself standing back, waiting to see if Alexia would come to him and hug him. He wanted her to be the way she had been with him before he left.

He'd been wrong to leave her behind. By the look on her face, Mavis was thinking the same thing. If a friend couldn't forgive him, how would his little girl?

"I'm ..." Mavis reached out and brought him close. "You must have missed her terribly. It won't... I mean, it wouldn't have been easy without her." Pinned in Mavis's embrace, a spasm worried his lower back.

They stood together until she let him go.

She brushed at her cheek with the back of her hand. Her hair had a few streaks of grey, her face was paler than usual. She took a deep breath and smiled weakly. "It's just such a surprise."

"It was time."

"I'm making some soup. Do you want some?" She closed the front door, rubbed at her arms, said summer had gone by too quickly.

He stood on the doormat as if not sure he'd be allowed to come in. "Is she here?"

Mavis turned and looked at the grandfather clock. "She'll be home in a couple of minutes." She sighed, then put her arm in his. "She's missed you."

The kitchen smelled of fresh-baked bread and felt like home, more home than his mother's kitchen, or that awful motel room. His stomach growled, but he didn't feel like eating. He sat at the kitchen table, listened to Mavis talk about how Alexia was doing in school, the friends she'd made, the baking they'd done, all the books they'd read. "I've missed a lot," he said. His fingers drummed at his thighs. "I get it."

Mavis turned. They looked at each other, then she turned away again. "It's just that she's such a great kid," Mavis said. "So interested and curious."

She wasn't telling him anything he didn't already know.

"I've taken pictures for you," she said as she threw some chopped parsley into the soup, "so you can see." She brushed one hand against the other.

Under his breath he rehearsed what he'd say to Alexia.

"I'm sorry, I didn't hear you." Mavis turned to face him. "Say again?"

He heard the front door open and slam shut. "I'm home, Aunty."

He pushed back his chair. His breath quickened. Calm down, he said to himself. Hearing her voice, he knew he'd made the right decision. At least once in his life. He couldn't have a life anywhere without her. He had to make her believe it.

"Come in here quick, Ali," Mavis said.

He rubbed his hands on his jeans. He listened to her in the hallway, watched the spot where she'd come through the door. His eyes would be the first thing she saw. She'd know he loved her. She'd know he was back to stay. His eyes would tell her everything.

Her sounds got louder: a huff as she kicked her shoes off, the bang as they knocked against the closet door, her sigh as she struggled with her coat. "It sticks to my fleece," she said. "I hate that coat." God, how he'd missed that voice. Her feet sliding as she came down the hallway. His arms dangled at his sides. His eyes ached staring at the blank doorway.

She ran to Mavis and hugged her. She hadn't seen him at all. He was sure he hadn't looked away. How could she have missed him? He was standing by the kitchen table. Of course, she couldn't see him. The island blocked her view.

"Wait until I tell you what happened!"

Mavis turned Alexia around and walked her to the other side of the island.

Alexia stared at him. She glanced over at Mavis as if to ask a question, then turned back to him. He could see a crease form on her forehead, just above her eyes.

"Are you finished working?" she asked, tucking her hands behind her back.

"I'm here to stay," he said.

"When she's got a question, her gaze can slice you open," her grade three teacher had told him. Nicolai understood now what she'd meant.

Mavis gave Alexia a slight nudge and turned towards the stove. Mavis pulled her apron up to her face, wiped her eyes.

Alexia ran her hand over her long hair as if to make sure she looked presentable.

Just like her mother, he thought. You'll always be perfect to me, *paidi mou*. The actual words didn't come out of his mouth. Her face was red. She liked to run. That hadn't changed. She'd probably run all the way home.

"I'm really happy to see you," he said softly, walking towards her.

She took a step back.

He stopped. Let her come to you, he told himself. "I've missed you," he said.

"Why did you hang up on me?"

"I'm sorry, *paidi mou,*" he said. He held her gaze, hoped she'd see it in his eyes. He wouldn't turn away now.

She shrugged, stared at her feet.

"I wanted to come back as soon as I could."

"Really?" She looked at him, again.

He nodded. He gazed beyond her, caught a glimpse of Mavis, her back still turned. He wanted to speak up, but his mouth was dry. He could use a glass of water.

Alexia shuffled towards him.

It's all right, he thought. I'm here now. I won't leave you again. Believe me, please. Please.

Her arms reached up to him. He hugged her close.

His knees felt like water. He wondered if his legs would collapse beneath him and he'd drop in front of her. "You've been running," he said, pulling away. "I can tell." He smiled and dropped down onto the chair.

"I'll clean up," she said, and shrugged.

"I missed you," he said again as if he were speaking Greek and these were the only words he remembered of his language. He held his breath.

"It's okay, Daddy," Alexia said and put her hand in his. "I know."

Nicolai agreed to stay with Stuart and Mavis until he was able to find a place. Alexia seemed happy with the arrangement for now. He went back to work, redoubled his efforts to build his public relations company, hired more staff, made presentations and went to meetings. He looked through the real estate ads for a place of their own.

They went to the fall fair and bake sale. On Halloween, they got dressed up and planned a route. It felt like a job, but one he wanted to do well.

"Do you want me to take her out?" Mavis asked.

"I'm back now, Mavis. Stop worrying," he said sharply. I screwed up before. I know that, he thought. But, I'm her father. And I'm here now. You don't have to worry, anymore. It's going to be fine. "You did a great job with her," he added, as an afterthought.

Mavis shrugged. "I'll get over it. Alexia's the one you should be worried about."

On Saturdays and sometimes on Sundays, too, he'd take Alexia out for the day. They'd look at houses and condominiums, grab a quick sandwich at lunch, see more places in the afternoon and eventually stop for dinner.

"You pick the restaurant," he said, one late Saturday afternoon. "We'll go anywhere you want to go."

"You pick," she said. "It doesn't matter to me."

"How about Greek?"

"Aren't you sick of that?"

They drove around the West End, Nicolai gazing up at the condominiums on Beach Avenue.

"Let's get a house where we can have a dog," she said again.

"How about that diner on Davie?" he said. "Let's go there."

She shrugged. "Okay."

Nicolai glanced over. The seat belt lay against her bony collarbone, holding her tight against the back of the seat. "Dogs are a big responsibility," he said. "You're too young. You've never had a pet."

"I'd look after it," she said stubbornly.

He glanced over at her. He got the message. She was blaming him. She didn't think he'd looked after her. He was trying, though. Maybe she couldn't see that? "Wouldn't it be nice to be by the water?" Nicolai asked. "In a condominium, we wouldn't have to take care of anything. Someone else would do all the work. We'd have more time."

"I don't mind doing stuff, Daddy. We'd do it together."

Like her mother, he thought. But not her mother. "I'm sorry, *paidi mou,* but I don't want another house. It's too much work. I'm busy at work. And you're busy at school," he said. "I don't want you to worry about anything else."

At the diner, they sat across from each other. She picked at her dinner and watched him closely. "You've got lots and lots of work, right?" Alexia said, and put her hand on his forearm.

He gulped the last drop of wine in his glass, patted his chin. "This is pretty incredible." He pointed to his half-eaten hamburger. "Best burger I've had in a while."

"I mean there's enough work here." She sat on her hands. "Right?"

He took another bite, shook his head, mumbled and began to cough.

She stood up beside him quickly and patted his back. She handed him a glass of water and said, "Don't talk with your mouth full."

He sipped water, wiped away a tear. "When did you become the parent?" he asked, through another coughing spurt. He cleared his throat. "I'm okay, *paidi mou*. Sit down, please." He flicked away a tear.

She stared at him for several seconds until he nodded. "Don't worry so much," he said. "Everything is okay now."

"That's what you said before."

She stood beside her chair, looking down at her plate. He followed her gaze to the uneaten burger. He told himself to reassure her. The two of them would be fine.

He nudged her so she had to look directly into his eyes. "That won't happen again. I'm not leaving. Not without you."

She nodded, but didn't smile. She sat down.

He tickled her. She giggled, pushing him away.

"Now eat before you disappear. You're like your..." He pushed his shoulders back, knocked his chair forward, pulling himself closer to the table.

"Like who?"

He grabbed his burger, brought it to his mouth, changed his mind and dropped it back on the plate.

"Who?"

"It still hurts to talk about her."

"I don't want us to forget Mom." Her hands sat on her lap curled up into fists.

He took her hands, kissed each and folded them within his. "We never will," he said and hugged her. "Not ever."

Nicolai continued to search for a place to live and after a few months found a penthouse condominium on Beach Avenue. He visited the place four times. He lay on his back on the floor in the living room, his head propped up on the pillow of his arms, and stared at the endless ocean.

He took Alexia to see it one night just before sunset. "Look," he said, pointing to the pink sky beyond the floor-to-ceiling windows. They stood side by side, his arm over her shoulder.

"Do they allow dogs?" she asked, turning away.

"We'll have this every single night." He smiled.

"It's not a very big living room, is it? I mean for a dog to run around."

He turned. "Let's check out your bedroom."

"Did you already buy it, Daddy?"

"I wanted you to look at it." He had put an offer in that morning. He could pull out of the deal if he had to, but he thought she'd like it. What was not to like?

"If you like it," she said and reached for his hand, "it's okay with me."

He squeezed her hand, smiled.

Once the paperwork went through, Nicolai had the condominium painted and decorated professionally. He wanted it to be perfect. He sprinkled holy water in each room. This new home would be blessed. It would be protected and would take care of both of them.

He wanted to get moved in as soon as possible. He appreciated Mavis and Stuart taking both Alexia and him in, but their worried looks made him feel like he was on probation. Why didn't anyone believe him? He was back to stay. Everything was fine.

When Nicolai walked down the hall of Mavis's house to Alexia's room to see if she was ready to go, he found Mavis and Alexia sitting on the bed, Alexia's hand on Mavis's leg. Mavis blew her nose. Nicolai leaned back, stood outside the open door.

"We're not going very far," Alexia said.

"That's right." Mavis blew her nose again.

Nicolai shook his head. What was the big deal? He'd talked to Mavis, thought he'd reassured her, told her how much he'd appreciated what she'd done for Alexia, for him. He knocked on the doorframe and walked into the room. "Ready to go?"

"One last thing, Daddy," Alexia said, pointing to a box on the table.

"I'll see you outside," he said. "We should get going."

"Oh, I almost forgot," Mavis said. "You got a letter this morning. It's on the kitchen counter." Alexia stood up. Mavis gave her a hug.

"I'll grab it on my way out."

He helped Alexia unpack after they arrived at the condominium and when she said she wasn't hungry, he asked her if she wanted to take a bath.

"I'm pretty tired."

"We'll be happy here," he said. "You'll see."

She nodded, kissed him and went to bed. He sat on the living room floor, flicked on the gas fireplace and opened the letter from Achilles.

Have you forgotten about us?

I'm trying, Nicolai said to himself.

In the next paragraph Achilles said he was still looking for more investors and things were *promising*. Nicolai smiled. Good old Achilles. He would never change.

Achilles went on to list the people he'd talked to, the amount of money they had promised, when he hoped to hear back from them and how he planned to follow up. He sent along some pictures of other light standards. Nicolai flipped through the clippings and shook his head. They all looked the same: ornate design, old-fashioned, high-end. Achilles would never get it. This wasn't the look Nicolai was going for.

He skimmed through Achilles's hopeful projections, picking up small clusters of words. Thank God I didn't get in any deeper, Nicolai thought. There's no way this project is ever going to get off the ground. At least I have the land. It might be worth something one day. That's better than nothing. He continued picking up the gist of Achilles's ramblings until he wasn't sure he understood what had been written. He rubbed his eyes and reread the last two paragraphs.

So they are blaming me for what happened. Because we were together before, they think it is my fault. But you and I know the truth. Now I understand why you left in such a hurry.

What was Achilles saying?

Why don't you talk some sense into your cousin? Tell her to get rid of it. Things will go better for her. It's a problem no one needs. She seems to have forgotten. We are a small village. Everyone talks and they look at me as if I'm the father.

He leaned back onto his elbows, pushed hard against the floor. His mind was blank. His elbows began to shake. He pushed harder. Shit!

He heard Alexia's footsteps behind him.

He turned.

She stood behind him shivering, her feet bare. "Can I get a glass of water?"

He stuffed the letter in his pant's pocket. "You're not asleep yet?"

"I can't find a comfy spot in my new bed. And it's cold."

"Let's see what we can do," he said and led her into the kitchen to get her some water. The letter crinkled in his pocket. He rubbed at her shoulders. "We need to get something warm inside you." He wasn't going to leave her. He wasn't going to hurt her again. And he wasn't going to let anyone else hurt her either. Focus, he told himself. Focus. Don't think about that letter. Not now.

He made Alexia a peanut butter and banana sandwich and gave her a cup of hot water with a piece of lemon. "My mother used to give me a cup of hot lemon water when I was cold." He got a comforter out of the closet and wrapped it around her.

"When can we go and see them?" she asked.

"I don't know," he said, shifting his gaze away from her questioning eyes. "We have too many things to do right here. And you've got a new school to start on Monday."

"I'm not sure about the school. What it'll be like."

He wiped some peanut butter off the counter. He picked up the dirty knife as if he meant to throttle it. Damn Achilles! Was this some kind of blackmail? Or was it true? It could be true.

"Daddy, are you listening?"

Nicolai sat down with her at the kitchen table. He forced himself to look at her, calm his voice. "You'll make lots of friends," he said. "You'll be part of the gang soon enough. You'll see."

She put her hands over his. "You're tapping again."

When had he picked up the spoon? He couldn't say. He put it down. "The noise fills up the room, doesn't it?"

He tucked her into bed and kissed her forehead, then went into his own room, got into bed with his clothes on and pulled the covers over his head. Those few moments with Alexia had given him a bit of reprieve. But that damn letter was still in his pocket. He heard it every time he moved. He threw off the covers and dug it out.

We met one day away from the village. It wasn't easy to arrange, but Achilles has his ways. She says she's moving away. Going to Aigio or Patras where no one knows her. But how will she survive? That woman has always been so headstrong. It is for this reason she can't get along with anyone.

Fuck! Fuck! Fuck! All this bullshit. What am I going to do? What the hell am I going to do?

Nicolai crumpled up the letter and threw it against the wall. He paced, picked up the letter again, smoothed it out and reread Achilles's words. Maybe it's not mine, he thought. It was possible.

He heard a tap. "Still can't sleep?" He pushed the letter under his mattress and opened his bedroom door.

"I just wanted to make sure you were still here."

He folded Alexia into his arms. "Where else would I be?"

She shrugged, touching his face.

"Sleep in here with me tonight," he said, bundling her in under the covers. "Until you get used to our new place. Okay?"

She nodded, looked beyond him. Fear. Disappointment. What else was written on her face? He felt a rush of impatience. Why didn't she get it? He wasn't going to leave again. He wasn't. He pulled the blanket over them hard, lifting the bedding at the bottom end and exposing his feet. He kicked at the sheets. Alexia lay still. He felt her stare.

Alexia fell asleep tucked in close to him. He listened to her shallow breathing and resolved to tear up Achilles's letter tomorrow after he made Alexia's breakfast.

They settled into a routine. Nicolai scheduled his work commitments so he could pick up Alexia after school. When he wasn't able to, he phoned the school and she walked home. He'd come home to find her in a chair in the living room staring out the window. "What's wrong?" he asked her the first time it happened.

She shrugged. "I didn't know what to do."

"You could have started your homework."

"I wasn't sure." She sat very still, wouldn't look at him.

"You mean you didn't know where to start?"

"I guess."

He went to her, crouched down in front of her, wrapping her in his arms. She was so withdrawn, he was afraid she'd reject his effort. But then he felt her hands, light on his shoulders, and was reassured. "Should we go for a walk?" he asked.

"Do you want to?"

"Or we could do something else," he said. "Anything you want."

"I should do my homework," she said, but didn't move.

"Sometimes I'm late, *paidi mou*. It doesn't mean any more than that."

"I know."

Years passed. Still, each time he wasn't able to pick her up at school, he'd come home and find her quiet and distant. Sometimes her mood lasted for days. He'd hear a creak outside his bedroom door late at night and knew she'd be standing outside. On those nights, he'd exaggerate his snoring. He hoped the sound of him would reassure her. He thought he'd convince her with all the things they did together: going to her practices, cheering louder than anyone at her basketball games, taking her to her favourite restaurants, planning weekends to the Gulf Islands. He'd show her he was a good father, and eventually she'd understand there was nothing to worry about. She'd forget he'd ever left her behind.

Sometimes he did think about Dimitria and the child, where they were, what they were doing. What did the child look like? What did the child like to do? Would he ever feel its hand in his, like he used to when Alexia was a child? Alexia was too grown-up for all that now. Sometimes, for long stretches at a time, he could distract himself with work or planning a weekend to the mountains with Alexia. But then he'd see a child playing in the park with her friends and he'd watch, wondering what his own flesh and blood was doing at the moment, so far away.

"Why don't you change your address?" Mavis said, handing him another one of the flimsy grey envelopes with the words *Air Mail* repeated over and over again around its border. "It's been almost five years."

"I'll get to it," he said every time. "I'm busy."

At first, he ripped up all the letters without reading them. But they kept coming. A new one arrived, thicker than the rest. Nicolai listened to the rain drum at his window and fingered the letter. Alexia was asleep. What could it hurt? He slid his finger under the lip of the envelope. Pictures scattered at his feet. He gathered them, checked under the bed to make sure he hadn't missed one. The beach, his property in Greece, now had a concrete promenade lined with old-fashioned light standards. It wasn't what he wanted. But he hadn't stuck around, had he?

The last picture was of a little girl about four or five years old with long straight hair pinned back off her face with pink ribbons. She had olive skin and dark eyes, though one eye seemed a bit lighter. She looked like Dimitria. He lay down and covered his eyes with his arm. The picture dangled from his fingers. Yes, she looked like Dimitria, but her cheekbones, her chin, they looked so much like his when he was her age.

He thought about the night he'd given Dimitria and Achilles a ride back to Diakofto. Achilles had insisted on being dropped off first, but thinking back, he had to admit he'd wanted to be alone with her. He had wanted her, like he did when they were kids playing in her bedroom. He hadn't thought about that in a long time. Every kid experimented. It was natural. Innocent. Nothing happened except a bit of touching and awkward kissing. He'd never given it much thought, certainly didn't think of it in the same way Dimitria had. When they got together again, in Greece, Dimitria had told him she was glad that she was finally going to lose herself to him. It was what she wanted. "You were my first love," she'd said. "Remember when we were kids? I waited all this time for you to come back so I could be yours. I knew you would."

He looked at the back of the picture. *Theodora, 5 years old.* Her name was Theodora. She had a name. He had a picture. How could he ignore her now?

He got up and went to the window. Maybe somehow they could make it work. He tried to imagine bringing Dimitria and the child to Vancouver. Maybe they could have some kind of life together. Alexia would love a little sister. They'd be a family. He shook his head, dislodging the image. "Don't be ridiculous. You don't love her," he said out loud. Does it matter? he wondered. The child. Theodora is more important.

He picked up the letter. There were only a few words. *As you can see work progresses and time passes with everything.*

Achilles included Dimitria's address and phone number. *I include it in every letter in the hopes you will come to your senses and return. They need you.*

Nicolai gazed at the clock on his nightstand. It was already morning in Greece. He folded the letter and told himself he'd call tomorrow.

What would he say? That he had so much. Of course, he would share it with them. Make their lives better. But what if she wanted more? He could only give so much. Sara understood that. Sometimes he forgot what she looked like, the way she held him and listened to him go on and on. She was right here on his nightstand and still he sometimes worried he'd forget her, or worse, that Alexia might. He couldn't give anyone more. But he could help the child. *Theodora.* He could do that. Alexia wouldn't need to know. He would keep everything separate. For now. Maybe later, who knew?

He pulled the letter from its hiding spot at the back of the drawer and picked up the phone. After the first ring, he hung up, shoved his hands in his armpits until he calmed down. He was being silly. She probably wasn't even home. He dialled again.

A little girl answered. Dimitria came on the line, apologized that her daughter had grabbed the phone and said hello two or three times. He said nothing. "The person doesn't want to talk to us," he heard Dimitria say.

"It's me," he said.

There was a hesitation, dead air. "I understand," she said finally.

He wondered where Theodora was in relation to her mother and then heard the little girl whine, "Mommy, I'm hot. When can we go?"

"We will in a moment," she said. "Let me finish here first."

"I can call back."

"No."

"How are you?" he asked.

"We're well," she said.

"Achilles sent me a picture."

"I told him not to," Dimitria said. "We can take care of ourselves."

"I can help."

"Look, Achilles wants you to come back," she said. "He sends you these things to entice you. But we are fine. Believe me. She doesn't know you."

"Maybe we should change that."

"It's too late," Dimitria said. "There's someone else. And besides, you remember what you said to me before you left? You were talking about the time we were children. You said, 'we were just playing house'. And you were right. We played house as children and we went farther, too far, as adults. But it was never more than a game."

"We could do something," Nicolai said. "I mean for the child's sake."

"Please don't call us again," she said and hung up.

"Are you sick, Daddy? You slept in."

He pulled the pillow off his head. She was standing by his bed, backpack over her shoulders. "I had trouble getting to sleep. What time is it?"

"Time for me to go to school." She gathered up his pants and threw them on the chair, his socks and shirt went into the hamper. "Look at all this stuff!" She picked up something from the floor as he got out of bed. "Who's that?"

He wanted to grab the picture out of her hand and tear it up. "A friend," he said, working to keep his voice calm. "It came in the mail."

"Cute kid," Alexia said. She put the picture on his bedside table beside Sara's framed picture. "Can we get going?"

In the years that followed, Achilles sent more pictures, more letters. Nothing happened with the promenade. The money dried up. Achilles couldn't find any more investors and Nicolai wasn't going to sink any more into the project. And that was that. Achilles's parents died and he inherited their house; he invited Nicolai to come and stay with him any time he wanted. Theodora grew. He kept one picture of her in his desk. He wasn't sure why this one over all the others. She sat on a blanket on the beach, smiling at the camera, hopeful.

One day, he told himself, he'd go back. With Alexia. He'd take care of whatever Theodora needed then. She'd be older. She'd be able to make up her own mind. He didn't go back when his own father and mother died. Still, there might come a time when he would. He spent late nights when he couldn't sleep and some afternoons when he got home early from work writing letters to Theodora. It helped him to say the things he wanted to say. Things he would say if she were here with him.

I know I haven't been around. I have no explanation for that. Nothing that would make any sense to you. I'm not sure I understand it myself.

Wait until you meet Alexia. She's your sister. I know you'll love each other, even though I made such a mess of everything. I know you will. She takes charge, she makes things happen, stubborn as anything. I wonder what you're like. One day, maybe I'll be lucky enough to meet you and find out myself.

Alexia is growing up so fast. I miss the little girl who wouldn't let go of my hand.

He never mailed those letters. He wasn't sure why he kept writing them.

Alexia became an independent teenager obsessed with doing well in school. "I need to do my homework, Dad," she would say when he'd ask her if she wanted to go to a movie.

"There's no better mark than an A, you know," he'd say and laugh. "And you've got those in spades."

"It doesn't happen by itself," she said.

He continued to help her with her homework, but he sensed that while she listened when he dispensed his advice, she had no intention of following it. When had things changed? She used to sit close beside him, walk hand in hand, listen to everything he had to say. But she was a teenager now. So serious and focused. She didn't need him anymore. Someone had told him once that a parent only had a few years when their child looked up to them, adored them without question. Time passes. Maybe his father had said it. But he wasn't someone who said those kinds of things. Nicolai must have heard it somewhere else.

He called on a new client one day and met a young woman in charge of her father's manufacturing company. He thought it was just another business dinner. Then he felt her leg against his. "Come up to my apartment," she said.

"I can't commit to anything," he said.

"Is one night too much of a commitment?" She laughed.

How could someone find him attractive after all these years? He hadn't thought about himself like that. Alexia wasn't a child anymore. Maybe it was his turn to have some fun.

As quickly as it ignited, the first fling burned out and he discovered there were other young women who were interested. He liked the way they looked at him. They were eager to get to know him. And he was excited about getting to know them. But he didn't want complications, or disappointments, or regrets. Everyone takes care of themselves. No one gets hurt or disillusioned. We keep it light and fun. He always made that clear at the outset. He told them about Sara, insisted he was only interested in enjoying their company, wasn't sure how long anything would last.

Each new woman agreed at first, but when all was said and done, it always ended the same way, with them trying to pin him down to get more serious. "Women are like that," he told Stuart over drinks one night, after another one of Nicolai's breakups. Stuart nodded, but Nicolai knew he didn't really understand. Stuart and Mavis had been married for such a long time. He didn't know anything about this game. "They try all kinds of things to get you to do what they want," Nicolai said.

2010

Maria shook her head. She opened her hands to Alexia as if to plead. “You are young. So smart. So beautiful. So perfect. We only guide you,” Maria said. “Why make the same mistakes we made?”

“I won’t,” she said, leaning against the kitchen counter for support.

Maria placed her hand on Alexia’s shoulder. “We’ve all said this before.”

“I should go.” She walked towards the door.

“How can you know how things work?” She stood on Maria’s front steps. You all want too damn much, she thought. Dad wants me to talk to Theodora. You and Christina don’t. And every time I ask a question, I find out more crap about this family. About him. He went back to Greece to be with Dimitria. His first love. For all I know, his only love. How pathetic. He didn’t give a damn about me. I was a kid. A stupid little kid.

Maria was like the rest of them. Sure, she was open about stuff, but she didn’t want any gossip about the family either. “Think of the shame this will bring.” What about doing the right thing? That never occurs to these people.

Alexia walked up the alleyway to where she’d parked her moped, got on and rode in the direction of Achilles’s favourite bar. Where was the harm in it? At least Achilles paid attention to her. It had been a long time since anyone treated her like a woman. Dan and her colleagues saw her as one of the guys. A perfect work buddy. That's me. Perfect. The perfect daughter. The perfect lawyer. Where did that ever get me? "I know what I'm doing," Alexia had said to Maria. "I'm so sick and tired of taking care of things, always doing what's expected."

Alexia accelerated, lurching forward as the moped begrudged her foot's demand for more speed. Perfect, Maria had said. I don't think so. Achilles was an old, self-centred lech, but she wasn't looking for anything permanent. Just a bit of a mindless escape. Was that so bad?

She parked the moped, clipped her helmet around the handlebars.

The lights in the tavern were dim and cigarette smoke enveloped the room in low floating haze. Upbeat, fast-strumming *bouzouki* music played in the background. She put a hand over one ear to dull the noise. The heavy bass pounded in her chest.

Her eyes adjusted. Achilles sat at the bar with his back to her, a glass of beer in front of him. The bartender wiped glasses, nodded as if he could hear what Achilles was saying. Neither noticed her walk in.

She stroked his back and kissed his cheek. "Have you forgotten me already?"

"My little bird returns." He scooped her close, leaning in to kiss her mouth.

She turned. He pecked her cheek and tightened his arm around her waist.

"*Paristani ton yoe,*" the bartender said.

Alexia pushed Achilles away. "Yes, he acts just like that. A magnet for women."

"I do not know my own strength." Achilles grabbed a pistachio from the bowl in front of him. He cracked it open with his fingernail and tossed the shell on to the heap of discarded bits he'd piled on the counter. He threw the pistachio up and opened his mouth to catch it. He swallowed it whole.

She pulled up a stool and ordered a beer. The bartender ducked under the counter and brought back a bottle and a filmy glass. He disappeared into the back.

Alexia sipped from the bottle, listening to the clatter of dishes.

Achilles stroked her hand. She pulled it away, tucked both hands under her legs and gazed at the multi-coloured, half-filled bottles of alcohol on the shelf in front her.

They left the bar, his arm inside hers as they walked up the street to where she had parked the moped. He nattered on about the boardwalk project he had in the works. "You will see. I have important friends who believe." He hugged her.

You're pretty damn sure of yourself, she thought. She smelled cigarette smoke on his sweater and stale beer on his breath. She squeezed in closer. What the hell. She wasn't a little girl anymore, even though everyone here treated her like one.

He gazed into the distance. "It's a magnificent place. People will come from all over." His arm loosened its hold on her. She leaned into him. He looked at her and smiled, squeezed her close. He kissed the top of her head. "Let me show you."

"Of course," she said.

He kissed the inside of her hand. His beard tickled her palm. She caught a quick glimpse of the tiny spot of scalp at his crown and felt a tenderness she hadn't felt for him before.

She eased her hand away, put on her helmet. She felt his stare. She didn't look at him. She dug into her pocket for the keys.

He touched her forearm and signalled to toss him the keys. "It is a man's responsibility to drive a woman wherever she needs to go. It is our role in this life."

What era do you come from? she wondered, shaking her head. He smiled, boyish and charming. She gazed down at the ground. She shrugged. Get off the soapbox once in your life. It's not like you're going to change him. And besides, this isn't a big deal. Let him believe what he wants. You're not marrying the guy. Just going for a ride. She handed him the keys.

He started the moped, and she slipped on behind him. He leaned against her; put his hand around her thigh to hold her in place. Her stomach seemed to drop away. His back warmed her. Putting her hands against his chest, she held him as he eased the moped forward. Her jacket rode up, exposing her lower back. Air played on her bare skin. She didn't pull her jacket down. She gripped him closer. As they rode through the dark streets, his hand loosened its hold on her leg.

He took her hand and led her down the concrete boardwalk, jumping over the spots where the cement had buckled and cracked. Large gaps had opened up, dropping to the stones and sand below. Water gurgled against the rocks. Across the inlet, lights flickered.

Some of the streetlights along the walkway sputtered on and off. The sky was clear and a half-moon gave enough light for Alexia to see Diakofto's splintered mountains. The breeze had disappeared. Moths flitted in and out of the light. Achilles nipped kisses from her when she tried to ask a question about his plans for the boardwalk.

"What do you think of the lights?" He squeezed her hand.

She followed his eyes up to one. It flashed bright as if for her benefit. He smiled.

She wasn't sure why Achilles was so pleased with himself. "Some fresh light bulbs might help. And some of these things look like they haven't been hooked up. Dangling bits don't exactly add anything."

Cupping her face in his hands, he kissed each of her eyelids. "People don't worry about these things when they have the ocean in front of them."

She held onto his hands. "How many people actually walk down here? What's here? What do you like about it?"

He kissed her forehead. "You think too much," he said, dropping his hands. He walked ahead.

He'd asked her a question. What was she supposed to do? Act like she didn't have an opinion? She noticed the slight sway of his walk, like an aging mare with a sagging rear.

"Okay," she said. "I get it. I'll walk home. Return my keys whenever." She jumped off the boardwalk and onto the beach. She jogged towards the road, her feet slipping in the sand, her shoes filling with tiny stones. She told herself she should be home. It was late. Christina would be worried. She'd probably called Maria and half the town by now. It would serve them right though. They'd think twice about keeping their stupid secrets from her.

"You don't have to be this way." He ran beside her, quick and agile like her father had been before he got sick. She picked up her pace, stared at the shadow of the road she could see a short distance in front of her.

He pulled at her arm.

She stopped. "If you want a parrot, I'm not that girl." She met his gaze defiantly, like she dealt with all her adversaries around the negotiating table. But like a disobedient child, she kept her hands behind her back.

"I want the woman," he said, stroking her face. He pressed his mouth against hers.

She stepped back and he released her. Running her tongue over her lip, she sucked her own salty blood. "Being gentle is okay, you know."

He shrugged.

Maybe he wasn't as sure of himself as he liked to pretend, she thought. She went to him. His tongue slithered over her lip, into her mouth.

He lay her down on the sand, kissing her breasts and stomach through her blouse. He tugged at the zipper of her pants with his mouth. It didn't budge. He tried again, yanking hard. He gave up, tried to lift her blouse. She held it down. "Right here?"

Achilles stroked his beard. He sat up without looking at her, crossed his legs and leaned against his knees. He picked up a small stone and threw it. It fell a few feet away.

She adjusted her blouse and sat up. What was he thinking?

"The fire is ready. There is no shame in this," he said. He wiped his hands against his shirt, pulled her down again and edged himself on top.

Her body arched upward as he kissed her neck.

He pulled at her zipper, again. He tugged her pants down. She slipped one leg free. Her pants now hung from the other leg. She tried to kick them away, but he whispered to leave them where they were. "We might have to react quickly," he said.

"What?"

"People talk," he said. I have to live here." He drew back her underwear, but didn't take them off.

She laughed.

He pulled himself up on his hands and hovered above her. "Have I done anything funny?" he asked. "You do not like what Achilles is doing?"

She stared up at the moon. "Even you worry about what people say?"

"Achilles? No," he said. "I have what I need without taking chances."

He bent down over her, forced her to look at him.

She turned her head. He stuck his tongue in her ear. She tried to squirm away. He held her head steady, sucked her earlobe. She twisted, finally giving him her mouth.

He pecked at her lips as he unzipped his pants, held her underwear to one side, pushing at her until he found her. She rocked up to meet him. Burying his face against her shoulder, his arms lay on the ground like a halo around her head. His beard rubbed at the tender spot below her collarbone, sand branded her backside. She stared at one bright star in the sky. It glimmered like a laugh.

A few seconds later, Achilles gasped. His full weight dropped on her. His arms closed in around her ears and muffled the sound of the ocean, all sound. His chest moved up and down in a slow, steady rhythm. She lay still, pierced to the ground, aware of how his zipper pinched her pubic bone, how the metal snagged at her skin. Her lips were dry. She bit and nibbled at her lip until she felt the skin rip open.

He heaved himself up onto his knees, used a handkerchief he'd pulled out of his pocket to wipe himself. He adjusted his sweater and zipped his pants, brushing sand away, then smoothed his hands over his hair and beard. He hummed. Slipping the soiled handkerchief into his shirt pocket, he stood up. "This was good for both of us. Yes." He gazed out in the direction of the boardwalk.

Alexia supported herself on her elbows. Watching Achilles, she remembered how her father would look at himself in the mirror whenever he got ready for work. He'd comb his hair, pulling it back into an elastic band. He'd make sure a few strands hung down around his face. He'd run his tongue over his teeth, brushing them a second time, then he'd drip his cologne onto his hands, slapping it on his face and the back of his neck. He'd check the wrinkles on his forehead and around his mouth, say no one liked an old guy. She'd tell him he was handsome. What else would the perfect daughter say to her father? She'd wanted him to be happy.

He'd smile and kiss her forehead.

She ran her fingers over her forehead. Sometimes she still felt his kiss. She sat up. This is ridiculous. He's gone. He never thought or worried about her as much as she worried about him.

Achilles pulled out another handkerchief from his pants pocket and handed it to her. "We should get back," he said. "*Ella, paidi mou.*"

She stroked her cheek with the handkerchief, smelled lavender.

Achilles stood with his legs apart, one hand on each hip. She hadn't noticed that angry stare in him before. The hunt was over for him, she thought. He got what he wanted. Now, he wanted to get going. She understood that. She'd done it herself before. They weren't that different. Don't worry, I don't feel like hanging around either. It wasn't the escape she'd hoped for, but it would have to do.

The handkerchief had been carefully pressed. Standing up, she adjusted her underwear and pulled up her pants. Sand sprinkled down and semen dribbled from her. She was cold and felt clammy. She needed to be home with Christina and Solon. They were her family. All she had. They pissed her off, yes. But, she was no angel either.

She handed the handkerchief back to Achilles, folded and unused.

"Do not worry," he said, pressing the handkerchief towards her. "I have a woman. She does my cleaning."

"I do for myself," Alexia said. The ocean cracked behind her. She didn't move.

"Maybe a storm comes tomorrow," he said.

She shrugged. The breeze had picked up. It pushed at her.

"There will always be women who want to take care of me," he said, putting his arm around her. "Should we meet here tomorrow night if there is no rain?"

She held out her hand. "How about my keys?"

"Good idea," he said. "We shouldn't be seen together. Why invite troubles?" He pulled out the keys and handed them to her.

"We can come to this spot and accidentally run into each other anytime you want. We do that well, yes?"

"I don't think it's a good idea," she said. "My family."

"You are like your father." He pulled away. "He worried about what his sisters thought, what his father said, who was talking about him, and so on. It paralyzed him." He put both hands in his pockets, gave her his back to ponder. He stared out at the ocean.

She jerked his arm until he faced her. "You knew my father?"

"It will be daylight soon," he said, gazing beyond her. "We have to go."

"Not until you tell me how you knew him." She stood in front of him.

"He was my partner on this project. That's all."

He walked away from her. She yanked him back.

"I knew him since we were kids. We were good friends once."

"What else?"

He turned to face the boardwalk. "He gets himself in trouble and leaves. That is why we have a construction zone here, as you call it, and not the dream." He threw his hands up, again. "You are a child. How can you understand?"

"A child you had no trouble fucking." She shoved him.

"If he was a good father, he should have come back to take care of her," he said. "I told him. He had no excuses. I told him."

"You mean he didn't know?" She grabbed his arms and meant to shake him. She tightened her grip. Her hands hurt, but she wouldn't let go.

He wrenched himself out of her grasp. "Dimitria did not want him to know. I am the one who wrote to him."

"Because you wanted him to come back for this stupid project of yours," Alexia said. "You didn't give a damn about Dimitria or Theodora."

"They all wanted to protect poor Nicolai," he said without meeting her eyes. "Someone had to tell him the truth."

"Who tried to protect him? Dimitria, his family, who?"

"We could have made this town," he said.

"Why didn't you tell me this before?" You're a womanizer and a damn liar, she thought. We're not alike. I may screw the odd married guy, but at least I'm honest.

He put his hands on her shoulders. "Achilles is a simple man with a dream. There is nothing difficult to understand with me. What you see is all."

"You couldn't convince my father," she said. "You thought you'd convince me?"

He grinned in that crooked adolescent way she so hated in weak men. She shoved him away. He stumbled backwards. I'm so sick of selfish, needy men who just expect you to take care of them, she thought.

"Do not be like this," he said, his arms open. "Tonight, you saw how good we are together."

"Give me a break," she said and walked away.

"Let us talk," he mumbled. "Maybe you could change old Achilles."

Picking up her pace, she began to run, the sand biting at her heels.

2009

Nicolai thrashed out of his jacket and heard the tear of fabric under his armpit. Armani isn't what it used to be, he muttered. He threw the jacket on the sand and yanked at his tie until it hung limp around his neck. Sitting down, he kicked off his shoes and flung them as far as he could. He'd been tired when he'd left the doctor's office, but had left his car parked there anyway and managed to walk for two hours until he reached this spot on Beach Avenue just below his condominium. The sun warmed his face. He dug wells in the sand with his heels, then tossed fistfuls of sand over his feet until they were completely covered. A seagull stood on a patch of brown grass close by, staring at him with its beady eyes.

Where had all the time gone? When Alexia was a little girl, she needed him to take care of her. He shook his head. No, she didn't. Stop fooling yourself. Too late for that crap. His feet were baking. He leaned back on his elbows, burying his feet deeper. She'd gone to a university at the other end of the country even though he'd tried to convince her to stay in Vancouver. She had to take more courses, complete another exam after her degree so she could practise law in British Columbia, and at first she wasn't sure she wanted to come back. "I have friends here, Dad," she said. But eventually she came home. It didn't stop her from pushing him away. She'd bought her own condominium, gone to a start-up company even after he'd tried to talk her out of both those moves.

They were good decisions, though. He saw that now. She knew what was best. She always did. So much time had slipped away. His headstrong, serious little girl was now a stubborn, self-assured woman.

He had a year left. "Give or take," the doctor had said. He was the third doctor Nicolai had gone to see. The first doctor had been right all along. "You don't know what you're talking about," Nicolai had said to him. "I feel fine."

"You will for a while."

The seagull picked at the grass, keeping an eye on Nicolai. He sat up and shooed the seagull away. It hopped a couple of feet further from him and squawked.

"Shut up." He pretended to throw something at the bird. It stared at him, but didn't move. Nicolai shook his head. "Why listen to me?"

"Were you talking to me?" a woman's voice asked.

He turned, but his buried feet refused to move. He kicked at the sand, slipping further.

"Looks like you're stuck." She pulled her earplugs out and kept jogging on the spot. "I thought you were talking to me."

He finally extricated himself and stood up. "Talking to myself like an old man." He wiped his hands on his pants. "I'm Nicolai," he said, extending his hand. When she took it, he cupped his other hand over hers.

"Erica," she said. She stopped jogging, gazed beyond him to the ocean.

He turned towards the water, his arms at his sides. "I'm sorry. I interrupted your run."

"I wasn't into it today," she said. "You shouldn't force stuff."

"I don't know." He picked up his jacket and shook it out. Sand fell, blowing up with the breeze. She rubbed her eyes. He apologized, told her he was an idiot, touching her arm to make sure she was okay.

"You're one of those guys who apologizes when you've done nothing wrong."

"It comes with being a husband and a father." He walked over to his shoes, picked them up and tucked them under his arm. The seagull flew off.

"How long have you been married?" She put her hand on his forearm as if to try to get his attention. He used the same gesture. For some reason, it drove Alexia crazy. He smiled.

"What?" she asked.

"Thinking about my daughter. My wife died many years ago."

"And you never remarried?"

He shook his head. He'd been asked this so many times by so many other women. Erica had the same moist softness in her eyes, anticipating, like the others, his answer. He'd always made it clear. That's probably why some of them had hoped for more. "That grin of yours, the way you hold yourself," an old girlfriend told him once long after she'd left him and married someone else. "I don't know what it is. It's like all we see is that little boy in you screaming, 'Take care of me.'"

"I'm heading up the street for a smoothie," Erica said. "Want to join me?"

He nodded. He wiped his right foot against the bottom of his pants and slipped into his shoe. He held onto Erica's shoulder as he rubbed the sand off the other foot.

"No socks?"

"They cramp my style." He put on the other shoe.

"Cool."

Erica did most of the talking. Nicolai sipped at his smoothie, trying to pay attention. He nodded whenever he thought she was about to stop. She was enrolled at Emily Carr and was working on her portfolio and an exhibition of her paintings. She jogged, did yoga, hung out with friends, and took care of herself. "We never know," she said. "I want to keep the house in order."

He should do the same thing. He should tell Alexia the truth so they could prepare together. How much had that helped him when Sara died? Not one bit. Instead, he'd worried, fussed and hoped that things could be different. Mostly, he'd been angry with her. "If you just keep doing things, you'll get better. Wait and see," he said when Sara reminded him again about the will.

"There you go again. Why not concentrate on the here and now?" he said. "Wills are for old people."

She leaned against the counter. "To make it clear."

"You've always kept us organized," he said. "Why change things now? It will only invite what we don't want."

She'd wrapped him in her arms. "It will all work out."

"Hey, are you still with me?" Erica asked.

"I should get going," he said, dropping his business card on the table. "Give me a call. I'll buy you dinner sometime."

She picked up the card, tucked it into the pocket of her jogging pants. She sucked the dregs of her smoothie through her straw.

It was raining outside. He pulled up his collar and walked fast, ducking under overhangs and awnings. He waited in the rain until he flagged a cab to take him back to his car.

When he got home he took off his wet clothes and stood in the hot shower for twenty minutes until he warmed up. He dried off, threw on some sweats and an extra sweater and sat on the living room floor with a bottle of *oúzo* and a small tumbler. He couldn't see the ocean in the dark. Lights flickered from Kits beach. He wasn't going to put Alexia through what he'd gone through with Sara. Alexia was busy with her own law practice, and maybe even had a boyfriend she didn't want him to know about just yet. He'd tell her eventually. They'd make the arrangements when the time was right. There wasn't any rush.

He gazed at the clock. He had to phone her. He called Alexia at eight o'clock every night and if he didn't, she'd know something was wrong.

Nicolai dialled her number.

"Hey, Dad," she said when she picked up the phone.

"It could have been someone else."

"No one else calls me every night."

"I need to change my routine," he said.

"I like it just the way it is."

"I bet you didn't count on the old man retiring." His voice cracked and he cleared his throat, looked up at the ceiling, as if she was standing in front of him and he had to avoid her stare. If she were here, she would know he wasn't telling her all of it.

"What?" she asked. "When did this happen?"

He gulped a mouthful of *ouzo*, began to cough.

"Are you all right?" she asked. "Should I come over?"

"The *ouzo* went down the wrong way," he gasped, taking a small sip, and clearing his throat. He squeezed his eyes shut. Tears bothered his cheek. "I've been thinking about it for a long time." He cleared his throat again.

"You built that business," she said. "Who else could run it?"

"I didn't say I was going to do it right away." He swallowed.

"But what will you do?"

"Spend more time with you, *paidi mou*. Relax a bit. It's time, isn't it?"

"There's nothing wrong?"

"What?" he said, chuckling. He swallowed hard to suppress another cough. "It's time for your old man to think about taking a break."

He pictured her sitting in her living room, staring out her window, legs folded to one side, the telephone at her ear. He heard her get up off the leather couch. She was pacing in front of her large window, looking out into the dark and thinking. She was a smart girl. He couldn't give himself away. "So who did you beat up today?" he asked.

"If there was something wrong, you'd tell me, right, Dad?"

"What could be wrong?" he asked. "I never planned to work forever. Priorities change. That's life, *paidi mou*."

"If you say so."

After she hung up, he held the phone to his forehead. He'd get his affairs in order. It was bloody well time.

He took a sip of his *ouzo*. It burned his mouth and throat. He gulped hard. Who else needed to know? Stuart. He'd get the will ready. And he'd tell Stuart about Theodora. It was time he came clean about that with Stuart, with someone.

Steve, his VP of operations, had often said he'd buy the company whenever Nicolai was ready to sell. Steve would be surprised. He deserved a chance to run the show.

Nicolai had always enjoyed making friends with clients and staff. He loved the office parties, the large gatherings, everyone sitting around the boardroom talking and laughing. No room to get hurt, no way to disappoint or be disappointed. Simple. That's how he liked his relationships. He briefly thought about his parents. After he left Greece that last time, he'd never seen them again. His family, Sara and Alexia, were the closest he'd ever been to anyone. Why had he been so stubborn with his father, his sisters?

Sure, his clients thought he was just a loveable Greek. They were impressed with his thoughtfulness, how he would remember a client's wife's birthday and send a small gift.

He'd had a good time, but that's all it was. Fun. His father had told him life was more than just having fun. Ha. He showed him.

He'd had letters and a few Christmas cards from his sisters over the years. He sent cards with pictures of Alexia. *We're doing very well. Alexia is captain of her basketball team. She's very serious. She works too hard. Alexia's been accepted to university. Alexia graduated today. She's practising law.* After he sent a card, he'd sprinkle holy water on Alexia to protect her from the "evil eye," as he told her. When she became a teenager, she'd scoff at his Greek superstitions. She was too smart for that sort of thing. He'd rub holy water on her picture, pray to God. "You didn't keep Sara safe. Okay, maybe I deserved that. Please do this favour for me. Keep Alexia safe. Don't let anything bad happen to her. I beg you." Then he would cross himself, kiss his fingers, like he was kissing the hand of God Himself.

He laughed at himself now. You could take the boy out of the village.

His sisters had never mentioned Theodora to him. He knew they knew about her and about Dimitria. This was the way it was in the village. There was no such thing as a secret. He knew what they would do if he told them about his illness. They would tell him to come home. They would pamper him, feed him until he burst. "All you need is some food from your country," they'd say, as if that could fix everything. They would sit around the kitchen table laughing like they were kids. Stop it! he told himself. That's just wishful thinking. The truth was, if he went back, his sisters would be worried that their neighbours or their families would get a whiff of the gossip about him and the talk would start. They wouldn't want any part of him. And who could blame them? Besides, he didn't need those troubles either. Not anymore.

The only news he ever received about Dimitria and Theodora was a few lines from Achilles. Those letters mostly complained about what hadn't happened with the boardwalk, blamed Nicolai. Once every few letters, Achilles mentioned a bit of news about

Theodora. She'd started school, finished school, was an artist like her mother and was getting married. "Wouldn't you like to be at her wedding? It's an opportunity."

Theodora. He wrote her a letter every single week. On Fridays he put the right number of stamps on the envelope and walked down to the mailbox. He fiddled with the letter in his pocket, but never pulled it out. When he got home, he stuck it with the rest of the letters under an elastic band and threw them in a drawer. Eventually, he put them in a shoebox, wrapped Sara's ribbons around it. One of these days, he'd tell Alexia what he wanted her to do. And if she found the box before he could talk to her, she would recognize the ribbons and know he never forgot Sara. He always kept her ribbons close. Everything would work out. She'd understand this was a message for her.

Dimitria had told him not to call again. And she'd said she was with someone else. He'd convinced himself not to interfere. He sipped the *ouzo*, stretched out his legs.

What would he have said to Alexia? She was so young. How could he explain that Dimitria was his cousin? He couldn't justify it to himself even now. He had left the mess behind because it was best for all of them. Dimitria had moved away and made a new life for herself, leaving the scandal behind too. The talk in the village likely subsided. Things worked out for everyone. He hadn't put his parents and sisters through any of it. Overall, he hadn't caused a hell of a lot of damage. That was a good thing. He'd expected more from himself once, but that was when Sara was still alive. After that, he got realistic.

The phone rang. He sat up. "Yes?"

"How about Saturday night?" the female voice on the other end said.

"Excuse me?"

"How about that dinner you promised? Does Saturday work for you?"

"Why not?" He smiled. He might as well enjoy himself. He wrote down Erica's address and phone number.

He grabbed a box of *galaktoboureko* and took it over to Alexia's place one Saturday morning a few months later. He told her he'd finalized the sale of his company and Stuart had tied up all the legal loose ends. He was a free man. His new girlfriend was keeping him busy with yoga, jogging and art exhibits. He was happy.

"She must be running you into the ground," Alexia said. She leaned across the kitchen table and stroked his face. "Is she feeding you?"

"Stop blaming Erica," he said, looking down at his plate. "I'm just getting old."

"I haven't always been fair with your girlfriends," Alexia said.

He shrugged, sipped the apricot juice he'd brought for them. "I can't stay too long this morning." He took a bite of his *galaktoboureko*. "We're off to the art gallery later."

Alexia reached for his hand. "Have a good time, Dad."

Nicolai had been in bed for several days. When he started to actually feel sick, he went downhill quickly. He heard Erica put her key in the door, Alexia turning her away. "Not now, he's asleep," Alexia said.

"But all I want to do is sit with him," Erica said.

"That's what I'm here for," Alexia said. "Come back a little later."

He heard Alexia pace outside his door. "*Paidi mou,*" he called out.

She went to him and helped him sit up, put a couple of pillows behind his back.

"She's a friend."

"You need to get better first."

"I'm not going to get better."

"You will," she said, pulling his sheets and blanket. She ran her hand over the blanket, smoothing out the wrinkles. "It'll just take a little time."

He shook his head and his face scrunched up in pain.

"It's almost time for your medicine."

She walked into his bathroom. He heard her twisting the top off the bottle. He had to tell her before he fell asleep again. The pain was too much and he needed the medication, but it left him sleepy. He wasn't sure he'd say what he needed to say. It hadn't been a year. Only six months. And he was reduced to a helpless man. He should have told her before this.

She handed him the pills, held his head up to put the glass to his mouth. "You'll feel better soon. You have to have a positive attitude."

"I used to say that to your mother," he said, falling back against the pillow.

"You don't know what you're saying. You're not well." Alexia held his hand. He heard his own raspy breathing. He was sure he'd said what he'd promised himself he would say. She tightened her grip on his hand. She must have heard him. He coughed as he opened his mouth to say something else. He heard only the whisper of his voice. "You have a sister."

Alexia patted his hand in the same way she used to when she was little. "You're stuck with me, Dad. There's no one else." Staring into her eyes, he saw the same fear and confusion he'd seen there the night her mother died, the night he left for Greece so long ago. Those other times too, when he hadn't been able to pick her up after school. He wished he could make things right, explain stuff, be what she needed. He'd left it too bloody late. *Coward.*

He grabbed her hand, pulling her close. Her breath was sweet and her skin creamy soft like her mother's.

"No one knows," he said. "Too many secrets. I'm sorry. So many things."

"Dad, you've been dreaming. It's the morphine. It's okay. When you're better, you'll see."

"*Paidi mou,* I'm telling you."

"It's just a bad dream. Lay back now. Rest and get better."

"It's true, Alexia. I'm sorry."

She dropped his hand, stood and turned her back to him. He wanted to tell her not to go, not to give up on him. He had done so badly by her, by Theodora.

"I'm sorry. Can't explain. Don't live like me." *Be with your family, embrace them, don't be afraid of shame or talk or getting too close. You can do better than me. Don't be afraid.* He hoped she heard him. He should have been honest with her. His daughter was a smart, compassionate woman. She could understand and forgive anything. Why hadn't he figured this out before?

2010

Alexia rubbed her hands on her pants, but the sand stuck to her palms. She wiped her hands again. She couldn't see much, but she was sure her hands were coated. She reached for the handle. It rattled. She squeezed her eyes shut. Quiet. She pushed her shoulder against the door. It began to open, then scraped to a halt against the floor. She winced, hoped Christina hadn't heard.

She was thankful that Christina was good to her word. "We do not need to lock houses," Christina had said to Alexia when she first arrived in Diakofto. No, just your damn secrets. Why hadn't they told Nicolai about Theodora? There was no way gossip like that wouldn't have reached them. And what did they do? They kept it to themselves, hoped he would never find out. Fat chance. Achilles couldn't get a letter off fast enough. Who knew when and how Achilles told him.

Achilles.

What had she been thinking? She'd left her moped parked on the beach and run the long way home, sprinting faster every time she saw his silly, self-satisfied grin. The spot close to her shoulder felt tender. She touched it, closing her eyes. Damn it. Another image. Achilles crawling on top of her, moving back and forth until she felt she might suffocate. His face buried in her shoulder, his beard rubbing her raw.

Her panties were wet and cold. Damn it all. Just get inside. Don't wake anybody. Deal with it in the morning. She sniffed her blouse. His heady smell was still there, mixing with her sweat.

She leaned her forehead against the door. She took a deep breath, peeked inside the house. She could see the outline of the stairs. Her room was just at the top of them. The smell of meat, no doubt tonight's dinner, ruined because of her. Did they have to be so nice to her? They'd welcomed her into their home. And she repaid them by going behind their backs, digging up their secrets, screwing the local playboy.

Alexia pulled up on the handle, raising the door. Her hand slipped off and the door fell against the floor with a thud. Damn. She wiped her hand again. She grabbed the handle, lifted the door, opened it and crept in. She held her breath, listened. Nothing. She closed the door behind her.

The smell of meat was stronger. She hadn't eaten anything since lunch. A salad. "Straight out of the garden," Christina had said as she'd ripped apart the lettuce. That smile of Christina's, always ready and willing to reassure Alexia. Her stomach groaned. Can't think about that now.

She looked up the stairs. The house was still. She pulled off one shoe, then the other. Sand spilled. She turned towards the door, put her shoes on the mat, bent down and swept the sand with her hands into the corner.

She put her foot on the first step and stopped. The step was cool against the bottom of her foot. She told herself she'd have the covers over her head in a few minutes. This nightmare would be over.

"I made lamb for you tonight," Christina said. A light clicked on in the kitchen.

Alexia jumped. She really didn't want to deal with Christina tonight. She closed her eyes and shook her head. Face this head on. It was her best shot. She stepped back.

A small lamp sat on the kitchen table. Alexia hadn't seen it before. Maybe Christina had brought it down from her bedroom.

The lamp's muted light cast shadows in the kitchen. Christina sat hunched over the table, her back to Alexia, a Saran-wrapped plate in her hands. She turned it one way, then another, as if she was trying to figure out what it was. Alexia's mouth was dry. She licked her lips and walked over to the cupboard, took out a glass and filled it with water. She turned to face Christina.

Alexia took a sip of water. Don't back away, she told herself. You've screwed up, yes. But they don't need to know that part. She saw herself lying with her legs apart and her pants over one knee. She swallowed hard.

"I thought you didn't eat meat before Easter," Alexia said.

"This was for you."

Stop with that stupid plate, she thought. Look at me. Yell at me. Do whatever. Let's just get this over with. Alexia put the glass down. "Are you okay?" she asked.

Christina shrugged.

"You're up very early today," Alexia said. "Can I get you something, *Thia*? I can make you some coffee if you like. Or a cup of tea?" She turned towards the counter and knocked the glass over with her elbow. "Damn." She caught it before it hit the ground.

"You've done enough."

Alexia grabbed the rag in the sink and wiped the counter and cabinet. She put the glass in the sink and picked up the kettle. "Maybe tea would be good."

"Where have you been?" Christina's voice was quiet, lower than usual.

Alexia turned.

Christina pushed the plate away and put her hands in her lap.

"You know where I was, *Thia*," Alexia said. "I'll get the tea on." She put the kettle on the burner, turned the knob and struck a match. The gas flared quicker than she expected. She stumbled back from the stove and reached over to turn the element off. "Maybe it's too late for tea. Or too early. We should be in bed."

Christina pulled out a chair and motioned for Alexia to sit down.

"I'm really tired." Alexia stood against the counter, her arms crossed.

"You were not too tired to stay out all night."

Alexia edged the chair away from Christina, then sat down.

"Well?" Christina asked. She put her hand over Alexia's.

"I went to Maria's. You know that." Alexia pulled her hand away.

"Maria called me when you left there," Christina said. "That was hours ago."

"I went to the beach. A run." Alexia leaned towards Christina. You can't check that. So there.

"You went to the bar first. No?" she asked. "Where you met your friend Achilles."

Alexia stood up. "Are you following me?"

"Still you don't understand," Christina said.

"So I went for a drink. What's the big deal?" She looked away. There were still a few drops of water on the counter. She wanted to wipe them up with her sleeve.

"The owner of the bar is a friend of ours. He was worried about you." Christina pulled herself out of the chair. She put her hand on Alexia's shoulder. "We all are."

"If your idea of concern is keeping secrets, I don't want to be a part of it."

Christina's hand felt heavy against her shoulder. Alexia shrugged it off. "I can take care of myself."

"This is what a family does."

"Why didn't you tell me?"

"Tell you what?" Christina stood in front of Alexia, grasped her arms firmly. "You know everything now." Her mouth drooped in a wounded smile. "Have we not been good to you?"

"What does that have to do with anything?" Alexia stepped back.

Christina let go. "Keep your voice down." She cocked her head and looked towards the ceiling.

"Because you don't want Solon to wake up and hear that you knew all along about Theodora and never told my father. You lied to him. You all did."

"What are you saying?" Christina said. "There were rumours, but our cousin went away. We thought it was just talk. We put her out of our minds. Besides she had been seen with your friend so we put two and two together. We did not know until Achilles, I hate to have his name enter my mouth, came to see our father, God rest his soul, your *pappou*." She folded her hands together as though in prayer.

"What?" Alexia slumped down on one of the chairs.

"He sent that man out of our house and told him to stay away from us." Christina grabbed a handkerchief from her pocket and dabbed at her mouth. She sat down across from Alexia. "I heard my father talking one night with my mother. They agreed to send an envelope to our cousin at the beginning of every month to help take care of Theodora, but when they died, I found all of the envelopes had come back to them." She shook her head. "They had never been opened. I still have them."

"They didn't tell my father."

"What good would it have done?"

"We might have been a family."

"*Ella, paidi mou,* it was only a mistake that happened because your father was upset with us and our cousin took advantage of that." Christina threw her hands up at Alexia. "They were cousins. Where could they have lived together without shame falling on their heads, and on their children? On all of our heads. How could we explain?"

"They were ashamed of him and wanted to protect themselves."

"It is not so easy," Christina said, tilting back in her chair. "Don't blame them. It is my fault."

Christina laced her fingers. She looked away. "Nicolai had an argument with our father and moved out. I asked him to come back from Aigio," Christina said. "When he wouldn't come home, I refused to speak to him because I knew Solon's family would not allow our marriage if they knew what Nicolai was doing. It was this way in those days. I'm to be blamed for what happened between Nicolai and Dimitria."

"He came back to Greece for her," Alexia said. "They were childhood sweethearts. I don't know. After my mom died, he came running back here to find her. His real love."

"No, Alexia. Now, you are wrong. What happened when they were kids was nothing. They were caught playing house. All children do this. It is normal. No? Her father got angry. He talked to our father and that was all that happened. Nothing more. They didn't even see each other after that. Nicolai never knew that our father knew. But our father kept him away from her."

"Then, why did he come back here? Why didn't he bring me?"

"Nicolai was probably afraid of what our father might do. Maybe ruin you with his anger. I don't know. What I know for sure is your mother was his only love. This is probably why he never married again. I know this. I knew it when I visited you in Vancouver. He told me he was happy. It was the first time in our lives I heard him say this. And I knew it was true. And you know it, too."

All those women. Nothing lasted. God, why hadn't I figured this out before? I thought he just brought them home to make my life miserable. He even told me there could never be anyone else but Sara for him. Why didn't I listen?

"I knew how much he needed us and I betrayed him."

"Why didn't you call him? Tell him?"

Christina shrugged. "He never said a word to any of us, so we thought he didn't want to talk about it. No?"

Christina reached over. Alexia flinched.

"There is something in your hair," Christina said, pulling out a tiny, dried-out leaf. "See?" She passed the leaf to Alexia.

"I was running." Alexia took the leaf. She got up, stuck it in her pocket and took off her jacket. She walked out into the hallway and hung it on the coat rack. Christina followed.

"Did you fall too?"

"What do you mean?"

Christina tried to brush Alexia's back. Alexia turned. More damn sand. Alexia grabbed the broom from the front closet, turning away from Christina. "I told you I went to the beach." She swept the sand into a corner and left it. She leaned the broom against the wall and turned to the stairs, gripped the railing. "I need some sleep," she said.

"We will talk more after Easter."

Alexia turned back towards Christina. "You've all made such a mess."

"When you hide things, everything gets worse." She caught Alexia's eye. "You understand this better, now. No?" Christina walked back into the kitchen, sat down and turned out the lamp.

Alexia stood in the dark. She heard Christina sigh. Alexia crept up the stairs, closed her bedroom door behind her and got into bed.

She woke to a sound. Panting. The sheets had wrapped themselves around her arms, holding her down. Alexia kicked at the twisted sheets, the blanket. She sat up quickly. Her eyes adjusted. She was in her room, alone, her bedroom door closed. The old-fashioned key dangled from the lock. Had Christina come up to check on her? Was it someone else? The door to the terrace was opened. The curtains fluttered in the light breeze. The sun warmed the room. She told herself she should get up and close the shutters.

She shimmied out of her pants and blouse and dropped both on the floor. Sand rubbed against her as she pushed herself up towards the headboard. She leaned against the pillow, pulled the sheets up to cover herself. The blanket had fallen on the floor out of reach. She couldn't be bothered to retrieve it. She rubbed her foot over her shin. The sand seemed to multiply. She wiped her hands against the sheets. She'd have to shake everything out, wash all the bedding and her clothes, shower. Get up, she told herself. She lay still, encased in sand, her arms by her sides as if to hold the sheets, the dirt down.

She listened for the static on the radio downstairs. The house was quiet. It must be late morning. Solon was likely in the field. Maybe Christina had gone shopping. Outside her terrace door she heard a machine grind and pitch.

Stupid. Stupid. Stupid. Why had she done it? Achilles meant nothing to her. She was just another one of his conquests and maybe his ticket to more money for his boardwalk. Sure, she had needed a way to let off steam. There was a lot of crap she was dealing with in this family. An escape from it was a good idea. She did that sometimes. No harm done with a married man. But this was just stupid. She couldn't get his grin or the silly way he stroked his patchy beard out of her head. She squeezed her eyes closed. She hadn't used a condom, hadn't even thought about it. A man like that could be carrying any number of diseases. Jesus Christ. She slammed her fists on the bed until she tired herself out. This doesn't happen to me, she thought. Ever. Even when I have my fun, I control things. This time, I screwed up royally. It's got to be this place, these people. They're making me crazy.

Christina's words came back to Alexia. "When you hide things, everything gets worse." Alexia saw the way Christina tilted her head as if she knew Alexia understood what she was talking about. "You understand this better now. No?"

Okay, maybe he hasn't had that many women. Maybe it's all just talk. Maybe it's going to be okay. You can only fool yourself so long, she thought. But it was all she could do right now. At least, I'm on the pill, she told herself. I don't have to worry about that.

She threw the sheets off and swung her feet to the floor. The room began to spin. Her stomach rumbled. She held her head in her hands until the dizziness passed. She had to eat. Get moving, she told herself. Sitting around feeling sorry for herself wasn't going to change a thing.

Alexia walked down a couple of steps, then stopped to listen for any sound. Nothing. Christina wasn't at the sink washing dishes or at the stove stirring a pot of soup. Maybe she was in the garden. She probably wants to avoid me as much as I want to avoid her, Alexia thought.

She walked into the kitchen and saw him. Solon sat at the table with his back to her. He sipped his coffee. The paper lay untouched beside him. Maybe he hadn't heard her come down. She might still have a chance to get back upstairs before he noticed.

"This is no good," he said.

"What are you doing home, *Thio*?"

He didn't turn. "Today is Good Friday. We do not work. We pay our respects to the one who suffered for us, sacrificed his life for us." He cradled a cup in his large hands, brought it to his mouth, but didn't take a drink. He seemed smaller to her, his whiskers made his face look grey.

"I'd forgotten."

"You have too much on your mind," he said.

She walked to the counter, trying to act normal. Maybe he didn't know anything about what had happened with Christina. "Do you want me to make you another coffee?" she asked, turning to face him.

"The coffee is fine," he said. "These bad feelings between you and Christina are not." He put his cup down.

Christina had either told him or he'd overheard them last night. Alexia wasn't going to say a thing until she figured out what he knew. Then, if she had to, she'd mount a defence. There was no way to explain what she'd done, not even to herself. But if Solon pushed her, she'd come up with a story. She always did.

"She will not tell me what happened. I do not like to see her hurt." He didn't look at her. "No good."

She stared at her bare feet. They were cold.

His voice was a whisper as if he was talking to himself. "When I first married Christina, my family did not like her. She did everything to please them and still they thought she was not good enough. Her own family was not perfect, but I told her over and over again, I was not marrying them. She wanted everything to be good because I guess she did not have this in her family. But life is not this way. People make mistakes, others talk. Who cares? Everything passes and we go on." He took a sip of his coffee, put the cup down. "Shame." He turned to face her. "We Greeks are strange. Our only purpose in life is to avoid it," he said, shaking his head. "This is what is wrong with us. Look at what happens now with the economy. People would rather kill themselves than ask their family for help. We never have this before. It is against our religion. It is against everything we know. But people do it now. They kill themselves. Our need to avoid shame runs very deep."

He was right. Isn't that what she'd always done? She kept up a stupid façade of being perfect. Her father bragged to his friends and colleagues about her all the time. "Alexia has never gotten into any trouble, never given me one thing to worry about. She has her head on right." He never knew about her affairs. It was so damn hard to be so good all the time. She sometimes wished she could screw up big time and have him find out about it. Just once to see what he would do.

Solon got up and put his cup in the sink. As he walked past her, he lay his hand on her shoulder and gazed into her eyes. "If it is about Theodora, do what you think is right. We will survive. Talk to Christina and fix it. She only wants for you not to be hurt."

He pinched her cheek the way he did with small children. His eyes were soft and forgiving.

He closed the door behind him. Alexia sat in his chair. It was warm. Maybe these people could accept her just the way she was. She shook her head. She had to talk to Christina. Then, she'd talk to Theodora. She wasn't going to continue to lie to her about who she was and what she was doing in Greece. She owed her that much at least.

Alexia folded the last shirt in the pile of clean clothes on the bed. The laundry was done and her bed remade. She swept the floor in her room, then went downstairs and knocked the sand out of her shoes, threw them outside on the front step and swept the stairs, the hallway and kitchen to make sure she'd gotten rid of everything she had tramped in. She scrubbed the kitchen counter and washed down the cupboard doors. She picked up the statue of the Acropolis and the tiny doll dressed in traditional Greek folk costume in the living room, dusted them and set them back. It was needless work, but it gave her time to think about what she would say to Christina. She'd apologize, tell her she'd been stupid to get involved with Achilles. It was over. Christina didn't have to worry. She would tell her to stop blaming herself for what had happened between Nicolai and Dimitria. And finally, she'd set down why she was going to tell Theodora the truth.

She lay down on her bed, arms behind her head, to wait.

The door scuffed against the floor downstairs. Alexia sat up. Time to face the music. Start with an apology, she told herself. That's always a good way. Christina is probably too mad to listen. Maybe if I act like nothing happened, it'd be better. Maybe we could go back to the way we were. When has that ever worked for this family? Don't be an idiot. Stop trying to find an easy fix, a quick solution that you think would make everyone happy. That doesn't work. Do the right thing. A teacher had told her once, "You know how to stick to your guns, you're stubborn that way. That's good. Life shouldn't beat that out of you."

She took the stairs two at a time and came to an abrupt stop on the bottom step. Katarina's shopping cart sat in the middle of the narrow hallway. Christina bobbed into the cart, grabbed a bag. Katarina took a few more bags out of the cart. "If we move the cart to one side, I can help," Alexia said.

Christina didn't respond.

Alexia wondered if they'd heard her. "I can help," she tried again.

"Ah, Alexia," Katarina said. "Christina, let's move the cart closer to the door."

"It is fine where it is," Christina said.

Katarina caught Alexia's eye and shrugged.

Alexia reached over and tapped Christina's back. She moved forward and Alexia squeezed through. She reached for the bag in Christina's hand.

"I have it," Christina said. She walked into the kitchen, the bag tucked in close.

Alexia stood, her arms still reaching open in front of her.

"You could put your shoes away. We nearly fell over them. One of us could have broken a leg." Christina took the watermelon out of the bag and put it on the table.

"It was nothing," Katarina said. "I saw your shoes. There was no danger." She laced two bags around each of Alexia's wrists. "Be careful. Don't let them drop."

Alexia adjusted the bags so she held them in her hands and walked into the kitchen. "Where do you want these?" she asked.

Christina leaned over the counter. She made a choking sound.

"Are you all right, *Thia*?"

Christina began coughing hard, pointed to the table.

Alexia put the bags on the table and returned to Christina's side. She rubbed her back. "Why don't you sit down?"

Christina allowed herself to be led to the chair, her back and shoulders stiff and heaving.

"She bought many things," Katarina said. "Easter is important to us."

Alexia got a glass out of the cupboard, filled it with water and handed it to Christina.

She coughed into her handkerchief. Alexia held the glass for her. The coughing subsided. Christina took the glass. She wiped away a tear. Her eyes closed as she sipped water. Her jaw was very stiff, her cheeks soft.

Katarina brought in the rest of the bags. "She will be okay once she rests. She worries too much. This is what happens."

Alexia pulled out the zucchini from one of the bags. "I can put everything away," Alexia said. She put the zucchini on the table.

"But you don't know." Christina said. She stood up. "I will do it."

"I will follow your instructions." Alexia met Christina's eyes. "I will."

"This is my work." Christina grabbed the zucchini from the table and threw it into one of her vegetable baskets. She worked around Alexia.

Alexia watched her. "I can put the cake in the fridge."

"Fine. Okay."

"I don't know why she bought it," Katarina said.

"For Easter."

"But you're planning to make cookies and pies and a cake too." Katarina stood with her hands on her hips.

"The store-bought one is better," Christina said. "Bought is always better."

"It isn't." Katarina shook her head, her arms by her sides. "We've told her."

"These are the things that families say to one another to be polite." She took another sip of water, grabbed the handkerchief in her pocket and wiped her face. Her colour began to return.

"She bought the Canadian flour today for baking," Katarina said. "It's the only time she buys it because it is too expensive here. But it is the best."

"Why didn't you tell me, *Thia*? I could have brought some from Canada."

"The two of you are in my way," Christina said. "I have many things to do to prepare for tonight and the church. The dinner we will have tomorrow to break the fast."

"Don't pay attention to her this weekend, Alexia," Katarina said. "She gets nervous and worried and isn't her real self around Easter. She wants everything to be just so."

Christina threw her hands at Katarina. "I have work. Go." She turned her back.

"I can help you." Alexia touched Christina's forearm.

"This is my kitchen," Christina said. She turned on the water, grabbed the sliver of soap in the dish beside the sink and scrubbed her hands.

"But you could teach me some of these things."

"Not today," Christina said. She bit at one of her wet sleeves and pushed it up.

Katarina shook her head. "This is a good time for us to leave." Katarina put a hand on Alexia's shoulder. "Stay out of her way and things will get better." She dragged her cart outside and turned to shut the door behind them. "What happened?" She leaned into Alexia.

Alexia righted her overturned shoes and slipped into them. "I don't know."

"Don't worry." Katarina pinched her cheeks. "Go for a walk. It will pass."

The store windows were full of hand-made candles decorated with flowers, eggs and ribbons. They were part of the Easter celebration. People bought them as gifts to be taken to the Saturday night church service. They would be lit after midnight on Saturday night once the priest had made his declaration: *Christos Anesti*. Christ has risen. Then Easter would begin. Chocolate bunnies sat in refrigerators in the bakery window. Alexia wanted to enjoy the celebration. How could she relax when things weren't right with Christina?

There were more people in town this weekend than she'd seen before. Christina had told her that Greeks return to their village at Easter to spend time with family and friends.

A couple on the sidewalk in front of the bakery smiled at Alexia, between them a child of about five or six. Each held one of her hands, swinging her back and forth. The child laughed. Alexia gulped down tears.

A breeze gusted, catching her skirt. She held it down, walked past the couple and their child, her eyes fixed in the distance. She had that once. Her father's family was not going to be a replacement. Christina was never going to forgive her. Never. Run, a voice in her head said. Run now. Getting away had saved her in the past. Go back to what you know. Work and more work.

Alexia grabbed the cell phone out of her jacket and punched the numbers.

He picked up after the first ring. "You okay?" he asked.

Had he expected her call? She pressed on. "I think I've had enough of this place."

"What's going on, kiddo?" he asked, his voice soft. Where was that formal tone? She pictured him setting his file aside, sitting back in his leather chair. She heard some movement. Someone was probably at his office door and he was holding his hand up to stop them from coming in. She shook her head. She knew better. Dan was too driven to allow her problems to interfere with work.

She listened to his breathing and pictured him lacing his hair through his fingers. She smiled for the first time since last night.

She walked up the boardwalk along the beach, changed her mind and jumped down onto the sand. She cleared her throat. Why won't he say anything? Her hands were damp. She started talking just to fill the dead air. And then she couldn't stop herself. She told him about her father, his dying wish, about what she was doing in Greece, how she'd met and befriended Theodora, but hadn't told her the truth about who she was. She caught herself over and over again talking about Christina, what she did for her, her funny expressions, all the things that made her laugh. "I don't know if my aunt will ever talk to me again."

"Wow," he said.

"I'm so sorry," she said, suddenly realizing what she'd done. Why had she told him so much?

"What for?"

"Laying all of this on you," she said. "I didn't mean to."

He interrupted her. "Hey," he said. "It's a lot to deal with. Even for you."

She heard more rustling and she knew he was likely shuffling paper and wanted to get back to work. "I should let you go, you're busy." She sat down on the sand, took off her shoes. She sank into the sand. It gave in to her, making her feel warm.

"My day hasn't even started."

She glanced at her watch. "God, I am so stupid," she said. "I woke you."

"I had to answer the phone anyway." She heard him kick the sheets off.

"I'm sorry."

"Stop," Dan said. "The girl I know makes no apologies."

"I'm thinking of flying back next week," Alexia said. "It's time. That's really all I wanted to say. Just ignore the rest." She touched her face, felt her cheeks turn hot.

"As much as I want you back," Dan said, "and let me make this clear since it's the middle of the night and we're both being honest and all. As much as I want you back for me, not the office, I think you should stay and sort things out."

She gasped. Put her hand over her mouth. She gulped down the rushing tears.

"Are you still there?"

She swallowed and cleared her throat. "Yup."

"And you're okay with that?"

What did he look like propped up against his pillow? What would it feel like to have his arms around her? She realized that she'd thought about these questions before. "Yup."

"All right then, sort stuff out like only you can," he said. "I'll wait, kiddo."

Alexia came into the house. Neighbours had already begun to arrive for a drink and a chat. Her aunts and cousins walked in and found a spot on the couch or the floor to sit. They talked over each other, laughed. She went upstairs and changed for church. She brushed out her hair, left it down. "For me," Dan had said. She repeated the words with each stroke. When had she become so silly?

She heard Solon's voice. "We're ready to go."

Concentrate, she told herself. You've got to deal with one thing at a time. Christina. Be honest with her, stand your ground. She'll understand. Alexia went downstairs.

"Very beautiful," he said. "Isn't she, Christina?"

"Let's not give her the evil eye," Christina said. She knocked three times on the wooden table beside her, made a spitting sound, but didn't look at Alexia.

Maria said, "*Ella, paidi mou*. These are our old ways. You don't believe in this."

"Maybe she'll find her husband tonight?" Katarina said.

"Not in this village," Christina said.

Alexia smiled. They were all crazy, but they were hers. She loved them.

She felt an arm around her shoulder and settled back into the embrace. She thought about her father just then. His touch had the same warmth. He'd be happy they were together. She missed him.

She turned. Christina stood beside her. She dropped her arm and held onto Alexia's hand. "Solon is never right. But, today is different. You are very beautiful." Alexia met her gaze and nodded. She put her arms around Christina and held her close, breathed in her scent, a mix of flour and lavender.

"Women and their emotions," Solon said.

Christina shrugged. Alexia laughed.

"It is better this way." Solon kissed Christina's cheek, then moved towards the door. "The church isn't going to wait for us."

They poured out the doorway. The children ran ahead. Alexia could hear their laughter even though she was at the back of the procession. Maria and Katarina started off with their husbands, but ended up together behind the children. They walked arm in arm. Solon and Zak and Maria's husband kept well behind, but every once in a while, when Maria caught the discussion about politics, she turned and said, "Can't we stop even at Easter?"

"What do you women know?"

Maria laughed. "At least we know what is interesting to talk about."

Alexia put her arm into Christina's. "I'm sorry, *Thia*."

Christina shrugged. "I only worry for you."

"I haven't made good decisions lately." Alexia didn't say his name.

Christina stopped and turned towards her. "You are a smart girl," she said. "I know you will do what is right."

Alexia nodded. "I am going to tell Theodora the truth, *Thia*."

"There will be talk."

Alexia took Christina's hands in hers. "I will deal with it."

"But it involves all of us." Christina met Alexia's eyes.

"It's what he wanted. I can't run away from it. And it's what I want too."

Christina nodded. "I don't know what will happen to all of us."

"These secrets haven't helped any of us," Alexia said. "Maybe we should try a different way."

Christina stared at Alexia.

Alexia tilted her head. "What do you think?"

"You have a point. No?"

"And *Thia*, it's time to stop blaming yourself for what happened to Nicolai."

"Your father told me the same thing when I was in Canada."

"And you didn't believe him?"

"But," Christina said.

"There is no but," Alexia said. "It wasn't your fault."

Christina fluttered her eyes closed, then opened them. Alexia thought she saw a slight nod.

Christina lit a candle as they entered the church and found a seat. Alexia followed, taking the chair beside her. The men sat on one side, the women on the other.

The small church echoed with a low, persistent drone. Alexia felt the murmur of the men's chanting in her chest. She gazed up at the gold-encrusted ceiling. She followed her family's lead, standing, kneeling and sitting whenever they did. She fell into the rhythm of the service. She couldn't remember another time in her life when she'd been so overwhelmed and in awe at the same time. Then it came to her.

It was the first Easter after her mother died. Her father had come back from Greece months earlier and they'd settled into the new place. She'd been tired that Sunday and wasn't sure she wanted to go. She hadn't been to this church before. He'd insisted and taken her to a Greek Orthodox service. They'd sat close, his arm around her shoulders. The church in Vancouver was modern. It didn't separate the men and women. It was less formal, yet there were similarities, too. The chanting had vibrated in her chest that day. Her father's touch, the priest's voice, the men's voices made her feel safe, protected, loved. It was the first time since her mother died that she didn't feel alone, didn't feel like she had to take care of him, find a way to fix everything. The feeling hadn't lasted, but it did happen.

She heard a bell chime softly and stood up with everyone else. The priest moved down the aisle. Behind him, the massive wooden cross was lifted onto the shoulders of a dozen men, including her uncles and cousins. Each man took a section. They walked out of the church. The women followed. Streetlights and store lights had been turned off. People lined the streets on both sides and held candles, crossed themselves as the priest and the procession passed. A breeze came up. Alexia cupped her candle to protect the light. The flame burned brighter.

As they turned the corner, she saw Achilles on the stoop just in front of a bar. As they passed, Achilles had a beer in one hand and his arm around a woman Alexia remembered seeing before. The woman cupped a candle in her hands.

Alexia shook her head as she caught his eye.

He shrugged, held up his beer as if to toast her.

She nodded, turned her gaze to her family, walking on every side of her.

2010

Theodora sat cross-legged on the kitchen floor, her trousers a flimsy layer of protection against the cold slate. She looked around for her sweater. It hung on the chair in the opposite corner of the room. Too far. She leaned against the cupboard. The knob burrowed into her shoulder blade. She pressed harder into it. In her arms, stacks of unopened envelopes. Her name on each one.

The tap dripped. The hollow sound was louder than ever. "I'll get to it when I have some time," Andreas would say whenever she complained. He might never get to it now. Would he walk back through that kitchen door? Be here with her? "We bring trouble on our heads when we are noticed."

She shook her head. This was more trouble than Andreas could understand. Alexia was her sister. Not a friend. A half-sister. All this time, Alexia had kept it a secret, letting Theodora think she'd made a new friend. All of it, a lie.

She pushed herself against the knob. Her mother had said her father died before she was born. More lies. Stupid, trusting Theodora.

There *was* some hint. "I see it," Theodora had said to Dimitria. She was looking at one of her mother's sketches. One of the first ones she remembered. An angry, dark sea. And submerged at the bottom of one of the relentless waves: an outline. Cheekbones. Nose. A closed mouth. Eyes shut tight. Asleep or dead?

Her mother's back was turned away. She was busy with a new drawing. Theodora knew she shouldn't bother her, but she had to ask.

"It looks like a face."

"I put my hand down on the paper," Dimitria said not turning, "and never know what will happen. It appears. I don't know where he came from."

"But you know it's a man."

"Did I say that?"

Theodora made it into a game. She'd examine each of her mother's sketches to see where he'd appear. Sometimes he was buried in a cloud or a grove of trees. Other times, he was hidden in one corner outside the main scene. It took a bit of looking. But she'd always find him. It was strange that her mother didn't see him. She created him over and over again, yet never seemed to know he was there on the canvas. Theodora had been so proud of herself. She'd seen something no one else could see.

Theodora shook her head. Trusting. That's all. Nothing special. Just naïve.

She glanced over at the back door. No sign of Andreas.

A few hours ago, Alexia had come through that door. She'd suggested they go for a walk. She should have gone, left Elena to take care of Nicky. If she'd done that, she would have heard the news first, then had time to digest it, think about what she'd tell Andreas. She'd always known how to pick the right time to talk to him.

She'd invited Alexia into the kitchen. Elena was sitting at the kitchen table, her lips a straight line. Theodora had done something wrong again. She wasn't sure what. Maybe it was because she'd allowed Nicky to play on the floor. She talked quickly, filling the room with her voice.

"We'll have some apricot juice. You can meet my mother-in-law." She should have seen it in Alexia's eyes. Perhaps she had, but she needed a break from Elena. She'd been at the house all afternoon. She could use a friend to share the misery.

Alexia suggested they go into the other room to talk. "Or I could come back."

Elena pushed a chair toward Alexia, motioned for her to sit down. "I've heard about the Canadian friend for weeks. And now she wants to run away before I have the pleasure of meeting her."

Turning to grab some glasses from the cupboard, Theodora ignored Alexia's helpless smile. "It's okay. We can visit here," she said into the cupboard. She couldn't find the glasses she wanted. She stared at the dishes in front of her as if she had forgotten exactly what it was she was looking for.

Alexia dropped her bag at the door. Theodora jumped. She stared at the dishes. Not this cupboard, she said to herself. She flicked the door closed, opened another one and found the glasses she wanted.

Alexia came into the kitchen and sat down. Theodora filled the glasses and set them on the table. A few drops of juice spilled. She turned to grab a rag. "It's nothing," Alexia said. "Don't worry." She touched Theodora's arm. Alexia's hand comforted her.

Theodora nodded. Elena sighed.

Theodora handed Alexia a napkin, then passed one to Elena. In the middle of the table, Theodora put a plate of Easter cookies. She sat down beside Alexia. Elena sat opposite them, inscrutable.

"They look delicious." Alexia reached for a cookie. "I used to bake with my aunt. And my mom before that. I haven't done it in so long," Alexia said. "Maybe I should start again. Get some of your recipes."

"We are still in mourning. It is only Saturday. Christ rises tonight at midnight, not before," Elena said. "But you're not Greek. You can't understand these things." She choked out a laugh.

"I am Greek." Alexia put the cookie down on her napkin, wiped her fingers.

"Then, your family should have taught you our ways." Elena leaned and tapped the table with her index finger. "Yes or no?"

God, why must she always be this way? Theodora wondered. Even with people she doesn't know.

"My father practised his religion," Alexia said.

"And you?"

"Nothing was forced on me." Alexia turned toward Theodora.

Theodora smiled weakly.

"Then I blame him for not teaching you correctly. Children are never at fault. They are innocent. What do they know?" She leaned back in her chair and picked up Nicky. He pushed at her, wriggling back to the floor. "We won't have that happen with this one. I am here to make sure. He will understand our ways."

"*Ella,*" Theodora said. "She lives in Canada. She didn't grow up here."

"Yes, of course." Again, Elena tapped her finger against the table.

Theodora poured each of them some more juice. The cookies lay untouched. They sipped in silence. "Did you go to church yesterday for Good Friday?" Theodora asked, clearing her throat.

"Yes. I felt very small in all the tradition. It was very inspiring."

Elena nodded once as if in approval.

Steel crashed against steel. Elena held her heart, shook her head. She picked Nicky up again. His cars fell, battering the floor. He screamed in protest, reached out to Theodora. "I will take him upstairs," Elena said. "You visit."

"It's okay, Nicky," Theodora said. "Go with *yiayia*."

Elena disappeared with Nicky upstairs.

"I came to talk to you," Alexia said.

Theodora put her finger to her mouth. She stood up and went to the stairs. She heard Elena in Nicky's room.

"What's wrong?" she asked, sitting down at the table beside Alexia.

Alexia moved her chair closer. "I haven't told you the truth."

Theodora watched Alexia's face.

"I came to Greece to find you. It was my father's last wish."

"I don't understand. Why?"

"My father is your father. Your mother and my father were together. I don't know how else to say it. When he was in Greece. After my mother died."

She's staring at me, Theodora thought, saying things I don't understand. Why is she doing this? She couldn't look at Alexia anymore. Theodora stared at the half-empty glass of apricot juice in front of her. An orange film was drying, crusting. She couldn't see through the glass.

"The bag is for you. It's full of letters he wrote to you."

What bag? she wondered. She looked around, saw it sitting by the kitchen door. Confirmation of everything all the kids she grew up with used to say about her, about her mother. This can't be, Theodora thought. More shame. Even now.

She closed her eyes tight. She couldn't bring more shame on her family. I've done enough to embarrass Andreas. And he'd always protected her.

Theodora felt Alexia's hand on her arm. She stood up, grabbed the chair and tried to push it towards the table. It wouldn't fit back into place.

She heard someone on the stairs. Theodora rolled her eyes.

Elena came into the kitchen, seized her purse from the counter. She quickly walked towards the door without looking at either Theodora or Alexia. "He's down for his nap. I will go now."

"Elena, please," Theodora said, trying to stay calm, not plead.

Elena turned.

"Stay," Alexia said. "I interrupted your visit. It was a pleasure to meet you, Elena. I really must go."

"Come to Diakofto for Easter, tomorrow," Alexia said. "Meet us all." She squeezed Theodora's hand, smiled and left.

Is she oblivious to what she's done? Theodora wondered. She stood still, watching Elena. Could she convince Elena to keep this quiet? She needed to make sense of it herself first. Then she'd find a way to tell Andreas.

"She could have waited until after Easter," Elena said. She checked her lipstick in the compact mirror she always carried. The lines around her mouth released into a sly smile. She snapped the compact shut, threw it back in her purse. "I have things to do now," Elena said. She left brusquely, as if leaving a shop where the clerk was a stranger, one who tried to cheat her.

Theodora couldn't feel the legs beneath her. She held onto the counter. Elena would be off to the butcher shop, busy with Easter shoppers. She'd drag Andreas to the back of the shop. The sound of the freezers would mask her words, meant only for him. "I warned you about her." She would stand in front of him, her hand cuffing his wrist, making sure he didn't move. She'd make him hear the whole story. He'd bow his head. She'd put a hand to his cheek, so he looked at her. "There is no end to the trouble she causes," Elena would whisper. "Of course it's not her fault. It's her mother's, but what can we do now? I probably shouldn't tell you, but you're my son. I only want the best for you. This is my only reason. I can't watch you make one mistake after another."

In her rush, Elena had left the door ajar. Theodora shut it and saw the bag Alexia had left. She stood away from it, as if getting closer would burn her. Her breath came in short bursts. She had to calm herself down, think about what to do. Think. She took a deep breath, then another. Finally, she grabbed the bag and slid down against the cupboard. Maybe the answers were in these envelopes.

Theodora heard Nicky's faint whimper now. She supported herself against the cupboard and tried to get up. She got halfway, then sat down, hard. The envelopes dropped to the floor. Nicky would fall asleep again.

A sister. A father. Her fingers outlined the letters of his name. Her stomach felt hollow, her head light. It was too much. She pushed the envelopes away.

Andreas. He'd never been angry with her. Not really. Nervous and short sometimes, but that was about stress and work. This was different. She remembered the times he'd defended her against the taunts of the other kids. "You don't even know what a bastard is," Andreas would say to one of the bullies. "Look in the mirror." She survived all of it because of him.

Andreas had said, "You are stronger than I could ever be," just before she left the village for university. "I will suffer without you." When she told her mother she didn't want to go, Dimitria said, "You must always be able to take care of yourself. You can do that with an education. Rely on no one but yourself." Her mother had always had so much pride. What good had it done them?

Why had Alexia lied to her? Another stupid question. She was like some of those other kids Theodora knew in school. The ones who told her how much they liked her outfit or her hair. Then she'd overhear them in the bathroom, "And can you believe it? She really thought I was serious." They'd laugh. "Once a stupid bastard..." She never told her mother any of this.

Theodora thumped her head against the cupboard. Alexia had seemed different. She had. "I don't do a thing without assessing every angle," Alexia said to Theodora. It was so obvious. Theodora saw it in the way Alexia discussed every choice on the menu or the best spot to sit on the beach. Alexia was a strong, powerful woman who worried about every decision. It couldn't have been easy for her to carry out their father's wishes. Father. My father. She reached for one of the envelopes, sniffed it. The scent was of paper that had sat in the drawer of an old desk for too long. She stroked the sealed flap.

She got up, picked up each envelope, then put them back in the bag.

Theodora bathed Nicky in preparation for the Saturday night Easter service at the church.

"Papa?" Nicky asked. He navigated his toy ship through the bath water.

She shook her head. "He'll be home soon." She hoped it was true. Her hand quivered as she finished rinsing his back. She ran her fingers through his wet hair. She pulled him out of the tub, draped the towel over his shoulders, put on a diaper and helped him into a clean pair of trousers and the new shirt she'd bought him for Easter. She heard the back door jar open. "Thank God," she said. "Thank God." Nicky put his hands on her cheeks and made her look at him. She nodded. Did he know how worried she was? What was he trying to tell her?

Nicky toddled into his room.

She walked slowly down the stairs.

She stood at the entrance to the kitchen. Andreas sat at the table, his back turned away from her. His hair grazed the collar of his shirt. He had to make time for a haircut. Why was she thinking about that now? They had so much to discuss. He might never let her tell him what he should do again.

"You had an eventful day." He sighed.

Her heart beat in her ears. She had to make him see. Find the right words.

"What do you think about this business?" he asked. His large hands were laced in front of him, his back stiff like a frustrated teacher waiting for a student to give him the right answer.

"I want to get to know her," she said. "I want to know everything."

He stood up, turned to face her. His broad shoulders were slightly bent. He had bags under his eyes. His apron was spotted as always. "You didn't know about any of this," he said. "No matter what my mother says, I know that."

Where was he going with this? Theodora wondered.

"I have something to tell you too. And it won't make you happy either," he said and put his hands in his pockets, stood away.

Theodora took a deep breath. He's going to leave me.

"When my mother came to see me today, I knew I had to tell you. I can't keep doing this anymore. Being angry and worried."

"I understand," Theodora said. What else was there to say? She couldn't force him to stay.

"I can't keep this secret any longer," Andreas said. "I borrowed money from my mother to open the shop. Many years now. I wanted to tell you. I couldn't worry you. My feet were outside the blanket for so long. I promised you I would never do that. I exposed us financially. So you're not the only one with a secret. I'm sorry. I'm so sorry for everything. I want to put these secrets behind us. Do this for me. Okay?"

She nodded. Or at least she thought she had. She couldn't move.

"All I ever wanted to do was make you happy," he said.

In the church in Aigio, Andreas kissed Theodora before taking Nicky to sit on the men's side. Theodora went to where the other women were. She sat beside one of her sisters-in-law. When she saw Theodora, Elena turned to talk to a woman who sat behind her in the pews. Theodora listened to the priests chanting, ignored Elena's whispers. She looked around and found Andreas. He smiled and winked when she caught his eye.

The parishioners emptied out into the street behind the priest. The night was crisp and clear. It was a few minutes past midnight. The streetlights were off. The crowd formed a circle around the main stage, remaining quiet as the priest climbed the four short steps.

"*Christos Anesti,*" the priest announced, lighting the first candle. He turned and lit the candle of the person standing beside him. The flame was passed from one person to the next in the same way.

Theodora kissed Andreas. "*Xronia polla,*" she said.

"For both of us," he said. "Many, many years."

She closed her eyes for a moment, then opened them again. She'd done the same thing when they were children, to thank him, reassure him, show him how she felt. They each kissed Nicky. First his forehead, then his cheeks, then behind his neck. He giggled, pushing them away.

They stood around shaking their neighbours' hands. Elena was to one side. Theodora saw her. She went to Elena, hugged her and kissed her cheeks. "*Xronia polla.*"

Elena nodded. "I will see you back at the house in a few minutes."

Theodora felt his hand on her back. "We'll come tonight," Andreas said. "But tomorrow we go to Theodora's family in Diakofto."

"Easter should be with family," Elena said, looking around as if to see who had heard her son speak to her in such a way.

"Yes, I know," Andreas said.

2010

"It's time," Solon said. "And you wanted to help."

Alexia held herself on her elbows, squinting at the light from the hallway.

"We're just about ready."

"I'm awake," Alexia said. "I'll be down in a few minutes."

He closed the door. She flicked on the light on her nightstand, lay against the headboard. 5:30 a.m. Why hadn't she stayed and talked to Theodora yesterday? She'd kept herself up half the night thinking about it. She should have stayed, faced up to whatever anger or shock Theodora might have had. Alexia remembered what she had gone through herself when she'd found out about Theodora, how long it took for her to accept that she had a sister. She could help Theodora with all of this. It was too much for Theodora to handle by herself. Theodora needed her to be her big sister. And what had she done? She'd taken off. Damn it. It wasn't like she didn't know how to tackle things head on. She'd never wanted to cause Theodora more trouble. Or at least, that's what she told herself.

She flung the covers off. Maybe Theodora needed some time to think about it all. Giving her some space might have been the best thing to do. Please come today, she thought. Please. I don't want us to waste any more time. You have family, her father had said to her. She wished he were here with her. She'd say, I know.

Alexia pulled on her jeans, wiggled into a sweater. She stood in the middle of her room in the light of the one small lamp by her bed. I've taken my shot, she thought. I've told her the truth about who I was, what I'm doing here. Whatever happens, she was not going to give up on having a relationship with Theodora. She'd make Theodora see that this was important for both of them.

On the kitchen counter, a whole skinned lamb lay on sheets of newspaper, its feet tied together, its eyes hollow. Solon manoeuvred the long spit through its body. Zak waited on the other end of the lamb for the sharp metal to protrude. Christina and Katarina sat at the kitchen table, a bowl of meat parts in front of them. They dipped the bits into olive oil, pushing them onto another spit, one piece tight against the other.

"What's that?" Alexia asked.

"We call it a *souvla,"* Christina said.

"No, not the spit itself," Alexia said. She pointed to the meat. "That."

"The best part."

Katarina laughed. "The insides. *Kokoresti.*" Her oily hands pressed a hunk of liver onto the spit.

"I invited Theodora and her family," Alexia said. "I told her."

Solon stopped struggling with the spit. He nodded to Zak. They rested the lamb against the counter. He washed his hands in the sink, splashing water everywhere. He dried his hands on his pants. Christina stared at the hunks of innards floating in a pool of watery oil in the bowl.

"Easter is a time for a new beginning," Solon finally said.

Alexia met his gaze.

"Is this what you want?" he asked.

Alexia nodded. "It's time."

"You did the right thing," Solon said.

Christina rubbed the excess oil off her hands and into the bowl. She got up and walked to the sink, her hands held together. She grumbled under her breath.

"What is it, woman?" Solon said.

Christina turned to face Solon. "You don't worry about what people will say?"

He went to Christina. "I have never worried." He put a hand on her shoulder. "Who cares? Haven't we suffered enough? Paid enough?"

"But with your family?"

"I told you many times," he said. "What they thought or said never mattered to me. It was important to you. Not me. I have only cared about one person." He winked. "Always. Just one."

Christina shook her head, allowed the slightest smile. "That simple?"

He nodded, then turned towards the meat. "It won't cook itself," Solon said.

"Go," Christina said. "Who is stopping you?"

"Let's have the newest member of the family help carry the *souvla* to the fires."

Alexia took one end, Solon the other. They carried it out of the house and walked towards the field at the back. Maria's husband and some of the other neighbours tended the coals on several small fires. Alexia and Solon dropped the *souvla* on the spikes set across one of the fires. "Below are grape vines," Maria said. "Makes for tastier meat."

Alexia counted twelve fires. The men sat on large stones or logs, cranking their spits by hand. Others fanned the lambs with rosemary branches dipped in olive oil. Fat dripped onto the fire. Tiny sparks ignited. Just as quickly, they died away.

"You do this by hand?" Alexia asked. "How long does that take?"

"We all take turns. We share in the work and like life, the meat is better," Solon said. "Maybe six hours, maybe more."

"Ours is a good size," Maria said. "Not the biggest, but it's enough."

The sky turned pink as Alexia stood in front of the fires, listening to the chatter, the jokes, the stories. I could stand here all day, she thought.

She was introduced to daughters and sons of neighbours, home for Easter from Corfu, Athens and other places. She smiled, kissed cheeks and hugged people she'd never met before. Thoughts of Theodora edged in and out, never far away.

The lamb and *kokoresti* had been on for five hours. Her cousins took turns at the spit. Christina, Katarina and Maria brought snacks of devilled eggs. Other neighbours brought dips and wine. Plates of almonds, crackers and cookies sat on the tables set up in the field, beside the fires. It was all there to share. Alexia tried everything. She'd be too full to eat any of the lamb. But no, she told herself, she'd find room for everything.

Alexia practised how she'd introduce Theodora to Christina, Solon and the rest of the family. "This is our *thia*." She thought about things they could talk about, what she'd do if there were any uncomfortable silences. She was ready, but Theodora wasn't here. Theodora had called earlier, said they were coming. Alexia hadn't said more than *thank you,* and given her directions. Alexia hung up quickly. Maybe too quickly, she thought now.

She peered down the road. Saw nothing. She'd go into the house, perhaps try calling Theodora. Or maybe she would just wait. Theodora said she'd come. Be patient, Alexia told herself.

She'd only been in the house for a couple of minutes, but when she came out, everything had changed. Alexia stood in the doorway and watched the scene. Christina had Theodora wrapped in her arms. Katarina and Maria stood beside them, smiling and waiting their turn. Katarina patted her eyes with her apron. Nicky stood with his tiny hand in his father's hand, looking at the ground. Solon crouched down, asked Nicky a question. He gazed up to his father. His father nodded. Nicky took Solon's hand.

"This is for you," Andreas said. He handed Solon a package wrapped in brown paper. "Not for today, but for another time."

"It's nice to have a butcher in the family," Solon said. "We'll get the best from now on."

Theodora handed Christina a large box. It had a pretty red bow. Alexia knew it was a box of small cakes. It was a custom here to bring sweets for a special occasion. She couldn't stop smiling.

Katarina and Maria weaved their arms through Theodora's, guiding her to the house. Christina followed behind. They chatted, asked questions. Theodora didn't seem to mind at all. It reminded Alexia of the scene at the airport when she'd arrived in Greece weeks ago. She laughed to herself. I'd be better at it now, she thought. Thanks to them.

"So you've met the family," Alexia said, kissing Theodora on both cheeks.

"Yes," Theodora said as the wave of aunts carried her forward.

"We're not so bad." Christina draped one arm around Alexia's shoulders.

2010

Theodora insisted they read their father's letters together.

"But they're yours. He intended them for you," Alexia said.

"Haven't we learned enough about hiding things from each other?"

Alexia couldn't resist a smile. "You're right."

One night, a few days before her return flight to Vancouver, she went to Theodora's for dinner. Andreas met her at the door, Nicky in one arm, a packed bag in the other.

"Where are you going?" Alexia asked.

"To my mother's for dinner and the night," he said, tucking Nicky into his coat. "You will need this time together to talk, be with your father."

Andreas kissed Theodora, Nicky hugged her.

Theodora put a large bowl of Greek salad in the middle of the table. She'd set the plates down in front of them. They picked at the salad directly from the bowl. Alexia tore a piece of bread and handed it to Theodora. "So when are you coming?" Alexia asked.

"We've talked about it," Theodora said. "I want to come. Andreas has to leave the shop. We have to find someone."

"You will, though. Right?"

Theodora leaned over and stroked Alexia's arm. "Yes."

"We'll make it work as often as we can," Alexia said. "Right?"

Theodora nodded. "I know."

After dinner, Alexia offered to help Theodora clean up.

"Let's leave it and go upstairs. I've always wanted a party where you invite a friend to spend the night. You giggle, talk, share secrets. I don't know how you call it."

"A slumber party," Alexia said.

"Yes."

Theodora pulled out the letters.

Alexia sat cross-legged on Theodora's bed.

Theodora sat beside her. "What was he like?"

"He was carefree, loved having lots of friends and people around. He laughed a lot," Alexia said. She pictured him at one of the office parties he liked to throw. "Always the loudest one in the room."

They looked at each other and laughed as if they both understood he couldn't have been any other way.

They leaned against the headboard, Alexia's shoulder against Theodora's. Both wore light pants and peasant-style lacey tops. Alexia thought about all the clothes she'd brought from Vancouver. None of it appropriate for the heat, this place. Maybe those clothes weren't right for any place.

Alexia took the picture out of her pocket. "He had it. It's how I recognized you."

"My mother took that picture," Theodora said.

"Can I keep it? It's a great picture of you."

"That and more." Theodora leaned closer.

Alexia straightened her legs to give her more room.

Theodora pulled out the first letter.

No one could replace Sara. I was a fool to allow other women, including your mother, Theodora, to try. I'm sorry I was so selfish. I shouldn't have let it happen. But I'm not sorry we had you. I know you turned out as lovely as your mother always was.

"He was a kind man," Theodora said.

Alexia nodded. It had been a long time since she'd heard her mother's name, read anything he'd written. She could almost hear his voice.

I was afraid I'd ruin your life or your mother's if I came back. The gossip would have been terrible. And I was afraid for Alexia. I hurt her badly when I left her after her mother died. I realize now, I was always afraid.

Alexia ran her fingers through her hair. Theodora squeezed Alexia's leg.

There were letters about his business, what he liked and didn't like about his work, where he planned to vacation, what business trips lay ahead.

Alexia just started high school. You'd be proud of your older sister as I'm sure she'd be proud of you. She's out-debating every teacher and she's an incredible basketball player, too. You'll see her one day. She takes care of everything and everyone, even me. Never makes a fuss. I wish I was a better father.

"You would have loved him." Alexia swallowed. "I didn't like him sometimes, but I always loved him. He was a great father. I didn't tell him." She swallowed again.

Theodora squeezed Alexia's leg tenderly. "I can see."

They opened another letter.

Alexia doesn't know I'm sick. She's taken care of me long enough. Now, I have to protect her for a change. I hope the two of you will get to know each other one day. I made a lot of mistakes. I thought I'd be different than my father, more involved in the lives of my children. He'd had a hard life. I understand that now. He had reasons for the way he was. I have no excuses.

I ran away from my family and from you for stupid reasons. Be with your family, embrace them, don't be afraid of shame or talk or any of that nonsense. You can do better than me. Both you and Alexia can do so much better.

Alexia put the last few letters back in their envelopes and handed them to Theodora.

"There's one more," Theodora said, pulling out another envelope. It looked thicker than the rest.

This is yours. It's a beautiful piece of land where your mother used to work and get inspiration for her sketches. A friend of mine and I had an idea about it, once. I bought this piece of land and now it's yours. There's an old Greek saying, if you focus on your past glories it will only make you cry. Go forward. Don't look back.

Acknowledgments

I started this book with a few images, thoughts, really. The novel found its soul when I visited Kalavryta and the museum and listened to the testimonials of the victims and climbed Kappi Hill myself. Making a dream come true takes the unwavering faith and the kindness of many. I am very fortunate to have so many people to thank. They have stood by me through the six years of writing, editing, researching and reediting this novel. First I'd like to thank my Whistler critique group, Pam Barnsley, Katherine Fawcett, Sara Leach, Mary MacDonald, Libby McKeever, Sue Oakey, Nancy Routley, and Rebecca Wood Barrett. This group of talented writers has provided me with so much more than just their eagle eyes, their literary expertise, thoughtful questions and insightful comments. Thank you so much for your friendship, camaraderie and generosity. My Simon Fraser University critique group has also stuck with me. Thanks so much, Eric Brown, Jennifer Honeyburn, James Leslie, Linda Quennec and ElJean Wilson.

I'd also like to thank Annabel Lyon and Paulette Bourgeois for their review and critique of my first chapters, Lawrence Hill for encouraging me to finish the novel, Wayne Grady for listening when I rambled on about my characters, Merilyn Simonds who innocently asked to read my manuscript one day and then helped me bring the novel to a level I know I could never have taken it to on my own, and Caroline Adderson and Andreas Schroeder for providing me with sound publishing advice and leads. I owe you all so much more than I will ever be able to repay or adequately acknowledge. Thank you.

Thank you to Karen Haughian and the team at Signature Editions for taking a chance on an unknown author and a war tragedy forgotten by history. You've made my transition into the world of publishing exciting and seamless.

I'd like to thank friends and family for always inquiring about my writing and my novel. Thanks so much for your genuine interest and support.

Finally I'd like to thank the one who puts up with me day in, day out. Whenever I feel like my back is against the wall, I've taken on too much, nothing is going as planned, I find Dave beside me, encouraging me forward.

About the Author

Stella Leventoyannis Harvey's stories have appeared in *The Literary Leanings Anthology, The New Orphic Review, Emerge Magazine, The Question* and *The Dalhousie Review*. Her non-fiction has appeared in *Pique Newsmagazine* and the *Globe and Mail.*

A social worker by training, she ran a management consulting practice in Canada and abroad. She was born in Cairo, Egypt and moved to Calgary, Alberta as a child with her family. Much of her family still lives in Greece, where she visits often, indulging her love of Greek food and culture and honing her fluency in the language.

In 2001, Stella founded the Whistler Writers Group, also known as the Vicious Circle, which each year produces the Whistler Writers Festival under her direction.

Eco-Audit

Printing this book using Rolland Enviro100 Book instead of virgin fibres paper saved the following resources:

Trees	Solid Waste	Water	Air Emissions
7	395 kg	26,052 L	1,026 kg